"SWANWICK DRAMATIZES THE WORLD OF DINOSAURS WITH GREAT FLAIR AND KNOWLEDGE, EVEN LOVE. *BONES OF THE EARTH* DANCES ON THE EDGE OF AN ABYSS . . . [AN] ENTERTAINING AND DEFT PERFORMANCE."

The Philadelphia Inquirer

Praise for

MICHAEL SWANWICK
and
BONES OF THE EARTH

"Michael Swanwick is a true seer in the very best sense of that word."
David Zindell

"Beautifully intricate without ever becoming overcomplicated . . . *Bones of the Earth* is a complex novel with the grace of a ballet dancer and the power of the dinosaurs which inhabit it. It intrigues and engages on every front, with heartfelt characterizations, a high-stakes adventure storyline, and a lovely solution to the scientific mystery at its heart."
John Clute, Sifi.com

"Refreshing . . . compelling . . . masterfully controlled . . . acerbic and at times funny."
Locus

"A marvelous book. *Bones of the Earth* shows what the best science fiction can be: the ideas of science become a fascinating, hands-on reality—and that reality reveals new things about our humanity."
Hugo Award-winning author Vernon Vinge

"An important writer whose work is contributing to the shape of things to come."
Pat Cadigan

"This book is a dinosaur paleontologist's dream come true. After reading *Bones of the Earth,* I will be dreadfully disappointed when anyone enters my office and it is not 'Mr. Griffin' and his little surprise package."
Michael Brett-Surman, Ph.D.,
co-editor of *The Complete Dinosaur*

"Anchoring this caged inferno is the world of dinosaurs, which Swanwick dramatizes with great flair and knowledge, even love."
Philadelphia Inquirer

"Swanwick proves that sci-fi has plenty of room for wonder and literary values."
San Francisco Chronicle

"Swanwick is an intelligent writer; his intelligence limns every dark thought."
Washington Post Book World

"Solid storytelling . . . Swanwick is a seasoned sci-fi pro . . . and he approaches *Bones of the Earth* with an ingrained sense of story tension leavened with fun . . . Enjoy."
Fort Worth Star-Telegram

"Swanwick's redevelopment of his Hugo Award winner, *Scherzo with Tyrannosaur,* bulges with intelligent speculation and intriguing plot twists; fans of the author, the original short story, dinosaur buffs, and time-travel aficionados will pounce."
Kirkus Reviews

"Time travel stories make no sense. That's their appeal. To find yourself living before your birth or after your death is such an affront to the laws of cause and effect that no one can be expected to keep all the paradoxes straight. Far from being put off by this difficulty, Michael Swanwick finds it exhilarating . . . Even when he is busily stirring up his subplots and paradoxes, his focus never strays."
New York Times Book Review

"Swanwick has emerged as one of the country's most respected authors."
Philadelphia Inquirer Magazine

Also by
Michael Swanwick

STATIONS OF THE TIDE
JACK FAUST
THE IRON DRAGON'S DAUGHTER

MICHAEL SWANWICK

BONES OF THE EARTH

HarperTorch
An Imprint of HarperCollins*Publishers*

HarperTorch
An Imprint of HarperCollins*Publishers*
10 East 53rd Street
New York, New York 10022-5299

Chapter opening illustration courtesy of the Peabody Museum of Natural History, Yale University, New Haven, CT
ISBN: 0-380-81289-4

First HarperTorch paperback printing: March 2003
First Eos hardcover printing: March 2002

Printed in the United States of America

Visit HarperTorch on the World Wide Web at www.harpercollins.com

10 9 8 7 6 5 4 3 2 1

This book is dedicated to all good teachers everywhere, most particularly those of the William Levering School and Central High School in Philadelphia, to whom more is owed than can ever be repaid.

Special thanks are due to Ralph Chapman, Linda Deck, Tom Holtz, Pete Tillman, and Bob Walters for giving generously of their time and knowledge. They are, of course, not responsible for any errors I may have made, just as I am not responsible for anything rendered invalid by discoveries they or their colleagues may make after this book reaches print. I am also grateful to Harry Turtledove for help with Greek nomenclature, to Suzette Haden Elgin for management strategies of the Lakota Sioux, to Charles Sheffield for the future history of the Earth, to William Gibson for the Rolex Milgauss (nice watch, Bill!), and to my favorite goddaughter in the known universe, Alicia Ma, for naming Lai-tsz. I am most indebted, as always, to the M.C. Porter Endowment for the Arts, most particularly for help writing the abstract for the infrasound paper.

Era	Period	Epoch		Age	M Years Ago
CENOZOIC					0 to 65
MESOZOIC	Cretaceous	LATE	Senonian	Maastrichtian	65 to 71
				Campanian	71 to 83
				Santonian	83 to 86
				Coniacian	86 to 89
			Gallic	Turonian	89 to 93
				Cenomanian	93 to 99
		EARLY		Albian	99 to 112
				Aptian	112 to 121
				Barrmian	121 to 127
			Neocomian	Hauterivian	127 to 132
				Valanginian	132 to 137
				Berriasian	137 to 144
	Jurassic	LATE	Malm	Tithonian	144 to 151
				Kimmeridgian	151 to 154
				Oxfordian	154 to 159
		MIDDLE	Dogger	Callovian	159 to 164
				Bathonian	164 to 169
				Bajocian	169 to 177
				Aalenian	177 to 180
		EARLY	Lias	Toarcian	180 to 190
				Pliensbachian	190 to 195
				Sinemurian	195 to 202
				Hettangian	202 to 206
	Triassic	LATE	Tr3	Rhaetian	206 to 210
				Norian	210 to 221
				Carnian	221 to 227
		MIDDLE	Tr2	Ladinian	227 to 234
				Anisian	234 to 242
		EARLY	Scythian	Olenekian	242 to 245
				Induan	245 to 248
PALEOZOIC					248 to 570

BONES OF THE EARTH

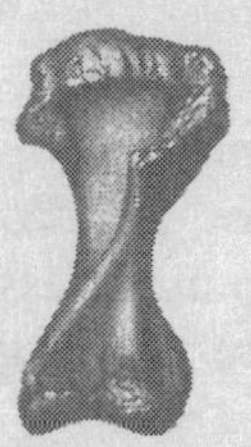

1

Predation Event

Washington, D.C.: Cenozoic era. Quaternary period. Holocene epoch. Modern age. 2010 C.E.

If the whole tangled affair could be said to have a beginning at all, it began on that cold, blustery afternoon in late October when the man with the Igloo cooler walked into Richard Leyster's office. His handshake was firm, and he set the cooler casually down on a tabletop between a lime-green inflatable tyrannosaur and a tray of unsorted hadrosaur teeth without asking permission first. His smile was utterly without warmth. He said his name was Griffin and that he had come to offer Leyster a new position.

Leyster laughed and, sitting back on the edge of his desk, put down the man's card without looking at it. "You could hardly have chosen a worse time to make the offer."

"Oh?" Griffin shifted a stack of AutoCAD boxes from a chair to the floor. His suit was expensive; he tugged at the knees as he sat, to protect the cloth. He had a heavy, inexpressive face. "Why is that?"

"Well, to begin with, the Smithsonian gave me my current position while I was still finishing up my doctorate. That's one hell of an honor, and I'd look pretty damn ungrateful to move on after less than three years service. I realize you're offering more money—"

"I haven't mentioned salary yet."

"The Smithsonian is acutely aware of what an honor it is to work for them," Leyster said dryly. "One of our technicians moonlights selling beer at Orioles games. Guess which job pays him more?"

"There are other inducements besides money."

"Which is precisely why you're wasting your time. I was on a dig this summer in Wyoming where we uncovered a trackway that's just . . . well, it's the sort of find that comes along once in a lifetime—*if* you're lucky. Whatever you're offering couldn't possibly be worth my walking away from it."

For a long moment, Griffin said nothing. Swiveling in his chair, he stared out the window. Following his gaze, Leyster saw only the dark sky, the slick orange tiles on the rooftops opposite, the taxis throwing up gray rooster tails behind themselves on Constitution Avenue, the wet leaves clinging to the glass. Then, turning back, Griffin asked, "Could I see?"

"Do you really want to?" Leyster was surprised. Griffin didn't seem the sort to be interested in original research. A bureaucrat, an arranger, an organizer, yes. A politician, possibly. But never a scientist. Griffin hadn't even arranged for this meeting as a scientist would, with the name of a mutual colleague and his professional affiliation held high, but through the administrative apparatus of the Museum. Some apparatchik, he couldn't even remember who, had called and said that somebody had applied pressure to somebody else up the line, and, figuring it was easier to take the meeting than hear out the explanation, he'd said he'd do it.

"I wouldn't ask if I didn't."

With a mental shrug, Leyster booted up first his computer and then the trackway program, routing the image to a high-density monitor hung on the wall. The image was as detailed as modern technology could make it. He had provided multiple photographs of each track and Ralph Chapman, down the hall, had come up with a 3-D merge-and-justify routine for them. The program began at the far end of the trackway.

"What do you see?" he asked.

"Footprints," Griffin said, "in mud."

"So they were, once. Which is what makes them so exciting. When you dig up fossil bones, that's the record of a dead animal. But here, this—this was made by *living* animals. They were alive and breathing the day they made these, and for one of them it was a very significant day indeed. Let me walk you through it."

He held one hand on the trackball, so he could scroll through the program as he talked. "One hundred forty million years ago, an *Apatosaurus*—

what used to known as *Brontosaurus,* before the taxon was reattributed—is out for a stroll along the shores of a shallow lake. See how steady the apatosaur's prints are, how placidly it ambles along. It is not yet aware that it's being hunted."

Griffin gravely folded his hands as Leyster scrolled down the trackway. They were enormous hands, even for a man of his bulk, and strangely expressive.

"Now look at these smaller sets of prints *here* and *here,* coming out of the forest and following along to either side of the apatosaur's prints. These belong to a hunting pair of *Allosaurus fragilis.* Killer dinosaurs twelve meters long, with enormous sharp claws on their hands and feet, and teeth as large as daggers but with a serrated edge. They move more swiftly than their prey, but they're not running yet—they're stalking. Notice how they've already positioned themselves so they can come up on it from either side.

"Here, the apatosaur becomes aware of its danger. Perhaps the wind shifts and it smells the allosaurs. Maybe the creatures scream as they attack. We'll never know. Whatever alerted it left no trace in the fossil record.

"It runs.

"See how the distance between strides increases. And see how back *here,* the same thing happens to the allosaur tracks. They've gone into an all-out sprint. They're charging, much like a lion charges its prey. Only, their prey is as big as a mountain and they themselves are so large and fierce they could eat lions for breakfast.

"Now look, see how there's a little skip here in the one allosaur's tracks, and an identical one here in the other's. They're matching strides with the apatosaur. For the rest of the chase, they're all three running in lockstep. The allosaurs are in position to leap."

He was paying no attention at all to his auditor now, caught up once again in the drama of the fossil. Life pursued by death. It was an experience common to all creatures, but somehow it always came as a surprise when it actually happened.

"Could the apatosaur outrun them? It's possible. If it could get up to speed quickly enough. But something that big simply can't accelerate as fast as the allosaurs can. So it has to turn—*here,* where the three tracks converge—and fight."

He double-clicked the trackball's right button to zoom up so that they could see a larger area in the screen.

"This is where things get interesting. Look how confused the trackway is—all these trampled places, all this churned-up mud. That's what makes this fossil unique. It's the actual record of the fight itself. Look at those footprints—hundreds of them!—where the apatosaur is struggling with its attackers. See how deep these paired footprints are? I haven't worked out the ergonomics yet, but it's possible the brute actually rears up on its hind legs and then falls forward again, trying to crush its tormentors. If it can only take advantage of its immense weight, it can still win the battle.

"Alas for our friend, it does not. Over here,

where the mud is pushed every which way, is where poor Patty falls. Wham! Leaving one hell of a nice body print, incidentally. *This* and *this* are definitely tail thrashes. She's a game creature, is Patty. But the fight is all over now, however much longer it lasts. Once the apatosaur is down, that's it. These little beauties are never going to let her get up again."

He zoomed outward again, revealing yet more of the mudstone that had once been ancient lakeside. The trackway was, all told, over half a mile long. His back still ached at the thought of all the work it had taken first to uncover it—unearthing representative samples for the first two-thirds, skipping and sampling until at the end it got exciting and they had to excavate the whole damned thing—and then, when their photographs were taken and measurements done, to rebury it under layers of Paleomat and sterile sand in order to protect the tracks from rain and snow and commercial fossil hunters.

"And then, over here—" This was the exciting part, and involuntarily his voice rose. There was nothing he loved so much as a scientific puzzle, and this trackway was the mother of all brainteasers. Besides the allosaur prints, there were also traces of secondary scavengers—birds, smaller dinos, even a few mammals—criss-crossing one another in such exuberant profusion that it seemed they might never be untangled. He welcomed the challenge. He looked forward to the work. "—this section is where our unfortunate Patty dies, and is eaten by the allosaurs.

"The incredible thing, though, is that some of the

scattered bones were pressed into the mud deeply and firmly enough in the process to leave clean impressions. We made rubber molds from them—an ulna, parts of a femur, three vertebrae—enough to make a positive identification. The first direct, noninferential identification of a dinosaur footprint ever!"

"That explains how you know it's an apatosaur. What about the allosaurs?"

Leyster grinned, and enlarged the image so that a single vertebra's imprint dominated the screen. A double-click of the trackball's left button and—God bless Ralph!—the boneprint inverted, changing it from a negative to a positive image. He zoomed in on the caudal articular process. "If you look closely, you can actually see an allosaur tooth embedded in the bone and broken off. No signs of healing. One of those bad boys lost it, either during the attack or while gnawing on the corpse."

Those enormous hands applauded softly, sardonically. "Astounding." There was a kind of disconnect between what Griffin said and the way he said it. He sounded like an actor in a dying play. He held himself like a man who had heard it all before. He was, Leyster realized with a shock that was almost physical, bored. Bored! How could anyone intelligent enough to follow his explanation possibly be bored by it? Carelessly, Griffin said, "Doubtless there's a book in it for you."

"This *is* a book; it's better than any book! There's never been anything like it. I'll be studying it for years."

Leyster had already consulted with ranchers

who had lost livestock to wolves and mountain lions and were only too familiar with the physical trace of predation sites. A friend at the National Museum of the American Indian had promised to get him in touch with a professional guide, a Navajo who, she claimed, could track a trout through water or a hawk through a cloud. There was no telling how much information might yet be coaxed out of this one specimen.

"Let me tell you something. When I uncovered this, when I first realized what I had, it was the single most profound moment of my life." That was out on Burning Woman Ridge, with the mountains to one side of him and hardscrabble ranchlands to the other, and the hottest, bluest sky in all creation overhead. He'd felt everything draw away from him then, the happy chatter of his crew, the grate of shovels in dirt, leaving him alone in a kind of holy stillness. There wasn't a sound or motion anywhere, not even a puff of wind. He felt the presence of God. "And I thought finding this, *all by itself,* justifies my existence on Earth. And you want me to give it up? Oh, no. I think not."

"On the contrary," Griffin said. "I have a much clearer idea of the value of your find than you do. And what I have to offer is better. Much better."

"With all due respect, Mr. Griffin . . ."

Griffin raised both hands, palms forward. "Please. Hear me out."

"All right."

The room was empty and Griffin had closed the door behind him on entering. He slowly looked around him before speaking anyway. Then he cleared his throat, apologized for doing so, and said, "Let me begin by spelling out the terms of the contract, just to save me the trouble later on. You'll be allowed to stay in your present position, and arrangements will be made to borrow your services for the project six aggregate months out of the year. You'll continue to be paid by the government, so I'm afraid there won't be any increase in your salary. Sorry."

He's enjoying this, thought Leyster. Science bores him to death, but having opposition to overcome brings him back to life. Ordinarily, Leyster didn't find people very interesting. But Griffin was different. He studied the impassive planes of the man's face, looking for a point of entry, a beginning to understanding, the least flicker of a hint as to what made him work. Leyster knew himself to be a methodical researcher; give him one end of a tangled thread and he wouldn't let go until he'd unraveled the entire snarl. All he needed was enough time and that one loose end.

And then Griffin did an extraordinary thing. It was the smallest of gestures, one Leyster wouldn't have noticed under ordinary circumstances. Now he found it riveting. Without looking, Griffin brushed back his sleeve to reveal a thick stainless steel watch. He clamped his hand over it, hiding the dial completely. Then he glanced down at the back of his hand.

He didn't release the watch until he had looked away.

Leyster had found his opening. Prodding gently, he said, "So far, you haven't made much of a case."

"It gets worse," Griffin said. So he had a sense of humor! Astonishing. "There are restrictions. You won't be allowed to publish. Oh, findings based on your own fieldwork, of course"—he waved a dismissive hand at the HDTV screen—"that sort of stuff you may publish whenever. Provided it is first cleared by an internal committee to ensure you're not taking advantage of information gained while working for us. Further, you won't even be allowed to talk about your work with us. It will be classified. We'll need your permission to have the FBI run a security check on you. Strictly routine. I assure you, it will turn up nothing embarrassing."

"A security check? For paleontology? What the hell are you talking about?"

"I should also mention that there is a serious possibility of violent death."

"Violent death. This is going to start making sense any minute now, right?"

"A man comes into your office"—Griffin leaned forward conspiratorially—"and suggests that he has a very special job to offer you. By its very nature he can't tell you much about it until you've committed yourself heart and soul. But he suggests—hints, rather—that it's your chance to be a part of the greatest scientific adventure since Darwin's voyage on H.M.S. *Beagle*. What would you think?"

"Well, he'd certainly have my interest."

"If it were true," Griffin said with heavy irony.

"Yes," Leyster agreed. "If it were true."

Griffin smiled. On his coarse-featured face, it looked sad. "Well, then, I believe I've told you all you need to know."

Leyster waited, but he said no more.

"Forgive me for saying so, but this is the damnedest pitch I've ever heard in my life. You haven't said one thing to make your offer attractive to me—quite the opposite. You say that I'll need FBI clearance, that I won't be allowed to publish, that I might . . . Frankly, I can't think of a set of arguments that would be less conducive to my coming to work for you."

There was an amused glint in Griffin's eye, as if Leyster's reaction were precisely what he had been hoping to provoke.

Or was this only what he wanted Leyster to think?

No, that was a paranoid line of reasoning. It was not the way Leyster normally thought, not the way he *liked* to think. He was accustomed to questioning an essentially impassive universe. The physical world might be maddeningly close-lipped about its secrets, but it didn't lie, and it never actively tried to deceive you.

Still, the corrupting influence of the man was such that it was hard *not* to think along such lines.

Again, Griffin clamped his hand over his watch. Glancing down at it, he said, "You'll take the position anyway."

"And the reasoning upon which you base this extraordinary conclusion is—?"

Griffin put the cooler on Leyster's desk. "This is a gift. There's only one string attached—you will not show it to anyone or tell anybody about it. Beyond that—" He twisted his mouth disparagingly. "Do whatever it takes to convince you it's genuine.

Cut it open. Take it apart. There are plenty more where that came from. But no photographs, please. Or you'll never get another one to play with again."

Then he was gone.

Alone, Leyster thought: I won't open it. The best possible course of action would be ditch this thing in the nearest Dumpster. Whatever Griffin was peddling, it could only mean trouble. FBI probes, internal committees, censorship, death. He didn't need that kind of grief. Just this once, he was going to curb his curiosity and leave well enough alone.

He opened the cooler.

For a long, still moment, he stared at what was contained within, packed in ice. Then, dazedly, he reached inside and removed it. The flesh was cool under his hands. The skin moved slightly; he could feel the bones and muscles underneath.

It was the head of a *Stegosaurus*.

A gust of wind made the window boom gently. A freshet of rain rattled on the glass. Cars hummed quietly by on the street below. Somebody in the hallway laughed.

Eventually, volition returned. He lifted the thing from the cooler and set it down on the workbench, atop a stack of *Journal of Vertebrate Paleontology* reprints. It was roughly eighteen inches long, six inches high, and six inches wide. Slowly, he passed his hands over its surface.

The flesh was cool and yielding. He could feel the give of muscles underneath it, and the hardness of bone beneath them. One thumb slipped inadvertently onto the creature's gums and felt the smoothness of teeth. The beak was like horn; it had a sharp edge. Almost in passing, he noted that it *did* have cheeks.

He peeled back an eyelid. Its eyes were golden.

Leyster found himself crying.

Without even bothering to wipe away the tears, not caring if he were crying or not, he flipped open a workbook, and began assembling tools. A number four scalpel with a number twenty blade. A heavy pair of Stille-Horsley bone-cutting forceps. A charriere saw. Some chisels and a heavy mallet. These were left over from last summer when Susan What's-Her-Name, one of the interns from Johns Hopkins, had sat quietly in the corner week after week, working with a komodo dragon that had recently passed away at the National Zoo to prepare an atlas of its soft tissues. Exactly the kind of painstaking and necessary work one prays somebody *else* will perform.

He swept the worktable clear of its contents—books and floppies, a pair of calipers, paper cutter, bags of pretzels, snapshots from the dig—and set the head in its center.

Carefully he laid out the tools. Scalpel, forceps, saw. What happened to those calipers he'd had out here? He picked them up off the floor. After a moment's hesitation, he tossed the mallet and chisel aside. They were for speedy work. It would be better to take his time.

Where to begin?

He began by making a single long incision along

the top of the head, from the edge of the beak all the way back to the foramen magnum—the hole where the spinal cord leaves the braincase. Gently, then, he peeled away the skin, revealing dark red muscles, lightly sheened with silver.

Craniocaudal musculature, he wrote in the workbook, and swiftly sketched it in.

When the muscular structure was all recorded, he took up the scalpel again and cut through the muscles to the skull beneath. He picked up the bone saw. Then he put it down, and picked up the forceps. He felt like a vandal doing so—like the guy who took a hammer to Michelangelo's *Pietà*. But, damn it, he already *knew* what a stego's skull looked like.

He began cutting away the bone. It made a flat, crunching sound, like stiff plastic breaking.

The brain case opened up before him.

The stegosaur's brain was a light orange-brown so delicately pale it was almost ivory, with a bright tracery of blood vessels across its surface. It was a small thing, of course—even for a dinosaur, a stegosaur was an extraordinarily stupid brute—and he was familiar with its shape from the close examination of brain casts taken from the fossil skulls of its kindred.

But this was scientific Terra Incognita. Nothing was known about the interior of a dinosaur's brain, or its microstructure. Would he find its brain similar to those of birds and crocodiles or more like those of mammals? There was so much to learn here! He needed to chart and record the pneumatic structures in the skull cavity. And the tongue! How muscular was it? He should dissect an eye to see the number of types of color receptors it had.

Also whether this thing had nasal turbinates. Was there room enough for them? Their purpose was to trap and recover moisture from each exhaled breath. A warm-blooded animal, with its high rate of respiration, would need complex turbinates to help keep the lungs from drying out. A cold-blooded animal, needing less rehydration, might not have turbinates at all.

The argument over whether dinosaurs were warm-blooded or cold-blooded had been raging for decades before Leyster was even born. It was possible he could settle the whole matter here and now.

But first there was the brain. He felt like Columbus, staring at the long, dark horizontal line of a new continent. *Here Be Dragons.* His scalpel hesitated over the ruptured head.

It descended.

Weariness caused Leyster to stagger and briefly lose consciousness and recover himself all in an instant.

He shook his head, blankly wondering where he was and why he felt so tired. Then the room swam into focus and he felt the silence of the building around him. The Elvis clock an old girlfriend had given him, with its pink jacket and swiveling hips, said that it was 3:12 A.M. He'd been working on the brain without food or rest for over twelve hours.

There were several collection jars before him, each with a section of the brain preserved in formaldehyde. His workbook was almost filled with notes and drawings. He picked it up and glanced down at a page near the beginning:

> *Opening the cranial cavity reveals that the brain is short and deep with strong cerebral and pontine flexures and a steep caudodorsal edge. The small cerebral hemispheres have a transverse diameter slightly in excess of the medulla oblongata. Though the optic lobes and the olfactory lobe are quite large, the cerebellum is strikingly small.*

He recognized the tidy, economical lettering as his own, but had no memory whatsoever of writing those words, or any of those on the dozens of pages that followed.

"I've got to stop," he said aloud. "The condition I'm in, I can't be trusted not to screw things up."

He listened to the words carefully, and decided that they made sense. Wearily, he wrapped up the head in aluminum foil and placed it in the refrigerator, ejecting a month-old carton of grapefruit juice and a six-pack of Diet Pepsis to make room for it. He didn't have a padlock, but a little rummaging came up with a long orange extension cord, which he wrapped around the refrigerator several times. With a Magic Marker he wrote, *Danger!!! Botulism experiment in progress—DO NOT OPEN!!!* on a sheet of paper, and taped it to the door.

Now he could go home.

But now that the head—the impossible, glorious

head—was no longer in front of him soaking up his every thought, he was faced with the problem of its existence.

Where had it come from? What could possibly explain such a miracle? How could such a thing exist?

Time travel? No.

He'd read a physics paper once, purporting to demonstrate the theoretical possibility of time travel. It required the construction of an extremely long, large, and dense cylinder massing as much as the Milky Way Galaxy, and rotating at half the speed of light. But even if such a monster could be built—and it couldn't—it would still be of dubious utility. An object shot past its surface at exactly the right angle would indeed travel into either the past or the future, depending on whether it was traveling with the cylinder's rotation or against it. But how far it would go, there was no predicting. And a quick jaunt to the Mesozoic was out of the question—nothing could travel to a time before the cylinder was created or after its destruction.

In any event, current physics wasn't up to building a time machine, and wouldn't be for at least another millennium. If ever.

Could someone have employed recombinant engineering to reassemble fragments of dinosaur DNA like in that movie he used to love back when he was a kid? Again, no. It was a pleasant fantasy. But DNA was fragile. It broke down too quickly. The most that had ever been recovered inside fossil amber had been tiny fragments of insect genes. That business of patching together the fragments?

Ridiculous. It would be like trying to reconstruct Shakespeare's plays from the ashes of a burnt folio, one that yielded only the words *never* and *foul* and *the*. Except that the ashes came not from a single folio, but from a hundred-thousand volume library that would have included Mickey Spillane and Dorothy Sayers, Horace Walpole and Jeane Dixon, the *Congressional Record* and the complete works of Stephen King.

It wasn't going to happen.

One's time could be better spent, alas, trying to restore the *Venus de Milo* by searching the beaches of the Mediterranean for the marble grains that had once been its arms.

Could it be a fake?

This was the least likely possibility of all. He had cut the animal apart himself, gotten its blood on his hands, felt the grain and give of its muscles. It had recently been a living creature.

In his work, Leyster followed the biological journals closely. He knew exactly what was possible and what was not. Build a pseudo-dinosaur? From scratch? Scientists were lucky if they could put together a virus. The simplest amoeba was worlds beyond them.

So that was that. There were only three possible explanations, and each one was more impossible than the next.

Griffin knew the answer, though! Griffin knew, and could tell, and had left behind his card. Where was it? It was somewhere on his desk.

He snatched up the card. It read:

H. JAMISON GRIFFIN
ADMINISTRATIVE OFFICER

Nothing more. There was no address. No phone number. No fax. No e-mail. It didn't even list his organization.

Griffin had left no way to get in touch with him.

Leyster grabbed the phone, punched up an outside line, and dialed directory assistance. Simultaneously, he booted up his Internet account. There were millions of records out there. The days when a man could accomplish anything at all without leaving any trace of himself behind were long gone. He'd find Griffin for sure.

But after an hour, he had to admit defeat. Griffin's name was listed in no directory Leyster could locate. He worked for no known government agency. So far as Leyster could tell, he had never posted a comment of any kind on any subject whatsoever, or been referred to, however fleetingly, by anyone.

The man did not seem to exist.

In the end, Leyster could only wait. Wait, and hope that the bastard would return.

And what if he didn't? What if he never came back?

These were the questions that Leyster was to ask himself a hundred times a day, every day for a year and a half. The time it took Griffin to get around to ending his silence with a phone call.

2

The Riddle of Achilles

Crystal City, Virginia: Cenozoic era. Quaternary period. Holocene epoch. Modern age. 2012 C.E.

Leyster was the only person in the van who wasn't peering out the windows, excitedly drawing attention to advertisements and the new Metrobuses, leaning into the glass when they passed a construction site. They'd all been given the day's *Washington Post* at the Pentagon, and it was a toss-up whether the comics or the editorial pages amused them more. He could understand their nostalgia, but he couldn't feel it.

To him, it was just the present.

The man beside him turned a cheerful round face his way and stuck out a hand. "Hi! I'm Bill Metzger, and this is my wife, Cedella. We're from ten years forward." The woman, smiling, leaned over her husband to shake hands as well. She was noticeably younger than he. It was, if not a May–December marriage, at least a June–October one.

"I'm not on the program, but Cedella's going to be reading a paper on the nasal turbinates of lambeosaurine hadrosaurs."

"Really? That's interesting. My paper deals with the nasal turbinates of stegosaurs. And their throat and tongue structure. And a little bit about their brains."

"That sounds familiar." Cedella flipped rapidly through her abstracts. "Wasn't that one I wanted to . . ." She stopped. "Oh! You're *Richard Leyster!* Oh, my goodness. I want to tell you that your book was so—"

Her husband cleared his throat meaningfully.

"Book?"

"Oh, right. It wouldn't be out yet." She turned to look out the window again. "Can you imagine wearing such hideous clothes? And yet they didn't seem so bad at the time."

Cedella had the most gorgeous Jamaican accent Leyster had ever heard, as rich as caramel pudding, as clear and precise as an algebraic equation. It was a pleasure just to hear her speak.

"Maybe I should hop out and look you up," Bill said. The marine in the front seat glanced sharply at him, but said nothing. "You were a hot little number then, funky clothes or no."

"What do you mean *were?*" She swatted him with her newspaper, and he laughed. "I ought to let you try, old man. I wasn't all tired out looking after you back then—you'd have a heart attack for certain. And it would serve you right."

"At least I'd die happy."

"But what about me? What would I do with the

rest of my evening? After the ambulance had hauled your worthless carcass away?"

"You could watch TV."

"There's nothing good on that early in the evening."

The two of them were so happily, sweetly absorbed in each other that Leyster felt sour and crabbed by contrast. He couldn't help marveling at how fluidly and naturally the words flowed between them. Conversation was never easy for him. He never knew what to say to people.

Bill turned back to him. "Forgive my wayward wife. This is our first trip through time, and I think everybody here's a little giddy."

"Not everybody. Some of us live here."

"Yes, yes, that's hard to keep in mind, forgive me." Bill looked out the window again, marveling at what seemed to Leyster a perfectly ordinary tract of row houses. "I can't believe how much has changed in only ten years. So very many things are going to happen in the next decade!"

"Anything important?"

"Compared to this? Compared to time travel? Nothing. Nothing at all."

The marine guard who, they'd been told, had orders to shoot anyone who tried to leave the van before being told to, and to whom they had also been directed to say nothing of their origins or destination, looked uncomfortable.

Orientation was held in the Crystal Gateway Marriott. It was easily the strangest conference Leyster had ever attended.

In some ways it was the best. One advantage of time travel was that the *Proceedings* could be made available at the beginning of the conference. It still took a year or more for the papers to be assembled, edited, and printed, but the books themselves could then be shipped back and sold at the registration table, so they could be carried from talk to talk, and annotated as the papers were presented.

On the negative side, Leyster recognized only a fraction of those present. Paleontology was a small world—there were only two or three thousand professionals in existence at any given moment. Most conferences, he knew everyone of importance, and was at least vaguely familiar with the faces of the rest. Here, though, with professionals recruited across the span of twenty-some years, there were many who were strange to him. Even those he thought he knew had aged and changed to the point where he didn't feel comfortable approaching them. He was no longer certain who anybody was.

He snagged a bear claw from the buffet, and joined the line for coffee. Bill and Cedella got in line behind him, Bill with a slap on his shoulder, and Cedella with a bright flash of teeth. He was grateful for their company.

Cedella made a face when she took her first sip of coffee. "This stuff is as bad as ever. If we can put a man on the moon and travel a hundred million years into the past, why can't we make a decent cup of coffee?"

"If you think that's bad, you should try the decaf."

"How this man suffers." She turned to Leyster. "Do you see how he suffers?"

"I've been thinking about my book. It's almost done, only I'm stuck on a title. I was thinking maybe *Tracks of Time* . . ."

"Oh, but that's not the—"

Bill cleared his throat, and Cedella fell silent. "We're really not supposed to say," he said gently. "I do apologize, but they were quite firm on that score."

"Come! The morning keynote speech starts in a few minutes. I want to get a good seat."

Leyster trailed after them into the Grand Ballroom. There was a happy buzz of anticipation in the room. Everyone was anxious to get things started. When the conference was over, they'd begin preparations for their first field trips back into deep time, to encounter in the flesh what they now knew only from impressions in stone. They were like so many fledglings nervously standing on their cliff face ledge, knowing that soon they would step over the edge, spread wings, and fly.

The seats filled up. Somebody dimmed the lights.

Griffin took the podium. He looked much older than Leyster recalled him being.

"First slide, please."

The slide showed the cartoon caveman Alley Oop, caressing the head of his faithful dinosaur mount, Dinny. There was light laughter.

"In just a moment we'll get to what I believe is technically known as 'the good stuff.' And what we have is spectacular. In addition to the papers, there will be a film program tonight—actual footage of live dinosaurs from the Triassic, Jurassic, and Cretaceous. The film has been chosen by your fellow vertebrate paleontologists from generation two, and they've taken care that all your favorites will be there. I can guarantee you—there *will* be surprises."

Several in the audience applauded.

"However, before we can proceed, I am required to share with you a few of the rules of the road. Everyone here has already been told the penalties for violating secrecy. Today I'm going to explain why those penalties are so Draconian. Now, our physicists have requested that I share with you as little of the mechanics of time travel as possible. Slide?"

The new slide showed a dense throng of mathematical notations. Leyster assumed they were not taken from the actual equations of time travel, but they could have been no more incomprehensible if they had been.

"No problem."

Laughter.

"In order to hold such conferences as this one, we will be shuttling researchers back and forth across a period of the next century or so. It's bound to occur to a few of you that there's a wealth of information to be gleaned from a copy of next year's newspaper. Lottery numbers. World Cup winners. Stock prices. What's to keep you from jotting down a few numbers and taking advantage of them? Only one thing:

"Paradox.

"A paradox is anything self-contradictory and yet irreconcilable. For example, the barber of Seville, who shaves everyone in town who doesn't shave himself. Does he shave himself or not? The statement, 'This sentence is a lie.' True or false? A little closer to the bone, a man goes into the past and kills his grandfather as a child, thus preventing his own birth. How can he exist, then, to commit the murder in the first place?

"Without time travel, paradoxes are pleasant logical puzzles which can be neatly despatched with a tweak in the rules of logic dealing with self-reference. However, once it's possible to physically invade the childhood of one's grandparents, the resolution of paradoxes becomes vitally important. So we've given this some serious thought."

Griffin paused, frowning down at his notes for a beat. Nobody made a sound. Leyster did not feel any particular warmth or charisma from the man, but he was clearly alone in this. The entire room was with Griffin.

"It turns out that paradox is deeply embedded in the nature of existence. The two are profoundly interrelated.

"Third slide." Another cartoon, this one of an athletic man in Greek skirt and lace-up sandals running furiously toward a turtle crawling away from him on the road ahead.

"Consider Zeno's first paradox. Achilles, the fastest man in the world, wishes to overtake a tortoise on the road ahead of him. He races toward it as swiftly as he can. However, by the time he reaches where the tortoise was, the tortoise is no longer there. It has moved a little further down the road. No problem. He simply races to that new spot. However, when he arrives there, he finds again that the tortoise has moved away. No matter how many times he tries, he can never catch up with the tortoise."

Griffin produced a tennis ball from the pocket of his jacket. He tossed it lightly into the air, caught it on the way down. "Consider also, Zeno's third paradox. Achilles draws his bow and shoots an arrow at a tree. The tree is not far distant. But in order for the arrow to reach the tree, it must first travel half the distance from the bow to the tree. In order to reach that midway point, it must travel half of *that* distance. And so on. In order to arrive anywhere, the arrow must perform an infinite number of operations. Which will take it an infinite amount of time. Obviously, it can never move."

Suddenly he threw the ball as hard as he could. With a soft *boom,* it hit the closed ballroom doors and bounced away, up the aisle.

"Nevertheless—it moves. Paradox can and does happen. This is the riddle of Achilles. How can the seemingly self-contradictory exist so easily in this world?

"And to this riddle we have no answer.

"Now, in just a minute, I'm going to leave the room, and take a limo back to the Pentagon. The trip takes roughly half an hour. I'll travel an hour into the past—so that I'll emerge from the Pentagon exactly one half hour ago. A car will be waiting for me. I'll ride it back here to the Marriott. The driver will let me off at the front door. I'll walk through the lobby, down the hall, and to the closed doors of the Grand Ballroom."

Heads were already beginning to swivel.

"And I'll enter the room . . . *now.*"

The doors opened and Griffin strode in, smiling jauntily and waving as he made his way to the stage.

The two identical men shook hands.

"Griffin, good to see you."

"Good to see *you,* Griffin." The earlier Griffin addressed the audience: "As you can see, it is indeed possible for the same object to be in two places at the same time." He handed the later Griffin the microphone. "And now I must leave to take that limo I told you about earlier, because—well, I'll let my one-hour-older self tell you why. With age comes wisdom, you know."

Down the aisle Griffin went. He stooped to pick up the tennis ball along the way, and then disappeared through the double doors.

His other self reached into a pocket and set that same tennis ball atop the podium. "There goes the pragmatic resolution of our dilemma. By making a simple loop in time, I was able to witness the same moment from two different perspectives. Causality was not violated. There was no paradox involved.

"Similarly, all your actions in the past—all your *future* actions, everything you *will* do—have already existed for millions of years, and are a part of what led inevitably to this present moment.

Don't obsess about the repercussions of simple actions. Step on as many butterflies as you wish—the present is safe.

"However, suppose when I entered the room just now, I decided to behave differently than I had witnessed myself behaving the first time. Suppose that rather than shake hands, I'd decided to punch myself out. Suppose then my earlier self had become so irate that he refused to travel into the past. What then?"

"It couldn't have happened!" somebody called from the audience. "It didn't—so it couldn't."

"So common sense would tell you. However—slide!" The incomprehensible physical equations again filled the screen. "Common sense has very little to do with physics. Unhappily, paradox is only too possible.

"Let's imagine that when I came into this room, with this tennis ball in my pocket, I kicked the original of it out of my way in the aisle, sending it skittering in among this amiable sea of friendly faces. This would have prevented my earlier self from picking it up in the first place. Where, then, would *this* tennis ball have come from? Suppose also that I subsequently took this ball and gave it to my earlier self to take back in time so I could bring it here to pass back into time." He tossed the ball back and forth between his hands. "Where did it come from? Where does it go? If it came spontaneously into being, as a miracle of quantum physics, then why does it have the Spalding logo stamped into its side?"

Nobody laughed. A few in the audience cleared their throats uncomfortably.

"Either of those instances—the refusal to perform a previously witnessed act, or the tennis ball from nowhere—would have been a massive violation of cause and effect. There are extremely good reasons why this cannot be allowed to occur. I am not permitted even to hint at these reasons, but I can assure you that we take them very seriously indeed.

"The bottom line is simply this: Could you go back in time and kill your own grandfather? Yes and no. Yes, it could happen. There's nothing in the physical nature of reality to prevent it. No, we won't permit it to happen.

"We have means of detecting a paradox before it actually happens—and, again, I won't tell you what they are. But any threat to this precious and fragile enterprise will be nipped in the bud, I can assure you that. And those responsible will be punished. No exceptions. And no clemency, either."

He slipped the tennis ball back in his pocket. "Any questions?"

A spry old gent who might have been the father of someone Leyster once worked with, stood. "What if, in spite of your best efforts, a paradox slips by you?"

"The entire project would be canceled. Retroactively. By which I mean that this wonderful opportunity will then have never been placed before you. It's harsh, but—I have been assured by those who know—absolutely necessary."

A woman stood. "What would become of us, then?"

"Cut free from causality, our entire history from that moment onward would become a timelike loop and dissolve."

"Excuse me. What does that mean?"

Griffin smiled. "No comment."

Leyster thrust up his hand.

"Mr. Leyster. Somehow I knew that you would be one of those asking questions."

"This technology—whatever it is—must be expensive."

"Extremely so."

"So why us?

"Is that a complaint?" Griffin asked. Amid laughter, he clamped a hand over his watch, glanced down, and then up again. "Any further questions?"

Leyster remained standing. "I just don't understand why this technology is being made available for our use. Why paleontologists? Why not the military, the CIA . . ." He fumbled for another plausible alternative, ". . . politicians? We all know how little money was spent last year on fieldwork, worldwide. Why are we suddenly important enough to rate the big bucks?"

There were annoyed sounds from the audience.

Griffin frowned. "I fail to see why you're opposed to this project."

"I'm not—"

"No, listen to me! I've come here bearing the greatest gift that anyone has ever received, and it's being presented to you at no cost whatsoever. Yes, there are a few strings attached. But, my God, they're extremely light, and what you get—the opportunity to study real, living dinosaurs—is so extraordinary, that I'd think you'd be grateful!"

"I only—"

People were actually shouting at him now. The crowd belonged to Griffin. It was more than the fact that he controlled access to the one thing they all wanted more than anything else. He knew how to manipulate them. A salesman had once told Leyster that the first thing he did was to find out a prospect's name. Once the name was dropped into the spiel, he said, the prospect was halfway to being sold. What Griffin was doing was more complex than that. But no more sincere.

They don't want to know, he thought. They've received something they know they don't deserve, and they're not willing to ask the price. They're afraid it might be too high. "I really feel that we—"

"Sit down!" somebody shouted.

Blushing with confusion, he sat.

Griffin held up both hands for calm. "Please. Please. Let's remember that in science, no questions are forbidden. Our Mr. Leyster had a perfect right to ask. Unfortunately, reasons of security prevent me from answering. Now, as I mentioned before, there will be films tonight, and if you'll look at your schedules, you'll see that you have three hours for dinner. I must ask you not to leave the hotel.

"In the meantime—a lot of you have been working with materials provided from the Mesozoic past. Let's hear those papers."

The applause was enthusiastic. Griffin leaned forward into it, almost bowing.

After lunch, Leyster returned to the Grand Ballroom for the afternoon keynote. He looked around for the Metzgers. Only a few of the seats were filled, but there were plenty of people in the back of the room, networking and politicking, leaning against walls and looking skeptical, speaking earnestly up at those leaners, and reaching into paper bags to bring forth the polished skull of a troodontid or the brightly feathered wing and toothed beak of an *Archaeopteryx*.

There was no use trying to be a part of the influence-swapping until he sorted out who was who, the major players from the bright young grad students who would hang in for a season or three before realizing that the money was elsewhere, the influential patriarchs of major institutions who spent so much time in administration they never published anything from the shy nondescripts who averted their heads to hide the eyes that burned with passionate insight.

A husky man with white hair cropped short over his pink scalp to disguise his incipient baldness came up behind Leyster and pounded him on the back. "You bastard! You look so young! I don't know how you do it."

"I think I *am* young. This is my home year, so—Monk? Is that you?"

James Montgomery Kavanagh—Monk to his friends—had studied with Leyster at Cornell. At one point they'd even been roommates, though neither of them recalled that year with much fondness. But he looked so haggard! So tired. He must have been recruited a full twenty years in the future.

Monk squeezed his shoulder, released him. "Quite an exciting morning, hey? I enjoyed your paper, by the way. Couldn't stay for the questions, unfortunately. Too bad more people didn't turn out for it."

"I've had fewer."

"You were up against a *Tyrannosaurus* hatchling. Nobody thinks all that highly of Hitchcock's work, but she had slides everybody wanted to see. Hell, I only came because it was you. Which papers are you planning to take in this afternoon?"

"I thought—"

"Skip the *Baryonyx* thing. Total nonsense. And Tom Holtz's chat on taxonomy. Cladistics is like New York City. It'll be something impressive, once they're done building it. Good to see Tom still producing useful work after all these years, though. You'd think he'd be retired by now."

"What do you know about the afternoon speaker?"

"Gertrude Salley? Oh, *she'll* put on a show. What a character. Brilliant in some ways, but . . . well, she likes to take chances. Willing to publish her findings before they've been entirely found. She's a splitter—never met a taxon she didn't like. If she could, she'd assign her right and left hands to different species. And not too careful about where she gets her data, if you catch my meaning. You have to keep a sharp eye on your specimens when Rude Salley's around."

"I never heard of her. Where's she from?"

"About thirty–forty years forward. I don't know the exact date. She must be in grammar school or maybe junior high right now. She works a generation or two ahead of us."

"Um. Then we're not supposed to be talking about her in this kind of detail, are we? Griffin said . . ."

"They can't stop gossip! They make a token attempt, but let's get real. It's tolerated. So long as no hard data get passed along with it. The impulse is too deeply embedded in human nature, hey?" Without pausing, he said, "Well, I could listen to you forever, Dick, but I've got a career to think about. People to suck up to and serious ass to kiss. Take care, okay? All right."

And he was gone.

The Metzgers had come up to Leyster sometime during the encounter, and stood listening in silence. Bill stared wonderingly after him. Cedella shook her head. "Wow."

"He's mellowed," Leyster said. "You should have seen him back in college."

Gertrude Salley was a strikingly handsome woman. She wore a Nile green silk outfit with mid-length skirt and buttons up the side. Leyster had never seen clothes of quite that cut. But he didn't need the string of pearls about her neck to tell him that they were, for her time, impeccably conservative. They just had that look.

Her address was entitled "The Traffic Moves the Policeman," and according to the *Proceedings* it was about the coevolution of the super-sauropods—the seismosaurs and titanosaurs of such tremendous size that they made a camarasaur look dainty—and the Mesozoic forests. Leyster didn't think much of the topic.

But then she began to speak.

"I know so much you need to know," she said. "So very much! I've read all your books, and thousands of your papers, and in the forty-five minutes allotted to me, I have no doubt whatsoever that I could drop enough information to save you all decades of effort.

"But I am not allowed to do so, and even if I were, I wouldn't. Why? Because so much of what I know is based on basic research that you yourselves will do. Good science is hard work, and everything we in generations two and three have achieved is built upon your efforts. If I told you your discoveries, would you be willing to sink half your life into verifying them? Or would you simply initial the data and pass 'em forward? We'd end up with one of Griffin's paradoxes . . . information that comes out of nowhere. And information that comes out of nowhere is not reliable, for it doesn't connect anywhere with the facts.

"What can I offer you, then? Not facts, but modes of thinking. I can lay out for you a few theories I have which are, alas, unprovable, and through them, perhaps, indicate a few fruitful ways of looking at things.

"Consider the Titanosauridae. They were by far the predominant sauropods of the Late Cretaceous, and so ecologically pivotal that in their time a forest could be defined as a body of trees surrounded by herbivores . . ."

And she was off, leaping like a salmon from idea to idea. Hers was the kind of fast and playful intellect that enjoyed tossing a stone into the pond of received wisdom, just to see the frogs jump. And speaking, as she did, from a vantage of fifty years, it was impossible to tell which of her notions were crazy, and which were the result of radical new discoveries. When she spoke of mountains dancing to the music of sauropods, Leyster was positive that was metaphor at best; when she claimed that ceratopsians were farmed by their predators, he was not so sure. That guff about birds he didn't buy at all.

Leyster was riveted.

Too soon, she finished, saying, "But if I can tell you nothing else, I can tell you how valuable your work is—or rather, will be. Sir Isaac Newton said, *If I have been able to see farther than others, it is because I stood on the shoulders of giants.* Well, today I have the rare opportunity of standing in the presence of giants. And the even rarer opportunity of being able to thank them. Thank you. Thank you for all you will do."

She stood down to tumultuous applause, and did not stay for questions.

Cedella leaned over and said in Leyster's ear, "I just discovered who I want to be when I grow up."

The afternoon passed in the usual happy blur, moved along by the surge and flow of attendees hurrying from room to room between sessions. There were three tracks running simultaneously and not a single paper that didn't conflict with at least one more that Leyster needed to hear. When the last one ended shortly before five, he wandered out to the lobby, head abuzz with all he had learned, looking for someone to form a dinner party with. The Metzgers, or possibly old Tom Holtz. But when he got there, the lobby was crowded with police and security personnel.

The Metzgers were being arrested.

Cedella held her chin high, eyes ablaze with scornful defiance. Bill simply looked deflated, a little man in a suit suddenly too large for him. Knots of shocked scientists stood in the entryways and watched as the two were led away by state troopers.

"I'm sorry, sir, you can't come in here," said a young officer when he automatically moved toward his friends. An admonishing hand closed about his upper arm. Turning, he saw Monk.

"What happened?"

"It's called note-passing," Monk said. "They caught the woman red-handed. Leaned up against the mail slot and slipped the letter in behind her back while her husband pretended to have a heart attack. Sad thing, isn't it?"

There was a brass mailbox built into the reception counter. The manager was unlocking it under the supervision of two FBI agents and a representative of the postal service.

"I was talking to one of Griffin's people. He told

me they got the memo a week ago detailing how to set up the sting. What happens is, Griffin will gather everybody's reports, write up a memo summarizing them, and post it back to his people seven days in the past. Pretty slick, actually."

"I don't understand. They seemed like good people. I just can't picture them doing something like this."

"Well, that's what makes it so sad. The wife's mother has schizophrenia. Painful case, apparently. Committed suicide eight, maybe nine years from now, just weeks before the new neural mediators came on the market. Ironic, hey? So when they learned they were coming back, the husband got hold of a few pills and the wife popped them into an envelope along with a letter to her younger self, and . . . well, what you saw."

Leyster stared hard at Monk. "When did you have the time to learn all this?"

"This isn't my first trip. People gossip. I told you that before."

"You son of a bitch. You *knew*. You knew this would happen, and you did nothing to prevent it."

"Hey. I couldn't, remember? That would have created a paradox."

"You could have told Bill. Just a word in his ear: 'Griffin knows what you're planning.' "

"Yeah, that would've worked just fine. It would've stopped them and the whole goddamned project as well! Do you want that? I sure as hell don't."

Leyster spun on his heel, and went into the bar.

* * *

The bartender poured him a single malt, and he carried it into a dim booth in the back. He thought about the Metzgers, and he thought about Monk. He thought about his own culpability. Finally, to keep himself from thinking about those things any more, he got out a pen and started to write words on the napkin. Burning Woman. Predators. Cretaceous. Death.

A woman slid into the booth opposite him.

It was Gertrude Salley. She was more than two decades older than he, but he couldn't help thinking what a good-looking woman she was. The gloom was kind to her.

"You're trying to think of a title for your book."

"How did you know that?"

Her eyes were piercing, flatly lustrous, like a hawk's. Amazing eyes that told him nothing about that hard intelligence burning within her skull. "I know quite a lot about you. I'm not permitted to tell you how." She put an ironic spin on the word *permitted,* to let him know how little hold such rules had on her. "Nor who we were—or will be—to each other."

"Who are we, then?"

There was a small silver scar, shaped like a crescent moon, by the corner of her mouth. It rose and fell with her predatory smile. "A week from now you'll go back for the first time. I envy you that. The excitement of starting from scratch, of knowing that everything you see, everything you discover, is new and important."

"Is it . . ." He couldn't quite put his question

into words. It wouldn't come out right. ". . . as good as I want it to be?"

"Oh, yes." She closed her eyes briefly, and when they opened they were amazing all over again. "The air is richer and the greens are greener and at night there are so many stars in the sky that it's terrifying. The Mesozoic *swarms* with life. You can't appreciate how thinned-out and impoverished our time is until you go back. Rain forests are nothing. They're not even in the running. Stretch out your arm."

He obeyed.

"With my own eyes, I have seen a plesiosaur give birth. This hand"—she held it up to show him, and then reached out to slowly stroke the length of his arm—"stroked her living neck as she lay quivering in the shallows afterward." She offered her hand to him, palm upward. "You may touch it, if you wish."

Almost jokingly, he touched her palm with his fingertips. She closed her hand around them. Her knee brushed against his, and for a second he thought it was an accident.

"Touch my face," she said.

He touched her face. Her flesh was softer than a young woman's, not near so taut. She raised her chin and moved her head against his palm, like a cat, and he felt himself harden. He wanted her.

Salley smiled. Those wide lips moving up in slow synchronicity with the lidding of her eyes. He felt the passion radiating from her like heat from a flame. He wanted to look away. He could not look away.

"Who are we to each other? Are we—?"

"Shhh." The sound was so soft and low as to be a caress. "You always ask too many questions, Richard."

"I need to know."

"Then find out," she said. "Come to my room. I know what you like. I know where to touch you. I *know* I can make you happy."

As if in a dream, he left the bar with her. They went up the elevator together, fingers intertwined, bodies not quite touching. They drifted hand in hand down the hall to her room. The difference in their ages added a touch of perversity to the whole thing which, strangely enough, he found himself liking. Leyster was not a sexual adventurer. He had summer affairs when he was in the field, and videotapes to get him through the winters. This was utterly unlike anything he'd ever done before.

How serious was their relationship, he wondered, in the shared time that lay in his future and her past? It was serious enough for her to go into her own pre-history in search of him. Maybe they were married. Maybe she was his widow. He wanted it to be real. He wanted everything from her.

At the door Salley released his hand to get out her key. He seized her and spun her around. They kissed, his tongue in her, and then hers inside him. Her body was soft and matronly; she ground it hard against his. He touched her face, that magical silvery moon of a scar. She did not close her eyes, not even for an instant.

He saw how she looked at him. It took his breath away.

At last, with a contented sigh, she pulled away. "I have a gift for you."

"Mmmm?"

"The title for your book. I brought along a copy of it."

She opened the door.

A small table had been set up so that it would be the first thing he saw on entering the room. A light shone down upon the book set on end upon it.

First he saw his name, and then he saw the strip of black electrician's tape covering the title. Then he saw the man in the chair behind it.

It was Griffin. He looked considerably younger than he had that morning.

Three security men materialized in the hall behind them. Two took Salley by the arms. The third pushed Leyster into the room and pulled the door shut behind them both.

"Once again, Mr. Leyster, you've made a terrible mess of things." Griffin tipped the book over, and stood. "Leaving it for others to clean up after you."

Muffled by the door, Salley's angry voice dwindled down the hall. "What are they going to do with her?" Leyster demanded. He made a move toward the door. But the security man stood between him and it, sad-eyed and competent. Leyster had never been much of a brawler. He turned back to Griffin.

"Nothing bad. A limousine has been called to take her back to the Pentagon. They'll return her to her proper time, and that's it. Oh, a reprimand will be placed in her file for trying to leak information back in time. But Ms. Salley doesn't much care about that."

"You had no right!" Leyster found he was quivering, with shock, with fear, with anger. "No right at all."

"You, sir, are a fucking idiot." Griffin reached into his jacket and took out a folded sheet of paper. "A woman twice your age tells you a couple of lies and you waltz right up to her bedroom. You think Dr. Salley is your friend? Well, think again." He unfolded the paper and thrust it at Leyster. "Read it and weep."

It was a photocopy of a page from *Science,* dated April 2032. At the top of the page was the title, "A Re-Evaluation of the Burning Woman Predation Site." The paper was authored by G. C. Salley.

Leyster read the abstract, disbelieving, and as he read, the room grew unsteady around him. There was a roaring noise in his ears, as if all the universe were laughing at him.

"That paper is the single most virulent refutation of your book ever printed. And the woman who wrote it almost got to screw you twice. You can open the door now, Jimmy."

Leyster made no move toward the doorway. "You're letting me off with a warning. Why didn't you do that with the Metzgers?"

"The—?"

"Husband-wife team, attempted causal violation," the security man said quickly. "Captured 2012, convicted in 2022, released in 2030."

Griffin seized his wrist and stared down at it, hard. "The world is not a fair place, Mr. Leyster." He looked up again. "We did it the way we did because according to the records, that's the way we did it. The rules against paradox bind us as tightly as they do you."

3

Lagerstätten

Hilltop Station: Mesozoic era. Cretaceous period. Senonian epoch. Maastrichtian age. 67 My B.C.E.

Griffin went straight from the orientation lecture to the Mesozoic. The phoniness of the thing, the charade of shaking hands with himself in particular, had depressed him. He needed to refuel. So, opting to avoid the snares and responsibilities of booking travel through his office, he took a local forward thirty years, and used his clout to slip into a VIP tour group headed for the deep past.

They emerged from the funnel and out into the rich air and hot sun of the late Cretaceous. Dinosaurs still walked the Earth, though they wouldn't for long, and shallow seas so moderated the climate that even the poles were free of ice. Not counting Tent City, where the researchers slept, there were only thirty-seven structures in all the world where one could honestly claim to be indoors.

He was home.

His fellow excursionists were the usual mix of predator capitalists, over-affluent politicians, and decorated heroes of genocidal wars, with a North American admiral and her loud wife thrown in for good measure. Griffin disappeared into the group and let it carry him along. He had the gift for being unobtrusive, when he wanted.

Their guide was what the loud American had, in a sarcastic aside, called "your basic science babe," blond and fetching in khaki shorts, linen blouse, and white cowboy hat. One had to look hard to see that she was actually rather plain. A couple of the gents, smiling secret fantasies at her backside, preferred not to look that hard. Griffin emerged from private thoughts to discover that she was talking.

". . . first thing that people ask is 'Where are the dinosaurs?' " She smiled dazzlingly and swept out an arm. "Well, they're all around you . . . the *birds!*"

In his weary state, the group seemed to Griffin like a cheapjack tourist construction made of bamboo, bright paper, and string, with a crank to turn that would jolt the two-dimensional cutout people into a crude semblance of human life. The guide gave the crank a turn and it chuckled, peered about hopefully, lifted a camera and then decided not to shoot.

"Yes, birds are indeed dinosaurs. Technically speaking, they're derived theropods, and thus they are distantly related to *Tyrannosaurus rex,* and kissing cousins to the dromaeosaurids. Even the birds back home in the twenty-first century are dinosaurs. But the behavior of Mesozoic birds is strikingly different from that of modern birds, and many have toothed beaks. Oh, look! There's a Quetzalcoatlus!"

Crank.

Hands lifted to shade eyes, mouths gaped to let *oohs* and *ohs* escape, the camera swung up and went *whirr*. The girl stood smiling and silent until their reactions had played out, then said, "Now, please follow me up to the top of the observation platform."

Obediently, they shuffled after her, so many celebredons following in the wake of a lithe young nobodysaurus that the least of them could buy and sell by the job lot. Yet such was the power of organizational structure that they meekly did as she directed.

"But when can we see *real* dinosaurs?" somebody asked.

"We'll be able to see non-avian dinosaurs through field glasses from the top of the tower," the guide said pleasantly. "There's also a photo safari arranged for those of you who want to get up close and personal with the animals."

Hilltop Station was situated atop a volcanic plug, steep enough on three sides to keep off everything but the swarms of midges and mosquitos that rose from the southwestern swamps every evening at sundown. The fourth side sloped gently downward to the flood plain, where most of their research took place. From the top of the observation platform, it was possible to see over the rooftops to the horizon in every direction.

". . . and if any of you have questions, I'd be only too happy to answer them."

"What about the theory of evolution?"

Griffin leaned against the rail, savoring the light breeze that pushed back against him. The sky was thronged with birds, semibirds, and pterosaurs: The Mesozoic truly was the first great age of flight. He stared out over the flood plain, with its scattered stands of ancestral sycamore and gum, metasequoia and cypress. Winding rivers shone like silver, dwindling to threads as they reached for the thin blue line along the horizon that was the Western Interior Seaway.

"I beg your pardon?"

"Have they proved the theory of evolution yet?" It was the American wife, of course. "Or is it still just a theory?"

Someone poked Griffin with a pair of binoculars, but he waved them away. He didn't need optics to know the dinosaurs were there. There would be ankylosaurs browsing on the berry bushes along the river banks, and herds of triceratopses speckling the flowered plains. Anatotitans ambled between copses of dromaeosaur-haunted poplar or stripped the leaves from cycads and dawn beeches. Lambeosaurs foraged in the swamps. There were mangroves along the seashore, where troodons hunted small arboreal mammals, and—invisible from here—deltas at the mouths of the rivers, where edmontosaurs built their communal nests, safe from the land-bound tyrannosaurs.

"A theory," said the guide, "is the best available

explanation, satisfying all known facts, of a phenomenon. Evolution has held up to two hundred years of rigorous questioning, in which scientists have come up with enormous amounts of information supporting it, and not one shred of disproof. In the paleontological community, it is universally accepted as true."

"But you don't have a complete record of one of these creatures changing from one thing into another! Why is that?"

"That's a very good question," the guide said, though Griffin knew that it was anything but. "And to answer it, I'll have to teach you a German word, *lagerstätten*. That's quite a mouthful, isn't it? It means 'mother lode.' " She had modulated her chirpy delivery into a practiced sincerity that Griffin found almost equally grating.

"Before time travel, we had to rely on the fossil record, which is extraordinarily patchy. So few fossils are formed, and of these so few survive erosion, and of those, so very few are found! But occasionally, paleontologists stumbled upon *lagerstätten,* fossil deposits of extraordinary richness and completeness. These deposits were like snapshots, giving us a very good idea of what life was like for an extremely brief period of time. But a find like the Solnhofen limestone or the Burgess shale was incredibly rare, and great periods of time were hidden from us."

"But not now," the American said.

"So you would think. But there are only a dozen or so stations like this one scattered through the 175 million years of the Mesozoic. So that the stations themselves are essentially *lagerstätten*—fabulously rich sources of knowledge, separated by gulfs of time so vast that we'll never fill in all the blank spots, try though we might."

The American nodded to herself. "So it will never be proved."

"Anybody can deny anything. But there's good news! One of our long-term projects is to make a series of brief forays into the time between stations, sampling twenty to thirty species once every hundred thousand years. The genetic baselines we establish will be the equivalent of taking a photograph of a rosebud once a minute in order to create a film of it blossoming. Which should be enough, I would think, to convince even the most hard-headed skeptic. That's a lot of work, though, and the results won't be in for quite a while. So we'll just have to wait." Her smile bloomed again, like a time-lapsed flower. "Are there any further questions? No? Well, then, next on our . . ."

The guide was a grad student, of course; otherwise she wouldn't've been stuck with the tour. Griffin made a mental note to find out her name and check her file. She had a real talent for this kind of blarney and was young and foolish enough not to keep that fact a secret. At this rate, she would find herself doing more and more public relations until by incremental degrees she was squeezed out of real paleobiology entirely. Griffin had seen it happen before. Something similar had happened to him.

The platform began emptying around him. Griffin leaned back into the wind and closed his eyes.

His original thought had been to borrow a land rover and drive it west, through the Lost Expedition Foothills and beyond, into the Rockies. Or maybe he could take a jetcopter to Beringia and then backpack north. Or else commandeer a research boat out on the Western Interior or the Tethys. He could do some diving among the clam reefs, maybe even troll for sea monsters. He had months of accumulated vacation leave that he could dip into.

He stood without moving, savoring the sweetness of marsh and flowering brushwood wafted upslope by the gentle east wind.

Then he realized there was somebody standing at his shoulder.

He turned, and there was Jimmy Boyle, sleepy eyes and all.

"Good to have you back again, sir."

"Jimmy," he said, "since when has it been policy to let creationists come through on our VIP tours?"

"She's just a sympathizer, sir," Jimmy Boyle said. "The type who goes to church on Sunday, takes her minister's word for what the Bible does and doesn't say, and would be shocked if you told her he was an ignorant wanker who couldn't find his willie if he used both hands. Harmless, really."

"Harmless."

"Yes, sir."

"Well, I don't think it's harmless at all. People spout this nonsense and it spreads. It metastasises. Damp down a tumor here with carefully ordered arguments, and it sprouts up in a dozen new places. It's easy for them; they can just make up their facts."

Jimmy said nothing.

"What I found most depressing was that not one of the crowd of august decision-makers in the tour thought there was anything outrageous about her questions. They stood there, nodding and smiling, as if it were perfectly reasonable to be doubting evolution with dinosaurs all around them."

"Well, they're from the 2040s, after all, sir. You know what it's like then."

Griffin turned to face west. The mountains, he thought. Definitely the mountains. There were critters out there that no man had ever seen, even after all these decades. The mountain packies hadn't been adequately studied; he could get a paper or two out of it. He'd bring along his rod and reel and catch a few sabre-tooth salmon. It would be fun.

At last his underling's silence had gone on too long for him to ignore. "All right, Jimmy," he said. "What is it? Why were you waiting for me?"

"The Old Man was here."

"Oh, Christ." In Griffin's experience, it was always bad news when the Old Man was involved. A funding crisis in the 2090s. A memo from a hundred million years upstream. A rumble of displeasure from the Unchanging. "What is it this time?"

"He said you'd be coming here, and that there was something I should show you."

They stood staring down at a wooden crate lying atop a long table in the only conference room in the world. There were five of them: Griffin, Jimmy, the security team of Molly Gerhard and Tom Navarro, and Amy Cho, an academic kept on retainer for exactly such incidents.

"Who do you think it's meant to be?" Griffin asked.

"Adam would be my guess, sir. But I'll defer to Miss Cho on this one."

Amy Cho was a heavy matriarch of a woman, who gripped the knob of her cane with gnarled and overlapping hands. "Adam, yes. He's certainly the most totemic choice. Myself, I'd throw in a brass dagger and an iron ring, and attribute the thing to Tubal-Cain. The first metal smith. Son of Lamech. But any nameless peasant drudge would suffice, so long as he died in the Flood." She smiled humorlessly. "Even a woman would do."

It was a human skeleton, and it was beautiful. The light sent prismatic smears of color dancing across the stone surfaces sticking out of the packing pellets.

"What's it made of? Opal?"

"Yes, sir."

"It must have cost a god-damned fortune."

"That it must, sir."

There were many ways to make a fossil. Not all of them were honest. This one had begun as a human skeleton. Somebody had buried it in silt within a pressurized low-temperature water oven of the sort that forgers called a "permineralizer."

The device had several functions. First, it served as an incubator for bacteria living inside the bones themselves. Gently it encouraged them to grow and form biofilms—cooperative structures in the shapes of pipes and channels that brought water and oxygen to every part of the bone, and carried away the waste products. Then it fed them a slow but steady trickle of highly mineralized water. Forgers usually favored calcites and siderites to produce the characteristic pale or red-black luster of common fossils. But in this case, they had gone with silicates to achieve the sort of pre-Reformation splendor that wouldn't have looked out of place in the Vatican.

Warm and coddled inside their box, the bacteria happily ate, drank, and multiplied, until no organics at all remained in the bone. Then they died. Each one left in its place a tiny lump of minerals, taken in with the water they consumed but of no metabolic use to them whatsoever, and thus discarded.

In this way microscopic creatures excreted perfect replicas of the bones of a creature millions of times their size.

"Walk me through this one," Griffin said. "Exactly what were they planning to do with this thing?"

"Well, first they'd bury it, sir. Likely they've identified a fossil bed in the late twenty-first century that was laid down right about now. Couldn't say where that would be."

"Holy Redeemer Ranch," Amy Cho said. "They train their own paleontologists there. Last year they graduated six Ph.D.s in Deluge Biology. They excavated quite a nice *Chasmosaurus* skeleton, and then ground it to powder in the hope that they would get variant radiometric readings from different portions of the same bones, thus disproving traditional dating methods." She hobbled over to a chair, and slowly began to sit. Jimmy hurried to offer her a hand. "They didn't. Which is why they never published their findings."

Seated at last, she added, "I went to a prayer breakfast there once. Had a lovely time."

"What I want to know," Molly Gerhard said, "is what possible good this would do them." Molly was the younger of the security officers, a redhead, all but quivering for action. Tom Navarro was a bland and burly man, and clearly the mentor of the team. He was the falconer, and she the hawk he flew from his hand. "They plant some bones. So what?"

"It is the Grail," Amy Cho said, "of creation science. Actual human bones fossilized *in situ* within rock strata previously documented by geologists as being tens of millions of years old. In their frame of reference, of course, these sediments were laid down about 4,500 years ago, and the dinos are merely animals that drowned during the Flood. So if a human skeleton is found among the dinosaurs, that's incontrovertible proof that they're right and we're wrong."

"It could be a scientist," Molly said dubiously. "Wandered away from his camp and met a mishap."

"Billions and billions of dinosaurs to produce just a few thousand fossils, while a solitary lost scientist is fossilized and recovered ages later? Nobody's going to buy that," Tom said gently. "I wouldn't."

Griffin felt an overwhelming urge to check the time, and clamped a hand over his watch so that when he looked, as he inevitably must, he wouldn't see the dial. It didn't pay to give in to these impulses. He knew that from long experience.

He looked up. "How long was it in storage before it was found?"

"Six months."

"Then whoever was supposed to retrieve it, didn't."

"Likely he got scared off. Something happened to make him think we were watching for him," Jimmy said. "Or her," he amended when Amy Cho scowled. "I would, however, like to draw your attention to a particularly clever little bit of business. Notice the label."

Those on the right side of the crate moved closer to look. Molly walked around to join them.

" 'Martin Marietta,' " Griffin read aloud. " 'Ptolemy Surveyor Launch System Tripod. Caution: To Be Operated By Trained Personnel Only.' "

"The Ptolemy is an orbital surveying system. It can be launched in the field by just three people: two to carry the rocket, and a third to set up the tripod. One of the first things we do when we establish a baseline station is send up a satellite to make maps. Thing is, it was a very good system in its time, but that time is past."

"Refresh my memory. What's our sister date back home?"

"2048, sir."

"Well, that's something, anyway." For Griffin, the great operational divide was not between the human era and the Mesozoic, but between those times with a home date prior to 2034, when time travel was a secret, and those after, when it was common knowledge. He never liked working pre-2034 dates. He hated secrecy.

"We advanced to Mercator-class mapping satellites in late 2047. So the labeling on this crate was particularly good. It was something just obsolete enough that nobody would use it, but not so far out of date they'd be surprised it was shipped through. Cunning stuff, methinks."

"Thank you, Jimmy. Does anybody have anything more?" Griffin waited. "All right, then, let's put it together. We've got a box of sacred bones, somebody who knows which nondescript patch of land here-and-now is going to be fossil-rich sandstone at Holy Redeemer Ranch sixty-seven million years in the future, and the very specific knowledge that a Martin Marietta Ptolemy launch system was newly obsolete. All of which adds up to—what?"

"It means we've got a creationist mole among our people," Molly said.

"A *deep* creationist!" Cho thumped her cane for emphasis. "Not a garden-or-cómmon-or-everyday creationist, but a deep creationist."

"What's the difference, then?"

"They're the ones who believe in violence. They're the ones who kill people."

There was a moment's silence as they all absorbed this information.

"What options are open to us?" Griffin asked at last. "Can we go back and intercept this thing when it's delivered? Most importantly, can we capture the mole before he does something else?"

"There haven't been any disappearances or unexplained absences in the last six months among the scientists, sir. Which is where our mole would be nestled. So no, we can't."

Molly glanced quickly at Tom and said, "I've gone over the records. There's nothing on who delivered this crate, when it arrived, who signed for it. It simply shows up on the inventory one day. And we know that *some*thing frightened off our mole."

"Have you gone through everything?"

"Yes, sir, I have. There's a great deal of silence surrounding the arrival of the crate. Somebody—and I have every reason to believe it's us—has gone to a lot of trouble to create that silence."

"Is it a big enough silence to inject an operation into? Realistically speaking, is there enough space there for us to operate a sting?"

Everybody leaned ever so slightly forward to hear Molly's answer. Eyes gleamed. Even Amy Cho showed a feral flash of teeth.

"Yes," she said. "Yes, I'm sure of it."

When they had finished making plans and all had been given their orders, Griffin dismissed them and went to his office. No matter where or when Griffin found himself, his office always looked the same. He insisted upon it. Desk *here* and liquor cabinet *there*. Active memos in the top left hand drawer in order of issuance. Backup documentation one drawer down. Forms, letterhead, and a ream of cream-colored heavy bond at the bottom. From the Triassic to the Holocene, from Pangaea through the breakup of the supercontinent into what eventually became the modern configuration of continents, he liked to find his pencils sharp and where he expected them to be.

It had been a good day's work. Briefly, he felt content. Then he read halfway down the first of the active memos, and his stomach soured.

It was a schedule for a series of lectures in which generation-one celebrities visited generation-two and generation-three research stations to lecture young scientists on the history of their field. He always scanned these carefully because the temptation for a researcher to pass information back to a formative idol was so great.

The third lecturer listed was Richard Leyster.

Among those slated to attend was Gertrude Salley.

He slammed open a drawer, drew out a sheet of letterhead, and began drafting a memo. *To all concerned: The third lecture on the attached sheet has been permanently canceled. All care will be taken henceforth that Salley and Leyster are not to be given the opportunity to . . .*

The door opened and closed behind him. The room filled with a familiar presence.

"Don't stand up," the Old Man said.

"I wasn't going to."

The Old Man walked over to the liquor cabinet and poured himself a shot of bourbon. He raised it to his nose and sniffed, but did not drink.

Then he picked up the memo Griffin had been working on, and tore it in half.

Griffin closed his eyes. "Why?"

"You've been listening to rumors again." The Old Man dropped the torn halves on the desk. "Otherwise you wouldn't be trying to keep those two apart."

"So I pay attention to rumors. I'm just playing the edges. If I want to get anything accomplished, I've got to play the edges. What other chance have I got?"

"There are no edges here." The Old Man put down his glass to remove a folder from his attaché. "Here's the report on the probe you've set into motion today. It doesn't catch your mole. He has to expose himself. You'll have to let him act out his intentions."

"Don't tell me any more. Leave me room to maneuver."

The Old Man shook his head. "Read the report. Then play it the way it's written."

Reluctantly, Griffin opened the folder. He turned the cover page, folded it flat, and began to read.

Halfway down the first page, he stopped.

"You've made a mistake here. I wasn't supposed to see the list of casualties."

"That was deliberate. I felt you were ready."

"*Damn* you," Griffin said vehemently. He could see no operational or administrative reason why he should know this information. Only malice could account for its disclosure. "Why implicate me in this? There's a big difference between sending people into a dangerous situation, and sending them out to die."

"Not so big as you might think."

"It's murder, plain and simple."

The Old Man said nothing to this, nor did Griffin expect him to. He slowly read through to the very end of the report, sighed, and said, "So that's why Leyster hates me. God help me. If I'd known, I would've been easier on the poor bastard."

"These things happen."

"Because we allow them to!"

"They happen because they happen. We dare not interfere. Don't pretend you don't know why."

To this, Griffin had no reply.

The Old Man went to the window and adjusted the blinds. Griffin winced as the late afternoon sun hit his eyes. Outside, a land rover had arrived and was surrounded by enthusiastic grad students. He gestured with his still-untouched glass. "Look at them. So young and full of energy. Not a one of them has the faintest notion how contingent their universe is."

He twisted the blinds shut again, leaving Griffin dazzled and blinded. "They're all going to die. Sooner or later. Everyone dies."

"But not because of me. Damn it, I won't do it! I'll tear the whole rotten system apart with my bare hands first. I swear I will!"

But it was empty bluster, and they both knew it.

"Everybody dies. So much of growing up consists of coming to grips with this fact." The Old Man again put down his glass and opened his attaché. This time he emerged with a brown paper bag, which he upended over the desk. The object it contained rolled noisily out. "This is for you."

It was a human skull.

The skull had not been long in the ground—a few decades at most. A patch of fine green moss discolored one cheek. There were fillings in the teeth.

Griffin's mouth went dry. "Whose is it?"

"Whose do you think?" The Old Man crumpled up the bag and stuffed it in a pocket. Then he drank down the bourbon he'd been holding all this while, abandoned the glass, and turned to leave. At the door, he paused and said, "*Memento mori*. Remember you must die."

He closed the door quietly behind him, leaving Griffin staring, horrified, at the skull the Old Man had given him.

His own.

Crossing the compound toward the building housing the time funnel, Griffin saw the young paleontologist who had been his guide that morning, helping move a newly-captured velociraptor from the land rover to one of the outdoor pens in the rear of the animal colony. He stopped to watch. She was one of three who had choke-sticks looped around its throat. It struggled ferociously, but could not reach any of them with its wickedly sharp claws. A wrangler stood by with an electric rifle in case it broke loose.

She was glowing with sweat and exertion, and grinning like a madwoman. It was obvious to Griffin that this was the single finest moment of her life to date.

"Are you coming, sir?"

"In a minute, Jimmy. You go ahead. I'll be right with you."

He waited until the animal had been successfully caged, and then approached the young woman. "That was a fine job you did this morning, leading the tour group."

"Uh . . . thank you, sir."

"I am not without influence. I want you to know that I'm going to recommend you for a promotion to full-time public relations. There are no guarantees, of course. But if you persevere, I can see you heading up the entire department in not that many years." The woman stared at him in bafflement. He placed a hand on her shoulder.

"Keep up the good work. We're proud of you."

Then he strode off, careful not to look back. In his mind, he could see her turning to the nearest bystander, and asking *Who was that?* He could see her eyes widen with horror at the answer.

Sometimes in order to achieve any good whatsoever, you simply had to lie to people.

Griffin hated that too.

4

Cuckoo's Nest

Bohemia Station: Mesozoic era. Jurassic period. Malm epoch. Tithonian age. 150 My B.C.E.

Salley awoke to the sound of camptosaurs singing.

She sighed and stretched out on her cot, one arm brushing against the mosquito netting, but did not get up. Salley never awoke easily. Not even on a day like today.

A day when she intended to change the world.

Nobody knew why camptosaurs sang. Salley thought it was out of joy, pure and simple. But that was going to be hard to prove. So she had other theories as well, some published and others she had simply made known. She had learned at an early age that it was not how often you were wrong that counted in science, but how often you were right. One startling hit covered a multitude of bad guesses.

So she had also posited that camptosaurs sang as a means of keeping the herd together. That their song was simply phatic noise, a way of reassuring each other that everything was okay. That by announcing their numbers, they warned predators away—be off, sirrah, we are too many for you! That they were comparing the taste and savor of the vegetation.

Honest to God, though, it sounded to her like joy.

Outside, an internal combustion engine roared to life. Two people walked past her tent, sleepily arguing the phylogenetic position of segnosaurs. Somebody rang the breakfast bell. Like a slumbering beast, the camp stirred lazily and shook itself out of its drowse.

Salley turned over on her stomach, reached under the netting, and felt around on the floor for her clothes. She really ought to do some picking up while the day was young—the tent would be hot as an oven by noon, and by the time it cooled down she expected to be long gone. But the way she saw it, you only had so much organization in your life. You had to choose: Invest it in your research, or fritter it away on housework.

Her socks were clean enough to wear for a second day, which seemed to her a particularly good omen.

The mess tent was filling up with chatter and coffee fumes. Salley snagged a tray and stood in line for sausages and grits.

She chose an empty table in an obscure corner of the dining tarp, half hoping Monk Kavanagh would sleep late and she could have some privacy for a change. But no such luck. She'd barely begun eating when he slid onto the bench beside her and flicked on his recorder.

The historian was a bald and hulking old man with a pink face as soft and crinkled as tissue paper and a tidy white mustache. He greeted her with an obnoxious little smirk that was evidently meant to be endearing. "You look like you've had a rough night."

"Being in the field is a lot like Girl Scout camp. Except Girl Scouts usually don't have next-door neighbors who like to invite their boyfriends into their tents and have screaming orgasms into the small hours of the morning."

"Oh? Anybody of note?"

Salley shut her eyes and took a long sip of coffee. "Okay, where was I?"

"You'd just been asked to leave the university."

"God! What a fucking mess. Do we really have to talk about that?"

"Well, it's part of our history, after all."

Four years ago, Salley had been caught up in an intellectual-theft scandal that almost destroyed her career. She had been sleeping with her advisor, a man better known for his fieldwork than his teaching skills, and some of his ideas found their way into one of her papers.

"Didn't he go over the paper first?"

"Of course he did. We went over it together, discussing the issues, and he went off on one his rants. That's when he mentioned his ideas and their application to what I was saying. He as good as *told* me to use them."

"There's a story that you two were in bed together when he went over the paper."

"Oh yeah. You'd have to know Timmy to understand. He said that sex helped to focus him. I know how stupid that sounds. But I was infatuated. I thought he was a cross between Charles Darwin and Jesus of Nazareth."

Monk nodded encouragingly.

"I had no idea I was doing anything wrong. The notion that ideas could belong to people was—I thought that the truth belonged to everybody. And I honestly did try to show him the final draft. He just waved it off. He said he trusted me. The bastard."

"You were asked to leave, and then the next semester you popped up at Yale. How did that happen?"

"I went to see the department head, and cried until he agreed to call in a favor." She shoved a sausage in her mouth and chewed it to nothing. "It was the single most humiliating experience in my life."

"That would have been Dr. Martelli, I believe."

"I swore to myself then and there that I'd never cry in public or sleep with another paleontologist again, so long as I lived. And I haven't."

"Well, you're young. Martelli was one of your on-line mentors, wasn't he?"

"Everybody was. I mean, not to be immodest, but when I was a teenager, I was everybody's favorite wannabe. God bless the Web. I was in correspondence with half the vertebrate paleontologists in the world."

"Here. Look this over." Monk placed a sheet of paper by her plate. "Tell me if I got anything wrong."

Salley shifted the spoon to her left hand so she could keep on eating, picked up the paper, and read:

Everyone who knew her agreed that Gertrude "gave good daughter." Except, of course, her own parents. At age five she took a pair of shears to the family Atlas and made silhouette dinosaurs. That same year she told her mother she wanted to marry a stegosaur when she grew up. At age seven she threw a fit when her parents wouldn't take her to China to dig for fossils for summer vacation. It was a relief to them when, in junior high, she discovered the listservs on the Web and jumped in with both feet, asking naive questions and posing wild hypotheses. One of these—her notion that dinosaurs were secondarily flightless—she wrote up and submitted to the scientific journals when she was fifteen. To her outrage, it was not accepted. By then she was the indulged and spoiled daughter to a generation of paleontologists. At eighteen she was accepted by the University of Chicago. At twenty-one she was involved in a serious academic scandal. At twenty-three she was briefly famous when she announced her discovery of a "feathered pseudosuchian" fossil. Though initially accepted by the popular press, it was met with skepticism in the scientific community. At age twenty-four she met and took an instant dislike to Richard

Leyster. At twenty-five her "pseudosuchian" had been widely discredited, the paper she published criticizing Leyster's work, though controversial, was not highly regarded, and Gertrude, no longer the youngest dinosaur expert in existence, was staring hard into the abyss of failure.

Salley mopped up the last of her grits with a bit of toast, and returned the paper. "I never use my given name. I'd prefer you called me Salley, okay?"

"Ah." He made a note on the paper. "Anything else?"

"Monk, are you going to have any actual science in your book?"

"Science? It's all science."

"What I've seen so far is just chitchat and gossip." She finished her coffee and picked up her tray. "Come on. I've got something to pick up over to the animal colony, and then I'll show you some real research. Maybe you'll learn something."

The animal colony was a windowless prefab with corrugated metal walls and a noisy air-handling system. "We call this Bird Valhalla," Salley said. She opened the door, and the warm scent of bird droppings touched their faces. "Looks like the 4-H poultry shed at the state fair, doesn't it?"

Archies screamed and lashed the bars of their cages with clawed wings as the door slammed shut. They were boldly patterned birds with long feathered tails, vicious little teeth, and dispositions to match. Their plumage was orange and brown and red.

An absorbed-looking young man put down a sack marked *Archaeopteryx Chow,* turned, and blinked with surprise to see them there. "Hey, Salley."

"Monk, this is Raymond. Raymond, Monk—he's writing a book about Bohemia Station."

"Oh, yeah? He should've been here yesterday. We pumped the hall full of tiny helium-filled bubbles, and flew a couple of archies down it, so we could photograph the vortices of their flight. Got some nice shots. *National Geographic* quality. Not that we're allowed to submit anything to a public forum."

"Let me guess—they were all continuous vortexes, right?"

"Uh . . . yeah."

"So you've just proved that an archie can fly fast, but not slow. Brilliant. It would've taken me ten seconds of direct observation to tell you the same thing."

Birds, with the exception of hummingbirds, which flew unlike anything else, had only two modes of flight—slow and bat-out-of-hell fast. The slow mode left pairs of loop-shaped whorls in the air behind them, while the disturbance of the fast mode was continuous. Slow flight was the more difficult mode to achieve, a refinement of primal flight that wouldn't appear for tens of millions of years yet.

"It was Dr. Jorgenson's experiment. I just helped run it." To Monk, he said, "If you're writing a book, that means you're from later in the century than we are. How long do we have to wait before we can publish our work?"

"I'm really not allowed to say."

"This idiot secrecy really screws up everything," Raymond said sullenly. "You can't do decent science when you can't publish. That's all fucked up. We had a group from the Royal Tyrrell through here last week, and they'd never even heard of our work. What kind of peer review is that? It's nuts."

Monk smirked. "I agree with you completely. If it were up to me—"

"Much as I enjoy listening to you guys whinge," Salley said, "Lydia Pell's expecting me to spell her at the blind. You want me to pick up another archie while we're there?"

"Uh . . . yeah, thanks. We can always use more. Jorgenson keeps letting ours go."

"You got it." She snagged an animal carrier and turned to leave. "Come on, Monk. Let's go look at the wildlife."

It was a glorious day to be trudging along the dunes. The sky was purest blue and a light breeze came off the Tethys Sea. Every now and then an archie would burst screaming out of the shrubbery at the edge of the trees and flap wildly away, low over the sand. An archaeopteryx rarely flew higher than the treetops. The upper air still belonged to pterosaurs.

Occasionally they flushed a small feathered runner of one variety or another from the brush, but these were rarer. Once they saw two sandpeepers—small compsognathids, not much larger than crows—fighting over a scrap of rotting meat on the beach.

Salley pointed them out. "Dinos. Small. No feathers. What does that tell you?"

"There are *lots* of feathered dinosaurs. Even you won't deny that."

"All birds have feathers. But only some dinosaurs. That's because feathers are a primitive condition for the ancestors of dinosaurs and birds. Birds kept the feathers, dinosaurs mostly lost 'em."

"Secondary featherlessness?" He laughed. "Is this anything like your secondarily flightless *Apatosaurus*?"

"Cut me some slack—I was fifteen when I wrote that paper suggesting that dinosaurs were descended from volant reptiles."

"But they've gone back to the Triassic, and nobody's found a living specimen of your hypothetical ancestor. How do you explain that?"

"Tell me something, Monk. How many important scientists—*important* ones—do you think made it to the senior prom?"

"I honestly can't say I've given it much thought."

"Hardly any. Here's something I've observed—the most popular kids in high school never become much of anything. They peak in their senior year. It's the dweebs, geeks, and misfits, the fringe types, the loners, who grow up to be Elvis Presley or Richard Feynman or Georgia O'Keeffe. And, similarly, it isn't the successful organisms that evolve into totally new forms. The successful organisms stay where they are, growing more and more perfectly adapted to their ecological niche until something shakes that niche and they all die. It's the fringe types that suddenly come up out of nowhere to fill the world with herds of triceratopses."

"Well, that's one way of looking . . ."

"The first feathered animal, whatever it was, was small and obscure. It developed something that gave it a very slight edge in a very marginal niche, and then it stayed in the shadows for a long time. Until God rolled the dice again, and scrambled all the niches. Dinosaurs were like that, back in the Triassic—just one nerdy group of archosaurs out of many, and far from the most successful one. My feathered pseudosuchian, too.

"Those guys back in the Triassic are looking in all the obvious places. Wrong. If I ever get the goddamned bureaucracy to post me back that far, you can bet I'll be poking around behind the bleachers and out on the fire escape."

Monk shook his head admiringly. "You never give up, do you?"

"I beg your pardon."

"Admit it. The evidence so far is all against you. Odds are, you're completely wrong."

"Wait and see, Monk. Wait and see."

From ahead, where the dunes gave way to salt marshes, came the low warbling sound that a camptosaur herd makes when something spooks it.

Monk shivered and glanced nervously inland, where the brush gave way to scrub pines. "It's not dangerous out here, I hope?"

Camptosaurs were skittish beasts, as likely to be frightened by their own imaginations as by a carnivore. But Salley felt no obligation to spell things out to Monk. "You're not much of a field man, are you?" she said amiably.

They walked on in silence for a time. The trail across the dunes was faint, but definite. In all the world, only humans made trails like that, running parallel to the seashore. Salley thought of all the human trails the researchers had made, radiating out in a dwindling fan from Bohemia Station. It got her to thinking about dino trails. There were thousands of them in the brush. If they could be mapped and classified by user species, what a wealth of behavioral information it would reveal! Too much and too tedious work for her to do by herself, of course. But if she could get a couple of grad students assigned to her . . .

"At age twenty-three, you were almost famous."

"Huh? Oh. Yes."

"Why don't you tell me the whole story?"

"Well, I had the fossil, and nobody would even *look* at it. So I decided to do an end-run around the process. I spent a day calling up every major news outlet in the hemisphere and saying, 'This is Dr. G. C. Salley, of Yale University. I'm calling to announce an extraordinary discovery.' Then I'd very carefully explain to them that since the last quarter of the twentieth century it has been generally accepted by the scientific community that birds were directly descended from dinosaurs and that therefore dinosaurs were no longer extinct. You have to spell things out for the press—you can't rely on them to know even the simplest things."

"And then?"

"Then I explained about my fossil. I told them that this meant that birds were not descended from dinosaurs, but from animals that existed before dinosaurs evolved. That birds were at best a sister clade to dinosaurs. And I capped it by declaring, 'Dinosaurs are extinct *again!*' They ate it up and licked the spoon afterwards."

The musky smells of the dunes, with their hints of cinnamon and bayberry, took on a darker tinge of sulfur and rotting vegetation. They'd come to the edge of the salt marsh. The trail divided here into two barely-visible tracks, one leading into the marsh and one into the woods. "We head inland here."

Cycads and low conifers rose up to either side of the trail. They passed into green shadow, walking single file and listening for predators.

Salley wondered how much it would cost to put a Global Positioning System in place. Then anytime a researcher used an animal trail, it could be automatically tracked and recorded, and dumped in a database for analysis back in the twenty-first century. The only trouble would be how to identify which individual trails were made by which animals. But that was grad student work again, and it was easier to get grad students when you didn't have to arrange funding to take them out into the field.

"How would you handle it today?" Monk asked abruptly.

"Handle what?"

"Your feathered fossil. If you had it to do all over again."

She pretended to think, briefly, though she'd gone over the scenario in her mind so many times it almost felt as though it had already happened. "Well, today I've still got a touch of residual fame, so I'd call a press conference instead of working the phones. I'd get myself all glammed up to help ensure they gave the story some coverage. And this time I'd make sure I had a *real good* specimen. The one I had was too fragmented. They said it was a mosaic of different species jumbled together. They said the feather trace was just dendrites. I should've gone back out and dug until I found something complete. Something flashy. Something that nobody could deny."

"That's the key, then?"

"A killer specimen. You got it."

The trail twisted, and there ahead of them was the blind. The walls were made of small tree trunks lashed together, and the roof was thatched with cycad leaves. It sat at the edge of the woods, overlooking a browse plain that had recently been eaten clear by sauropods and now held only low vegetation. "Last man-made structure for 7,900 miles," Salley said. "Lydia built it herself with a hatchet and a ball of twine."

Lydia Pell was sitting in her blind, knitting and reading a book propped up on the shelf beneath the window slit. She put down her knitting and turned off the book when they came in. Salley introduced her to Monk, and then said, "Tell him what you're up to here."

Lydia was round-faced and plump, in a middle-aged way. She opened up two camp chairs for her guests, and said, "Well, it's quite a story. I was making my rounds and, among other things, I had in mind to check up on a widow fisher whose nest I had found, when—"

"Widow fisher?" Monk asked.

"*Eogripeus hoffmannii.* It means 'dawn-fisher.' Named after Phil Hoffmann because it was one of his students who identified it as a basal spinosaur, maybe even the node taxon for the clade." She put a finger to her chin and smiled so he would understand that the student was herself. "A great big thing with a narrow little snout like a crocodile's. Out in the field, we just call them fishers. This particular fisher was a widow because her mate had been eaten by allosaurs a couple of days before."

"Ahh. I see. Go on."

"Well, anyway, I spotted an allosaur behaving oddly. I thought at first she was injured because she was moving so awkwardly. Like this." She stood up and leaned forward, arms tucked up and butt thrust out backward, and made a few comically clumsy steps. "I quickly realized that what I had here was a gravid allosaur—one that was heavy with eggs. But what made her movements so strange wasn't the fact that she was pregnant, but that she was peering around like this." She swung her head back and forth, in a furtive and guilty manner. "Believe it or not, she was *sneaking around!*"

Salley laughed and, after an instant's hesitation, so did Monk.

"Well, exactly. An eleven-meter-long carnivore trying to look inconspicuous is one funny sight.

But also an interesting one. Just what was she up to? Why was she sniffing and searching around like that?

"It turned out she was looking for the fisher's nest. When she found it, I thought she would eat the eggs—which would've been intriguing in itself—but instead, she squatted down over them and with surprising delicacy deposited one egg of her own. And then she left."

"Nest parasitism?" Monk asked.

"Yes. Just like a cuckoo. I picked out a good site, built this blind, and hunkered down to observe."

"Show him the nest," Salley suggested.

Obligingly, Lydia Pell handed Monk her binoculars. "Straight out," she said, "where the land begins to rise. You see that little stand of cycads? Good. Right in the middle of it, there's a darker green spot, and that's the widow. Can you make her out?"

"No."

"Be patient. Keep looking."

"I don't . . . whoah! She just sat up." A bright streak of blue rose up from the cycads—the silvery underbelly of the fisher. She craned her neck to its utmost, peering anxiously into the woods. Then, with a clumsy surge, she stood. Her narrow snout turned one way and then the other. "What's she doing?"

"She's looking around for her mate. A fisher is not a brilliant animal, I'm afraid. Just look at those big-mama hips! All butt and no brain."

"Her back blends in with the shrubs perfectly."

He returned the glasses. "But why is her belly that color?"

"A fisher spends a lot of its time crouching over the water," Salley said promptly. "The light belly makes it less noticeable to the fish." To Lydia Pell, she said, "Tell him the rest of your story."

"Oh, yes. Well, eventually her eggs hatched. The poor widow had to go fishing to feed her hatchlings, and that meant leaving them alone several times a day. Life is not easy for a single mom. Still, it was convenient for me. I was able to monitor the nest on a daily basis.

"The allosaur hatched a good two days later than the others. It was a little bigger than its siblings, and it seemed to me—though I wasn't close enough to be sure—that it got more than its share of fish.

"The next day, there was one fewer hatchling in the nest."

Monk whistled.

"Cain-and-Abel syndrome, exactly right! Every day since, there's been one fewer fisher hatchling. Like clockwork, one fewer every day. Now there's only the one overfed allosaur chick and still the poor misguided widow fisher keeps bringing it fish. How long will the hatchling keep working this scam? Will the widow ever wise up? It's quite a soap opera, you've got to admit."

"How much longer does it have to run?"

"Well, fisher chicks normally leave the nest three weeks after they hatch, so not very long I expect. Unfortunately, I'm expected to be back at Columbia tomorrow, prepping for this year's classes. Which is why I asked Salley to take over here for me."

Monk looked sharply at Salley. She said, "You'd think it would be just as easy to return you to the opening of the school year two weeks from now as it is today."

"That's exactly what I said. But would they do it for me? No. Bureaucrats! 'One day home time for every day deep time. No exceptions.' "

"I hate that kind of thinking. I hate dishonesty. I hate deception. Most of all, I hate secrecy. If I were in your position, I'd hunker down and make them drag me away."

"Well, that's you, isn't it, Salley? Not all of us are such terrible rebels. My things are packed and waiting by the time funnel. This time tomorrow I'll be facing a campus full of freshly-scrubbed, vacuous young faces. I—well! No use dragging things out. It's time I left." She slapped her knees and stood.

They followed her outside.

"Have I left anything? Hat, water bottle . . . You can have the camp chairs. I see you're collecting archies again. Jorgenson doesn't appreciate you, Salley."

"Is there anything I need to know?"

"The widow leaves her nest three or four times a day. Wait until she's out of sight—you'll have at least twenty minutes before she returns. You only need to check on the nest once a day, I expect. When the allosaur leaves, write up your notes and ship them forward. I'll see you get second credit on the paper."

"I look forward to it," Salley said.

Lydia Pell gave Salley a quick hug. "I'm so grateful," she said. "This work means so much to me, and I wouldn't trust it to anyone else."

At last, she left.

"Okay," Salley sighed. "Now we wait. Switch on your machine. We might as well make the most of it."

Hours passed. The interview droned on.

"Where did you find the fossil in the first place?"

"I acquired it at a mineral and fossil shop. On the drive home from a summer dig. I stopped off in—well, never mind where—and struck up a conversation with the proprietor. Naomi was an amateur fossil hunter, and she asked me to identify a batch of specimens she'd picked up, and this was among them. I asked where she'd acquired it, and she got out the maps, and promised to lead me to the spot in the spring."

"You told her how valuable it was, of course."

"Of course."

"But she just gave it to you, anyway."

"Yes."

"You must've hit it off pretty well."

They'd set up business at a table in the enclosed porch in back of the shop—Naomi lived in back and upstairs of the store—going through shoe boxes and coffee-cans of fossils, and slabs of rock wrapped in newspaper. After two hours, with almost everything classified, Salley leaned back in her chair and, staring through the screens, saw a few cottonwoods, a car up on cinder blocks, and the empty gravel parking lot behind a shabby roadhouse some distance down the highway.

Naomi returned from the kitchen with a teapot, and saw her glance. "Not much to look at, I'm afraid," she said. "It gets pretty lonely out here sometimes."

"I'll bet." Salley held a rock up to the light and put it down with the other miscellaneous crocodilian scutes. "How'd you get stuck here?"

"Oh, well, you know." Naomi wore a sleeveless top and a loose skirt that brushed against her ankles. She was a lean woman with sharp features, angular and nervous, with large brown eyes. "See, I bought this place with a friend, but she . . ."

Salley unwrapped one final slab. She took one look, drew in her breath, and stopped listening.

The bones had fossilized in a disarticulated jumble, and then been further damaged by Naomi's clumsy extraction. But they were still readable. One fragmentary ulna was broken open, revealing a hollow interior. The skull had held together better than might be expected, and showed avian hallmarks in lateral aspect, including what might be a modified diapsid condition. There was a fragment of jaw nearby with distinctly unavian teeth.

And winding through the matrix, like a halo around the mangled remains, was a dark feather trace.

"Where did this come from?" she asked, hiding her excitement.

"Up Copperhead Creek, there's a Triassic outcropping. It's one of my favorite fossiling sites. I could take you there, if you like."

Salley, bent low over the fossil, said, "Yes, I'd like that very much."

"You would? You can? Really?" Naomi set down her cup so rapidly that Salley jumped at the sound. She looked up, expecting to see it shatter.

Their eyes met.

Naomi blushed, and turned away in confusion.

My God, Salley thought. She's flirting. With me. Well, that explained those big, googly eyes. That explained her nervousness. That explained any number of odd things she'd said.

In a sudden flash of insight, then, she saw exactly how it must be for Naomi. This poor, lonely woman. Still carrying a torch for the friend who'd saddled her with this business, and then left. And now a hotshot young vertebrate paleontologist comes breezing through her life, bronze-skinned and windblown from a summer spent digging up *Elasmosaurus* skeletons, with a rusted-out old Ford Windstar crammed with fossils and a head full of sacred lore. Small wonder she'd be infatuated.

This kind of empathy was not typical of Salley, and she resented experiencing it now. It made her want to do something for the poor cow. It almost made her wish she were the type who'd feel obliged to give the woman a mercy fuck on the way out.

But she wasn't. And what a mess that would be if she were. Salley didn't believe in an irrational emotional life—not since that mess with Timmy.

She firmly believed that if everyone were ruled by self-interest, there'd be a lot less human misery in the world.

"I have to be back at Yale by Tuesday," she said carefully.

"Oh." Naomi stared down at her hands, clasped about the tea cup.

"Still . . . maybe this spring?" Despising herself, she looked the woman direct in her eyes and smiled. "I bet it's lovely out here in the springtime."

Those eyes lit up with hope. Next time, they said, she would surely be bolder, braver, able to seize the opportunity. "Of course," she said. "I've got camping equipment, a tent. We could spend a few days."

"Good. I'd like that." Standing, Salley reached out and squeezed Naomi's hand. The woman actually shivered. Oh God, Salley thought, you've got it bad. She picked up the fossil.

Casually, she said, "Mind if I borrow this? I'll return it next time I'm through."

None of which she told Monk, of course. He'd've put it in his book—and where was the science in *that?*

There was a sudden flash of blue on the far side of the browse plain. "Whoops, there she goes!" Salley waited until the fisher had disappeared into the forest, and grabbed the carrier. "Come on!"

They ran across the browse plain.

The nest was a shallow depression scratched in the dirt and ringed with the dead leaves and forest litter with which the fisher had covered the eggs while they were hatching. A flattened area beside it was where she had rested while shading her children from the sun and protecting them from predators.

In the center was the allosaur.

The hatchling was appalling and adorable all at once. Looking at it, one saw first the downy white fluffy that covered its body and then those large and liquid eyes. Then, with a *shreep* like a giant's fingernails scraping slate, that horror of a mouth opened to reveal its needle-sharp teeth. It was an ugly little brute, and at the same time as cuddly as a children's toy.

She leaned over the nest to admire the appalling creature. "Watch this," she said to Monk. "Here's how you handle an allosaur hatchling."

She fluttered one hand in front of the creature, and when it lunged forward, snapping, whipped it away. Her other hand swooped down to nab it behind the neck.

Deftly, she popped it into the carrier, and snapped shut the door.

"You're just going to take it? I thought—"

She turned on him, sternly. "Okay, Kavanagh. I've shown you my dirty laundry, I've answered every question you could think of, down to the color of my pubic hair. I haven't held back a thing. Now it's payback time. How are we going to do this?"

He took a deep breath. "I'll bring the carrier with me—I'm rated to bring back living specimens to any time period after 2034. In transit, we swap

ID cards—they don't check them as closely when you're returning from deep time—and I'll hand off the specimen to you. You get off at 2034. I'll go on to your originally planned time."

Doubt touched Salley then, and she said, "It sounds pretty touch-and-go to me. You're sure this will work?"

"In my time-frame—it already has."

Fierce elation filled her, like liquid fire, and she blurted out, "You know! You *know* what I'm going to do, don't you?"

That irritating little smirk again. "My dear young lady. Why do you think I'm here in the first place?"

5

Island Hopping

College Park, Maryland: Cenozoic era. Quaternary period. Holocene epoch. Modern age. 2034 C.E.

Richard Leyster returned from the Triassic sunburned, windswept, and in a foul mood. All the way to the University of Maryland, he stared sullenly at the passing traffic. It was only as the driver pulled into the ring campus that he roused himself to ask, "Have you ever noticed how many limos there are in the D.C. area with tinted windows?"

"Ambassadors from central Africa. Assistant Deputy Secretaries of HUD. Lobbyists with delusions of importance," Molly Gerhard said casually. She had observed the same thing herself, and didn't want Leyster to move on to the next questions: How many time travelers *were* there loose in the world? From when? For what purposes? It didn't do to ask because Griffin wouldn't tell, and once you became sensitized to the possibilities, paranoia invariably followed. Molly had a mild case of it herself.

To distract him, she said, "You've been staring out the window as if you found the modern world horrifying. Having trouble readjusting?"

"I'd forgotten how muggy the summers here could be. And the puddles. They're everywhere. Water that sits on the ground and doesn't evaporate. It feels unnatural."

"Well, we just had a rainstorm."

"The midcontinental deserts of Pangaea are the bleakest, emptiest, driest land anybody's ever seen. There are cycads adapted for the conditions, and they're these leafless, leathery-black stumps sticking up out of nothing but rocks and red sand. That's all.

"But every so often, a storm cloud manages to penetrate to the supercontinental interior. Rain pours down on the sand and washes through the gullies, and the instant it stops, the desert comes to life. I almost said 'blooms,' but of course it doesn't bloom. Flowering plants don't appear until the late Cretaceous. But that doesn't matter. The cycads put out leaves. Desert ferns appear—ephemeral things, like nothing living today. The air is suddenly full of coelurosauravids."

"What are those?"

"Primitive diapsids with ribs that stick way out to either side, supporting a flap of skin. They scuttle up the cycads and launch themselves from the tops, little stiff-winged gliders. I've seen them as thick as mayflies.

"Burrowers emerge from the sand—horn-beaked eosuchians the size of your hand. They frolic and mate in lakes a mile wide and an inch deep, so many that they lash the water to a froth. There's something with a head like a block of wood that's not quite a proper turtle yet, with the plates of its shell still unfused, and yet with its own clunky kind of charm. It's a day of carnival, all bright colors and music, flight and feeding and dropping seeds and depositing eggs. And then, just as suddenly as it began, it's all over, and you'd swear there was no life anywhere this side of the horizon.

"It's a beauty like nobody has ever seen."

"Wow."

"You bet wow. And I got dragged away from *there* to—" Leyster caught himself. "Well, it's not your fault, I suppose. You're just one of Griffin's creatures. What's my schedule?"

The driver parked the limo in one of the student lots and hurried around to open Leyster's door. An undistinguished brick building squatted behind some low bushes nearby. Save for the remnants of the old Agricultural College, the campus dated back to the 1960s and it looked it. As they walked across the lot, Molly flicked open her administrative assistant and began to read.

Leyster was first scheduled to meet informally with an honors colloquium of generation-three grad students. Then there was tea with the head of the Department of Geology. After which he'd give a formal talk to a gathering of generation-two recruits. "Both groups are still time virgins," Molly said. "The gen-two kids have been brought forward from the recent past, and the gen-three guys were shipped back from the near future. But none of them have been to the Mesozoic yet. So they're all pretty excited. Oh, and neither batch is supposed to know about the other."

"Why on earth would you schedule two separate groups for the same time?"

Molly Gerhard shrugged. "Probably because this is when the university let us have the buildings. But it could just as well be simply because that's what we did. A lot of the system runs on predestination."

Leyster grunted.

"For the colloquium, all that's expected of you is to mingle with the kids. Larry"—that was the driver—"will be on hand to make sure nobody tells you anything you shouldn't know. I expect you'll find the gen-three group pretty interesting. They're the first to be recruited knowing that time travel exists. They grew up with titanosaurs on TV and ceratopsians in the zoos."

"Well, let's get it over with."

The generation-three recruits had taken over a student lounge, and were sprawled over the couches or sitting cross-legged on the floor with the television at their center of focus. In one corner, a live archaeopteryx was shackled to a segment of log by a short length of chain.

Leyster paused in the doorway. "*Those* are going to be vertebrate paleontologists?"

"What did you expect? They're most of them from the 2040s, after all."

"What's that they're watching?"

"Nobody told you? Today's July 17, 2034."

If there was an Independence Day for paleontologists, it was today. This was when Salley held her famous press conference, announcing—as if it were her right—the existence of time travel. After today, paleontologists could publish their work, talk about it in public, show footage of a juvenile triceratops being mobbed by dromaeosaurs, sign movie contracts, make public appeals for funding, become media stars. Today was when a quiet and rather dry science, whose practitioners had once been slandered by a physicist as "less scientists than stamp collectors," went Hollywood.

Before Leyster could react to the news, two of the group's lecturers saw him and hurried forward with outstretched arms. He faded into their handshakes. Molly turned her back on him, hit her mark, and begin working the room.

"Hi. I'm Dick Leyster's niece, Molly Gerhard."

"I'm Tamara. He's Caligula." The girl pulled a dead rat out of a paper bag and dangled it over the archie. With a shriek, the little horror leaped for it. "You one of our merry little crew?"

"No, I don't have the educational background, I'm afraid. Though sometimes I think maybe I'd like to get a job with you guys. If something turns up."

"If you're Leyster's niece, I guess it will. Hey, Jamal! Say hello to Leyster's niece."

Jamal sat precariously balanced in a stuffed chair with one broken leg. "Hello to Leyster's niece." He leaned forward, hand extended, and the chair overtoppled forward, to be stopped by an agile little hop of his foot and a grin that was equal parts cocky and shy. "So the prim in the ugly clothes is Leyster? Go figure."

"Jamal has an MBA in dinosaur merchandising. We're pretty sure he's the first."

"Is there money in dino merchandising?"

"You'd be surprised. Let's say you've got a new critter—something glam, a giant European carnivore, let's say. You've got three resources you can sell. First the name. *Euroraptor westinghousei* for a modest sponsorship, *Exxonraptor europensis* for the big bucks. Then there's the copyrightable likeness, including film, photos, and little plastic toys. Finally and most valuable of the lot, there's the public focus on your beastie—all that interest and attention which can be used to subtly rub the sponsor's name in the public's face. But you've got to move fast. You want to have the package on the corporate desk before word hits the street. That rush of media attention is extremely ephemeral."

"Jamal's going to be a billionaire."

"You bet I am. You just watch me, girl."

"Who else is here?" Molly Gerhard asked Tamara. "Introduce me around."

"Well, I don't know most of them. But, lessee, there's Manuel. Sylvia. The tall, weedy one is Nils. Gillian Harrowsmith. Lai-tsz. Over there in the corner is Robo Boy."

"Robo Boy?"

"Raymond Bois. If you knew him, you'd understand. Jason, with his back to us. Allis—"

"Shhh!" Jamal said. "It's coming on."

There was a fast round of shushings, while on the screen a camera focused on the empty lobby of the *Geographic* building. Molly Gerhard recalled hearing that Salley had chosen the site because she knew an administrator there who'd let her have it on short notice. She hadn't told him how big an event it would be, of course. A narrator was saying something, but there was still too much chatter to hear.

"Here she comes!" somebody shouted.

"God, this takes me back."

"Hush up, I want to listen."

There were whistles and hoots as Salley hit the screen. To Molly's eye, she was dressed almost self-parodically, safari jacket over white blouse, Aussie hat at a jaunty angle; still, on camera it looked good. She was carrying a wire cage, draped in cloth.

"Look at how much make-up she's wearing!"

"She's cute. In a twenty-years-out-of-date kind of way."

"Turn it up!" Somebody touched the controls and Salley's voice filled the room:

—for coming here. It is my extreme pleasure to be able to announce a development of the utmost importance to science.

The moment was coming up fast. Smiling, she bent to remove the cloth from the cage, and one of the girls squealed, "Oh my God, she's wearing a push-up bra!"

"Is she really? She isn't really."

"Trust me on this one, sweetie."

But first, I must show you my very special friend. She was born one hundred fifty million years ago, and she's still only a hatchling.

With a flourish, she whipped away the cloth.

As one, the students cheered.

A baby allosaur looked up, blinking and confused, at the camera. Its eyes were large and green. Because it was young, its snout was still short. But when it opened its mouth, it revealed a murderous array of knife-sharp teeth. Except for its face and claws, it was covered with soft, downy white feathers.

It was mesmerizing. It short-circuited every instinctive reaction Molly had.

But she wasn't here to watch TV.

Molly drew back a little, alertly watching the interactions between students, noting who hung together, and which individuals sat adamantly alone. Filing away everything for future reference. Generation three was the single most likely source group for their mole—recruited from a period when the existence of researchers in the Mesozoic was open knowledge but still new enough to be shocking to the radical fundamentalists. Not that she believed her target would be unveiled that easily. She was only establishing a presence today. Still, every little bit helped.

No, just the Mesozoic. Nothing closer. Nothing further away.

She noticed how Leyster leaned forward in his chair and stared at Salley, frowning and unblinking. One of his colleagues touched his sleeve, and he shook it off impatiently. The poor bastard really had it bad.

I don't know why. You'll have to ask the physicists. I'm just a dino girl.

Applause and whoops of laughter.

Something beeped. Her administrative assistant, in phone mode. She stepped out into the hallway to take the call. It was Tom Navarro.

"I'm in California with Amy Cho," he said. "Grab a conference room—we've hit the jackpot. We've been approached by a defector from Holy Redeemer Ranch."

"Holy shit. But wait. I can't get away from this until it's over—it would draw too much attention to me. Can you stall him for half an hour or so?"

"No problem, we'll just let him stew. The flesh comes off the bone so much easier that way."

She slipped back into the lounge to find that the press conference was over. The students were Monday-morning quarterbacking Salley's performance.

"Very shrewd indeed," the weedy one said. Nils, loosely aligned with Manuel and Katie, though there seemed to be something going on between him and Caligula's Tamara.

"If she's so shrewd, why doesn't she copyright the hatchling? All those plush allosaurs with felt teeth and fake feathers. It makes my teeth ache to think how much she's missing out on." Jamal, self-centered and opportunistic, though everybody seemed to like him—Gillian in particular.

"I had a doll like that when I was little."

"She's not a natural blond, is she?"

"According to Kavanaugh's book, she is." Tamara dangled another rat over her archaeopteryx.

Caligula snatched the rat and flung it down to

the floor. Then he stood on the creature's head with one foot, and tore messily at its stomach with his beak.

Jamal grimaced down at it. "Oh God. Oh, gross. Rat innards all over the carpet again."

The teleconference room was a good sixty years old and timelessly bland, though the equipment itself was contemporary. Molly double-checked that the camera was off-line, and then turned on the video wall.

The defector was sitting bitterly in a chair behind a conference table, staring straight ahead of himself at nothing. He rarely blinked.

"When will Griffin be here?" he asked peevishly. He was dressed entirely in black, and had cultivated a small, devilish goatee. All in all, he was the single most Satanic-looking individual Molly Gerhard had ever seen. She was surprised he wasn't wearing an inverted crucifix on a chain around his neck.

Tom Navarro, sitting to the man's left, put down some papers and pushed his glasses up on his forehead. "Just be patient."

On the defector's right, Amy Cho sat smiling down at the top of her cane, tightly clutched by those pale, blue-veined hands. Without looking up, she made a comforting, clucking noise.

The defector scowled.

Okay, kiddies, Molly thought. It's show time!

She dimmed the lights to give her an indistinct background, put her administrative assistant on the table before her, and switched it to steno mode.

Then she snapped on the camera. "All right," she said. "What do you have for me?"

"Who's this?" the defector demanded. "I was supposed to talk to Griffin. Why isn't he here?"

She'd wondered that herself. "I am Mr. Griffin's associate," she said emotionlessly. "Unfortunately, he can't be here at this time. But anything you can tell him, you can tell me."

"This is bullshit! I came here in good faith and you—"

"We have yet to establish that you have anything worth hearing," Tom Navarro said. "The burden of proof is on you."

"That's bullshit too! How could I even *know* about your operation if it weren't riddled with double agents? Your press conference announcing time travel is going on right now! I didn't come here to be treated like a child!"

"You're absolutely right, dear," Amy Cho said. "But you're here now, and you have a message that needs to be heard. So why don't you just tell us it? We'd all be delighted to listen."

"All right," he said. "All right! But no more of this good-cop bad-cop routine, okay? I expect you to keep this guy muzzled." This last was directed at Molly.

Bingo! she thought. He'd accepted her authority. Their little psychodrama was now firmly on course. But she was careful not to let her elation show. Outwardly, she allowed herself only the smallest of nods. "Go on."

"Okay, I stared work at the Ranch four years ago—"

"From the beginning, please," Molly Gerhard said. "So we have a more complete picture."

The defector grimaced and began again.

He was a film maker. After graduating from London University in 2023, he'd returned to the States and the usual round of rejection and menial industry jobs an aspirant director could expect, before drifting into Christian video. He'd had some success with Sunday school tapes and inspirational packages for aspirant missionaries. He specialized in morality tales of people rescued from drugs, alcohol, and situation ethics by a strict literal reading of the Bible. He was always careful to have those transforming passages read aloud by a stern father-figure, who could then explain what they meant. He was particularly proud of that touch.

He'd had success, but no money. Religious producers were notoriously miserly, slow to pay off a contract and quick to point out the spiritual benefits of poverty and hard work.

Nor was there recognition to be had. The Jew-dominated secular film industry, of course, paid no attention to fundamentalist films. None of his work was reviewed, listed, or even noted in their cinematography journals. Awards? Forget it.

So when he was approached by one of the Ranch's recruiters, he listened. The money wasn't great, they told him, but it was reliable. He'd be doing important work. He'd have his own studio.

The Ranch started him out with a documentary of an expedition to Mount Ararat in search of Noah's Ark. Six weeks in Armenia, sleeping in tents and coddling the inflated egos of self-styled archaeologists who didn't even know that the mountain's name dated back not to the Flood but to a prestige-seeking Christian monarch in the fourth century A.D. After that, he made a series of training films showing how to forge fossils. Then revisionist biographies of Darwin and Huxley identifying them as Freemasons and hinting at incest and murder. He admitted that these were speculations.

"Didn't that bother you?" Tom Navarro asked abruptly.

"Didn't what bother me?"

"Slandering Darwin and Huxley. They neither of them did any of the terrible things you claim."

"They *could* have. Without God, all things are possible. They were both atheists. Why shouldn't they do whatever evil things entered into their heads?"

"But they didn't."

"But they could have."

"*If* we can keep to the topic—" Molly said crisply. Amy Cho, sputtering with indignation, looked like she was about to take her cane to Tom. To the defector, Molly said, "Please continue."

"Yes." The defector placed his hands together, as if in prayer, bowed his head over them, and then looked up through his dark eyebrows at her. He looked like a second-rate stage magician building up suspense for his next illusion. "As you say."

Finally, they trusted him enough to let him film a demolitions expert assembling a bomb.

"Who was he?" Tom wanted to know.

"I have no idea. They brought him in. I filmed him. End of story."

The video had been made under almost comically excessive secrecy. He was taken blindfolded at night to a cabin in the mountains to film a man wearing thin gloves and a ski mask while he slowly and lovingly assembled a bomb to the accompaniment of a synthetic-voice narrative. He hired actors to play the parts of Ranch strategists in what they thought were scripted fictions, then muffled their voices and electronically altered their faces, to protect those strategists even further.

"How many videos did you make?" Tom Navarro asked. "When did you start?"

"We made a lot. How to build a bomb. How to plant it. How to infiltrate a hostile organization. Hiding your faith. Passing yourself off as a godless humanist. I lost count. Maybe one a month for the past year?"

"That's a lot of work for so little time," Amy Cho observed.

"No third takes, no re-shoots, no catering," the defector said with a touch of pride. "It may not be pretty, but it's efficient. I gave them good value, and I brought their films in under budget."

"And they dumped you."

"We had a falling-out, yes."

Molly checked the transcript on her administrative assistant. "We seem to have skipped over the cause of your dismissal."

"He was running a porn site," Tom said. "Anonymously, it goes without saying. The Ranch probably would've never found out if he hadn't gotten the fifteen-year-old daughter of one of their administrators involved."

The defector glanced at him scornfully. "It was her own idea, made freely and without coercion. It wasn't exploitative at all."

"It was a so-called 'Christian porn site,' " Tom explained. "That had to be what made them angriest. They hate those things. They think the very name is rank hypocrisy. Know what? I think they have a point."

"I'm having trouble picturing such a thing," Molly said.

"Biblical scenes. Girls in short skirts kneeling in church. The joys of wedded bliss. Saints being flogged and tortured."

"Those were faked. Do I really have to put up with this?"

"We're only establishing why they let you go," Tom said. "I hear the folks at the Ranch are saying some pretty harsh things about you."

"They should talk. *They're* not Christians! Christians are supposed to forgive. I made a mistake and I admitted it. Did they forgive me? After all my work? Like hell they did."

"Of course, dear," Amy Cho said. "Tom, you're not to behave like this."

Tom turned away from the defector, as if in anger, but really, Molly knew from long experience with him, to hide his smile.

Hours later, the preliminary interview was finally done.

"What a piece of work," Molly said to her partner afterward, when only the two of them were left in their respective conference rooms. "How much do you think we can get out of him?"

"Well, he doesn't know a third as much as he thinks he does, and he'll have to be coddled in order to tell us half of that. The Ranch has been careful to keep him away from their mole, and the only times he's actually met any of their operatives, they made sure he didn't learn their identities. On the other hand, he knows exactly what kind of explosives they'll be using, the type of incident they hope to create, and which scientists are their most likely targets."

"So he really can be as useful as I think?"

"*Oh*, yes."

By the time Molly Gerhard joined the afternoon session, it was almost over. She didn't mind. She'd heard Leyster—an older Leyster, admittedly—present it several times before. He invariably began by observing that his lecture before this later, better-informed generation should have been titled "A Fossil Speaks."

Then, after polite laughter, he'd say, "I admit to feeling a little uncomfortable speaking to you. I've only been in the field—exposed to the living reality of the Dinosauria—for a little over a year, and everyone here is a full lifetime ahead of me. So much of what I think I know is surely outdated by now! What could I possibly have to contribute to your understanding?"

He'd look down briefly, then, as if in thought. "A few years ago, my time—a few decades in yours—I was involved with what seemed to me the most wonderfully informative fossil anybody had ever found. I'm speaking of the Burning Woman predation site, which I wrote about in a book called *The Claws That Grab*. Some of you may have read it." He always looked surprised when they applauded the book. "Uh . . . Thank you. It seemed to me to provide a perfect test case for calibrating our earlier observations. How close did we come? How short did we fall? We could not, for obvious reasons, hope to locate the original site, but predation was not uncommon in the Mesozoic . . ."

From which point, he'd get down to specifics about the Burning Woman tracks, what aspects he'd read correctly and which had turned out to be wrong in surprising ways. He was not a brilliant speaker. He fumbled words and dropped sentences and went back and started to re-read them and stopped midway through to apologize. But the students never minded. He knew what they needed to hear. He showed them what it was like to think brilliantly about their discipline.

That lecture always lit a fire in them.

She entered the lecture hall just as the question-and-answer session ended. There was a tremendous roar of applause, and while the front rows converged upon the speaker, the back rows emptied quickly into the hallway outside. There the students clustered into knots, excitedly discussing what they'd just heard.

Molly Gerhard experienced a kind of culture shock, encountering these sober gen-twos after the more freewheeling gen-threes. It was like traveling back to the Victorian era. Port and cigars in the library, and scientists who wore formal clothes to autopsies.

Leyster moved slowly up the aisle, chatting with anyone who approached him. He was back among his own.

Molly's primary mission today was to make an impression on as many grad students as possible, so that when she popped up in the Mesozoic, it wouldn't seem suspicious. Somebody would remember meeting her and she wouldn't be an inexplicably unqualified stranger but, rather, Dick Leyster's unqualified niece. A clear-cut case of nepotism and not a mystery at all.

She closed her eyes, listening for the loudest voice of the many in the hall. Then she headed straight for the clique of students from which it originated, and waltzed right in.

"—body talks about land bridges," the speaker was saying. She almost didn't recognize Salley, who was apparently trying out a new and transient look involving red dye and a razor cut. "That's because their teachers made such a big deal about the Bering Strait land bridge in grammar school. But land bridges between continents are rare. The more common way of getting around is island hopping."

"You mean, swimming from island to island?" somebody asked.

"The islands would have to be damned close together for that. No, I'm talking plate tectonics.

There are a couple of ways it could happen. You could have a microplate raft off across the ocean. The Baha Southern California microplate is moving up the coast, but if it were heading westward, it would fetch up against Siberia in a few tens of millions of years—these things happen. Or you could have a new island chain formed by a plate margin coming up. The dinos could cross the ocean without even being aware of it."

"Is this commonly accepted," Molly asked, "or is it your own theory?"

Salley stopped. "Excuse me. Who did you say you were?"

"Molly Gerhard. I'm Dick Leyster's niece."

"Wait. You *know* Leyster? Personally."

"Well, I should, he's—"

Taking Molly's elbow, Salley steered herself away from the others, leaving the conversation unfinished. "What's he like?"

"Um . . . Stern, a little shy, kind of internal, you know?"

"I'm not interested in that kind of cult-of-personality crap," Salley said impatiently. "Tell me what he's like as a researcher."

"Well, I'm not a paleontologist myself—"

"I can tell." Salley dropped her arm as Leyster's group moved past them. Abandoning Molly, she went hurrying after.

In *Just a Dino Girl,* Monk Kavanaugh had written of this very lecture that "Salley sat in the back row, enraptured. There was so much going on in Leyster's brain! She knew there were things he suspected, or speculated, or intuited, that he was not about to say aloud because he could not prove them. She wanted to pry these secret possibilities out of him. She wanted to see him fly."

By sheer luck, Molly had chanced upon a moment that was famous in paleontological gossip. She decided to tag along. She had never seen anything happen that would later wind up in a book.

She caught up just as Salley held up a battered, much-read copy of Leyster's book and asked for his autograph. She saw Leyster's modest smile, the way his hand dipped automatically into a pocket for his pen. "It's not really very good," he said. "It was the best I could do, given what we knew then, but so much of what we knew then was wrong."

Then, overriding her polite protests, he asked, "Do you want it inscribed? Yes? How should I make it out?"

"To G. S. Salley. I don't use my—"

"You!" He slammed the book shut and shoved it back into her hands. "Can't I get *rid* of you?"

He turned his back on her, and strode away. Molly, watching, saw Salley's look of bewilderment harden into anger. Then she too spun around, and stormed off in the opposite direction.

Just a Dino Girl also told how Salley, returning to her own time, would condense Leyster's talk into a tightly-argued critique of his original work and submit it for publication to a geosciences journal. By luck, nobody involved in the peer review was in on the secret of time travel or, if they were, had heard Leyster's lecture. She was careful not to use any information that wasn't available in her own time, and so avoided the wrath of Griffin's people. The paper, when it came out, did much to augment her professional luster and to diminish Leyster's as well.

Molly had less than an hour before she had to escort Leyster back to D.C. She filled it as well as she could.

On the way to the limo, they turned a corner and almost walked into Salley. Leyster turned his head away. Salley's face went white.

You've given her a knife, Molly thought. Then you spat in her face, and dared her to use it. That would be bad enough. But now you've turned your back on her. As if she were harmless.

Leyster really was a royal screw-up. But Molly didn't say that. Nor did she tell him that he was a primary target of the Ranch's terrorists. Molly never said anything without a definite end in mind.

6

Feeding Strategies

Xanadu Station: Mesozoic era. Cretaceous period. Gallic epoch. Turonian age. 95 My B.C.E.

Tom and Molly's report lay unread on Griffin's desk, the first of fifteen such from the team he'd assembled to deal with the creation terrorist threat. All fifteen were from different times, and they were all marked *Urgent*. He wasn't sure yet which he would read, and in what order. He wasn't sure how much he wanted to know.

The mere fact of opening a report had an almost metaphysical dimension. It collapsed the infinite range of possibilities that *might yet be* into a single unalterable account of *what was*. It turned the future into the past. It traded the lively play of free will for the iron shackles of determinism.

Sometimes ignorance was your only friend.

"Sir?" It was Jimmy Boyle. "The Undersea Ball is about to begin."

Griffin hated fund-raisers. But it was his misfortune to be good at this sort of thing. "Is my tux in fashion?" he asked. "Exactly when is this lot from, anyway?"

"The 2090s, sir. Your suit is twenty years out of date, the same as everyone else's. You'll fit right in."

"You haven't seen the Old Man snooping around, have you?"

"Are you expecting him?"

"Good Lord, I hope not. But I've got a feeling about tonight. Something bad is going to happen. I wouldn't be one bit surprised if this weren't the night that the Unchanging finally decided to revoke our time travel privileges."

Jimmy's habitually sad face twisted into a homely smile. "You just don't like formal affairs." The older Jimmy got, the more comforting his presence was. He was close to retirement age now, ripe with wisdom, and, through experience, grown almost infinitely tolerant. "You always talk like this before one."

"That's true enough. Do you have my cheat sheet?"

Wordlessly, Jimmy handed it over.

Griffin turned his back on the reports, leaving them all unread. But as he did, his arm swung up and without thinking he glanced down at his watch: 8:10 P.M. personal time. 3:17 P.M. local time.

It was his own private superstition that as long as he didn't know what time it was, things were still fluid enough for him to maintain some semblance of control over events. It seemed a poor omen to start the evening with this small defeat.

The view from Xanadu was like none other in the Mesozoic. Griffin knew. He'd been everywhere, from the lush green stillness of the Induan era at its outset to the desolation of Ring Station, a hundred years into the aftermath of the Chicxulub impactor strike that ended it. Xanadu was special.

Sunk in the shallow waters of the Tethys Sea, Xanadu was a bubble of blue-green glass anchored and buttressed by rudist reefs that twenty-second-century biotechnicians had shaped and trained to their purposes. From the outside, it looked like a Japanese fishing float partially encrusted in barnacles. Within, one stood bathed in shifting, watery light and immersed in a wealth of life.

It was altogether beautiful.

A pianist played Cole Porter in the background. Guests were arriving, being shown to their tables, politely considering the ocean around them, the giant strands of seaweed, the swarms of ammonites, the jewellike teleosts in rich profusion.

But then an armada of waiters swept into the room, trays held high, bringing in the *hors d'oeuvres*: pliosaur wrapped in kelp, beluga caviar smeared over sliced hesperornis egg, grilled and shredded enigmasaur on toast, a dozen delicacies more.

It was like a conjuring trick. Attention shifted and in an instant nobody was looking out at the wonder surrounding them.

Except for one. A thirteen-year-old girl stood by the window, drinking it all in. She had a pocket guide and, now and then when something flashed by, she'd hold it up quickly to catch the image and get an ID. As Griffin watched, a twenty-foot-long fish swam slowly up and eyed her malevolently through the glass.

It was ugly as sin. Sharp teeth jutted out between enormous lips of a mouth that thrust sharply downward. Those teeth, that mouth, and its unblinking, indignant gaze gave the fish a pugnacious appearance. But either the guide wasn't working properly, or she couldn't get the right angle, because whenever the girl looked down at it, her eyes flashed with annoyance and she held it up again.

Snagging a glass of champagne from a passing tray, Griffin strolled over to her side. "*Xiphactinus audax,*" he said. "Commonly known as the bulldog fish. For obvious reasons."

"Thank you," she said solemnly. "It's a predator, isn't it?"

"With those teeth? You bet. *Xiphactinus* is unusual in that, unlike a shark, it swallows its prey whole. The fish go down alive and struggling."

"That doesn't seem like a very good feeding strategy, does it? How do they keep their prey from damaging them?"

"Sometimes they don't. Sometimes they choke on something they swallowed, and then they die. The bulldog fish is not a perfect predator. Still, enough survive to keep the species going."

With a sudden flick of its fins, the bulldog fish was gone. The girl turned to face him for the first time.

He offered his hand. "My name's Griffin."

They shook. "I am pleased to meet you, Mr. Griffin. My name is Esme Borst-Campbell. Are you a paleontologist?"

"I used to be, but I got promoted. Now I'm just a bureaucratic functionary."

"Oh," she said, disappointedly. "I was hoping you'd be sitting at our table."

"I'm honored that you'd want me there." Tickets to the Ball went for a hundred thousand dollars a seat, figured at year 2010 values, and in addition to the silent auction before the meal and the dancing afterwards, those who bought an entire table for six—as the Borst-Campbells had—were given their very own paleontologist, as a sort of party favor.

"I'm just afraid that I'll be stuck with somebody boring who'll want to talk about *dinosaurs* all evening." She managed to invest the word with an immense amount of scorn.

"You don't like dinosaurs?"

"It's rather a boy thing, isn't it? Killer monsters with dagger teeth, creatures so big they could crush people underfoot. What I like about marine biology is how connected everything is. Biology and botany, vertebrates and invertebrates, chemistry and physics, behaviorism and ecology, geology and tidal mechanics—all the sciences come together in the ocean. Visibly. No matter what you're interested in, you can study it here."

"And what are you interested in?"

"Everything!" Esme blurted. Then, embarrassed, "I shouldn't have said that. I'm sorry."

"No, no, you were right to say that." It ranked, in Griffin's estimation, among the best things he had ever heard anybody say. "But about your problem. Let me see." He glanced at his cheat sheet. The first item on it, printed in his own neat hand, read *Esme—Richard L.* "You're in luck. You have Dr. Leyster. The two of you will get along just fine."

"He doesn't like dinosaurs?"

"Well, he does, but I'll tell you what to do."

"What?"

"When you're introduced, look him in the eye and tell him you think dinosaur paleontology is inferior to paleoichthyology."

"Won't that offend him?"

"He'll be intrigued. He's a scientist—he'll want to know why. And he's a natural teacher—by the time you're done telling him, he'll be itching to encourage your interest. Once he's started talking about paleomarine life, you won't be able to shut him up."

Skeptically, Esme said, "Will that work?"

"Trust me, I know the man." Griffin gestured with his glass toward the distant kelp forest. "Now look out there, where the water gets murky. See where the shadows seem to be moving? Those are plesiosaurs, feeding on shrimp. Every now and then, if you watch, you'll see one lazily loop up to the surface for air, and back down for more food."

In companionable silence, they stared into the depths together, watching the shadows move. Eventually it was time for him to give the opening address, and Griffin sent the child back to her table. The plesiosaurs were gone by then.

* * *

Somebody handed him a microphone, and he tapped it twice for attention. He was standing before the window with a galaxy of ammonites to his back, shells flashing as they jetted swiftly by, too many to count.

"Ladies and gentlemen," he said, "let me welcome you to the Turonian Age—the time when clams ruled the seas!" He paused for polite laughter, then continued.

"Believe it or not, despite all the wondrous creatures that surround us—the plesiosaurs, mosasaurs, and giant sharks—the primary purpose of Xanadu Station is to study the rudist clams that make up the reefs surrounding us.

"Why? Because these creatures achieved something remarkable and then mysteriously lost it. Rudist clams began as simple burrowers. But then they learned how to join together in colonies and form reefs. Their shells are corrugated with little bubbles, so it took them less time than other shellfish to lay down calcium. Because they grew fast, they quickly came to dominate the ocean ecosphere. Yet shortly before the end of the Cretaceous, for reasons we do not yet understand, they went extinct. It was only because of this that corals were later able to learn the same trick and filled the reef-building niche, where they remain into the modern age. We cannot explain why this happened. We're here to find out."

He paused, and flashed a sincere grin. "But that's not to say you have to spend the evening watching clams! We have a lot of marine life scheduled for you tonight, beginning with a pair of mosasaurs that should be closing in on us right . . . about . . . now!"

The lights dimmed. Now the tables were illumined only by what sunlight found its way down through the water. Griffin lit up his microphone, swept it around to draw everyone's eyes, and pointed it straight outward. Softly, he said, "Here they come."

From the depths of the kelp forest, two mosasaurs swam straight toward the station. They were thirty-five feet long, demon lizard-fish with nightmare-toothed jaws and dark, sardonic eyes.

They were terrifying.

Even from the safe confines of the station, they were horrific things to see descend upon you. Diners stirred uneasily. Chairs scraped against the floor.

But the mosasaurs were safely under control. In a little room not far away, two wranglers sat, joysticks in hand, controlling the creatures. Biochip interfaces had been planted deep in the reptiles' brains, so that the wranglers could see through their eyes and move their bodies as easily as their own. This pair were their primary herding tools, used daily, and through practice grown assured and responsive.

The mosasaurs twisted, parted, and then converged again. With startling speed, they bore down upon Xanadu and the diners within.

Griffin glanced over at the Borst-Campbell table. While her parents and their guests were intent upon the show, Esme had eyes only for Leyster. She leaned raptly into his murmured words. The paleontologist's hands moved in a circle, describing the flat, lid-like top of a rudist clam, then fluttered underneath that lid to depict the rudist's mantle, which formed a friendly home for complex colonies of symbiotic algae.

The mosasaurs rushed down upon the station with such reckless force that it seemed they must surely crash into the glass walls. But at the last possible instant, they parted to barrel-roll left and right, simultaneously slashing their heads in a savage (and utterly gratuitous) display of teeth. The diners gasped. Then they were gone.

Esme hadn't even looked up.

The worst of it was that she was right. This wasn't science, any more than stunt flying was war. It was merely the whimsical exercise of power.

"There'll be more surprises throughout the evening," he said. "In the meantime, enjoy your meal."

Griffin faded back to applause, and began the round of table hopping. A joke here, a word of praise there. It's banana oil makes the world go round.

Mostly he wanted to keep an eye on the scientists. Griffin thought of them as his problem children. He knew all their faults. This one drank too much and that one was a terrible bore. The meek-looking one was an aggressive womanizer, and the grandmotherly one swore like a sailor. They were all gaping at the lighting fixtures, clusters of museum-grade coiled clams and flaring trumpet shells polished to translucence and appointed with brass fittings. Griffin was sure they were wondering how big an expedition they could fund if they were ripped down and sold.

Waiters slipped in and out of existence. They'd scurry behind the screen hiding the entrance to the time funnel and then pop out immediately on the other side with heavily-laden trays. Pentaceratopsian steaks smothered in mushrooms for those who liked red meat. *Confuciusornis* almondine for those who preferred white. Radicchio and truffles for the vegetarians.

All to the accompaniment of music, pleasant chitchat, and a view that could be matched nowhere else.

Gertrude Salley had been assigned a table as far from Leyster's as Griffin could arrange. The seating plan seemed to be working out well. She certainly was charming her patrons. Right now she was flapping her arms to demonstrate how pteranodons managed to take off from the surface of the ocean. Everyone was laughing, of course, but in a respectful way. Salley knew exactly how far she could go without losing her audience.

Then Griffin's silent beeper went off, and he had to duck out of the late Cretaceous and back into the kitchen, up home in the year 2082.

Young Jimmy Boyle was waiting for him.

Where the old Jimmy Boyle by his very presence radiated competence and calm strength, his younger version was a real pain in the ass. He had a loud mouth, and a special talent for creating chaos.

This time was no exception. The kitchen was swarming with police. In one corner, a man stood very straight, eyes raised, repeating the Lord's

Prayer while his hands were glue-cuffed behind his back. A woman lay on the floor, weeping and clutching her leg as a medbot built a stretcher around her. Both the man and the woman were dressed as waiters. Somebody who had to be the chef was saying, "—outrageous! You must get all these people out of my kitchen. I cannot work with them underfoot!"

"Fucking Americans," Jimmy Boyle said. He meant his two captives. "Think they still own the world."

"The kids in Bomb Disposal will be wanting these, sir," an officer said politely. He held several pieces of what had been a coffee samovar. "For analytical purposes."

"Yeah, right, go ahead." To Griffin, Jimmy Boyle said, "Almost touchingly old-tech, sir. Gelignite, a wind-up clock, and a friction striker. Still, enough to punch a hole right through every window in Xanadu. If you hadn't notified me—"

Griffin waved him silent. "Good work, Boyle," he said, in a voice meant to be heard by everyone in the room. He clapped a hand over the man's shoulder, turning him away from the others. In a voice so low Jimmy Boyle was forced to bow his head to hear, he added, "You asshole. This isn't this way it's done. You were supposed to write up a report afterwards, and forward it to me the day before the Undersea Ball. *Then,* if I thought it was important to do so, I'd've put in an appearance. It wasn't your place to make this decision."

"Well, I thought you'd be wanting to know about this as soon as possible."

"What I wanted was for you to be capable of taking care of this sort of fiasco by yourself. Now, can you do the job or not?"

Jimmy Boyle stiffened. "By damn, sir, you know I can."

"Then do it."

With Griffin looking on, Jimmy Boyle spoke with the chef. First he offered to hire another caterer to finish the supper if she wasn't up to the job. It would be easy enough for him to go a week or two into her past and have somebody waiting outside ready to take over right now. Then he asked what additional resources would be needed to keep things on track. Finally, he assured her that she'd have replacement waiters in five minutes.

Boyle then signed off with the police and let them take the two creation terrorists away. He called the waitstaff together, and spoke briefly and intensely about what had happened, and the need to maintain their professional standards. Then he routed a call for two replacements several hours into the local past, and had them briefed and on duty within the time he'd promised the chef.

Then, finally, Griffin felt free to leave.

It had been an ugly one. And a close one, too. But he didn't mention either fact to Jimmy Boyle. The boy had to learn to think for himself, and the sooner the better.

Before going back down the funnel, Griffin dropped into his office and wrote two memos: One was to the woman responsible for the seating arrangements, telling her to shift Leyster to the Borst-Campbell table and Salley to the furthest table from him. The second was to Leyster himself, two days before the Ball, directing him to drop a shark's tooth in his pocket when he went. A big one. The sort of thing a precocious thirteen-year-old marine biologist wannabe would like.

Then he returned to Xanadu.

He arrived just as the tables were being cleared for dessert and coffee. He nodded to the pianist, who began to play. Another cue, and the lights faded to nothing.

On the surface above, it was bright afternoon. The dinner was an evening function and neatly calculated for a local time when just enough light filtered down this deep into the water to provide a dim, sunset-level illumination.

Griffin took the microphone out of his pocket and moved to the front of the room. "Folks, we just got lucky." Heads craned.

Outside, a pod of plesiosaurs flew lazily by the window like great, long-necked, four-winged penguins, drawing a murmurous *ooh* from the diners. They were the most graceful creatures Griffin had ever seen, and that included whales. In his estimation, compared to plesiosaurs, whales were all bulk and no beauty.

"Here before you, we have three adults and five juvenile *Elasmosaurus,* the largest of the plesiosaurs, and the greatest of the reptiles ever to grace the seas. They're neither as fast, nor as fierce as the mosasaurs we saw earlier. Yet I think you'll agree with me that the sight of these animals alone makes tonight memorable."

He didn't mention that it was skillful use of the biochipped mosasaurs that had gently herded the plesiosaurs inward, toward the station. The reefs were rich with life here and the mosasaurs were out of sight, so the creatures began to feed. Plesiosaurs had almost no memory. They lived in the moment.

Griffin paused for a count of ten, relishing the beauty of those long, long necks as the plesiosaurs darted about, catching fish. Then he said, "There'll be dancing soon. In the meantime, please feel free to stand and walk over to the windows. Enjoy."

Somebody stood, a second and third followed, and then the room was filled with pleasant confusion. Griffin pocketed the microphone and checked his cheat sheet. Then he walked over to Esme's table.

The adults were gone. Only Leyster and Esme remained. She was speaking to Leyster so earnestly she didn't even notice his approach.

"But my teacher said that men and women pursue different reproductive strategies. That men try to scatter their seed as widely as they can, but women have more at stake, so they try to limit access to a single male."

"With all due respect," Leyster said, "your teacher is full of it. No species could survive very long if the males and females had different reproductive strategies."

"Yes, I suppose that's—oh, hello, Mr. Griffin!"

"I was just checking up to make sure our Mr. Leyster wasn't boring you."

"He could never do *that!*" Esme spoke with such conviction that Leyster actually blushed. "He was telling me about Dr. Salley's work with plesiosaurs. Have you heard of that?"

"Well . . ." He had, but was surprised Leyster would bring it up.

One of the oldest puzzles in paleontology was whether plesiosaurs were viviparous or oviparous—whether they gave birth to their young alive or laid eggs. Fossil mosasaurs had been found which had died in the act of giving birth. Nothing like that had ever been found for plesiosaurs. Nor had fossilized plesiosaur eggs been found.

Salley had tagged a dozen females with radio transmitters, and spent several months out in small boats, observing them. Whenever one showed up with a newborn tagging alongside her, she went over the GPS maps to see where it had been.

"She found that when it's time the female will leave the ocean, not onto land, but up a freshwater river," Esme said. "The male follows after her. She goes as far as she can, until the river's so shallow she can't go any further. That's where she gives birth. The land carnivores can't get at her in the water. There aren't any aquatic carnivores large enough to threaten her that far upriver. And the male swims back and forth to the downriver side, to make sure nothing comes up after her.

"Isn't that neat?"

Griffin, who had read Salley's original paper, as well as the later popularization, had to agree.

Aloud, however, he said, "You know why I'm here, don't you, Esme?"

It was as if the sun had gone behind a cloud. "It's time for me to leave."

"Alas."

Somebody came up to the table and stood silently waiting for the conversation to end. A servant. His posture was too good for him to be anything else.

"This was the best night of my life," the girl said fervently. "When I grow up, I'm going to be a paleoicthyologist. A marine ecologist, not a wrangler or a specialist. I want to know *everything* about the Tethys."

Leyster was smiling mistily. The kid had really gotten to him. He must've been a lot like her when he was that age. "Oh, wait. I almost forgot to give you this." His hand dipped into a pocket, emerged with the shark's tooth, dropped it in her palm.

She stared down at it in wonder.

The stranger offered Esme his hand. Evidently, her parents were staying to dance.

The girl left.

She'd had a conversion experience. Griffin knew exactly how it felt. He'd had his standing in front of the Zallinger "Age of Reptiles" mural in the Peabody Museum in New Haven. That was before time travel, when paintings of dinosaurs were about as real as you could get. Nowadays he could point out a hundred inaccuracies in how the dinosaurs were depicted. But on that distant sun-dusty morning in the Atlantis of his youth, he just stood staring at those magnificent brutes, head filled with wonder, until his mother dragged him away.

Thinking about Esme and what would become of her made him sad. For an instant he felt the weight of all his years, every petty accommodation, every unworthy expedience.

Minutes after Esme left, a young woman in a short red dress arrived. She hadn't been here earlier—Griffin would have noticed. He snatched out his cheat sheet and, stomach souring, read the final item.

As he'd suspected, it was Esme again.

Esme, ten years older.

She'd been a beautiful child. It should be no surprise that she was a beautiful young woman.

She looked around the room anxiously. Her gaze passed right over Griffin. Evidently, she had forgotten him years ago. But when she saw Leyster, her face lit up and she headed straight toward him.

The band began to play. People began to dance. Griffin watched from the far side of the room as Esme explained to Leyster who she was.

She wore a shark's tooth around her neck on a silken cord.

"Who's the chippie talking to Leyster?"

Griffin turned. It was Salley. She was smiling in a way he couldn't read. "It's a sad story."

"Then tell me it on the dance floor."

She took his hand and led him away.

A slow dance is a slow dance the world around. Briefly, Griffin was able to forget himself. Then Salley said, "Well?"

He explained about the girl. "It really is a pity. Esme was so full of curiosity and enthusiasm when she was a child. She'd make a great biologist. But it was her misfortune to be born wealthy. She had dreams. But her parents had too much money to allow *that*."

"She could've broken away," Salley said dismissively. "Hell, she still could. She's young."

"She won't."

"How do you know?"

Griffin knew because he'd glanced through the personnel records for the next hundred years and Esme's name wasn't there anywhere. "It's what happened."

"Why's she back here?"

"I suppose she's reliving her moment of glory. The last time she seriously thought she might make a life for herself."

Salley watched how the girl put her arms around Leyster's neck, how she stared deeply into his eyes. Leyster looked spooked. He was definitely out of his depth. "She's just a headhunter."

"She doesn't get to be what she wanted. Why not let her have her consolation prize?"

"So she gets her trophy fuck?" Salley said scornfully. "Much good it will do either of them. He looks ashamed of himself already."

"Well, things don't always work out the way we'd like them to."

They danced for a time. Salley put her head on Griffin's shoulder, and said, "How'd she get back here in the first place?"

"We don't publicize it, but occasionally, we'll

make that kind of arrangement. For a considerable fee. Under carefully controlled circumstances."

"Tell me something, Griffin. How did I get that *Allosaurus* hatchling past all your security people?"

"You were lucky. It won't happen again."

She drew back and looked at him coldly. "Don't give me that. I waltzed right through. People turned their backs. Halls were empty. Everything fell into place. How?"

He smiled. "Well . . . thwarted, as I so often am, by bureaucracy, I came to feel that all this secrecy was . . . an unnecessary burden. So I may have given Monk a few hints and pointed him in your direction."

"You shithead." She pressed her body against his. They couldn't have been any closer if they tried. "Why make me jump through hoops? Why make everything so convoluted and baroque?"

He shrugged. "Welcome to my world."

"They say that once in her life, every woman should fall in love with a *real bastard*." She looked deeply in his eyes. "I wonder if you're mine."

He drew back from her a little. "You're drunk."

"Lucky you," she murmured. "Lucky, lucky you."

Hours later, personal time, Griffin returned to his office. The lights were on. Other than himself, there was only one person he trusted with the key. "Jimmy," he said as he opened the door, "I swear my body aches in places I never—"

His chair swivelled around.

"We need to talk," the Old Man said.

Griffin stopped. Then he shut the door behind him. He went to the liquor cabinet and poured himself a shot of 90-proof Bulleit. The Old Man, he noted, had been there before him. "So talk."

The Old Man lifted the top report from the stack and read: " 'Defector said priority was given to opportunities to assassinate high-profile individuals, to which end a short list had been made of opportunities. Primary among these were fundraisers.' "

He dropped the report on the desk. "Had you bothered to read this, you'd know that Holy Redeemer's hit list of people they particularly want to take out has our two favorite media hounds, Salley and Leyster, in positions one and two. You should not have been taken by surprise today. You should have known to keep those two apart."

"So? Jimmy caught the terrorists. You notified him to do so. The system worked as well as it ever does. Meanwhile, I get to keep my options open."

The Old Man stood, steadying himself with one hand on the desktop. Griffin had to wonder how much he'd had to drink already. "We caught two fucking outside operatives, and we've still got a mole in our operation. How did they know about the Ball? Who told them which caterer would be handling it?" He slammed the pile of reports with his fist. "You have no options. Read these. All. Now."

Griffin took his seat.

Griffin was a fast reader. Still, it took him over an hour to absorb everything. When he was done, he covered his eyes with his hands. "You want me to use Leyster and Salley as bait."

"Yes."

"Knowing what will happen to them."

"Yes."

"You're prepared to let people die."

"Yes."

"It's a god-damned filthy thing to do."

"From my perspective, it *was* a god-damned filthy thing to do. You'll do it, though. I'm sure of that much."

Griffin stared long and hard into the Old Man's eyes.

Those eyes fascinated and repulsed Griffin. They were deepest brown, and nested in a lifetime's accumulation of wrinkles. He'd been working with the Old Man since he was first recruited for the project, and they were still a mystery to him, absolutely opaque. They made him feel like a mouse being stared down by a snake.

He hadn't touched his bourbon yet. But when he reached for it, the Old Man took the glass and poured it back into the decanter. He capped it and put it back in the cabinet. "You don't need that stuff."

"*You've* been drinking it."

"Yeah, well, I'm a lot older than you are."

Griffin wasn't sure how old the Old Man was. There were longevity treatments available for those who played the game, and the Old Man had been playing this lousy game so long he practically ran it. All Griffin knew for sure was that he and the Old Man were one and the same person.

Overcome with loathing, Griffin said, "You

know, I could slit my wrists tonight, and then where would you be?"

That hit home. For a long moment the Old Man did not speak. Possibly he was thinking of the consequences of such a major paradox. It would bring their sponsors down on them like so many angry hornets. The Unchanging would yank time travel out of human hands—retroactively. Everything connected with it would be looped out of reality and into the disintegrative medium of quantum uncertainty. Xanadu and a score of other research stations up and down the Mesozoic would dissolve into the realm of might-have-been. The research and findings of hundreds of scientists would vanish from human knowing. Everything Griffin had spent his life working to accomplish would be undone.

He didn't know that he'd regret that.

"Listen," the Old Man said at last. "You remember that day in the Peabody?"

"You know I do."

"I stood there in front of that mural wishing with all my heart—all *your* heart—that I could see a real, living dinosaur. But even then, even as an eight-year-old, I knew it wasn't going to happen. That some things could never be."

Griffin said nothing.

"God hands you a miracle," the Old Man said, "you don't throw it back in his face."

Then he left.

Griffin remained.

Thinking of the Old Man's eyes. Eyes so deep you could drown in them. Eyes so dark you couldn't tell how many corpses already lay submerged within them. After all these years working with him, Griffin still couldn't tell if those were the eyes of a saint or those of the most evil man in the world.

Griffin thought of those eyes.

His own eyes.

Loathing himself, he set to work.

7

Protective Coloration

Survival Station: Mesozoic era. Triassic period. Tr3 epoch. Carnian age. 225 My B.C.E.

The important thing was to maintain a scientific frame of mind. He was being tested. When Griffin popped out of the time funnel early, with his Irish shadow in tow, Robo Boy knew exactly how to act and what to say.

"They trapped a dwarf coelophysid in the highlands the other day." He accepted their credentials through the slot in the cage door and carefully compared the photos against their faces. "Everybody was all excited." He checked their names against the schedule on his clipboard. "It was less than two feet long." He ran the papers through a text verifier, waited for the light to flash green. "They're calling it *Nanogojirasaurus.*" The light flashed. "But Maria thinks it's just a juvenile."

He unlocked the heavy, iron-barred door and they stepped out of the cage. A monotonous rain was drumming on the supply room's roof. The shelves were thronged with boxes and bundles. A single lightbulb overhead filled the empty spaces between them with shadows and mystery.

"Why aren't the chairs set up yet?" Griffin asked. He clamped a hand over his wrist, glared down at it, and said, "I can't spare much time. I'm only stopping over on my way to the Induan."

"You weren't supposed to arrive for another two hours," Robo Boy pointed out.

The Irishman took the clipboard from his hands, scribbled out what Robo Boy had written, and wrote a later time above it. "Sometimes things don't happen exactly when it says they did in the record. It's a security measure."

The buzzer sounded, announcing another arrival.

With a heavy iron *clank,* a new car filled the cage. Robo Boy snatched back his clipboard.

Salley stepped out of the cage.

"They trapped a dwarf coelophysid in the highlands the other day," he said, holding out his hand for the woman's credentials. "Everybody was all excited."

"It was a juvenile," Salley said. "I read Maria Caporelli's paper about it. I'm gen-two, remember?" To Griffin, she said, "Can't you cut through all of this bureaucratic rigamarole for me?"

"Of course." Griffin nodded to the Irishman, who leaned forward and threw the latch. Salley stepped out into the room.

"*Hey!*" Robo Boy objected. But the Irishman clapped a hand on his shoulder and quietly said, "Let me give you a wee bit of advice, son. Don't try so hard. You'll get a lot further in life if you cut people a little slack."

Robo Boy flushed and retreated, as he always did, into his work. First he set up four chairs. Then the folding table. Finally, glasses and a pitcher of water that had been chilled by keeping the jerrycan right next to the cage.

Meetings were held in the storage room because it was so much cooler than outside. The time funnel acted as a heat sink, sucking warmth from the ambient air and re-radiating it out into the darkness between stations. Nobody knew exactly where the heat went. The funnel itself had been mathematically modeled as a multidimensional crack in time, and no one had yet figured out a way to probe beyond its walls.

While Griffin neatly positioned papers across the tabletop and Salley poured herself a glass of water, Robo Boy returned the jerrycan to its place beside the time beacon. The beacon was an integral part of the funnel mechanism, anchoring the funnel to this particular instant. Without it, they would be unfindable, an infinitesimally small instant of duration in the shoreless ocean of time. Occasionally he thought how easy it would be to smash the beacon and maroon them all. Always he was stopped by the thought of spending the rest of his life with Darwinian atheists.

The door outside slammed open.

"Hello?" Somebody stood blinking in the steaming wash of hot and humid air. "Anybody here?"

Leyster stepped into the room.

He closed the door behind him, and hung up his slicker on a peg alongside it. Then he turned and saw Salley.

"Hello, Leyster." A tentative smile, there and gone. She looked quickly away. Leyster, in his turn, muttered something polite and scraped up a chair.

Was it as obvious to everyone else, Robo Boy wondered? The way the two of them were so painfully conscious of each other? How their gazes danced about the room, toward and away from each other, without ever actually connecting? Surely they were all aware of it, whether they acknowledged it or not.

"You two know each other," Griffin said. "There's no reason to pretend otherwise. However, I'm sure you'll agree that the Baseline Project is important enough to set aside whatever personal—" He stopped, and said to Robo Boy, "Why are you still here?"

"I was running inventory." He waved his clipboard at the shelves.

"Can it be done another time?"

"Yes."

"Then leave."

Robo Boy put the flimsies of his time transit report form into an envelope pre-stamped TTR(TR3/Carnian) and stuck it into the outgoing mailbox. He took his slicker off its hook.

The Irishman leaned back against the shelves, arms folded, and stared at Robo Boy speculatively.

A stab of fear shot through him. He'd been found out! But no, if he had, they'd have arrested him long ago. He assumed the stubborn look his mother had always called his "pig face" and went out into the rain, letting the door slam behind him.

He didn't look back, but he knew from experience that the Irishman's attention had already shifted away from him. He had that effect on people. They thought he was a jerk.

He knew how to act like a jerk because he used to be one.

"Hey, Robo Boy," somebody said in a friendly way. A girl matched strides with him. It was Leyster's cousin, Molly. She wore a transparent hooded slicker over basic paleo-drag: khaki shorts, blouse, and a battered hat.

"My name is Raymond," he said stiffly. "I don't know why everybody persists in calling me by that ridiculous nickname."

"I dunno. It suits you. Listen, I wanted to ask your advice about getting a job."

"My advice? Nobody asks for my advice."

"Well, everybody says you've had more transfers than anyone, so I figured you'd know the ropes. Hey, have you heard the rumors?"

"What rumors?"

"About Leyster and Salley and the Baseline Project."

Molly was, in Robo Boy's estimation, as harmless as anyone could be, a chatterbox and a bit of an airhead and not much else. Still, he didn't want her to know how interested he might be in the Baseline Project. So he sighed in a way that he knew from experience girls didn't like, and waved a hand at the mud and tents and spare utilitarian structures of the camp, and said, "Tell me something. Why would you *want* a job in a place like this?"

"I just love dinosaurs, I guess."

"Then you're in the wrong place. The Carnian is—" They'd come to the cook tent. It was where he'd been headed all along. "Look, why don't we go inside and discuss it there?"

Molly smiled brightly. "Okay!" She led the way in.

Robo Boy followed, scowling down at her ass. Molly had curly red hair. He thought she wasn't wearing a bra, but she wore her blouse so loosely he couldn't be sure.

"The Carnian is a lousy place to look for dinosaurs," he explained over a cup of tea. "That's one reason everyone is so worked up over the gojirasaur—they're rare. All the action here is in synapsids and non-dinosaurian archosaurs. They're the ones who are busily speciating and competing for dominance of the community. The early dinosaurs are just bit players. But a funny thing is about to happen. The synapsids are going to take a major hit in the evolutionary sweepstakes. Most lines will die out completely. The only ones that'll survive into the Jurassic are mammals, and then only because they colonized the small-animal niche. Which is where they'll be stuck until the end of the Mesozoic and the onset of the Cenozoic. Following this so far?"

Molly nodded.

"Okay, now the non-dino archosaurs also suffer a reduction in diversity. But among the archosaurs is a group called the pseudosuchians, and their descendants include all the crocodilians. So they do pretty well. And dinosaurs come up winners. From the Triassic on, the Mesozoic belongs to them.

"But it's important to understand that whatever favored dinos was opportunistic, not competitive."

"Which means?"

"It means they didn't supplant their rivals because they were inherently superior. Some of those archosaur groups are as hot-blooded as any dino. But the volcanic event that opened up the Atlantic Ocean changed the environment in ways that favored dinosaurs over their rivals. They just got lucky."

He folded his arms smugly.

It was a good performance. He'd rattled off the lies as if he meant them, pedantically and with just the right touch of condescension. It astonished him how carefully Molly listened.

But then she said, "So do you think I could get a job in supplies, like you? I mean, it looks pretty simple. You just move things around with a fork lift, right?"

"No, I do not." He didn't have to fake his irritation. "They use fork lifts at the far end, where there's plenty of electrical energy. *I* use a hand truck." Supplies were shipped down the funnel in bundles lashed to pallets, and thus he measured the work in pallets. Three pallets was a light day, and ten was more work than he could do without help. "Everything gets loaded and unloaded by hand."

"Cool. So how did you get your position in the first place?"

"I was transferred."

It was easy to get transfers if you were a hard worker and willing to take on the grunt jobs nobody else wanted. Robo Boy was careful to make himself unpopular so that when he applied for a transfer, nobody ever made a strong effort to keep him. He had wandered from job to job, seemingly aimlessly, until he ended up deep in the Triassic, with complete control over the supplies and shipping, and, not coincidentally, one nexus of the time funnel.

"Well, how did you get your first gig?"

"I started out with a masters in geology. I got really good grades. I wrote my thesis on some stratigraphic problems that the people here were interested in."

"That doesn't sound like a terribly viable option for me," Molly said.

"No, it doesn't. Now what's all this about Leyster and Salley?" He crossed his arms and leaned back, masking his interest with a skeptical expression.

Molly flashed that brainless smile of hers. "They're going to be working on the Baseline Project. Together. If you can imagine that."

"I find that hard to—wait a minute. That's supposed to be a gen-three project."

"Griffin's promoting them both. At least that's the offer he's putting on the table. But can you picture either of them turning him down? Leyster's pre-2034, so he'll have to be shifted forward in time. But that's not much of a sacrifice for him. Most of his friends are in paleontology, and I'm the only one in the family he's actually close to."

"I can't picture those two working together. Who gets to be the boss?"

"Neither. Both. One's in charge of the camp, and the other's in charge of specimen collection. Lucky for them, they'll be bossing around a batch of grad students so green they won't have any idea what a fucked-up arrangement that is."

"Huh," Robo Boy said.

Briefly, he wondered how Molly had come into possession of such juicy inside dirt. Surely not from the notoriously close-mouthed Leyster. Did she have contacts in Administration?

He would have liked to ask her. But that wouldn't be in character.

That was on Tuesday. Three days later a big rhynchosaur roast was held to celebrate the end of survival training. Everybody had too much beer, and then they built a campfire to sit around, though the nights never really got cold enough to need it. Leyster got up and made a little speech, and then introduced their guest-lecturer.

Sylvia Davenport was a generation-three researcher from Ring Station, located a hundred years into the aftermath. She stood by the campfire and talked to the new recruits about the K-T extinctions. Robo Boy listened scornfully from the shadows.

The upper Triassic was buggy and humid. The survival camp was, anyway, and he didn't really care what it was like elsewhere. He never left the camp on expeditions or field trips, but stayed at home always, operating the commissary.

"We've looked," Davenport said. "Enough dinosaurs survived the Event to repopulate the Earth with their kind within the millennium. Yet ten years later, there were only a fraction of the number of those that survived, and in a century, they were extinct. Why? Other animals adapted. Hell, there were *dinosaurs* that adapted—the birds. Why didn't the rest? Non-avian dinosaurs had already survived the worst of it. Why couldn't they adapt?"

Robo Boy leaned forward and narrowed his eyes. This was a trick he had learned in school. It made him look engrossed in the subject and allowed his mind the freedom to wander.

He shut out the speaker's voice. Directly behind him, Leyster was murmuring something to the woman beside him, a gloss on what Davenport had just said. Robo Boy shut him out too.

He sank into the blissful silence of his own thoughts.

He despised the scientists for their constant inquisitive chatter, the way they leapt freely from possibility to possibility, postulating, positing, and speculating, with never an assurance that truth lay truly underfoot, unchanging, solid, inviolate. He could not live that way. If he were to admit, however briefly, that their tentative and provisional way might be valid, all certainty would dissolve within him, leaving nothing but chaos and the Pit. Stranding him in that emotional anomie he had inhabited before his Third Birth as a Midnight Christian. So he held them at an ironic distance. He spoke to them as from behind a mask—the mask of the worthless man he had been. In this way his old life had some value. It moved his new life closer to its validation.

Briefly, he thought about the time he had caught a glimpse of an angel. Then he wondered exactly when and where they might be—where they *really* were, as opposed to the party line of their atheistic humanist leaders. By his best guess, Robo Boy figured they were roughly six thousand years in the past, sometime between the Fall and the Flood. Physically, the camp lay somewhere east of Eden, in a land without flowers.

How astonishing to be alive in the time of the Patriarchs!

Sodom and Gomorrah were still thriving cities. Giants walked the Earth. Somewhere, Methuselah was living out his thousand years. Tubal-Cain was inventing metallurgy. The young Noah, perhaps, was seeking out a virtuous woman to be his wife. He felt blessed to be alive at such a time, and he thanked God for this blessing, and for the events that had brought him here.

It was a book that had changed his life, and a single sentence within that book which had done the work. The book was *Darwin Antichrist,* which he had bought to laugh at, and the sentence was, "If time travel is real, then why haven't we found human footprints among the fossil dinosaur tracks?"

If time travel is real—

It had never occurred to him to doubt the consensus version of reality before that very instant. And once he began to doubt it, layer upon layer of the humanist fallacy started to peel away, until all the world was dark and empty and held together only by an incomprehensible network of conspiracies.

—then why haven't we found human footprints among the fossil dinosaur tracks?

Of course! He closed his eyes, blind as Paul on the road to Damascus, his mind racing ahead of the page, anticipating the arguments that would lead him through the labyrinth of his meaningless existence and out into the light.

Toward God.

He had never thought much of God before. A white-haired old man on a throne in the clouds, hung up on the Sunday school blackboard, that was it. Now he realized God as something more subtle than that, an all-justifying power that entered into his heart and mind and skin like liquid lightning and made him impervious to scorn and error alike.

He did not ask why an all-loving God would create a false fossil record in order to deceive men and lead them away from the revealed truth. Robo Boy simply accepted it.

After his conversion, he had moved from organization to organization, always finding them lacking in commitment and zeal. At last, though, he had discovered deep creationism and the Thrice-Born Brotherhood: born once in the flesh, again in Christ, and a third time as warriors. They understood that defending God sometimes required extreme methods. They had opened his eyes. Under their tutelage, he'd proudly abandoned the conventional prayer-at-bedtime and church-on-

Sunday beliefs he had been brought up in for a life of urgent commitment.

Before his conversion, the temptation to sin was omnipresent. He was weak. He lusted after women in his heart. Now, believing in prophecy and the inherent rightness of his vow of chastity, he was born again and yet again.

The strictness of his conviction and righteousness made it his duty to convict those non-believers still mired in disbelief, in skepticism, in the Darwinian heresy. Few of them realized how badly they needed saving. But he was on a rescue mission, and where the fate of the world was at stake, it hardly mattered what became of a few souls. Or their bodies.

Davenport stopped speaking. Somebody began to clap, and then the others joined in.

Nobody applauded as loudly as he did.

The next day's schedule had him working the time funnel in heavy rotation. First the juvenile gojirasaur was shipped forward as a present to the People's Paleozoological Garden in Beijing. The famous Dr. Wu himself brought a crew of wranglers, lean young grad students who squatted on their heels when they ate their lunches out of cardboard containers with chopsticks, and joked casually among themselves as they worked under his stern eye.

Leyster emerged from his obsessive checking and re-checking of the Baseline Project's provisions to shake the great man's hand, and receive a few words of recognition in exchange. Then the camp director showed up, and the three of them solemnly examined the caged gojirasaur while the wranglers stood back in silent witness to this moment of shared celebrity.

The theropod itself was a beautiful creature. Its skin was leaf-green, mottled with splotches of yellow. Even its eyes—alert and quietly watchful—were yellow. There was little room for it to move within the cage, and so it stood still. There was a tense menace to its calm, though. Once, a wrangler placed a hand carelessly upon the cage, and the gojirasaur almost bit off her fingers. She danced backwards from its snapping teeth while her peers laughed.

Then they slid iron bars through the underside of the cage and hoisted it inside the time funnel. The Chinese delegation placed themselves carefully within as well, and Robo Boy checked off their names and threw the switch.

They were gone.

Ten minutes later the buzzer sounded, and he had to muscle out two pallets of supplies: toilet paper, restaurant-size tins of food, brush hooks, shotgun shells, a remote-operated hovercam, canvas shower-bags, powdered soap, fungicide cream, tampons, a banjo, and a bundle of scientific journals. Nothing either interesting or unusual. But everything had to be accounted for, recorded, and stowed away.

At last Leyster's people began to arrive for the Baseline Project expedition. They trickled in by twos and threes, laughing and chatting, and they all got in the way of Robo Boy's re-packing of the pallets that Leyster had torn apart to make sure nothing had been left out. Several greeted him by name.

He spoke curtly when he could not avoid speaking at all. Only rarely did he look up from his clipboard. Robo Boy had a reputation for surliness, and it helped keep people at a distance.

Which was useful. Nobody was looking at him when he placed the time beacon carefully atop the third pallet, and lashed it tight with nylon cord. Nobody saw how nervous he was.

Ready hands helped him slide the pallet into the cage. He backed out, mumbling, "Okay, it's all yours."

"All right, gang, let's *move 'em out!*" Leyster shouted, and bounded inside. "Richard Leyster, present and accounted for," he told Robo Boy.

Robo Boy checked off their names, one by one, as they crowded into the cage. Somebody made a joke about stuffing college students into a telephone booth, and somebody else said, "Better than stuffing them into a tyrannosaur!" and they all laughed. He was careful not to make eye contact with anybody. He was afraid of what they might see in him if he did.

"That's everyone. You may fire when ready, Gridley," Leyster said.

"Wait a minute," Robo Boy said. "Where's Salley?"

"She's not on this expedition."

"Of course she is," Robo Boy said irritably. "I saw her name on the roster yesterday."

"Change of plans. Lydia Pell's taking her place."

Robo Boy stared dumbstruck at the roster, and for the first time looked at the dozen names as a whole. Salley's was not among them. Lydia Pell's was. It was a perverse miracle, a Satanic impossibility.

Fear clutched his heart. It was a trap! Molly must have fed him her information in order to force his hand. He saw that now. He'd believed her, and made his move prematurely, and was caught. In a second, Griffin's uniformed goons would come pouring into the room to seize him.

"Um . . . We're ready if you are," Leyster said.

He placed a hand on the switch, knowing how useless the gesture was.

He pulled.

They all went away.

For a long, silent minute, Robo Boy waited. He hoped it was the old Irishman who would come for him. He'd heard the young version was pretty brutal. They said he liked to break bones.

But nobody came into the room. The change in the roster hadn't been a trap, after all, but only the gnostic and unfathomable workings of Griffin's bureaucracy.

Which meant—he could hardly believe it—that he had succeeded! He might not have bagged Salley, but he'd gotten Leyster and eleven others, and that would have consequences back home in the present. They couldn't hush this one up! There would be hearings. With luck, they would expose time travel and Darwinism for the diabolically-inspired lies they were.

He had struck a blow for God. Now they could arrest him, torture him, kill him, and it wouldn't matter. He would die a martyr. Heaven, which would never have received him in his old, sinful state, was open to him at last. He was finally, truly, saved.

He leaned back against the wall, breathing shallowly.

Not long after, he heard a wolf-whistle outside.

"Oh, baby!" somebody cried happily. "I think I'm in love."

"You wish."

Salley swept into the room. She wore a red silk evening gown, and her hair was piled up elaborately on her head. Silver raptor teeth dangled from her earlobes.

"I have to be in Xanadu Station for a fund-raiser," she said, handing him a transit form. "Fire up your machine and send me forward."

His heart was still pounding like a jackhammer. But Robo Boy put on his pig face and went over the form slowly and carefully. Everything was in order.

Best to play it bland.

"I thought you were supposed to be on the Baseline Project expedition," he said.

"Yeah, well, plans change," Salley said carelessly. She stepped into the cage. The gate slammed shut. Automatically, he double-checked the authorization codes, did a visual confirmation of Salley's identity, and pulled the switch.

She was gone.

Thirty seconds later, Salley walked into the room again. She was a good twenty years older than the Gertrude Salley who had just left, and there was a small, moon-shaped scar by the corner of her mouth.

"Hey!" he said, genuinely shocked. "You can't be here! That's against the rules!"

"And you care about the rules one fuck of a lot, don't you, Robo Boy?" the woman said. Her eyes burned with wrath.

He shrank away from her. He couldn't help it.

"Two decades ago, when I was young and innocent, I was made co-head of the first Baseline Project expedition. It was a simple but important gig. Starting at a hundred thousand years before the end of the Cretaceous, we were going to perform a series of mapping, recording, and sampling functions. Atmosphere, mean global temperature, gene specimens from select species. Then we'd hop back a million years and do it all over again. Seven weeks to do the Maastrichtian. Another five to cover the top third of the Campanian. Am I boring you, Robo Boy?"

"I—I know all this."

"I'm sure you do. But something happened. There was an explosive device among our supplies. People died. Does any of this sound familiar to you?"

"I don't know what you're talking about!"

She curled her lip scornfully. "Yeah, I didn't *think* you did."

Then she spun on her heel and strode to the time funnel. She stepped into the cage, and pulled the door shut.

"You're not going anywhere! I'm calling Griffin. You're in big trouble now."

The woman took a plastic card from her purse and touched it to an inside wall. "Good-bye, Robo Boy," she said, "you little shit."

The car went away, and with it Salley.

The very first thing he had been told, when they trained him to operate the time funnel, was that under no conditions could the car be launched without his pulling the switch. It had never occurred to him that they would lie about such a thing.

Evidently they had.

For a long time he stood perfectly motionless. Thinking.

But finding no answers.

The important thing was to remain scientific. He must assume the language, behavior, and even the thought-patterns of his enemy. He must never let down his guard. He was a warrior. He was Thrice-Born. He was being tested.

His name was Raymond Bois. The girls all called him Robo Boy. He never could figure out why.

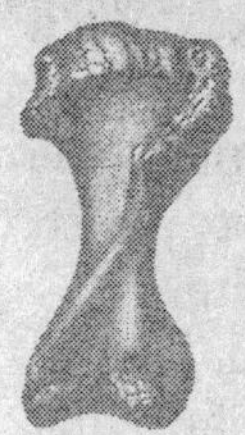

8

Hell Creek

Lost Expedition Foothills: Mesozoic era. Cretaceous period. Senonian epoch. Maastrichtian age. 65 My B.C.E.

They tumbled out of a hole in time into a bright, blue-skyed day, whooping with excitement. The team had been deposited on a gentle rise above a small, meandering stream, which the students inevitably decided to name Hell Creek, after the famous fossil-bearing formation.

Leyster consulted with Lydia Pell, and they agreed to let the group skylark for a bit before putting them to work. It was their first time in the Maastrichtian, after all. It was their first time in the field and on their own. They needed to gape and stare, to point wonderingly at the distant herd of titanosaurs that was browsing its way across the valley, to breathe deep of the fragrant air and do handstands and peer under logs and flip over rocks just to see what was underneath.

Then, when Pell judged they'd let off enough

steam, Leyster said, "Okay, let's get these things unpacked and sorted out." He waved an arm toward a stony bluff above Hell Creek. "We'll pitch our tents over there."

Everybody leapt to work. Jamal pulled the Ptolemy rocket launcher from the first pallet. "When do we send up the surveyor satellite?"

"No time like the present," Leyster said. He ran a thumb down his mental list of who'd had what training. "You and Lai-tsz take it off a safe distance. Nils can carry the tripod."

"Who gets to push the button?"

Leyster grinned. "Paper-scissors-rock works best for that kind of decision."

Twenty minutes later, the surveyor went up. Everybody stopped whatever they were doing to gawk as the dazzling pinprick of light curved up into the sky, tracing a thin line of smoke behind it.

"You have just launched the missile," a priggish voice said, a little too loudly. "Its electromagnetic signature has been picked up by a detector wired to this recording."

Leyster turned, puzzled. "What?"

"In sixty seconds, an explosive charge will destroy the time beacon. Please stand clear so you won't be hurt."

It was Robo Boy's voice.

The surreal intrusion of someone he knew to be millions of years distant bewildered Leyster for an instant. He watched, uncomprehending, as Lydia Pell tore at one of the pallets like a terrier, wildly throwing packs and boxes aside. She emerged with the time beacon.

"You have fifty seconds."

The voice came from the beacon itself.

There was a Swiss Army knife in Pell's hand. She shoved a blade into the seam of the beacon's casing and twisted, breaking it open.

"You have forty seconds."

The top half of the beacon went flying away. She reached down into the bottom half.

To Leyster's eye, there was nothing to differentiate one part of the beacon's innards from another. It was all chips, transistors, and multicolored wiring. But Lydia Pell clearly knew what she was looking for. She'd been an officer in the U.S. Navy before going for her postgraduate degree, he knew. Hadn't somebody said something about her having been in demolitions?

"You have thirty seconds. Please take this warning seriously."

She wrenched something free. The bottom half of the beacon fell to the ground.

Lydia Pell turned away from the others, and shouted over her shoulder, "Everybody get down! I'm going to throw—"

"You have twenty seconds," the device said.

Then it went off in her hands.

Gillian was saying something, but Leyster couldn't tell what. His ears rang terribly from the explosion. He couldn't hear a thing.

He was the first to reach Lydia Pell's body.

The terrible thing was that she wasn't dead. Her face was gray and streaked with blood. One hand had been almost blown away, and the other was hanging by a shred of flesh. What remained of her blouse was darkening to crimson. But she wasn't dead.

Leyster whipped off his belt and wrapped it around Lydia's wrist, above the exposed bone. I'm going to have nightmares about this, he thought as he pulled it tight. I'll never be able to get these images out of my mind. To the far side of the body, Gillian was making a tourniquet for the other arm.

Small fragments of the bomb specked Lydia Pell's face. One larger shard had torn quite a gouge in her cheek. A little higher and she would have lost an eye. Daljit knelt by her head and, bending low, began daintily extracting the fragments with a pair of tweezers.

Keep calm, Leyster thought. There would be trauma. There might be concussion. There was always shock. Keep her warm. Elevate the feet. Check for other wounds. Don't panic.

It took a while to stop the bleeding. But they did. Then they cushioned her head, and elevated her feet. They cleaned and bandaged her wounds. They made up a cot, and eased her onto it. Twelve willing hands gently carried the cot into a tent.

By the time Leyster could hear again, there was nothing more to do for her.

A light drizzle was falling.

Leyster slogged uphill, following what he sincerely hoped was an abandoned dromaeosaur trail. Lai-tsz trudged along behind him. At first they had talked about the paucity of local fauna, and why, in the week since the titanosaurs had left, they had not seen any dinosaurs. Then, as Smoke Hollow fell behind them, and they were confident they would not be overheard, their talk turned to more serious matters.

"Can the time beacon be repaired?" Leyster asked.

"God only knows."

"You're the only one here with any substantive knowledge of electronics."

"Substantive! I've torn apart a few computers, patched together a couple of motherboards, hyper-configged a new device or two. There's a big distance between that and repairing something that was probably built a thousand years in the future. In our home future, I mean. Sometime after the Third Millennium."

"So you're saying . . . what? Tell me you're not saying that you can't fix it."

"I'm saying I don't know. I'll do my best. But Pell ripped the hell out of the innards, getting that bomb out. Even if I *can* fix it, it'll take time."

"Listen," Leyster said. "If anybody asks, tell them you've got a handle on it. Say it'll take you a week or two, a month at the outside. I don't want the crew fixating on the possibility that we might be stranded here permanently. Morale is bad enough as it is."

Lai-tsz made a short, sharp sound midway between a laugh and a snort. "I'll say! Everybody's at each other's throats. Nils and Chuck almost got into a fight this morning over whose turn it was to take the dishes down to the stream and wash them. Gillian isn't speaking to Tamara, Matthew isn't speaking to Katie, and Daljit isn't speaking to anyone. And of course Jamal is being a real jerk. About the only stable ones left are thee and me, and sometimes I have my doubts about thee." She waited a beat, then said in a small voice, "Hey, come on. That was a joke. You were supposed to laugh."

"It's Lydia Pell," Leyster said seriously. "If only she wouldn't make those noises. If only she wouldn't scream. She's using up our morphine fast, and that's not good either. Sometimes I think it would be best for all of us if she just . . ."

They walked on in silence for a while. Then Lai-tsz said, "So tell me something, Richard. *Are* we stranded here for the rest of our lives?"

Leyster blew out his cheeks, said, "Well, unless you can fix that beacon or somebody comes to rescue us . . . yeah, we are."

"What are the chances of somebody coming to rescue us?"

"If they were going to rescue us, they'd've done it already. They would've popped up while the smoke was still in the air. Lydia Pell would be in a hospital now, with one hand reattached, and doctors working to grow a new hand to replace the other."

"Ah," Lai-tsz said, and nothing more.

They came to a branching in the path.

"This is where we part ways," Lai-tsz said. "There's a gingko grove to the east that's shedding fruit. I'll have a knapsack full of pits when you get back. You can help me shell them."

"Watch out for dromies."

"Hey, no problem. You should see me climb a tree."

"Um . . . dromaeosaurs can climb too. Rather well, in fact."

She dismissed his worries with a wave of her hand. "Say hello to the Purgatory shrews for me."

Leyster distractedly climbed the rest of the way up to Barren Ridge alone. He'd brought another day's worth of samples to place before the *Purgatorius* colony there. He called them Purgatory shrews, though of course they weren't shrews but ancestral primates. Still, they sure looked like shrews. And considering their insectivorous teeth, they had surprisingly catholic tastes. They liked almost everything he offered them.

He made the long trek from Smoke Hollow to Barren Ridge every other day to set out a new selection of roots, barks, and funguses at the foot of their favored tree. Purgatory shrews had the closest thing to human metabolisms of anything in the Mesozoic, and he figured that anything they ate would be safe enough for him to try.

Meat wasn't a problem. The team gigged frogs, snagged turtles, dug freshwater clams, caught fish, and even trapped a few large lizards; there was no shortage of edible flesh. What they would need most when their supplies ran out were fruits and greens.

The red bark was gone, and so were four of the tubers. A fifth, greenish one hadn't been touched at all. Leyster made a mental note to avoid it in the future.

He laid out his new samples, then turned and looked out over the valley.

Hell Creek was a steely glint visible only intermittently through the rain as it flowed down to the River Styx. The bottom lands to this side of the river, which had been browsed flat by the titanosaurs, were already lush with ferns and flowering plants. In this heat, things came up overnight. You could push a stone into the soil, and come morning you'd find a pebble bush.

Even in the rain, and partially obscured by mists, the valley was beautiful. Even with the sky low and gray, something in him thrilled to it.

Leyster didn't need a lot of company. It occurred to him that if it weren't for the others, he could be perfectly happy here. Or, rather, if he weren't responsible for their well-being, he could be happy.

He rued the argument he'd had with Jamal three days ago.

Jamal had taken it upon himself to start building a log-frame house, as they'd been taught in survival training. Without consulting anybody, he'd begun chopping down trees for its frame.

"Those are a little large for firewood," Leyster had said to him.

Jamal looked impatient. "They're for a long house. We're going to be here for a while. We need it."

"Yes, but we don't need it *right away*. What we need now are a better latrine, some storage baskets, a little investigation into plants that might be spun into cloth. I really think you ought to—"

Jamal flung down his axe in exasperation.

"What gives you the right to order us around?" he said. "This isn't an expedition anymore, this is about survival. Why the fuck should we take orders from you? Just because you're a couple of years older?"

"It's not a matter of giving orders. It's a matter of common sense."

"Whose sense? Huh? Your sense? Well, it's not my sense. I happen to think we need the house, and I'm going to build it."

"All by yourself? I really doubt it. You can cut the beams, but you can't assemble them without help," Leyster said. "Face it, we're all in this together. All this grandstanding and ego-tripping is perfectly useless."

"You think I'm grandstanding?"

"I know you are."

At which point Chuck had wandered up and said, "Hey. What's up?"

"Chuck!" Jamal said. "You'll help build the long house, won't you?"

"Uh . . . sure. Why not?"

"Because we have more important things to do," Leyster said testily. "Because we—" He stopped. Chuck was looking at him as if he weren't making any sense.

And then, out of weariness and frustration, he had flung up his hands and said, "Fine! Do it your way! What the hell do I care?" and stomped angrily off.

Even as he did it, he knew it was a big mistake.

* * *

So now the team was split into two factions—three, if you counted Daljit and Matthew, who'd gotten stuck with watching over Lydia Pell while she died, and consequently had little energy for anything else. Jamal, Katie, Gillian, Patrick, and Chuck made up the house-building faction. Leyster, Tamara, Lai-tsz, and Nils were the food-gatherers.

It worried Leyster that this split had occurred. But since he was perceived as being the head of one of the factions—and the smaller of the two, at that—he didn't have the credibility needed to patch up the rupture. It was a damn-fool situation to be in. It was completely counter-productive. But he couldn't begin to see how to undo this mess.

He sighed, and stared out unseeing into the distance.

It was then, as he was thinking no particular thought and experiencing no particular emotion, that a most extraordinary sensation came over Leyster. It was a feeling very much like awe. He felt the way he had on occasion felt as a child sitting in the pew in church on Sunday morning, a profound and oceanic inward shiver, as if suddenly made aware that God were peering over his shoulder.

Slowly, Leyster turned.

He froze.

At the very top of the ridge—it must have been there all along—stood a tyrannosaur.

It dominated the sky.

The beast's skin was forest green with streaks

of gold, like sunlight streaming down through the leaves. This, combined with its height, its immobility, and Leyster's distracted state, had rendered it invisible to him. He had simply failed to notice it.

Oh shit, Leyster said silently.

As if it had heard his thought, the tyrannosaur slowly swung its massive head about. Small, fierce eyes locked onto him. For an agonizing slice of eternity it studied Leyster with every grain of attention it had.

Then, with disdainful hauteur, it turned its head away, and resumed staring out across the valley.

Leyster was too terrified to move.

He'd stood beneath tyrannosaur skeletons in museums a hundred times imagining what it would be like to be the prey of such a monster. He'd pictured its ferocious attack, seen that devil skull dipping downward to munch him up in two crisp bites, felt his bones shatter under those brutally efficient teeth. This was far more terrifying than his most vivid imaginings.

His gaze went up to the many-toothed head so high above him. Then down to those taloned feet. All the world fell away from the creature. It was the crown and pinnacle of creation. Everything existed for its convenience. The valley held its face upward for its inspection.

It held the world fast in its claws.

He hadn't had the exposure to tyrannosaurs to know what sex this one was. It was absolutely unscientific, then, to assign it a gender. But Leyster lovingly remembered Stan, the first *Tyrannosaurus* skeleton he'd ever gotten to examine closely, and decided on the spot that this, his first living tyrannosaur, was also male.

The brute's calm was uncanny. He was still with the perfect stillness of an assassin at rest with his conscience. No doubts, no mercy, no hesitation sullied his thought. He was all Zen and murder, Death's favored child. He stood here because it pleased him.

His was a timeless universe. He did not permit change to enter it. Now and forever, he was king of Eden.

As quietly as he could, Leyster edged away. If the tyrannosaur noticed, he did not deign to show it. His eyes remained slitted, his head motionless. Only his throat moved, pulsing gently.

Trees rose up to obscure the animal. The trail twisted and the top of the ridge disappeared as well. Leyster turned and, with frequent glances over his shoulder, crept furtively downslope. A hundred yards down the trail, he was able at last to draw in a deep breath.

He had seen *Tyrannosaurus rex!*

And he was still alive!

Had the animal been hungry, of course, it would have been an entirely different story. Nevertheless, Leyster was filled with a strange and savage joy. He was so happy he wanted to sing, though the wiser side of him cautioned that he should put a few miles between himself and his new playmate before doing any such thing.

Would he now have to avoid Barren Ridge?

It was a tough call. Dinosaur skin wasn't anywhere

as glandular as that of mammals. Still, theropods had a distinctive smell, dry and pungent, like a mixture of cinnamon and toad. So, had the ridge been a regular stop on the tyrannosaur's rounds, Leyster would have known. He was a newcomer, then.

Even so, the overlook was a convenient spot. The Lord of the Valley might well decide to make it his regular perch. Before he dared find out if this were the case, Leyster would need to find a different approach. One where he could tell if the tyrannosaur were present long before putting himself within chomping distance.

In any event, best he avoid Barren Ridge for the next week or two. By then, the scent would tell the story one way or the other.

He hurried homeward to tell the others the news. They'd all have to take precautions. They'd all want to see.

It occurred to him that he would have to find a new *Purgatorius* colony now.

When Leyster strode into camp, humming the "Ode to Joy" to himself, there was no one about. The twin lines of tents were still and silent. A solitary dragonfly flew swiftly past him and was gone.

Somewhere in the distance the crazed-monkey laughter of a whooping loon rose up and then suddenly cut off, making the silence absolute. To one side of the camp was a stand of protomagnolias. The scent of their flowers hung heavy on the air.

"Hello?" he called.

A tent flap exploded open.

All in a rush, Daljit burst from Lydia Pell's tent. She was crying. She seized Leyster and buried her face in his shoulder. "Oh, Richard," she said. "Liddie's dead!"

Clumsily, he put his arms around her. He stroked her hair as if she were a sorrowing child. "We did everything we could," he said.

"She was a h-hero. She saved us all. W-when I heard the tape, I just *stood* there! I didn't d-do a thing!"

"There, there," he said awkwardly. "None of us did. Maybe it's just a form of pride to imagine we should have, rather than just accepting how extraordinary it was what she did." He was acutely aware of how pompous he sounded.

"You know what the w-worst part is? If Robo Boy had been a *competent* terrorist, she'd b-be alive now! That asshole! If she'd only had another t-twenty seconds . . ."

"There, now."

"I haven't felt like this since my m-mother died," Daljit said. "I suppose I'll be crying off and on for days this time too."

She pulled back from him. Her face was round and red. The tears had abruptly shut off, but there were circles under her eyes and she looked worn and weary. These days had been hardest on her and on Matthew. They'd been the only two with any medical experience, but it belatedly occurred to Leyster that this chore should have been shared out more fairly.

"I'll go wake up Matthew," she said. "He's resting in his tent. Will you tell the others?"

"Of course I will. Where are they?"

"Those who aren't out looking for food are up the hollow, working on Jamal's long house," she said. Then, with absolutely no transition at all, "This bickering can't go on."

"I know."

"It's stupid."

"Yes, it is."

"Well, don't just fucking *agree* with me. Do something about it! You've got to put an end to . . . I'm going to start crying again. Go on! Scoot!"

Weeping and hunched, she scuttled to Matthew's tent and disappeared within.

Leyster hesitated, then ducked into the tent she had just vacated. It was hot inside, and dark. He waited for his eyes to adjust, then approached Lydia Pell's cot.

Two flies were buzzing around her head. One tried to land, and he shooed it away.

In death, Lydia Pell had regained the face she had spent a lifetime creating. It was a serious, no-nonsense face, plain and round-cheeked. But one who knew her could see how amenable it would be to a smile or a wry twist of her features. He could see her now, looking up from her knitting with that one particular expression that said *would you believe it?* Followed by another that meant *well, people are funny.*

"Shoo," Leyster said absently. "Shoo, fly."

That face had been lost in pain in the ten days since the explosion. He was glad to see it back. He was doubly glad that Daljit had closed the eyes, so he didn't have to see them staring back at him from the far side of death.

"Good-bye, Liddie," he said softly. "I wish to God we had you with us now. You'd do so much better a job wrangling this bunch than I can. I miss you already. But I'm glad you're at peace now."

One fly landed, and began walking back and forth across the tender strip of flesh between her lips and nostrils. He raised a hand to shoo it away yet again, then thought the better of it. She was dead. Her body was no longer of any use to her.

"I'll get everybody together again. Somehow. I promise."

He could think of nothing more to say. He dried his eyes and left.

So Leyster walked, alone, up Smoke Hollow to the new campsite. The way darkened as the proto-magnolias gave way first to cedars and then to redwoods. The redwoods were still young and grew close together enough to serve as a barrier to the larger dinosaurs. Still, it might make sense to sharpen and lash together triads of logs into a line of *cheveaux-de-frise* to discourage any medium-size predators that might happen along. Or maybe they could plant thorn bushes. He sighed. There was so much to do! Chances that were worth taking for a month's stay just weren't tolerable over the span of a lifetime.

He stepped into the clearing around the long house. A thin curl of smoke rose up from the fire they kept banked to preserve the wood and their limited supply of matches.

"Hello!" Leyster called. "Anybody here?"

Jamal was standing on the ridgepole of the long house, shirt tied around his waist and a kerchief around his head. He waved jubilantly when he saw Leyster coming, and shouted, "We've finished thatching the roof! I'm putting up the satellite dish now. Come up and take a look. The others have gone out for more leaves."

Jamal, for all his faults, had extraordinary powers of organization and persuasion. He'd worked his faction hard and well. The long house frame was complete, and the palm-frond roof looked convincingly rainproof. Gazing up at it, Leyster for the first time actually believed in his heart of hearts that they were here for good. That they were never going home to the Cenozoic. That, for good or ill, this was their home now.

Leyster took his glasses off, ran a hand over his face, and put them back on. "Come on down!" he shouted. "I have something important to tell you!"

Jamal went to the edge of the roof and looked down at him. "What?"

"It's better said face-to-face," Leyster said. "Really."

With a puzzled scowl, Jamal squatted down and reached over to grab the frame.

At that moment, the rain began to pelt down harder. Leyster quickly stepped under the shelter of the half-built long house. The sky opened then, and the rain came down torrentially. It was dry in here, though. Jamal's gang had built a good roof.

With a rattle of dried fronds, Jamal jumped

down from a crosspiece of the frame. He landed with a thump. The momentary elation he had displayed on the rooftop was gone. His features were sullen and flooded with shadow. "Well?" he said challengingly. "What is it?"

9

Trace Fossils

Washington, D.C.: Cenozoic era. Quaternary period. Holocene epoch. Modern age. 2045 C.E.

They held the paper autopsy in a conference room that looked like every other conference room Molly Gerhard had ever seen.

Griffin's people had been given administrative space in the Herbert Hoover Building on Constitution Avenue. It was an inadequate run of offices squeezed from the Department of Commerce by DOD functionaries anxious to keep Griffin at arm's length from the Pentagon and the actual workings of time travel. Occasional use of the conference room was only grudgingly permitted by the Bureau of Export. But it had a snazzy new Japanese whiteboard, and a conference table, and that was all she really needed.

"Don't get your hopes too high," Tom Navarro said. "We have a very weak case here."

"I think it's stronger than you think," she said. "I'm betting we can sell it."

She laid the papers out on the table in strict chronological order, with Robo Boy's birth certificate in the upper left-hand corner, and her summary brief in the lower right.

She was reminded of a fossil slab that Leyster, in one of his mellower moods, had once shown her. It held the traces of pterosaurs dabbling in the mud of a shallow lake. To her uneducated eye, it had looked like nothing but random scratches. Leyster, however, had wanted to show her how paleontology had been done before time travel in order to demonstrate how much could be known from the very smallest of clues. So he had shown her the places where, swimming in shallow water, the pterosaurs had scuffed their feet against the lake bottom, leaving small parallel grooves with the occasional claw-tip shape among them. *Here* was a full pes print, and over *there* several manus prints. The pock marks were the imprints of beaks prodding in the mud for invertebrates. He had shown her the pterosaurs, no larger than ducks, dabbling in the water, disappearing suddenly as they dove for food, genially squabbling with each other for space. It had taken him an hour, but in that time he had re-created a world.

This, however, was her field of expertise, and within it she was as skilled as Leyster or any of his compatriots were in theirs. She knew how to trace a life and discern its hidden significance from the papers left behind in its wake. To another, they might be no more than scratches in mud. To her, they were the fossil trace of human emotion.

Griffin entered the conference room with Jimmy Boyle and Amy Cho in tow. Somehow, and despite the fact that he held the door for Amy Cho, he made them seem his entourage. Solicitously, he helped Amy down into a chair. He did not sit down himself, nor did Boyle. "All right," he said. "Impress me."

Molly started with the birth certificate. "Raymond Lawrence Bois. Born 9:17 A.M., February 14, 2019, in Akron City Hospital, Akron, Ohio. Father: Charles Raymond Bois. Mother: Lucinda Williams Bois, born Finley."

She tapped on the whiteboard, drew a time line down one side, and with her pointer squirted the date to one end:

14-02-19.

"He grew up in a vintage split-level in Franklin Township. Typical suburban childhood. Riding lawnmowers, memberships at the local pool."

Next came a series of school records, starting with Turkeyfoot Elementary. As she read through each one, she squirted the dates onto the time line. Hidden in here were the mysterious origins of personality, and if they left no trace, there was nothing to be done about it. She would have to go with externalities. "Look at those grades. This is one bright kid."

"Any disciplinary problems?" Griffin asked.

"Some. Nothing out of the ordinary. Now right here, sophomore year at Firestone High, he hits adolescence hard, and his grades go into a slump. Drops his AP classes and all extracurriculars. This continues until his senior year, when he finally realizes he needs the numbers to get into college, panics, and brings them back up.

"Fall of 2036, he enters Illinois State University. Normal, Illinois."

"So he finally got his act together, did he?"

"He was placed on academic pro his first semester, and never got out of it. At the end of his freshman year, he was in danger of flunking out. So he transferred to the University of Akron."

"Do they normally accept underachieving students?"

"His mother was a chemist at the Polymer Science Institute there. It seems likely she pulled a few strings."

"Ah."

"His grades remained lackluster. He was picked up by the campus police a couple of times for drunken behavior, once for public urination, once for grabbing a young lady's breast in a manner she found offensive." She put the individual dates up on the time line. A neat, unbroken row of numbers marched across the board. "No charges filed either time.

"I think by now we've got a pretty good picture of the sort of guy he was. Weak. Directionless. There was nothing he particularly wanted to do or achieve or become. He had the mental equipment, but lacked any goal that would make him actually exert himself. The only reason he didn't drop out was that his parents were paying the tab and college provided him with a comfortable existence. Nevertheless, it was as good as written that he was never going to get his degree. He was on a downward spiral.

"Now look *here.*" She put an enlargement of the transcript up on the whiteboard so they could all see it, and circled the relevant numbers. "Out of nowhere, he pulls himself up out of his tailspin. Look at those grades! He got an A in *French!* How he managed that after such a sloppy beginning, I'll never know. He can't have gotten much sleep. Where did that kind of discipline come from?"

She put the date of his finals up on the board, but left an open space before it, where she inserted a large red question mark. "There aren't a lot of things that can turn someone's life around like that. A hitch in the military. Marriage. Or getting religion."

"He found Jesus," Amy Cho said warmly. She struggled up out of her seat, and stamped her cane for emphasis. "He discovered the solace and strength of the Lord!"

"He certainly did. We may never know what triggered his conversion. But we know it happened, because during the time he was burning the midnight oil to bring his grades up, he also got involved in Campus Ministries. For about six weeks. Then, abruptly, he quit."

Amy Cho leaned heavily on the table with both hands and stared down at the transcript, as if it were a holy relic. "They were too *mild* for him! Liberals and Unitarians, weak tea the lot of them. He'd been touched by holy fire! He needed *sacrifice!* They offered him prayer meetings and recycling drives. He was looking for a cause that would consume him. One that would accept everything he had and demand more."

Nobody doubted that she knew what she was talking about.

"He worked in a furniture factory that summer. No absences, no tardiness. In his off hours, he apparently wrote a few papers for creationist on-line journals. Most of them have been erased, but we found one that another creationist group pirated for their own website. In it, he calculated how much water it would've taken to cover the Earth during the Flood, and put forward several speculations as to where that excess water might have gone. It differed from most such papers in that it adhered rigorously to known science. In the end, he admitted that none of his speculations could account for the discrepancy in figures, and concluded that God must have worked a miracle.

"Junior year. He changed his major from English Lit to Geology."

"How deeply involved was he in creationist circles at this time?"

"He was still hoping to discredit science using its own tools. He was an activist, but he hadn't hooked up with the Ranch yet. We know this because now is when his father died."

She added the date to the whiteboard:

2-14-39

"He didn't attend the funeral."

"There's no record that he did," Tom corrected her.

"There's no record he attended the funeral. If the Ranch had been grooming him at that point, he would have been there. He would have been very careful to sign the register."

"He was still a pilgrim," Amy Cho said. She stared down at the papers as if she could read things from them that no one else could. "He moved from creation science to deep creationism. He fell in with the Wrath of Gideon. They talk a good game, but they're riddled with informers, and everybody knows it. So he moved on. Finally, he discovered the Thrice-Born Brotherhood, and they recognized his potential."

"You can document this?" Griffin asked Molly.

"No, of course not. It's the separation of Church and State. Religious organizations don't have to file membership lists anywhere. These damned fundamentalists don't appreciate how unregulated they are."

"So this part of the presentation is speculative, then?"

"Well . . . yes. But"—she moved swiftly to her next suite of papers—"here, for his senior year, you'll note that his tuition check was posted from an apartment near the campus, rather than from his mother's house."

"Which means what?"

"She threw him out. He'd be hard enough to take as a failure. Imagine him burning with the righteousness of a new convert! But here's the interesting question: *Where did that money come from?* Not from Mom. The check is written on his own bank account. He couldn't possibly have earned enough over summer break to pay for it. For that matter, there's no record he had a summer job at all." She placed a red question mark on the time line to mark that summer. "So where was he?"

"Well?"

"We know one particularly well-funded group, don't we?" Amy Cho said. "Lots of rich old men hoping to squeeze through the eye of the needle. Capitalist carnivores desperate to lie down with the lambs before it's too late. Oh, Holy Redeemer Ranch does not lack for money."

"Is that all?" Griffin asked. "Suspicion, innuendo, and a complete lack of physical evidence?"

"Sir, there's a pattern here!" Molly squirted up the remaining dates, then faded them down so that the time line was dominated by the series of dark red question marks. "There's a Ranch-shaped gap in our boy's life. Every summer, every break, he disappears from the records. Do you have any idea how difficult that is? He doesn't use a credit card. He doesn't write checks. Where is he?"

"He's on retreat," Amy Cho said excitedly. "He's just spent nine months in the belly of Great Satan Academia, his soul in constant mortal peril from humanism and scientific rationalism. The very first thing they'd want to do is to offer prayers of thanks for his safe return. They'd kill the fatted calf. Followed by fasting and purification. Imagine how filthy the poor boy must feel, pretending to be one of the Devil's lackeys. Then, when he's cleansed and rested . . ."

"A few of the lads would take him out for a bit of Christian rage," Jimmy Boyle said. "They'd beat up a drug dealer or two, some faggots, maybe an abortionist if they've got one lined up. Just to keep the edge on him."

"I take it this is undocumented as well," Griffin said.

"It's what I'd do if I were running him. It's what anybody would do."

She had them now, everybody but Griffin. Unfortunately, she was running up against the end of her trail. This was the tricky part. She was not allowed to look very deeply into his post-recruitment history nor at any part of that history in any great detail.

She drew a thick slash across the time line. "Here's where we recruit him. We could hardly have avoided it. He'd been very carefully prepped. He had skills that we particularly wanted. He looked like a very attractive candidate.

"So what became of him? Almost immediately, he faded into obscurity. He made a competent but unimpressive job of the stratigraphic work that was expected of him. Transferred to Carnival Station and kept the animal register for a time. Transferred to Bohemia Station and ran the bird colony. Transferred to Mjolnir Station and spent a few months preparing skeletons for exhibitions. That's tedious work. Transferred to Origin Station and prepped tissue specimens. Even more tedious. Transferred to Sundance Station and maintained the boats. Transferred to Survival Station, where he now runs the commissary, stows supplies, and has complete access to the time funnel.

"That's a lot of transfers, and a lot of wasted potential. But in less than two years, personal time, it's got him exactly where he wants to be."

Time for the big wrap-up. Molly took a deep breath. "Sir, we're requesting—"

Griffin held out a hand to stop her.

"It's not good enough," he said. "There is no judge anywhere I can take this to and get a warrant from."

"I'm not requesting a warrant, just permission to run a proper investigation. Let me ask a few questions. Get the FBI to put a tracer on him one of those summers, see exactly where he goes. We know he's our mole. I'm just asking that you let me prove it."

"I'm afraid that can't be done."

"Why not?"

"Because it's not the way it *was* done. Jimmy? If you would."

While Molly tidied her papers into a pile, Jimmy Boyle placed one black binder before everybody's place. Then, almost ritually, he helped Amy Cho back into her seat.

They all opened their binders.

Griffin took Molly's pointer and erased everything from the whiteboard. He pulled up a new time line. "This is two years and three months of Robo Boy's life, from his own perspective. During this time, he bounces all over the Mesozoic, but we're ignoring that. Here to the left, it begins with his being recruited to join our merry little band of pranksters. To the right, at the end of our examined period, while he was working at Hilltop Station, is the date the opal man, Tubal-Cain or whoever it was supposed to be, was shipped. Okay? Robo Boy never picked it up. We had people watching, but he never came close to it. Something scared him off.

"Here, just before his transfer to Hilltop, is where our second sting is being placed. We've baited a trap with Salley and Leyster. He's going to strand them in the Maastrichtian. We're going to investigate. Again, there won't be the physical evidence to prove he was at fault. But three months later, when we yank the expedition back, we can use their testimony to convict him."

"Wait," Tom said. "Why would you place a second sting just before the first? No wonder Robo Boy was spooked."

"We already knew the first sting didn't work," Griffin said testily. "So we're placing the second sting as early as possible in order to minimize the time available to him. We want to get him out of our hair as quickly as possible, remember?"

Molly flipped through the material in the binder, scanning the headings and subheadings, reading the captions. The final page was a casualty list.

She looked up. "Five deaths?"

"A terrible thing," Griffin said. "But unavoidable."

"*Five deaths?* Unavoidable?"

"They all knew the risks." Griffin turned a page in his binder. "Tom, Molly, your part in this operation will be to—"

She stood so fast the chair toppled over behind her. "This isn't what I took this job to accomplish. I refuse to be a part of it."

"According to our files, you play your part as directed." He tapped his binder impatiently. "So, please, spare us this display of histrionics."

Jimmy Boyle's face was like stone. Amy Cho looked alarmed. Tom Navarro had raised his hands and was shaking his head. Calm down, he meant. Choose your fights carefully. Never do anything irrevocable when you're angry.

She ignored them all.

"You don't intimidate me, and you can't con me either. All this I-have-the-files-and-I-know-the-future bullshit doesn't cut it. I'm not going to go along with your filthy little plan. I'm going over your head. And if *that* doesn't work, I'll quit. So your files are wrong. One way or the other, they're wrong."

Griffin made an elaborately bored grimace and flicked his fingers toward the door. "Go. See how much good it does you."

In a rage, she left the room.

She stormed down the hall to the Old Man's office. Normally, the door was closed and the office was dark. But on her first day here, the Old Man had promised that the door would be open, "anytime you need to see me."

The door was open for her.

She went in.

The Old Man looked up from his work. It was uncanny how much he looked like Griffin while somehow feeling like a completely different person. More solitary, in a wolfish sort of way. More deeply scarred.

The fingertips of one hand lightly stroked the skull he kept on his desk. Involuntarily, she remembered the half-facetious rumor that it was a trophy from a hated enemy he had somehow defeated. "Come in," he said. "Close the door, have a seat. I've been expecting you."

She obeyed.

It was like entering an ogre's den. Thick curtains kept out the sunlight. Heavy wooden furniture held a clutter of mementos and framed photographs. He even had an *Quetzalcoatlus* skull propped up in the corner. It was as if he dwelt within his own hindbrain.

"Sir, I—"

He held up a hand. "I know why you're here. Give me credit for—" He stifled a yawn. "Give me that much credit, anyway. You're hoping that age has mellowed me. But if it hasn't, you think you're prepared to quit.

"Alas, it simply isn't that easy. Your Griffin made the decisions he did because *I* told him to. He didn't like it any more than you do. But he understood the necessity."

Molly's heart sank. She prided herself on being able to see deeper into a face than most, but the man was unreadable. He might be a saint or a devil. She honestly couldn't tell which. Looking into his eyes was like staring down a lightless road at midnight. There was no telling what might be down there. Those eyes had seen things she could not imagine.

She took a deep breath. "Then I'm afraid I must tender my resignation. Effective immediately."

"Let me show you something."

The Old Man removed a sheet of paper from a drawer. "This is a copy, of course. I just returned from a ceremony where you were presented the original." He slid it across the table to her.

It was a citation. The date had been blacked out, as had most of the text. But her name, in black Gothic letters was at the top, and several phrases remained. "For Exceptional Valor" was one.

"I can't tell you what you did—what you're going to do—and I can't tell you when you'll do it. But twenty people are alive because of your future actions. You got into security because you wanted to make a difference, right? Well, I just saw an old woman kiss your hand and thank you for saving the life of her son. You were embarrassed, but you were also pleased. You told me that that one instant justified your entire life."

"I don't believe you."

"Of course you do." He took the paper from her hands and returned it to his drawer. "You simply can't imagine what I could possibly say to keep you on board."

"No. I can't."

He looked at her with a strange glitter in his eye. He likes this, Molly thought. Corruption was the final pleasure of men such as he. Her original mission was lost. Now she wanted only to escape his presence before he managed to drag her down into the mire of complicity and guilt with him. She simply wanted to get out of this room unsoiled.

"Have you ever wondered," the Old Man asked, "where time travel came from?"

Carefully, she said, "Of course I have."

"Richard Leyster told me once that the technology couldn't possibly be of human origin. Nobody could build a time machine with today's physics, he said, or with any imaginable extension of it. It won't be feasible for at least a million years.

"As usual, his estimate was correct but conservative. In point of fact, time travel won't be invented for another forty-nine-point-six million years."

"Sir?" His words didn't make sense to her. She couldn't parse them out.

"What I'm telling you now is a government secret: Time travel is not a human invention. It is a gift from the Unchanging. And the Unchanging are not human."

"Then . . . what are they?"

"If you ever need to know, you'll be told. The operant fact is that the technology is on loan. As is ever the case with such gifts, there are a few strings. One of which is that we're not allowed to meddle with causality."

"Why?" Molly asked.

"I don't know. The physicists—some of them—tell me that if even one observed event were undone, all of time and existence would start to unravel. Not just the future, but the past as well, so that we'd be destabilizing all of existence, from alpha to omega, the Big Bang to the Cold Dark. Other physicists tell me no such thing, of course. The truth? The truth is that the Unchanging don't want us to do it.

"They've told us that if we ever violate their directives, they'll go back to the instant before giving us time travel, and withhold the offer. Think about that! Everything we've done and labored for these many years will come to nothing. Our lives, our experiences will dissolve into timelike loops and futility. The project will have never been.

"*Now*. You've met these people—the paleontologists. If you told them that the price of time travel was five deaths, what would they say? Would *they* think the price was too high?"

His face grew uncertain in her eyes. She squeezed them tight shut for the briefest instant. When she opened them again, she felt compelled to stand and turn away from him. On the wall was a photograph. It had been taken at the opening of the dinosaur compound in the National Zoo, and showed Griffin and the then-Speaker of the House stagily pulling opposite ends of a *T. rex* wishbone. She stared at their stiff poses, their insincere grins.

"I won't be a part of it. You cannot make me responsible for those deaths."

"You already are."

She shook her head. "What?"

"You remember that week you spent at Survival Station? Tom told you to make sure that Robo Boy heard that Leyster and Salley would be leading the first Baseline expedition. Tom got his directions from Jimmy, who was acting in response to a memo that Griffin should be writing up right now. You've already played your part."

The Old Man spread his hands. "Can you go back and undo everything you did and said back then? Well, no more can I undo these five deaths."

"I'll quit anyway! I won't be used like this!"

"Then twenty people die." Griffin smiled sadly

and spread his hands. "This is not a threat. Later in life, you'll happen to be the right person in the right place at the right time. Resign now, and you won't be there. Twenty people will die. Because you quit."

Molly squeezed her eyes tight, against her tears. "You are an evil, evil man," she said.

He made a warm, ambiguous sound that might have been a chuckle. "I know, dear. Believe me, I know."

10

Sexual Display

Lost Expedition Foothills: Mesozoic era. Cretaceous period.Senonian epoch. Maastrichtian age. 65 My B.C.E.

They buried Lydia Pell on a fern-covered knoll above Hell Creek. There was some argument over what religion she was, because she had once jokingly referred to herself as a "heretic Taoist." But then Katie went through her effects and found a pocket New Testament and a pendant cross made from three square-cut carpenter's nails, and that pretty well settled it that she was a Christian.

While those who had kept the night watch over her corpse slept, Leyster spent the morning searching Gillian's Bible for an appropriate passage. He'd considered "There were giants in the Earth," or the verse about Leviathan. But such attempts to fit in a reference to dinosaurs made him feel as if he were cheapening the grandeur and meaning of Lydia Pell's life by reducing it to the circumstances of her death. So in the end he settled for the Twenty-Third Psalm.

"The Lord is my shepherd," he began. "I shall not want." There were no sheep anywhere in the world, nor would there be for many tens of millions of years. Yet still, the words seemed appropriate. There was comfort in them.

The day was wet and miserable, but the rain was light and did not interfere with the ceremony. For most of the afternoon, everybody glumly carried stones from the creek to raise a small cairn over her grave, in order to keep scavengers away from her body. Just as they finished, the sun came out again.

Lai-tsz raised her head. "Listen," she said. "Do you hear that?"

A distant murmurous sound rose up from the far side of the river. It sounded a little like geese honking.

All in a group they hurried up to the top of the hollow, where a gap in the trees afforded a partial view of the valley. There they saw that the land beyond the River Styx was in motion. Tamara scrambled up a tree and shouted down, "The herds are *flooding* in! They're coming from all directions. More from the west than the east, though. I see hadrosaurs of some sort, and triceratopses too."

"I didn't bring my cameras!" wailed Patrick.

Tamara called down from the top of the tree, "Now they're crossing the river! Holy cow. It's incredible. They're putting up so much mist you can't see the half of them."

Several others went swarming up the trees to see for themselves.

"Can you give us an estimate of their numbers?" Leyster shouted up.

"No way! I keep losing sight of them among the trees. Or in the water. But there must be hundreds of them. Maybe thousands."

"Hundreds of hadrosaurs, or hundreds of triceratopses?"

"Both!"

"What are they doing on this side?"

"It's hard to tell. Milling about, mostly. Some of the hadrosaurs appear to be breaking into smaller groups. The triceratopses are clustering."

"So what do you think—are these guys migrating?"

"Actually, it looks like they're moving in to stay."

"They couldn't have chosen a better time for it," Katie commented. "All this young growth, freshly fertilized with titanosaur dung—it's herbivore heaven here."

"Damn." Leyster thought for a moment, then said, "I want to go down by the river and get a closer look at them." He was understating the case drastically. He *had* to go take a closer look. "Who here wants to go with me?"

Tamara swung down out of her tree so fast Leyster worried she would fall, singing, "Me! Me! Me!"

"Some of us should stay here," Jamal said dubiously. "To look after the camp. Also we've still got the walls to put up."

"Come with us," Leyster said quietly. "Nobody can say you haven't done your share of the work."

Jamal hesitated, then shook his head. "No, really. How can I expect anybody else to work, if I'm not willing to work myself?"

The party he put together was, to Leyster's profound disappointment, made up mostly of the food-gatherers and Daljit. Of the house-builders, only Patrick, loaded down with his cameras, broke ranks.

They moved cautiously, single file, like a jungle combat squad out of the twentieth century. Lai-tsz went first, toting one of the expedition's four shotguns. Leyster doubted it would do much good in a confrontation with a full-sized dinosaur, but the idea was that the noise would frighten a predator away.

He sincerely hoped that was true.

They were deep into the valley flatlands before they spotted their first dinos—a clutch of hadrosaurs delicately grazing on the tender young shoots that grew thickly along the verges of the creek.

As one, all binoculars went up.

The animals paid them no attention. Every now and then one would bob up on its two hind feet and look around warily, then dip back down again. Briefly, the startling orange markings on either side of its head would erupt into the air like a burst of flame, before disappearing again into the new growth. There was always at least one keeping watch.

"What are they?" Daljit asked quietly. "I mean, I know they're hadrosaurs, but what kind?"

Hadrosaurs, or duckbilled dinosaurs, made up a very large family grouping indeed, including dozens of known species spread throughout the Late Cretaceous. To call something a hadrosaur was like declaring a particular mammal was a feline without specifying whether it was a leopard or a house cat.

"Well, keep in mind that I'm a bone man at heart," Leyster said. "I'd have a much easier time if there weren't all that skin and muscle in the way." What he really needed was a *Peterson's Field Guide to the Late Maastrichtian Megafauna,* with diagnostic illustrations and little black lines pointing to all the field-marks. "Still, check out those heads. They're definitely hadrosaurines—the non-crested duckbills. And from the elongation and width of the snouts I'd have to say they were *Anatotitan.* What species of anatotitan, though, I don't know."

"They sure are active buggers," Daljit said. "Look at them bob up and down."

Crouching, they crept closer. Anatotitans were herbivores, of course. But they were also enormous. An animal half as big as a bus didn't have to be a carnivore to be dangerous.

They got within thirty yards before some unseen signal passed among the animals and, as one, they rose to their hind legs and moved swiftly away. They did not run, exactly, but their bounding gait was so quick that they were, nevertheless, gone in a moment.

"Come on," Leyster said. "Let's—"

Tamara was tugging at his sleeve. "Look!"

He looked back where she pointed.

The Lord of the Valley came striding upriver. Leyster recognized the tyrannosaur by its markings. It was his old acquaintance and none other.

The most dangerous predator the world had ever known glided swiftly through the low growth with a dreamlike lack of haste. His pace was unrushed, and yet his legs were so long, he moved with astonishing speed.

Silent as a shark, he strode after the fleeing anatotitans. He didn't even give the researchers a glance as he passed by.

"Holy shit," Patrick said flatly.

"Come on." Leyster gestured. "We've got a lot of land to cover. Let's get moving."

They headed west, parallel to the sluggish River Styx, being careful to keep to the forest side of the herds.

As they traveled, Leyster told the others something about hadrosaurs. They knew already that hadrosaurs were the most diverse and abundant group of large vertebrates in the northern hemisphere during the closing stages of the Late Cretaceous, and that they were the last major group of ornithopods to evolve in the Mesozoic. But he wanted them to understand that in many ways hadrosaurs were a blueprint for the dinosaurs of their future. That they were so well adapted to such a variety of ecosystems that if it hadn't been for the K-T event, their descendants might well have survived into modern times.

“So what makes them so special?” Patrick asked. “They sure don’t look like much. Why should they dominate the ecology?”

“Maybe because they’re ideal tyrannosaur chow,” Tamara said suddenly. “Look at ’em. Almost but not quite as big as a tyrannosaur, no armor or weaponry to speak of, and that great big fleshy neck just perfect for biting. One good chomp, and down it goes! If I were a rex, I’d take good care of *these* critters.”

Patrick scowled. “No, seriously.”

“Seriously?” Leyster said, “They’re generalists, like we are. You’ll notice that humans don’t have many specialized adaptations either. No armor, no horns, no claws. But we can find a way to get along wherever we find ourselves. Same thing with hadrosaurs. They—”

“Shush!” Lai-tsz said. “I hear something. Up ahead.”

A lone triceratops poked its head out of the distant wood. Cautiously, it eased out into the open. It ambled a short way into the meadow, then stopped. That massive head swung to one side, and then to the other, as it searched for enemies. Finally, convinced there were none, it grunted three times.

A pause. Then a second triceratops emerged from the woods. A third. A fourth. A ragged line of the brutes flowed out of the woods and into the ferns and flowers. Their frills were all as bright as butterflies, dominated by two black-rimmed orange circles, like great eyes.

"Triceratops herds have leaders!" Nils said. "Just like cattle."

"We can't conclude that yet," Leyster cautioned. "It looks good, but it'll take long and careful observation to make sure that what we think we're seeing is actually so."

"Look at those frills! Sexual display, you think?"

"Got to be."

Lai-tsz put down her glasses and, pointing at the leader, asked, "What's that swelling?"

The creature's face looked puffy. Twin nasal sacs to either side of its central horn were inflated like the cheeks of a bullfrog. Suddenly they deflated. *Gronk!*

Everybody laughed. Tamara fell over, whooping. "Oh God, can you believe it? What a noise! It sounds like a New Year's Eve noisemaker."

The triceratops pawed the earth.

Lai-tsz and Nils made shushing noises at Tamara. "Quiet! It's doing something." Patrick darted off to the side, camera out, looking for a good angle.

The animal's face pouches were inflating again. It took several deep, gulping breaths, shaking its head as it did so. "What do you think it's doing?" Lai-tsz asked Leyster.

"I don't know. It looks kind of like it's reinflating—"

Gronk!

Tamara clapped a hand over her mouth, cutting off a high-pitched laughter in mid-shriek.

"Look over there," Nils said. "Somebody else wants to get into the act." A second triceratops was approaching the first, slowly and meaningfully. "Intraspecific aggression, do you think? Dominance display? Are they going to fight?"

The first triceratops had his nasal sacs half inflated again. The second stopped within charging distance of him and then bowed its head. Slowly, ponderously, it rolled over onto its side.

"I don't think so," Leyster said wryly. "It looks more like a mating display."

"It's a girl!" Tamara cried.

Gronk!

Lying on the ground, one rear leg raised in the air, the female shivered.

"She's mesmerized!"

"C'mere, big boy."

"Oh, mamma. You know you want me."

With unhurried dignity, the male maneuvered himself alongside the female, one foreleg to either side of her tail. It paused then, seemingly baffled. The female made a plaintive sound, and he took a step backward, then another forward, trying to get himself into position. That didn't work either. But on his third attempt, he finally got their bellies properly aligned and slowly eased himself downward.

"Man, oh, man," Patrick muttered. "These shots are going to be great."

Ponderously, the two triceratopses began to mate.

It was sunset when they finally got back to camp and discovered that Jamal's crew had moved the contents of two of the tents into the long house, and lashed the tents' canvases to the frame to make walls. So up the slope they went, to share what they'd seen.

The interior of the long house was bright with artificial light. It looked infinitely welcoming. Of course, their flashlights, even with the solar rechargers, would only last so long. All the more reason to use them now. Brandish ye flashlights while ye may, Leyster thought. Old Time is still a-flying.

"Take your shoes off!" Katie called cheerfully as they entered. "There's a space for them by the door."

The interior was fragrant with the smell of ferns, which had been brought in by the armload and dumped over the floor, and with turtle soup, simmering in a kettle over the fire outside. Leyster and the others came in and sat.

"Welcome the intrepid dino hunters!" Chuck declared. "You're just in time for supper. Come in, sit down, tell us everything."

While Chuck distributed bowls and Katie ladled soup, Patrick passed around his camera, showing off a sequence of his best shots.

"What are these two *doing?*" Gillian asked incredulously when she saw the first picture of the two triceratops.

"Exactly what you think they're doing," Patrick said.

"The filthy things!" Gillian wagged a finger reprovingly. "Naughty-naughty."

"Dino porn. This stuff would be *so* marketable," Jamal mourned.

"But who would buy it?" Chuck asked. "I don't see much of a market."

"Are you kidding? It's sex, it's funny, and it's something you haven't seen before. It creates its own market. Why, the calendars alone . . ."

Everybody laughed. Jamal flushed, then ducked his head and grinned ruefully. "Well, it would!"

They continued the discussion through dinner. "So you lost the shotgun?" Matthew asked when they told the story of being scattered by the post-coital triceratops.

"I was caught by surprise!" Lai-tsz said. "We all were. But, damn it, they told us in survival training that the noise of a shotgun blast would scare off anything. So when I shot the gun off in the air, I wasn't expecting the thing to *charge!* It came barreling down on us, and we all just ran. If it had been a little faster, it would've gotten me." She shook her head. "There was definitely something wrong with that animal."

"Did you go back and look for the gun?"

"Yes, we did. All the ground was trampled into mud. It was like looking for a needle in a haystack."

"I'd rather lose all four shotguns than a single Swiss Army knife," Jamal observed. He turned to Leyster. "Still, that trike wasn't supposed to charge like that. Our instructor told us she'd frightened off ceratopsians herself, dozens of times. Why didn't it run?"

Leyster shrugged. "Back in grad school, Dr. Schmura used to say, 'The organism is always right.' Living things don't always do what they're supposed to. Some days sand fleas eat medusae and minnows attack sharks. When that happens, your job is to take good notes and hope that someday you'll be able to make sense out of it."

Hours passed as they quietly talked. It had been so long since they'd all been friends. Nobody wanted it to end.

"Hey, look what I found," Chuck said. He darted into a shadowy corner, and wrestled the skull of a juvenile triceratops into the center of the room. "I found it bleaching in the sun. You wouldn't believe how much work it was to drag it up here."

"Why on earth would you bother?" Tamara asked.

Chuck shrugged. "I always wanted one of these things. Now I have it." He lifted it up and held it before him, waggling it from side to side, as if it were in heat and courting a mate.

"What's that sound it made, again?"

"Gronk!"

"More like grawwnk! With a little glissando on the awwnk."

Chuck, who had early on assumed for himself the role of group clown, began to sing, ". . . darling, 'cause when you're near me . . ."

Katie picked up the tune, singing, "I'm in the . . . mooood . . . for love!"

Joke made, Chuck stopped. But Katie went on singing and, one by one, the others joined all in, singing the old romantic standard. Then, when that was done, they sang "Stormy Weather," and "Smoke Gets in Your Eyes."

Then Chuck, squatting behind the triceratops skull, began beating its frill with the flats of his hands, as if he were playing bongos. In a high, clear falsetto, he began to sing

In the 'zoic, the Mesozoic,
The T. rex *sleeps tonight . . .*

And Tamara added

In the mud of the Maas-tricht-i-an,
The shotgun rusts tonight.

Everyone else joined in on the doo-wop harmonies, singing

Ohhhh weeeeee weeeeee oh wim oh wey
Ohhhh weeeeee weeeeee oh wim oh wey

and

A-weema-weh, a-weemah-weh, a-weema-weh, a-weemeh-weh
A-weema-weh, a-weemah-weh, a-weema-weh, a-weemeh-weh

until the music filled the long house like a living spirit. Outside, the night was dark and filled with the furtive scurrying of small mammals. Within, there was the warmth of friendship and good times. People traded off verses, making them up extempore, so that when Daljit sang

Why don't you get a job with Mobil?
I hear that they pay well.

Lai-tsz replied

They've got great health care and pension plans,
Their profit sharing's swell.

Then, after the break, Chuck threw out

That's too risky, no I'll get tenure
With my new Ph.D.

And Tamara responded with

And if triceratops don't gore me,
I'll have job security!

They all collapsed, laughing, on the floor. It took them a few minutes to catch their breaths afterwards.

Leyster was about to suggest another song when suddenly Katie threw her blouse in the air. Patrick cheered and clapped, and then, as if that had been a prearranged signal, everybody was shucking clothes, struggling free of trousers, frantically untying bootlaces.

Leyster opened his mouth to say something.

But Tamara, sitting beside him, touched his arm and said in a voice so soft that only he could hear, "Please. Don't spoil it."

For an instant, Leyster did not know how to respond. Then he began to unbutton his shirt. By the time he had it off, somebody had already undone his fly and was tugging down his trousers. He kissed Gillian long and hard, and she pressed his hand between her legs. She was already moist. He slid a finger deep inside her.

It was strange, strange, to be so intimate so suddenly with somebody he'd never romanced.

Then Patrick murmured something which might have been, "Excuse me," and Gillian was guiding Patrick's head down where Leyster's hand had been. Tamara's mouth closed over the head of his cock, and he gasped softly. Beside him, Katie thrust her breast into his mouth.

His mouth caressed her nipple. It tasted so sweet.

Then things got confused. Confused and wonderful.

At breakfast the next morning, Leyster watched the subtle dance of small, shy smiles and light, fleeting touches that passed through the group. It astonished him. He'd awakened feeling ashamed and remorseful about what he'd done. Even though he'd never been a particularly religious person, it felt wrong, a violation of the way things should be.

The others clearly didn't feel that at all. Well, they were grad students. They were young. Their sexuality was still new to them, and malleable. They were open to new possibilities in a way that he, though almost of an age with them, could never be.

Still, it was important not to let his embarrassment show. They had finally made peace, and peace was precious. He must pretend to be as happy as they.

Sometimes deceit was the best policy.

So when Daljit squeezed his shoulder, Leyster gently leaned back against her for an instant. When Nils placed his hand on Katie's, Leyster briefly put his hand atop both of theirs. He stayed silent, and smiled, and was particularly careful not to flinch away from anyone's glance. He waited.

Until at last the psychologically right moment was come.

Mentally, he took a deep breath. Then he said, "I've been thinking about this whole leadership thing."

Several people stiffened. Jamal said, "Well, see, I didn't mean to . . ." His voice dwindled off.

"It's not like that. This isn't about who gets to lead. I just don't see why we need a leader at all." They were all watching him intently, unblinkingly. "When this was an expedition, sure, we needed somebody to divvy up chores and keep everyone on task. But things are different now. And, well, there are only eleven of us. Why shouldn't we just get together—like we are right now—and decide things as they come up?"

"Majority vote, you mean?" Lai-tsz asked.

"No. I don't think we should do anything unless everybody agrees on it. No dissenters, no abstentions."

"Can that work?" somebody asked.

"A friend of mine did some linguistic work with the Lakota Sioux," Daljit said. "She told me they were fiends for consensus. If they had a meeting to write up a press release, they insisted that everybody agree on the size of the envelopes and the color of the paper before they'd say a word about the actual content. My friend said it drove outsiders *nuts*. But it worked. She said that in the long run there was a lot less conflict that way."

"That's a lot of talking," Patrick said dubiously.

"Well, we've got a lot of time," Daljit said.

"I'm willing to cut down on my TV watching, if that's what it takes," Chuck offered.

A chuckle went around the circle.

Eventually, they adopted the motion by consensus. Then they moved on to the chores schedule.

Grievances were aired, compromises proposed, and adjustments made. At last Jamal slapped his hands together and said, "Well, I don't know about the rest of you, but I've got work to do. So if there isn't anything else on the agenda . . ."

"There's just one more thing," Leyster said. "I think we should be doing some real science. We've gotten so caught up in survival that we've forgotten why we're here. We came to do research. I think we should."

There was an instant's astonished silence. Then—

"Well, I was *wondering* when somebody would say that!"

"About time, too."

"I would've said it myself, but—"

"Okay," Tamara said. "We're all agreed. Fine. So how do we do this? What are we looking for?"

Everybody turned to Leyster.

He coughed, embarrassed. The authority of superior knowledge was different in kind from the authority of assumed power. Still, he felt a little awkward assuming it.

"That's not how it works," he said. "Konrad Lorenz didn't say to himself, 'I'm going to discover imprinting in baby ducks' and set out to gather evidence. He very carefully gathered data and studied it until it told him something. That's what we're going to do. Observe, record, discuss, analyze. Sooner or later, we'll learn something."

Patrick grinned slyly. "Yeah, but there's got to be stuff we're *hoping*, somewhere in the backs of our heads, to find out."

"Well, obviously, there's always the problem of why the dinosaurs died out."

"Whopping big rock. Tidal waves, firestorms, nuclear winter, no food. End of story."

"Crocodiles survived. Some of them were enormous. Birds survived, and cladistically speaking, they *are* dinosaurs. What made the non-avian dinosaurs so vulnerable to the K-T disaster? I can't help suspecting that it's related to the fact that during the last several million years of the Mesozoic, dinosaurs underwent a radical loss of diversity."

"There's plenty of dinos out there!" Katie objected.

"Lots of individuals. But compared to the old days, only a fraction the number of species. Leaving those that remain particularly susceptible to environmental change."

"I really can't see that," Patrick said. "They're so robust. They're so perfectly adapted to their environment."

"Maybe too well adapted. The species that die out are those that adapt themselves so perfectly to a specific niche that they can't survive if that niche suddenly changes or ceases to be. That's why so many species went extinct in the twentieth century, even though the kind of indiscriminate slaughter of animals that hunters engaged in during the nineteenth had pretty much ceased. When humans destroyed their habitat, they had nowhere to go."

They talked until noon. They could afford to. The long house was built, and they had enough food stored up for a week, even without dipping into the freeze-dried stuff. More, these were still students, however far they might be from a university. They needed the reassurance of learning, the familiar cadences of lecture and debate, to restore their sense of normality.

Finally, though, somebody realized that it was time for lunch and the dishes hadn't been washed, and everybody scattered to their assigned cooking and set-up chores.

Tamara lingered behind, to have a quiet word with Leyster.

"Well, my hat's off to you. You pulled us all together. I really didn't think you could do it."

Leyster took her hand, gently kissed one knuckle, and did not let it go. He felt like a fraud. He had become a paleontologist at least in part because he found dinosaurs comprehensible in a way that people were not. It was a terrible thing to be so deceitful. "I think last night had a lot to do with it."

"Last night was nice." She smiled, and he fleetingly wondered if it was possible she was putting on an act too. Then rejected the thought as paranoia. "But it just happened. This morning was premeditated."

"Maybe just a little," he admitted. "The problem was that when all you're trying to do is survive, the universe seems a cold and hostile place. We needed a purpose. To distract us from our awareness of being a single spark of human warmth in an infinite expanse of silence. One small candle in the infinite night of being."

"Do you really think science is purpose enough?"

"Yes, I do. I always have. Maybe it's because I was a lonely kid, and there were times when learning things was all that kept me going. The search for truth is not an unworthy reason to keep going."

"You make it sound so arbitrary."

"Maybe it is. Yet I persist in believing that knowledge is better than ignorance." He was silent for a moment. "I was in Uppsala, Sweden, once. In the floor of the Domkyrka, the Cathedral, there, I found Linnaeus's gravestone."

"Carl Linnaeus, you mean? The inventor of binomial nomenclature?"

"Yeah. It was a fine-grained gray stone with two fossil belemnites swimming across its surface, like pale comets. Linnaeus didn't even know what fossils were. During his lifetime, Voltaire quite seriously suggested they were the petrified remains of pilgrims' lunches. But there they were, like guardians assigned him by Nature in gratitude for his work." He let go of her hand. "Why should I find that comforting? Yet I do."

After lunch, Leyster stayed behind to work on the smokehouse, while Katie took a party out to make the first observations. They were all laughing and chattering, as they left, as cheerful as children and as heedless of the danger. Watching them, Leyster felt the same sickening fear for them that he imagined a parent must experience the first time a child is allowed to leave the house by itself.

He wanted so hard to protect them, and knew he could not. They were all buoyed up by what had happened last night. But all their confidence, all their joy, would not be enough to keep them safe. They would have to be continually on their guard. In this world, the night might belong to mammals, but dinosaurs ruled the day.

11

Chalk Talk

Xanadu Station: Mesozoic era. Cretaceous period. Gallic epoch. Turonian age. 95 My B.C.E.

The meeting room was built into a cliff overlooking the Tethys Sea. Ordinarily the view through the glass wall was enough to fill the soul and elevate the spirit, and even at the exorbitant rates charged for its use, the room was booked solid for every clear day until its scheduled demolition. Today, however, the weather was dreary. A dull rain spattered against the windows and turned the ocean water gray.

Griffin sat in a leather conference chair, thinking about chalk.

It was only vertebrate chauvinism that made people think dinosaurs were the most important living things of their time. From the mid-Cretaceous onward, one of the most significant and varied families of organisms on Earth was the calcareous algae. Though microscopically small, these spherical plants had armored themselves with ornately structured overlapping calcium plates. The warm seas contained galaxies of calcareous algae, living uneventful lives and shedding their cunning little shields when they died.

The exoskeletal debris from the algae and other nannoplankton, both vegetal and animal, was constantly filtering down through the water, an eternal snowfall that deposited as much as six inches of finely-grained chalk on the ocean floor in a thousand years. The white cliffs of Dover were the patient work of billions of generations of tiny creatures leading orderly and bourgeois lives. Hopscotch diagrams and sidewalk artists' naive copies of *The Last Supper,* grammar school sentence diagrams and physicists' equations, the sure kiss of a pool stick against a cue ball, the frictionless grip of a gymnast's hands upon the high bar, all depended on the anonymous contributions of these placid beings.

Griffin often meditated upon this. The thought that such transient lives served the diverse purposes of a higher order of life pleased him. He wondered sometimes if the human race would leave behind a legacy half so enduring. Such thoughts calmed him, usually.

Not today.

Today, everything was fucked. Griffin had come at last, as he'd always known he would, to a dead end. The fairy castle he had built out of playing cards and hope was trembling in the breeze. Any second now, it would collapse. Everything he'd worked for, the sacrifices he'd made, the hard and sometimes cruel decisions that had been forced on him—all was come to futility. Everything was fucked and done for.

The door opened and closed behind him. He did not need to look to know that Salley had entered the room. She came up behind him and placed her hands on his shoulders. Briefly, she kneaded the muscles. They were stiff and knotted.

"All right," she said. "What is it?"

There were so many responses he could have made. Almost at random, he said, "I've never hit a woman." He could see her ghostly reflection in the window wall, tall and regal as a queen. Below her he was slumped in his leather armchair like a defeated king waiting for the barbarians to arrive. Their eyes met in the glass. "Today, I almost hit you."

"Tell me why."

Griffin had been away from Salley for a week when he finally returned to his room in Xanadu. But for her, it had only been a half hour. He knew because, as he always did in such cases, he'd written himself a memo.

His plan was simply to say a quiet good-bye. Salley was scheduled to leave on the Baseline Project expedition in the morning. Knowing what hardships she would face, and how long it would be before her rescue, he wanted to say something that would linger. Something that would, on reflection, offer her a touch of secret hope when it looked like she was stranded forever.

But when he'd tried saying the carefully composed words, she'd stopped his mouth with kisses. She'd hooked a leg behind him and shoved him on the chest, tumbling him down on the bed. Then she took his shirt in both hands and pulled, scattering buttons in all directions. What happened then should have been every bit as much fun as he'd had the first time with her.

It wasn't, of course.

It made him feel guilty. There was no use denying that. But what choice did he have? Anything else would only have been that much crueler for her. So he was using her. So what? It hadn't been his decision. *She'd* seduced *him,* for Christ's sake! It would be different if it had been the other way around. But he wasn't going to carry the can for a situation that was entirely of her own making.

Griffin had been married before, both times to women who ended up making him feel confused and defensive. Women who introduced chaos and emotion into what should have been an orderly existence. Women toward whom—it could not be denied—his feelings were mixed, even now.

This was why relationships were such a bad idea.

For all his experience, however, he had to admit that Salley was a particularly exhausting woman. She made demands. She took up all of his attention. She melted every bone in his body. By the time she was done with him, he lacked the desire even to sit up.

To her, on the other hand, sex was clearly a tonic. It made her glow. Afterwards, she crouched over him, smiling, and, bending down, covered his face with soft kisses. "Don't try to get up," she said. "I'll show myself out."

"I really should make sure you get back to the Carnian in time to make your preparations."

"I'm already packed. I'm cleared to take the funnel back to half an hour before the expedition departs. All I have to do then is change my clothes."

"No, really, I can't let you . . ."

"Hush," she said. "Don't say a word. Let me watch you fall asleep, before I go."

Gratefully, suspecting nothing, he let sleep overcome him.

In the morning he awoke to find Salley rattling about in the kitchenette, brewing a pot of coffee. She was wearing one of his shirts, and whenever she reached for something, it rode up to reveal her bare bottom.

Griffin sat bolt upright, shocked fully awake. "What time is it? Why are you still here?" He snatched up his watch. It read 8:47 A.M. Disbelieving, he slid it on his wrist.

"Relax." She came into the room with two cups of coffee and handed him one. "There was a change in the expedition's roster. Lydia Pell took my place." She put down her cup and rummaged about in her purse. "Here. I brought you a copy of that day's traffic log."

Griffin unfolded the sheet one-handed and stared at it in disbelief. There was no denying its existence. Yet it simply could not be. He had seen that exact same sheet (the light blue flimsies were never duplicated nor their ID numbers reused) on his desk, with "Salley, G. C." at the top of the roster. Now her name was absent, and replaced by Lydia Pell's.

"You were supposed to be on that expedition. Goddamnit, you *were* on that expedition. It's documented. It's certain. I signed off on it myself. It's already happened." He placed his hand over his wrist and squeezed as hard as he could. "You've created a Class One time paradox."

Salley smiled. "Yes, I know."

"Tell me why," Salley repeated.

So he did. It took a very long time, and he had to oversimplify wildly, but he managed. He told her something about the Unchanging, and quite a bit more about Holy Redeemer Ranch, and went into some detail about why, though he knew who was responsible, he couldn't simply arrest the mole who'd planted the bomb in the expedition's supplies.

He'd expected Salley to be angry when she learned that he had been prepared to send her off on a doomed expedition. She was not. To his astonishment, she was hanging on his every word, transparently fascinated.

Without intending to, he was, he realized, playing to her weaknesses. He was giving her a glimpse behind the curtain, where the Wizard of Oz operated the secret machinery that ran the cosmos, and showing her exactly which levers were attached to what pulleys.

"The expedition is lost for good," he concluded. "The first time, the Unchanging lent us the equipment to pull off a recovery mission. They'll never do that now."

He didn't mention that, according to the final

reports, they'd recovered only seven people. That three had died as a result of injuries from the bomb, and two by misadventure thereafter. The sequence in which that had happened had, after all, been sundered from the main time line. In their frame of reference, it didn't exist.

"All of which assumes that our screwing around isn't going to destroy the universe," he added in bitter afterthought.

"I don't think we need worry about *that,*" Salley said. "And I doubt the Unchanging are really going to loop back on themselves and decide not to give us time travel. From what I was told, things will go on pretty much as they always have, paradox or no."

"Told! Who told you that?" He was collected enough now to ask the questions he'd dared not earlier when, in furious silence, he had thrown on his clothes and stormed out of his room. He was collected enough now to listen to her answers. "Who put such a crazy idea into your head?"

"I did."

"What?"

She laughed a small, self-conscious laugh. "It's a funny thing. There must be a hundred movies in which the hero sees her exact double walk into the room, and she's always stunned when it happens. But when it happened to me—when I looked up and saw myself walk into the tent, I had no idea who it was. It wasn't until she held up a pocket mirror and told me to compare faces that I realized she was me, only older. She told me—"

Griffin at last turned his face up toward Salley. "And you *believed* her?"

But of course Salley had believed her. The stranger was, after all, herself. What possible motive could she have for deceiving her? So she had agreed to drop out of the expedition, accepted the changed roster sheet, and promised to seduce Griffin after the fund-raiser, make certain he was too tired to see her home to the Carnian that night, and hand him the paper in the morning.

Nobody else who knew Salley at all well would have gone along with a fraction of that. Everyone else knew she was a terrible liar. Only she herself was unaware of how untrustworthy she was.

"It hardly matters how we got here," Salley said. "What matters is what we do now. I think we should hop up to the future and cut a deal. Everybody makes deals."

He shook his head. "Time travel was given to us under certain conditions. We've violated every rule there is."

"Okay, so we broke the rules. That's good! There are no more rules—they're broken. Anything is possible now. We'll find a solution. There has to be a solution. There always is."

"Not in *my* experience." They were, he realized, standing on opposite sides of the great divide that separates those who deal with scientific fact and those who deal with the consequences of human actions. Which is to say, those who believe in a rational universe and those who know that, given the existence of human beings, there is no such thing. "You and I belong to entirely different universes, did you know that?"

"Then come join me in mine," she said gently. "Yours doesn't work anymore."

It was true. God knows, it was true. Griffin felt something shift within himself. It was the rebirth not of hope (for he had never truly felt any hope) but of purpose. "Tell me something," he said. "What were you trying to accomplish? Your other self, I mean. What did she say to you that made you go along with her?"

Incredibly, Salley blushed.

"She told me that I love you."

When he had finished phrasing the invitations, Griffin glanced at his watch. Two minutes before the hour. He'd hold the meeting in two minutes, then. He filled in the spaces he'd left blank, and slid the papers into his attaché to give to a courier later.

There was a knock on the open door.

"Is it just the three of us, then?" Jimmy asked quietly. He nodded to Salley, and she smiled insincerely back at him.

"I've invited one more," Griffin said. "He ought to be arriving just about . . . now."

Jimmy strode in the door. He stopped as he saw himself.

"This isn't good," Jimmy said.

His older self looked extremely sad. "I have no memory of this at all. And it's not the sort of thing I'd forget."

Leaving unsaid, but understood: You've really stepped on your dick this time. Griffin and Jimmy had worked together so long that they no longer had to say such things. Each knew the other well enough to dispense with all but the essentials.

"Have a seat, both of you." Griffin picked up a piece of chalk. Presentation technology shifted so often in the twenty-first century, from electronic whiteboards to interflats, smartboards and body interpreters, that no one person could manage them all. But everybody knew how to use a blackboard.

He drew three parallel lines. "Okay, these are the pertinent segments of the Maastrichtian, the Turonian, and the Carnian."

Most of Griffin's publications were in the field of chronocybernetics. All of them were classified, at varying degrees of hardness. Some of them he suspected only *he* was cleared to read. But his single most useful contribution to the field was the invention of causal schematics. They were rather like a cross between cladograms and Feynman space-time diagrams, and were used to keep cause-and-effect events from becoming entangled.

Briskly, he overlaid the lines with a series of linked circles representing stable areas of operation. Then he cut through them with branching consequence lines. Completed, the schematic showed a major anomaly nested deep within Salley's actions. Young Jimmy drew his breath in when he saw that. His older counterpart leaned back, looking sour.

"There's our problem," Griffin said. "Comments?"

Jimmy eyed Salley coldly. "How the hell did she get into her own history? We have safeguards in place."

"She . . . Okay, let's call the older vector Gertrude, to avoid confusion. And to remind *you,*" he said to a glaring Salley, "that she is by no means to be mistaken for yourself. Not any longer. Gertrude would've needed All Access clearance. Which is obtainable only from the Old Man. How she managed that, we'll never know."

"Couldn't we—?"

"No. We can't. Gertrude has disappeared on the far side of the anomaly. Any vector of Salley we could reach would be the linear descendant or predecessor of the one here with us, and completely blameless."

The older Jimmy cleared his throat. "Are you sure?"

"Exactly what," Salley said, "are you implying?"

Griffin held up a hand for peace. "It's a fair question. Yes, I'm sure. Gertrude went to a great deal of effort to deceive Salley. Why? We don't know, and we can't even guess at her motives. So let's not waste time trying."

"What do we do now?" asked the older Jimmy. His younger self leaned forward.

"Whatever else, we've got an expedition to rescue. We need to speak with our sponsors."

"Not possible. Access to the Unchanging is the military's bailiwick. Even the Old Man has a tough time getting through to them."

"Then we'll have to do an end run. Meet them on their home turf." He paused significantly. "All of us."

"It'd be easier," young Jimmy said, "if you didn't take *her.*"

"That's not up for discussion." It had been a long time since Griffin had done anything that was out-and-out illegal—he preferred to work within the system. If he was going off-track, he wanted Salley with him, and Jimmy as well. Each was cunning in a way the other was not. And he was going to need all the help he could get. "Where do we start?"

Young Jimmy got up and erased everything Griffin had drawn on the board. Then he picked up a piece of chalk and drew a complex series of interlinking up-and-down lines. "The Subway of the Gods," he said with a sharkish grin. "Local stops. As per your memo, I brought along a list of weak links."

"Weak links?" Salley asked.

"When we set up security," Griffin said, "we made sure to stir in a few guards who were less than optimally bright. Just in case. None of them are on duty very long. You'd have to have hired them to know where they were."

"Now here," Jimmy tapped a node, "in 2103 is a perfect opportunity. Security officer Mankalita Harrison. Officious, ambitious, bottom of her class. Filling in for Sue Browder for a period of two days. Never met the Old Man. Best of all, we've kept those days almost perfectly undocumented. We can insert anything into that silence we want. But you'll need All Access clearance to pull it off. Is there any way you can get hold of the Old Man's ID?"

The Old Man was a creature of habit, and had been since he was a teenager. Sharpened pencils always to one side of the top drawer, a ream of cream-colored bond in the middle. Griffin knew where he would keep his authorization papers. He knew what the passcodes would be. "I can do it."

Old Jimmy cleared his throat. "I notice you assume the Old Man won't play along?"

"Trust me. He'll never cooperate on this one."

"Well, if you can get the ID, I can do the rest. We'll need documentation from—"

Old Jimmy threw Griffin a look. Griffin, in response, turned to young Jimmy, and said, "Okay. We've game-planned this sort of thing out. Take care of the paperwork and get the boys in the shop to build us the crate. We'll be leaving in fifteen minutes."

"The crate?" Salley asked.

Griffin ignored her. "Oh, and we'll need another person on the security team. Any recommendations?"

"I've heard good things about Molly Gerhard."

"Get her. She leaves us at age forty-something to start her own business. Requisition her as close to the end as you can. The older the better."

"Done." The young man got up and left.

Griffin turned to the remaining Jimmy. "All right," he said. "What is it?"

"I'm not sure I should . . ." He cocked an eyebrow toward Salley.

"I have no secrets from her. Speak openly."

Jimmy sighed and shook his head. "When you get to be my age, you lose your taste for *his* kind of games." He nodded toward the door on *his*. "Harry, I'm about to retire. I bought a bar on Long Island. Tomorrow is my last day."

"Then give me your last day. Find the Old Man's intercept point and keep him away from me until after the travel roster's been filed. Take him out for drinks. Get him talking about the old days."

Jimmy looked pained. "I understand how you feel. But there's no way you can convince me to take sides here."

Griffin studied Jimmy carefully, making him the focus of all his attention, to the perfect exclusion of everything else. He waited until Jimmy filled the universe, then said, "Do you remember that time in the Texas roadhouse, outside of San Antonio?"

Jimmy chuckled. He remembered, of course. It was a beat-up old redneck hangout with dollar bills stapled to the ceiling for decoration. They were in town for a rock and gem show where a generation-one geologist had planned to sell a fistful of particularly flashy *Caudipteryx* feathers to a private collector. This was in 2034, a week before Salley's press conference, and time travel was still a great secret. When the geologist checked into his hotel room, Griffin was there, Jimmy at his back, prepared to put the fear of God into the man. Later, they'd tossed the contraband out the rental car window on their way out of town.

They'd stopped in the roadhouse for a few beers and a game of pool (each played badly and fancied the other played worse), when a drunk came over and tried to pick a fight. "*Hey!*" he'd said. "Y'all ain't *faggots*, are you?" He was an unshaven, sloppy-fat yahoo, who wore a plaid shirt open over a stained tee. But he had the look of someone who worked for a living. Griffin judged there was real muscle under that paunch. " 'Cause you sure *look* like a pair a god-damned faggots!"

"Have a beer," Griffin suggested. "My treat."

The drunk stared at him in pop-eyed astonishment. He wove a little from side to side. "Y'all saying that I take drinks from faggots? You must think that I'm a faggot too."

Jimmy was bent over the pool table, lining up a shot. Without looking up, he said, "I don't have time for you. But that's my bottle over there on the bumper. You can cram it up your arse."

The drunk blinked. Then, with a roar, he ran at Jimmy, fist raised.

Jimmy stood and broke the cue stick over the man's head.

He fell like an ox.

Griffin looked down at the man. He lay very still. There was a trickle of blood coming out of one ear. He didn't seem to be breathing. "Maybe we should get out of here."

Jimmy took out his wallet and laid several twenties down on the felt. He put his beer bottle atop them. "This should pay for the stick," he said. There weren't a lot of people in the bar, but every one of them was watching him.

Nobody said a word as they left the place.

Out on the road, they drove in silence for a while. Then Jimmy said, "You're not going to like this."

"What?"

"I left my driver's license back in the bar. I had to leave it with the man to get the pool table."

"Think there's time to go back and get it?"

A police car, lights flashing, passed them, heading in the direction of the roadhouse.

"I don't suppose there is."

So they drove out to the airport and found a Cessna pilot who for two thousand dollars was willing to fly them back to D.C., no questions asked. There they ran out to the Pentagon, and looped back a day, so Jimmy could call the DMV to report his license had been stolen. After which, he and Griffin went out to a bar in Georgetown, where Jimmy broke a few things. They both spent the night in the drunk tank.

"That wasn't part of the plan," Griffin told Salley. "But when the police came, this fellow here got behind me and lifted me by the belt and shoved me right into them. We all fell over in a pile." They were both laughing by then.

"I just thought that as long I was going to be in jail, I might as well have company." Jimmy wiped the tears from his eyes. "In any event, it did give us a darling of an alibi."

"The Old Man had us on the carpet for that one. He chewed us both out good."

"Well, he had to, now didn't he?"

"Yes, but here's the thing." He paused until the laughter had died down. "On the way out, I turned and winked at him. He didn't wink back." He let the silence sit for a moment. "You get older, you get more conservative. You know how that is. Well, the Old Man's forgotten what it felt like to be young and wild. But not us. Not you, and not me. Yet."

For a long moment, Jimmy said nothing. Then he nodded. "All right. One last run."

He got up slowly, and left without so much as a word or a glance to Salley. As if she weren't present.

When he was gone, Salley said, "Did he die?"

"Did who die?"

"The man in the bar. The drunk."

He could see by her expression that she hadn't thought the story was very funny. He shrugged. "It was a long time ago. We never checked."

A minute later, young Jimmy was back, wearing a different set of clothes. He dollied in a large wooden packing crate, and showed them how it opened up. "This is how you'll be traveling," he told Salley. "Nothing fancy. We went for simplicity here. Padded on the inside. This little shelf acts as a seat. Hand grips here and here. And this clip holds a flashlight, in case you want to bring a book."

There was a bold orange-and-black sticker on the side reading THIS END UP, and another reading DANGER: OMNIVORE.

"I don't understand," Salley said. "Why would I have to go in a crate?"

"I'm afraid you won't like the answer," Griffin said uncomfortably.

"Don't tell me what I will or won't like."

"You see," Jimmy said, "we anticipated that something of this sort might come up and so we made preparations. There's a rider on the Old Man's clearance that allows me to be brought along as muscle. You, however, were not anticipated. There's simply no way you could possibly accompany us as a member of the security team."

Griffin wanted to tell Jimmy to moderate his manner. Salley had been simmering for a while now. She was ready to cause a scene. Griffin had enough experience with women to know this. But, though he mellowed in later life, Jimmy in his younger days was every bit as hard to handle as Salley herself.

"So?" Salley said.

That sharkish grin again. A jaunty nod toward the box. He was a sadistic little shit, was Jimmy, at this age. "So you'll be traveling as a biological specimen."

12

Nesting Behavior

Lost Expedition Foothills: Mesozoic era. Cretaceous period. Senonian epoch. Maastrichtian age. 65 My B.C.E.

The anatotitans were nesting on Egg Island. A mating pair of ankylosaurs was grumpily fossicking about in the shrubs along the river. And Her Ladyship was having a difficult time controlling her rambunctious young. They were at an age when they kept wandering away from the encampment, and she had to keep shooing them back.

Juvenile tyrannosaurs, unlike their aloof elders, were fiercely curious beings. They examined everything they saw, and attacked anything that moved. The mortality rate among juveniles was extremely high, but those who survived into adulthood were cagy and experienced creatures.

Jamal had built an observation platform high in the trees above Smoke Hollow, and another on Barren Ridge. Between them, it was possible to get a good overview of everything that happened in the valley. The Barren Ridge platform was the better of the two, however, because it afforded an excellent view of the tyrannosaur camp.

It was Leyster's turn on the Barren Ridge watch that day. Branches of the tree shook and rattled as Katie swung her way up to him. She popped over the edge of the platform and handed him a fried fish wrapped in leaves.

"Morning, dear. I brought you lunch." She gave him a peck on the cheek. "How are the children?"

"See for yourself." He handed her the binoculars. "She's lost another one. Scarface."

There were sixteen tyrannosaur juveniles remaining out of the original twenty, and they were all ugly as gargoyles. They were only two meters tall, and still young enough that their molt wasn't complete yet. Splotchy patches of hairy gray feathers clung here and there on all of them, looking for all the world like fungus infections.

"Here comes the breadwinner," Katie said.

The Lord of the Valley clambered awkwardly over the log-and-brushwood barrier he and his mate had shoved into a ring around the encampment. A bloody edmontosaur haunch dangled from his mouth.

The juveniles came running up to him, squawking with excitement. Avidly, they jumped (jumping was one thing an adult, with all that weight, could not do) and snapped at the meat.

With a grunt, the Lord let it drop to the ground.

The juveniles swarmed over the haunch, tearing at it so savagely their snouts were spattered with blood. Slasher got in the way of Adolf, and got her tail bitten for doing so. She squealed like a pig, then scrambled back to the meat, roughly shoving Attila and Lizzy Borden out of her way.

"That is not an edifying sight," Katie said. "How can you watch that and eat at the same time?"

Leyster dug into the fish with relish. Now that their supply of freeze-dried was gone, they were largely reliant on what they could catch or trap, and as a result there were times when they did not eat well at all. It made him appreciate the times when they did. "Hunger is an excellent sauce."

Privately, though, the sight of those little horrors feeding always made him glad there was a ravine between him and them.

Without putting the binoculars down, Katie said, "You know what I've always wondered?"

"What?"

"Why don't dinosaurs have external ears? Ears are ever so handy. It seems like they'd be much easier to evolve than, say, beaks. Or wings. So why don't the kids down there have great big floppy elephant ears?"

"Good question. I don't know. Here's another. Where do the dinosaurs go when they're not here? One day they're everywhere. Then, a morning later, you wake up and they're nowhere to be seen. Four months after that, you find a tyrannosaur pacing off the valley, and next thing you know, they're back. We're going to have to follow the herds next rainy season. Physically, I mean."

They'd tried monitoring the migrations over the

satellite downlink during the previous winter. But the Ptolemy system was designed primarily for mapping. Its resolution was poor, and, worse, it couldn't see through clouds. Which were, unfortunately, quite common in the rainy season. They'd been able to track only a general trend inland, where the herds dispersed and effectively disappeared from the screen.

Leyster yearned with all his heart to follow them. In the rainy season only the smaller dinosaurs—the feathered dinosaurs—remained to chastise the frogs, mammals, fish, and lizards. The river plain grew lush and thick as a jungle, but to Leyster it felt empty and soulless without the larger dinos. "We'll never understand these guys until we understand the patterns of their migration. Finding out has got to be our first order of business."

"Our second, actually. Chuck says we need veggies, so you've been drafted to lead an expedition to gather marsh tubers."

"Me! Why me? I was going to spend today making twine and re-reading *Much Ado About Nothing.*" He gestured toward the basket full of fiber and his volume of collected Shakespeare, lying beside the field observations notebook.

Katie smiled sweetly. "You're the one who found the tubers. Nobody else knows where they are." She moved the books to her side, and the basket to her lap. "I'll be happy to take over for you here, however."

Leyster recruited Patrick and Tamara to accompany him to Skeeter Marsh. Despite his grousing, he was glad to be going. It wasn't the lazy, productive day he'd planned, but food gathering was easy work, and entailed a long and pleasant walk through countryside he loved. It was even possible they'd spot something new in dinosaurian behavior.

Since they'd used up their shotgun shells long ago, he and Patrick carried clubs (in Leyster's case the shovel; in Patrick's an otherwise-useless gun) to protect themselves against chance attacks from dromaeosaurs. Dromies were the only carnivores so little reliant on smell that they'd attack a human being under normal circumstances. The stench of cookfire smoke that permeated their hair and clothing and skin protected them from pretty much everything else. Except the crocodiles, and those tended to stay by the water.

Tamara, of course, carried her spear. She had spent months during the rainy season laboriously grinding the head from an iron flange that had originally been a piece of bracing for their supplies. Then she had set the leaf-shaped product into a seasoned hardwood haft with a resin glue, and wrapped it tight with hadrosaur tendon.

The result was a murderous-looking weapon they all called "Tamara's Folly."

She carried it everywhere and worked on her throwing skills for at least an hour every day. She said it made her feel safe.

Nevertheless, they walked with a caution grown natural through long use. If the past year had taught them nothing else, it was that nothing was to be taken for granted.

As they walked, they talked quietly. This was the one aspect of their stranding that Leyster genuinely appreciated. It was like a never-ending seminar. Being a teacher wasn't a matter of handing knowledge down from Parnassus to the groundlings below. You learned from your students, from their questions and speculations, and sometimes even their misunderstandings. And this crew was sharp. He'd learned a lot from them.

"Does it seem to anybody else," Tamara asked, "that there's an awful lot of biomass tied up in the megafauna here? I mean, not only are there a lot of *species* in the valley, but there are a lot more *individuals* than you'd expect."

"Yeah!" Patrick said. "How can the land support them all? They must be feeding at a startling level of efficiency. They're constantly chomping down the new growth, and yet they never overgraze. How do they do that?"

"Sometimes small groups leave," Leyster pointed out. "We've seen them do that."

"Yes, and always just enough to keep things balanced here. That's spooky," Tamara said. "How do dim-brained animals like dinosaurs keep those kinds of balances, when real smart animals like human beings can't?"

"I dunno," Leyster said.

"Don't get me wrong," Tamara said. "But it seems like you say that a lot."

"Well, if suffering is the essence of the human condition, then the essence of the scientific condition must be ignorance." Leyster shrugged. "Any ecosystem is a dance of needs, a complex balancing of hungers. When all we had to work with was fossils, what we needed was to find more and better fossils. Now all we have to do is make more and better observations. You guys don't appreciate how easy you have it." A mosquito bit him on the arm. He slapped at it and said, "Hey, we're almost there."

They dug for tubers until their packs were full and their arms were sore. Then they took a break before heading back. Lying with his head against a log, watching dragonflies noisily mating in the air while Tamara plaited white blossoms into her hair, Leyster decided he was as close to happy as he had ever been.

Tamara and Patrick were lazily, reflexively, arguing about the function of the tyrannosaurs' tiny little two-fingered arms. Patrick had footage of Her Ladyship fussing over her dried mud mound of a nest and delicately turning over the eggs with them, and felt that settled it. Tamara held that that was only an incidental function, and was convinced that their primary use was as signaling devices for sexual display: I'm ready to mate. Or else: I'm not in the mood.

Leyster was about to weigh in with his own opinion when the phone rang.

"I've got it," Tamara said. She unzipped a pocket on her knapsack, and removed the carefully-swaddled device. Painstakingly, she unwrapped it. Then, walking a little distance away for privacy, she hit the talk button.

Leyster stood. He needed to take a leak. "Back in a minute," he said.

When Leyster returned, Patrick and Tamara were grinning ear to ear. "Well," he said. "Good news?"

"Lai-tsz just made an announcement," Patrick said. "She was going to wait until tonight when everyone was there, but then somebody said something and she just blurted it out. She's pregnant."

"What?! Pregnant? How?"

Patrick snorted and raised a sardonic eyebrow. Tamara looked impatient. "How do you think?"

Leyster sat down on the log. "God, I can't believe this. Wasn't she supposed to be on some kind of birth control?" He knew for a fact that she was. He'd seen her medical records. All the women in the party were on long-term birth control, the kind that took medical intervention to undo. "Who's the fath—?" He stopped. "I'm sorry, that's a really dumb question."

"Yes, it is," Tamara said. "You're *all* the father. Everybody's responsible. We're all its parents."

"You don't sound very happy about the news," Patrick said carefully.

"Happy? You expect me to be happy? Has anybody given any thought to what kind of life we can provide for this kid?"

"We haven't had the—"

"With eleven parents, it's a pretty sure thing she'll be pampered and spoiled," Tamara said. "Big deal. Kids are resilient."

"How about when she hits adolescence?"

Nobody said anything.

"Imagine being a teenage girl in a world full of nothing but your parents. No girlfriends. Nobody to confide in. No boyfriends, no dating, no high school prom. This is going to be one screwed-up child. When her sex drive kicks in, she's going to want to take part in our little physical therapy sessions. What do we tell her then?"

"I really don't think that—" Patrick began.

"Either we say yes or we tell her she can't. I don't know which is going to twist her around more."

"And *I* don't know why you're being so unpleasant," Tamara said.

"Okay, she gets through adolescence. Somehow. Now she's an adult. She's young and full of beans in a camp full of elders who are starting to slow down. Everything she wants to do is just a little too wild, a little too fast, a little too much for everyone else. Majority rule, of course. She's outvoted every time.

"Meanwhile, we keep on getting older. More and more of the work of caring for the rest of us falls upon her. She resents it, but there's nothing she can do about it. Where else can she go? So she drudges away, surly and unhappy. Until finally we begin to die off.

"At first, it's going to be a relief for her. She'll feel guilty about that, of course. It'll warp her even more. But she's still human. She'll be happy to see us go. But then as, one by one, the human world gets smaller, she'll slowly begin to realize exactly how lonely she's going to get. Until that bright day dawns when she's the last woman on Earth. Think about that! The last woman on Earth. Perfectly, absolutely, and abjectly alone. With maybe twenty years more left to live.

"Tell me this: Just how sane do you think she'll be by then? Just how human?"

Patrick slowly sucked in the air between his teeth. "Well, but . . . what's the alternative?"

"I'm afraid Lai-tsz's going to have to—"

To Leyster's absolute astonishment, Tamara balled up her fist, and hit him in the stomach. Hard.

He doubled over.

She stood over him, her face white with anger, and said, "That's not an alternative! And if it were, it wouldn't be *your* choice to make. 'Wasn't she supposed to be on some kind of birth control?' Jesus Christ, didn't you give ten seconds thought before sticking your dick into her? There's no form of birth control that works every time—women always have to take that into account, so why can't *men?*"

She snatched up her knapsack and spear.

"Anyway," she said over her shoulder, "the odds are that we'll all be dead in five years. So it doesn't really matter in the first place!"

She strode angrily away.

"Whew!" Patrick smiled embarrassedly. "That was brutal. Even if—forgive me for saying this—some of it was deserved." He helped Leyster stand up. "You okay?"

Leyster just shook his head.

So they weren't as careful as they usually were on the trip home. Tamara led, walking fast and staring straight ahead of herself until she was a small figure far ahead of them. Leyster and Patrick followed as best they could.

They walked along the river until they came to Hell Creek, and then turned inland. Leyster was idly watching some faraway troodons cracking open mussels when Patrick said, "Uh oh."

"What?" Leyster turned and saw a juvenile tyrannosaur—it was Scarface, the one that had wandered away that morning—standing almost motionless in the distance. Only its head moved.

It was tracking Tamara.

"Tamara!" Patrick bellowed, and gestured widely toward the tyrannosaur.

Tamara spun, saw the predator, and then looked wildly about for a place to flee. The land by the river was flat and almost featureless. There were not many natural sanctuaries or hiding places here.

"Thorns! Thorns!" Patrick shouted. He waved both hands upward and then forward, pointing to a distant thicket of thorn trees. If Tamara could reach them, there was a chance she could burrow deep into the center of the tangle, where the young tyrannosaur with its relatively thin hide would not care to follow.

All in one motion, Tamara shed her knapsack and began to run.

Scarface leapt forward, after her.

Tamara had always been a jock. She ran like a sprinter, knees high, her spear flashing up and down with her arms.

She was running, but not fast enough. The juvenile was coming straight toward her. And it was a lot faster than she could ever hope to be.

She couldn't possibly reach the thorn trees in time.

She wasn't going to make it.

As if from a great distance, Leyster saw himself race forward to place himself between her and Scarface. It was an instinctive action, one totally beyond his control. He was shocked to realize what he was doing.

When a tyrannosaur charged, he knew, it locked its attention entirely upon its desired prey. The anatotitans might scatter in a dozen directions, but it couldn't be distracted because it only wanted that hadrosaur which it had fixed upon. Not *that* one but *this* one. Nothing else would do.

Still, if he were right in front of Scarface when it reached him, even something as single-minded as a tyrannosaur would gobble him down.

That was Leyster's theory, anyway.

With a kind of dreamlike wonder, he saw Scarface bear down upon him. The tyrannosaur's mouth was open, the devil's own cutlery drawer of sharp, serrated teeth. He came to a halt directly before the brute. He braced his feet.

Leyster's body trembled with the need to flee. Run! it demanded.

But he stayed there.

The tyrannosaur splashed across the creek in two bounds. It was almost upon him. It grew and swelled in his sight, until there was nothing in the world at all but that enormous, demonic head. He could count all five silvery parallel slashes across its snout.

Then, incredibly, as it reached him, it lifted that great head upward and to the side, and then back again, so that he was effortlessly knocked out of the creature's way.

It was like being shoved aside by a Percheron. With a *slam* of pain Leyster stumbled back against Patrick, who was there, somehow, grabbing at his shoulders, trying to pull him away from the charging tyrannosaur.

He fell.

He'd been rejected. Scarface wanted Tamara and no other.

A strange sensation of mingled disappointment and relief flooded Leyster then. It wasn't his fault now, if Tamara died. He'd done all that was humanly possible.

But even as he fell, Leyster realized that he was still carrying the shovel. In his confusion, he'd forgotten to drop the thing. So, desperately, he swung it around with all his strength at the juvenile's legs.

Tyrannosaurs were built for speed. Their leg bones were hollow, like a bird's. If he could break a femur . . .

The shovel connected, but not solidly. It hit without breaking anything. But, still, it got tangled up in those powerful legs. With enormous force, it was wrenched out of his hands. Leyster was sent tumbling on the ground.

Somebody was screaming. Dazed, Leyster raised himself up on his arms to see Patrick, hysterically slamming the juvenile, over and over, with the butt of the shotgun. He didn't seem to be having much effect. Scarface was clumsily trying to struggle to its feet. It seemed not so much angry as bewildered by what was happening to it.

Then, out of nowhere, Tamara was standing in front of the monster. She looked like a warrior goddess, all rage and purpose. Her spear was raised up high above Scarface, gripped tightly in both hands. Her knuckles were white.

With all her strength, she drove the spear down through the center of the tyrannosaur's face.

It spasmed, and died.

Suddenly everything was very still.

Painfully, Leyster stood. "I think my rib is cracked."

"I think your head is cracked," Tamara said. "Just what were you trying to prove there? Attacking a tyrannosaur with a shovel! You idiot."

"I . . ." Everything felt unreal. "How did you get here? You were running . . ." He waved a hand toward the copse of thorn trees. ". . . that way."

"I turned around. I looked over my shoulder and saw what a stupid thing you were doing, and came back to bail you out."

Patrick started to laugh. "Oh, man," he said. "Did you see the look on that thing's face?"

"When you were beating on it with that—!"

"It was baffled! I thought I was the only one who—"

Then they were all hugging one another and thumping each other on the back, and crying and howling with laughter at the same time. There was a lifetime's worth of emotion inside them, trying to get out all at once.

"Right through the old antorbital fenestra!" Tamara crowed. "Right there in the middle of the skull where there are no bone plates at all. Nothing but soft tissue. The spear punched right into its brain. Hah! Leyster, you were right—practical anatomy *does* pay off." She got out her hunting knife, and knelt down by the tyrannosaur's corpse.

"What are you doing?" Leyster asked.

"Getting a tooth. I killed this sucker, I want a trophy, damn it!"

Patrick had his camera out. "Stand by the body," he told her. "Put your foot up on its head. Yeah, like that. Now show us a little cleavage. Ouch! Hey! No!" He laughed and dodged as she jabbed at him with the butt of her spear. "I'm telling ya, a little skin'll do wonders for your career."

He posed her again, and ran off several snaps. "Okay, one of those ought to be a keeper. Now all three of us together. Leyster, I want you to hold your shovel with the blade up."

He began to set up his tripod.

"We'd best take those pictures and get that tooth out fast," Leyster said. "I don't want to be anywhere near here when Mama comes looking for her little Baby Bunting."

Leyster worried about the Lord and Lady all the long and uneventful trek home. Still, when they came trudging up Smoke Hollow, and he saw the firelight from the long house and the last glint of the setting sun on the satellite dish, his spirits lifted. He felt good to be returning to it. He wanted to hear Tamara bragging about her exploits. He wanted to see Lai-tsz again. He wanted to see if she was showing yet. He wanted to share in the happiness he knew everyone would be feeling.

This is my home, he thought. These are my people. They are my tribe.

13

Ghost Lineage

Terminal City: Telezoic era. Eognotic period. Afrasia epoch. Orogenian age. 50 My C.E.

Poking about in the bluffs of a stream feeding into the Aegean River, Salley found something interesting. In an eroded cliff face, she had noticed a little syncline of a dark material that looked to be asphaltite. So, of course, she scrambled up to check it out. "Dead oil" often marked a bone-bed. She broke off a bit and sniffed it for kerogens. A green streak of corrosion led her to something small embedded in the rock and just recently exposed to the elements. She opened her knife and began to dig it out, so she could identify it.

It was flat and shaped roughly like a disk. She touched it to her tongue. Copper. A penny, perhaps. Maybe a washer of some kind.

For an instant she felt dizzy with how far she was from home.

The stratum, she realized, was metamorphic

macadam, a roadbed that had been squeezed and twisted by the millions-years-long collision of Africa into Europe that had thrown up the mighty Mediterranean Mountains dominating the horizon. Once it would have been thronged with tourists in rental cars and busloads of school children, motor scooters and moving vans, flatbed trucks with tiers of bright new automobiles, sports cars driving far too fast, junkers held together with bailing wire spouting black exhaust and carrying families of refugees from regional brushfire wars into a strange new world.

Now it took a sharp eye and careful analysis to determine that human beings had ever existed at all.

Carefully, she wrapped the bit of metal in her handkerchief. She could examine it more closely later. Then she flipped open her notepad to record the find, only to discover to her intense annoyance that her pen was out of ink.

"Dr. Salley!"

She turned to see who was calling.

It was the Irishman. He stood by the stream, waving for her to come down.

She shook her head and pointed beyond him, to where the stream poured into the Aegean. Several platybelodons were splashing and wallowing in the bright green river. They were wonderful beasts, basal proboscideans with great shovel-jaw tusks, and they clearly loved it here. They scooped up and ate the floating waterbushes with enormous gusto. There were little glints of gold about their necks. "Come on up! Enjoy the view!"

With a wry twist of his mouth, he started upslope.

Involuntarily, Salley touched her torc. She did not trust Jimmy Boyle. He was all calm and calculation. There was always a hint of coldness to his smile.

"Here you are." Jimmy plopped down alongside her, and waited to hear what she had to say. Jimmy was patient like that. Jimmy always had all the time in the world.

"Shouldn't you be with Griffin?"

"I could ask the same of you." He waited. Then, when she did not respond, he said, "He's concerned about you. We all are."

"I'm doing fine."

"Then why aren't you in Terminal City, helping with negotiations?"

"Because I'm of more use out here."

"Doing what?"

She shrugged. Down on the river road, a lone Unchanging was guiding a small herd of indricotheres toward their new habitat. *Indricotherium* was a bland and placid beast, as well as being the largest land mammal ever to exist. It stood fourteen feet high at the shoulder and looked something like a cross between a giraffe, an elephant, and a horse. Salley's heart soared at the sight of it.

She raised her glasses and stared briefly at the Unchanging, tall and serene, leading the indricotheres.

The Unchanging were beautiful too, in their way. They were thinner than El Greco's angels, and indistinguishable in their sexlessness. But Salley couldn't warm to them, the way she could to the beasts of the valley. They were too perfect. They lacked the stench and unpredictability of biological life.

The sun flashed off a gold circlet around one indricothere's neck, and she put the glasses down.

Again, she touched a hand to her torc.

Jimmy glanced at her shrewdly. "He's not using the controller, if that's what's bothering you," he said. "That's just not his style."

"Don't talk," she said, annoyed. "Just listen."

The first thing that impressed Salley about the Telezoic was how quiet it was. A stunned silence permeated the world, even when the birds were singing and the insects calling to one another across the distances. Something catastrophic had happened to the world within the last few million years. So far as she could tell, all the larger animals were gone. Mammals seemed to be entirely extinct. A thousand noises she was accustomed to were no more.

Except along the Aegean River, of course. Here, the Unchanging had imported great numbers of uintatheres, dinohyuses, giant sloths . . . a parade of whimsical creatures making up a sort of "greatest hits" selection of the Age of Mammals. With a few unexplained exceptions (such as her beloved platybelodons, which ranged freely up and down the river), the animals each had their own territory, sorted roughly in order of appearance, so that a trip downriver was like a journey through time. Salley had backpacked two days down the river road, past the glyptodons and megatheres of the Pleistocene, the gracile kyptocerases of the

Pliocene, the shansitheres of the Miocene, all the way into the Oligocene with its brontopses and indricotheres, before running low on food and turning back.

"I'm not hearing anything," Jimmy said.

"You hear everything. You just don't know what it means."

She wasn't sure how far back in time the stock went. Did it end after dwindling into the insignificant mammals—not a one of them larger than a badger—that crossed over the K-T boundary into the early Paleocene, where their betters could not, and so inherited the Earth? Or was there then a sudden irruption of dinosaurs? She knew which *she* would choose. But even on short acquaintance, she was certain that the Unchanging did not reason the way she did.

"It makes you think," Jimmy said. "All those millions of years those brutes were extinct, and now they're alive again."

"Hell of a ghost lineage," Salley agreed.

Jimmy cocked his head. "What's that when it's at home?"

"Sometimes you'll have a line that disappears from the fossil record for millions of years, and then pops up again in an entirely new era. During the interval, it looks to be extinct. But then an animal that's clearly its descendant pops up again in a distant age. They're obviously related, so we infer a succession of generations between them. That's a ghost lineage."

"Doctor," Jimmy said, "I'll be frank. I don't think there's a chance in hell you'd be much use to us. But Griffin thinks very highly of you, and wants you with him in Terminal City. It puts him off his stride that you're not."

"If it's that important to him, why didn't he mention it last night? We slept in the same bed."

Jimmy looked away. "He's not exactly rational when it comes to you."

"So. This little discussion wasn't his idea, was it?"

"A man thinks with his dick," Jimmy said, embarrassed. "That's why his friends have to look out for him."

Salley stood. "If Griffin wants me, he can always reel me in." She touched the torc again.

Jimmy stood as well, slapping at his trousers. "He doesn't play that kind of game, Dr. Salley. Honestly, he doesn't."

"Oh, wait. Before you go," she said. "Lend me your pen. Mine is out of ink."

Jimmy hesitated. "It belonged to my father."

"Don't worry. I'll give it back to you."

With obvious reluctance, he unclipped it from his pocket and handed it over. It was a Mont Blanc. "I'd be sorry to see anything happen to it," he said.

"I'll take good care of it. I promise."

When Jimmy was gone, Salley climbed back down to the stream. She'd intended to head upslope, toward the foothills of the Mediterraneans, but something about the day, the heat, the slant of the afternoon light, sapped her will. She found a fruit-maple tree that looked like it needed her to sit underneath it, and so she did.

Leaning back against the tree but not in its shade, half-drowsing in the dusty sunlight, Salley closed her eyes. She resurrected a fantasy of the sort she had long ago learned not to be ashamed of but to accept as a natural part of the complex workings of the human mind.

In her fantasy, she was working a cliff face in the badlands of Patagonia, delicately picking out the intact skull of a giganotosaur a good third again larger than had ever been found before. Which would catapult *Giganotosaurus* past its rivals and establish it, once and for all, as the largest land predator the world had ever known. Simultaneously, she was speaking via satellite uplink to the Society of Vertebrate Paleontology, for whose annual meeting in Denver she had been unwilling to abandon this astonishing find. And, of course, because the fossil was a complete and utter refutation of all his theories, she had Leyster kneeling before her—bound, blindfolded, and naked.

The SVP had just awarded her the Romer-Simpson medal, and she was making her acceptance speech.

In her fantasy, she was wearing a wide denim skirt instead of her usual jeans. With one hand, she pulled the skirt up above her knees. Then she seized Leyster by the hair and forced his head between her legs. She wasn't wearing any panties.

"Lick me," she whispered harshly in a moment when her speech was interrupted by spontaneous applause. Then, cunningly, "If you do a good enough job, I might let you go."

Which was a lie, but she wanted him to do his damnedest to please her.

Leyster was shockingly erect. She could tell by the earnest and enthusiastic way he ran his tongue up and down her cleft. By the small noises he made as he nuzzled and kissed her until she was moist and wide. By the barely-controlled ardor with which he licked and played with her clit.

But as he labored (and she spoke, to thunderous approval), the quality of his lovemaking changed profoundly. It became gentler, more lingering . . . romantic, even. This was—in her fantasy, she could tell—no longer an act of lust but one of love. In the heat of the act he had, all against his will, fallen in love with her. Inwardly he raged against it. But he was helpless before his desire, unable to resist the flood of his own consuming passion.

It was at that moment that she reached orgasm.

At the same time that she came in her fantasy, Salley grabbed the soft inner parts of her thighs—it was a point of pride with her never to touch her private parts at such moments—and squeezed as hard as she could, digging in with her nails until pain became pleasure and pleasure became release.

Afterwards, she leaned back, thinking about Griffin. She was aware of the irony of including Richard Leyster in her fantasies. But she didn't feel that this was in any way being unfaithful to Griffin. Just because you loved somebody didn't mean you had to fantasize about him.

She did love him. Salley inevitably fell for every man she had sex with. It was, she supposed, a genetic predisposition hardwired into her personality. But, still, the thought that this time was for real and forever was inherently odd.

Why him?

Griffin was such a *strange* man to fall for! She knew the smell of his cologne, and that he invariably wore Argyle socks (she had never before been involved with a man who even knew what Argyle socks were) and a hundred other things about him as well. She knew that the awful watch he wore was a Rolex Milgauss, self-winding, anti-magnetic, and originally designed to sell to nuclear power plant engineers. But she didn't really know him at all. His inner essence was still a mystery.

When Gertrude had popped into her life like a demented fairy godmother, she'd said, "Trust me. This is the one. He's everything you want. A week from now, you'll wonder how you ever lived without him."

But a week had gone by, and more than a week, and it was like every other relationship she'd ever been in. She was as confused as ever.

True love sure didn't feel anything like she'd thought it would.

Not half an hour later, Molly Gerhard strolled casually out of the forest. Salley trusted Molly-the-Spook even less than she did Jimmy. Molly came in under your radar. She was such a pleasant woman, so patient and understanding. So easy to talk to. She was the kind of person you wanted for a friend, someone to confide in and share all your innermost thoughts with.

"So," Molly Gerhard said. "How's it going?"

She'd put on a few pounds from her early days, and that only made her seem that much more comfortable and trustworthy. "I ran into Jimmy just now. Wow, is he looking sour. You really put a bee in his ear."

"If we're going to talk, let's not pretend you just happened to wander by, okay?"

Molly Gerhard grinned. "Can't put anything over on you, can I? Jimmy thought maybe you'd be a little more comfortable talking things over with me."

"Just us gals, huh?"

"Jimmy can be a real jerk," Molly Gerhard said. "Griffin too. I know I'm not supposed to talk about my boss like that."

"Not unless you want to establish rapport with his girlfriend, no."

"But we really do need to talk. Come back to the village. I'll make you a pot of tea."

"I was going to go upstream and . . ." Salley began. But suddenly she didn't want any such thing. "Oh, all right."

So far as Salley knew, nobody had bothered to give the village a name. It was a scattering of cottages with thatched roofs, indoor plumbing, and several appliances she couldn't figure out. She'd seen motels that were bigger. "We have conferences here sometimes," Griffin had explained.

"How come I've never heard of this?" she'd asked.

"They're for government types—planners, bureaucrats, politicians. Not paleontologists."

"Why is that?"

"To be perfectly frank, you're not important enough."

Upriver from the village loomed Terminal City, looking for all the world like a cliff of solid gold. When first she'd seen it from a distance, she'd thought it was two sea stacks miraculously stranded far inland, separated by a razor-straight line of sky and river. The color, she'd assumed, was reflection from the setting sun. Then that it was a structure built in imitation of eroded geological forms, rather like one of Ursula von Rydingsvard's sculptures, only of yellow bricks.

But no. It really was made of gold.

"You know what?" Molly Gerhard said, breaking into her thoughts. "This would be the perfect place for a honeymoon."

Salley snorted.

"Wrong thing to say, huh?" Molly Gerhard said quietly.

"There's my cottage. Let's go in. I'll make the tea."

Salley had just put the kettle on when she heard a familiar noise outside. She hurried to the ice box. "Here. Watch this," she said, and went to the back door with a cabbage in each hand.

Something big was moving out in the bushes. She underhanded the cabbages lightly in that direction. Molly Gerhard came up behind her and waited.

They didn't have to wait long before a glyptodon came lumbering out of the underbrush and onto the lawn.

Glyptodons were charming creatures, as armored as a turtle and as large as a Volkswagen. Their backs were covered with a pebbled shell that looked like a bowl turned upside down. They had matching armored yarmulkas atop their heads.

"Now that," Molly Gerhard said, "is one ugly critter."

"Are you nuts? It's gorgeous."

The glyptodon slowly approached the cabbages and examined them critically. Then it crunched first one and then the other in its beaked mouth, tossing its head as it ate. After which, it waddled away again. They were grouchy creatures, glyptodons were. They reminded her a lot of ankylosaurs.

And a little of Griffin.

The water was ready then, so she poured two cups and carried them to the kitchen table. "So," she said. "How are the talks?"

Molly Gerhard looked discouraged. "They *talk*. But they won't negotiate."

"I'm not surprised."

"How so?" Molly Gerhard leaned forward. "What have you figured out?"

"Nothing you wouldn't have learned if you'd been paying attention."

"What? What? Tell me."

Salley sipped her tea, and said nothing.

Molly Gerhard changed tactics. "Listen to me. We're running out of time. Our operational schedules are divided into cells, with an administrative intercept point for each one. We're in a Priority D era, so the op-cell we have to work with is eight days long. Are you with me so far?"

"I loathe bureaucratic jargon. Give it to me in English."

"We've been here six days. Two more, and the

Old Man finds us and shuts us down. Come with me to Terminal City. Help us find an answer."

"There's nothing to be learned there."

"And there is out here?"

"Yes," Salley said. "Have you taken a close look at the waterbushes?"

"Those things that clog the river? No."

"I have. They're an entirely new plant form. I think they're derived from kelp, believe it or not. Forget about the glyptodons. Waterbushes are much more important."

"I'm not following you."

"Let me put it this way. The biggest difference between the Mesozoic and the Cenozoic is not the absence of dinosaurs, but the presence of grass. Grass changed everything. It has amazing powers of recovery, which made large-scale grazing possible for the first time. Which in turn made animals like bisons and water buffalos possible. And therefore made predators like lions and tigers possible. Theoretically, birds could have evolved to fill the niches their bigger cousins vacated. How come mammals managed to make an end run around birds? Grass! It changed the rules. It made it impossible for the dinosaurs to come back."

"Oh-kaay. I think I'm following this. So what's the application to our present situation?"

"The waterbushes are something *new.* They change the rules. I want to see what they've made of the local ecosystem."

"It's a pretty dull ecosystem, I gather," Molly Gerhard said. "Lots of drab little birds. A few lizards, and I think I saw some crawdads. I don't see why you'd care, when you've got all these terrific mammals to look at. You've never seen them before, right? I'd think you'd be excited."

"I was, at first. But there's no context. It's like going to the fucking zoo. You see an elephant, some kangaroos, and a pond full of penguins and try to figure out what kind of ecosystem produced them. You know nothing about their behavior. You know nothing about what they're like in the wild. I want to see the Telezoic. I want to muck about in a functioning wilderness."

She did not tell Molly, but it was immediately obvious to her that this could not possibly be the Unchanging's home time. The environment was simply not damaged enough to be home to a technologically advanced civilization. Even if they'd reached a stage where they could restore the damaged biota, resurrect extinct plants and animals, recreate the delicate webs of interdependence, there was no way they could undo the physical damage—the mountains leveled, the minerals redistributed, pit mines dug deep into the earth.

There was no way they *would*.

"Well," Molly Gerhard said, "if you want to go look, why don't you?"

Salley lifted her chin, to make her torc more prominent.

With a stricken expression, Molly reached out to touch Salley's arm. "Oh, Salley. You don't really think . . ."

"Yes. I do."

* * *

The crate had been humiliating enough.

But when she'd emerged from it into Terminal City, Salley wasn't expecting to be put on a leash. The Unchanging, however, were astonishingly literal-minded. They had fit the torc around Salley's neck, and given Griffin the controller. He'd slipped it into his pocket. "I promise you," he'd said, as soon as the Unchanging were out of earshot, "I will never use it."

She stuck out her hand. "Fork it over, and I'll make damned sure you won't."

Griffin looked pained. "I can't do that. They'd know."

"You like this!" Salley spat. "You're *enjoying* it."

"Of course I'm not."

Arguing, they'd stepped through a transport gate and into the village.

They'd patched things up that night, and slept together, and even made love. But it still rankled. So, after a day's unhappy thought, she'd gone walkabout.

The mammals were delightful. She had to admit that. What she had originally thought a game preserve, but eventually concluded must be a quarantine area or holding pens for transshipment, was stocked with marvels. The kyptocerases alone—primitive, deerlike ungulates with two horns over their eyes and another pair on their noses—were well worth price of admission. She broke out laughing every time she saw one. They might have been invented by Dr. Seuss.

But whenever she'd started to wander away from the river, something had drawn her back.

She'd get bored, or tired, or distracted. A pattern began to emerge. So she started observing the animals themselves, to see how their torcs kept them in their designated areas.

And found that whenever they reached the limits of their range, they'd grow bored, or tired, or distracted, and turn back. Once or twice, she noticed them grow randy and amble off in search of a mate. Never outward. Always inward.

"Stop beating up on yourself, Salley," Molly Gerhard said. "Word of honor, Griffin isn't using the controller. Look. I don't even particularly like the man. But I swear to you, he wouldn't do that."

Salley was a romantic. It almost went without saying. Any person who squandered all her life and intellect on an underpaid career laboriously grinding fossils out of rocks just because these stones had once been the bones of an animal that millions of years ago had kicked Mesozoic butt was of necessity a romantic. It went with the territory. It was why so many paleontologists wore funny hats.

She wanted to believe Molly Gerhard.

But she wasn't about to turn off her brain to do so.

So, after she'd gotten rid of the woman, Salley went back to her creek and as far up it as she could before feeling so tired and weary that she simply couldn't go one step further. It was a bright little glen with ferns around the edges, and a clear mossy space under the trees she'd almost reached twice before, but never set foot upon.

She took Jimmy's Mont Blanc out of her pocket.

Then she threw it gently ahead of her, onto a

soft patch of moss. It glinted, bright and golden, in the sunlight.

It would be the easiest thing in the world to walk ahead and pick it up. Yet she did not. Go get it, she thought. Jimmy will be pissed if you lose it. It's important to him. Walk over and pick it up.

But she didn't. She simply didn't want to. No matter how important the pen was, she wasn't about to go after it.

Which was how she knew for sure that Griffin really *was* controlling her.

On her way back to her cottage, she picked up an axe from the tool shed by the woodpile. Then she went into the bedroom she and Griffin had shared and turned the bed into a pile of kindling. After which she dragged the mattress outside, piled the broken bedframe atop it, and doused it with cooking oil.

Then she set it afire.

She wasn't sure who she was angrier at—Griffin or herself. Griffin had lied to and betrayed her. Gertrude, on the other hand, had as good as made a whore of her. No man who was so afraid of what she might do that he'd use a device to control her could possibly be the great love of her life. She couldn't love such a man.

She couldn't even respect him.

Why wasn't the bastard here, so she could take this axe to *him?* It was typical of Griffin that when the time came to take the heat, he was nowhere to be found.

Gertrude too, for that matter.

Seething, she went into the bedroom to pack her few possessions into the travel case. Then she had to get this monstrosity off her neck. There had to be a metal saw or some bolt cutters around here somewhere. She'd . . .

She stopped.

There was an envelope on the dresser. Funny she hadn't seen it before. She picked it up. Something was written on it, in her own hand.

It was addressed to her.

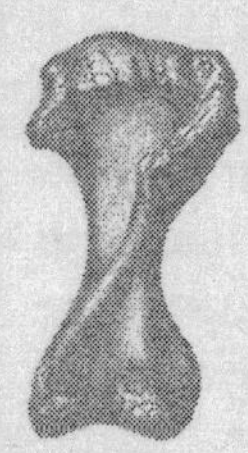

14

Intraspecific Communication

Lost Expedition Foothills: Mesozoic era. Cretaceous period. Senonian epoch. Maastrichtian age. 65 My B.C.E.

With dreamlike slowness, the great beasts browsed in the moonlight.

Oneirosaurus was the last and largest of the supersauropods. It was a late, final flowering of the Titanosaurinae, rare as rare, and a creature that all logic said properly belonged not in the late Cretaceous, but in the Jurassic, when giant sauropods were common. To see one was to refuse to believe it existed. To see five scattered across the river valley, as now, eating the jungle down to stubble, was a privilege Leyster knew he would cherish for the rest of his life.

Alone of all the creatures in the valley, *Oneirosaurus* never slept. It couldn't afford to. It had to keep eating, moving its little head steadily, monotonously, from side to side until all the vegetation within reach was gone, and then taking a ponderous step or two forward to repeat the process. All day and all night it did this, just to keep alive.

It was not much of a life, but one they seemed dimly to enjoy. And it was one that could last for centuries. Leyster had heard rumors that individuals had been identified as being over five hundred years old.

Wonderful as those giant gray shadow-beasts were to look at, though, he knew that Lai-tsz hadn't brought him out here for esthetic reasons. She was a pragmatist. Her mind just didn't work that way.

"So what is it that you wanted me to see?" he asked.

"Not to see. To hear. To feel."

"Then what—?"

"Shhh. Wait."

She wrapped her arms protectively around her swollen belly, and stared out over the land. Prospect Bluff had a view second only to Barren Ridge—and no carnivores nested here. A touch of wind blew her hair forward, and she raised her chin slightly, as if to meet it.

Leyster found himself wishing he had the skill to paint in oils, so he could capture her as she was then, with the land a symphony of grays behind her, and the River Styx a gleam of silver meandering through it. There was something heroic about a pregnant woman. She carried all the hopes and fears of a new life within her body. Nobody could deny that she was engaged in serious business.

After a while, Lai-tsz made a face and said, "Little Turok is active tonight."

"Have you decided on a name yet?"

"For the English name, I'm leaning toward Emily if it's a girl, and Nathaniel if it's a boy. For the Chinese—there! Listen!"

At first, Leyster heard nothing. He turned to Lai-tsz to say so, but something about her stance, the way she held her head, told him that *she*, at least could hear something. Whatever it was, though, had to be subtle and extremely easy to miss.

He willed himself perfectly still. He quieted all conscious thought.

He waited.

Slowly he became aware of a low, pervasive rumbling, like the inaudible undertones produced by the deepest pipes of a church organ. He felt more than heard it, in his chest and the pit of his stomach, a sound so deep into the bass that he had to wonder if he were fantasizing it.

"I . . . hear it, I think. Something. But what is it?"

Lai-tsz shivered in a kind of ecstasy. "Infrasound."

"What?"

"I didn't want to say anything before I got independent confirmation that there really *is* something there. They're speaking to each other infrasonically—with sound waves of such low frequency that you and I can't actually hear them."

"My God," Leyster said. "You mean they're communicating with each other?"

"With each other, with oneirosaurs outside the valley—who knows? Infrasound can travel for miles. They could be speaking with kin beyond the horizon. Elephants use infrasound to communicate with each other over huge distances."

"How did you discover this?"

"It's Turok's discovery, actually. The little floater grows very still whenever the oneirosaurs speak. Child-to-be would be bouncing around actively, and then suddenly stop, listening. After a while, I made the connection. Whenever Turok got still like that, there'd be an oneirosaur in sight. Either that, or else a tyrannosaur."

"Tyrannosaurs, too?"

"Yes, I really do think so."

Leyster laughed from sheer joy. "This is wonderful! You've made an incredible discovery." He seized her hand and kissed it fervently. If it hadn't been for young Turok, he would have picked her up and whirled her around in the air. "This is . . . it's *important!*"

"Yes. I know," Lai-tsz said complacently. Leyster understood that she was every bit as pleased as he was. She just didn't like to show it.

For a time, they stared after the oneirosaurs determinedly eating their way up the valley, sharing the moment without speaking. The moon shone down hazily through a sky strewn with wisps of cloud. There would be rain in the morning, and regrowth would begin. When the lesser herbivores returned, there would be new food in plenty for them.

"It's really quite marvelous," Leyster said at last, "how everything fits together. The oneirosaurs level and fertilize the valley just at the right time to maximize growth. And then they move on, rather than staying and monopolizing the limited resources."

"The herds should be returning soon."

"Yes."

"It's funny, though, how the first animals to return from the migrations were the tyrannosaurs. Followed so closely by the oneirosaurs. It's almost as if the one were leading the other."

Leyster was silent for a moment. Then he said, "You don't really believe that, though."

"I don't know. They both employ infrasound. It's quite possible there's interspecific as well as intraspecific communication going on. It's something we really ought to look into."

"How could we check? Could you build a device of some kind?"

"Oh, yeah, easily. We've got a couple of recorders, and all I'd have to do is speed up the playback to bring the ultrasonics up into audibility."

"You'd have to take time away from trying to repair the time beacon, though."

She threw him an odd look. "Oh, Richard," she said, as if it were a negligible thing. "I thought you knew. I gave up on that a long time ago."

To his amazement, he discovered that she was right. He knew she'd given up on their ever returning to their own time. He'd known it for months.

Finally, though, it was time to go home. They picked their way gingerly downslope and through the woods, guided by the fitful glimmer of one of their two remaining flashlights. Since Chuck had lost the third, two weeks ago, the flashlights had been put on the proscribed list of equipment that was never to leave the camp. But Lai-tsz's condition superceded all rules. Leyster held the flashlight for her, walking half a step ahead and to the side, to make sure the way was safe.

"I miss Daljit and Jamal," Lai-tsz said.

"They call every day."

"It's not the same."

For the end of the rainy season, Daljit and Jamal had determined to go inland to meet the migrating herds partway home, make a count of their numbers, and possibly gain some insight into their behavior. They would have liked to follow the migrating herds out at the beginning of the season and back again in the spring, but everybody agreed there simply weren't the resources yet to make that plan practical. So they'd compromised.

The Styx was tributary to the Eden River, which flowed through the Faraways (hardly mountains, but more than hills) at Water Gap. There, on an elevated spot above the migration trails Jamal and Daljit had set up their camp.

Two weeks they'd been waiting, while the herds didn't come. There had been a flurry of excitement as the oneirosaurs passed through—fifty of them; they'd broken into smaller groups since—preceded by swift waves of tyrannosaurs. But since then, nothing.

The trees opened up onto Smoke Hollow. "Odd," Leyster said. There was a light on in the long house. "People are still up?" They'd slipped away at sundown, explaining only that they'd be back late.

"Daljit and Jamal, remember? The evening

satellite window opens late tonight. If they came up with something interesting this afternoon, this would be their first chance to share it."

"You know, that satellite would be a lot more useful if it weren't out of range so often. Why isn't it in a geosynchrous orbit?"

"Well, two reasons, offhand. First, because it would take a lot more fuel to raise it to such a high orbit. Second, because a geosynchrous orbit is a lousy position for a mapping satellite."

"There's another thing. Why is a geosynchrous orbit so high? It would be a lot more convenient if it were lower."

"Because it—oh, you're teasing me!"

"It took you this long to figure that out?"

Mock-bickering, they entered the long house. Everyone squatted in a circle around Chuck, who was speaking on the phone.

Chuck looked up. His expression was uncharacteristically tense. "It's Daljit," he said. "Jamal's been hurt."

Luckily, Jamal's injury was nothing worse than a broken leg. Unluckily, it left Daljit and him in no condition to return home without help. This at a time when their food supplies were running low and the migrating dinosaurs had flushed most of the small game from their immediate neighborhood.

After much discussion, it was decided that the largest rescue party they could manage was three people. After more discussion, it was agreed that those three should be Leyster, for his orienteering skill, Tamara, because she was the best hunter, and Chuck, because the other two wanted him.

"Why me?" Chuck asked cautiously. He'd been feeling a little insecure of late. Losing the flashlight had hit his self-esteem hard.

"Because you'll keep our spirits up," Tamara said. Leyster nodded gravely.

A small flush of pleasure spread over Chuck's face.

In the morning, they packed their knapsacks, evenly dividing among them one poptent and three sleeping blankets, a coil of rope, knives, an axe, crocodile jerky and hadrosaur pemmican for food, a medicine kit, homebrew sun block and insect repellant, a Leica 8X20, a cell phone with solar recharger, map and compass, a friction lighter for starting fires, hooks and fishing line, a coil of snare wire, the butt end of a roll of duct tape in case anybody's shoes started falling apart, sunglasses, rain gear and a change of clothing apiece, toothbrushes, a towel, two pens and a notebook, a pot for boiling water, and three water bottles. They went over the list three times to make sure they hadn't left anything out, and then unfolded the map to plan their route.

"Originally, Daljit and Jamal traveled down to the mouth of the Styx, and then up the Eden River Valley," Gillian said. "With the herds coming down the valley right now, that's not advisable. You're going to have cut cross-country." She drew a straight line from Smoke Hollow to Water Gap with her finger. "That's about twenty-five miles."

"Piece of cake," Chuck said.

"We ought to be able to do that," Tamara said judiciously.

Leyster agreed. "How hard can it be?"

"It's all up-and-down terrain, low hills, a few ridges. There ought to be streams, but since it's mostly forested, the surveillance map doesn't show them. The phone has a built-in positional system, so anytime the satellite's above the horizon, you can locate yourself on the map."

"Nobody here's had a lot of experience in forested environments," Nils said. "We've spent so much time in the river valley, we've gotten used to its ways. But the gods of the hills are not the gods of the valley. Keep that in mind, okay, guys?"

"No fear," Leyster said. "Let's go."

Leyster took a compass reading from the top of Barren Ridge, and they started west-southwest. Each carried a spear in one hand and another tied to the back of their packs, all of them (except for Tamara's Folly) with points of sharpened tyrannosaur ivory. In addition, Leyster carried the axe in a holster on his left hip. He was careful to keep the compass away from it.

The forest closed around them, and the shouted farewells of their friends faded away.

They walked.

For the first few hours they didn't talk much, concentrating instead on making a good start. But the longer the silence lasted, the more time Leyster had to think. And the more he thought, the more he came up with speculations he wanted to know if the others shared.

Finally he said, "If tyrannosaurs and anatotitans *do* communicate with each other—and I'm not saying they do—what would they have to say to each other?"

" 'Surrender, Dorothy,' " Chuck said in a deep, rex-ish sort of voice. " 'I'll get you and your little dog, too.' "

Tamara tried to choke back her laughter, and snorted instead. Then she said, "You remember last year, after the titanosaurs had eaten their way through the valley and were gone, how the Lord of the Valley stalked around the perimeter? And then, a couple of days later, the herds came pouring in?"

"Yeah?"

"Suppose he was staking out his territory, the way hawks do. He makes his claim to the valley and everything in it. Then maybe he's actually calling the herds in. Telling them that the territory's ready."

"Why would they come, though?" asked Leyster, who'd been thinking along the same lines himself. "What's in it for them?"

"A nice lush valley with plenty to eat, and a promise that if any other tyrannosaurs try to move in on them, the Lord will kick their butts. We've seen him drive away several bachelor rexes over the past year."

"You've got to admit," Chuck said. "It makes for an attractive package. Good food, good company, an absolute minimum of predation. If I were a hadro, I'd go for it in an instant."

They were walking through a stretch of old-growth forest. The tree trunks were far apart from each other, and the floor was a soft and silent carpet of pine needles. They could talk quietly here, and without fear.

"As long as we're speculating," Tamara said, laying emphasis on that last word, "there could be any number of interspecific communication loops. Say the herds got too large for the carrying capacity of the valley, the rexes could split off smaller fragments of the herds and drive them away. We've seen behavior that looks very much like that."

"How would they know to do that?" Leyster asked quickly.

"Infrasound again," Tamara said. "If there's too much of it around, too many trikes and titans gossiping back and forth, the rexes get irritable."

"Only one thing can cure this headache," Chuck said. "Scaring the crap out of a few herbivores."

"Don't forget," Tamara said, "the behavior doesn't have to be intentionally mediated. Ants engage in complex social behavior, and their brains are negligible, even by dinosaur standards."

"Okay, but what's in it for the tyrannosaur?"

"Easy prey. The herds are too large to keep together in tight, compact groups. They have to spread out to forage. Old Rexie can step in and bag one at his convenience."

They were coming to the end of the old-growth forest. Ahead in the distance, the unvarying gloom brightened slightly, the diffuse effect of small shafts of light reaching through the canopy to the ground.

Leyster nodded. "I remember Dr. Salley gave a talk once in which she said that tyrannosaurs were farmers. I wonder if this is what she was talking about."

"I was there too!" Chuck said. "You remember she said that mountains danced to the music of sauropods? I bet she was right about that one too."

"Okay, now you've lost me."

"Me too."

"Hear me out. You know that continental drift isn't silent, right? Those huge tectonic plates moving a couple of inches a year put out long, slow sound waves—infrasound. Now, if two oneirosaurs can hear each other a hundred miles apart, why can't they hear the sound of the mountains moving and the plates shifting? And if they *do,* then there's a mechanism for their migration. They can use those sounds to guide themselves into the interior and back again every year.

"But that's not all! It would explain why all the non-avian dinosaurs died out at the K-T. There have been studies modeling the effects of the Chicxulub impactor and it would have struck the Earth like a *gong!* The infrasonic reverberations would have echoed back and forth for years."

"So?" Tamara asked.

"So, during a time of enormous environmental stress, the major dinosaurs would have been deaf. Unable to migrate. Unable to communicate with each other. They, and everything reliant upon them, would have been at an incredible disadvantage. Imagine if ants suddenly lost the ability to cooperate socially! That's where the dinosaurs would be."

There was a moment's silence. Then Tamara said, "Chuck, you've outdone yourself."

"It's inspired lunacy," Leyster agreed. Chuck looked crestfallen. "Right up there with continental drift, or the notion that birds might be descended from dinosaurs." Chuck brightened. "But it's also right up there with Eric Van Danniken and Lamarckian genetics. Until we've tested it out, it's just a nifty hypothesis, no more."

"So let's test it!"

"From here? I don't see how. It hasn't even happened yet. What kind of experiment could you . . . ?" He lapsed into silence, considering the problem. If they could somehow jam the natural infrasonic emissions of the Earth, and then transmit a false signal, it would be possible to see if the migrating dinosaurs then went astray. But that would require equipment well beyond anything Lai-tsz could donkey together out of instrument chips and bailing wire. If they knew what part of the brain processed the infrasonics and then isolated it surgically—but that was as much a fantasy as the first notion. If they . . .

Leyster walked mechanically forward, spinning off idea after idea, until finally he came to the conclusion that the notion was untestable with the resources at hand. It was a problem they'd never be able to tackle, unless they were someday, against all odds, rescued.

He wondered if it was possible that they someday *would* go home again. It seemed unlikely. But not impossible. In which case, at that long-ago orientation lecture, Salley would have been simply feeding them their own speculations, repackaged as hers. He smiled sadly. That would be typical of her.

He looked up and saw that Tamara was staring at him. Chuck had taken over the lead, and was some twenty paces ahead of them. "I was just thinking about that lecture Dr. Salley gave," he said.

"You've still got it for her, then?" she said quietly, so Chuck wouldn't hear. He as not at all surprised by the ease with which she read deeper into his private thoughts than he himself had. She was a perceptive woman, and they none of them had a lot of secrets from one another anymore.

"No, that was just a notion I had once. I got over that one a long time ago."

"Sure you did," Tamara said. But affectionately. There was no sting in her words.

"Hey, look!" Chuck called. "There's light ahead. A clearing!"

The clearing was filled with flowers, knee-high bushes, and a few musty-smelling sumacs. They were halfway across when they came too close to a toothbird nest. Chuck was in the lead, lustily singing "Waltzing Mathilda." Leyster came second, and Tamara brought up the rear, spear in one hand and compass in the other.

Two birds burst out of the undergrowth.

Screaming, the male—they could tell by the bright orange slashes on its wings—dove at Tamara's head. She flinched away, futilely slashing her spear in the air. It banked tightly, and dove at Chuck.

Meanwhile, the female ran straight at Leyster, wings out and claws extended. It climbed right up his pants and shirt. It happened so fast that the bird's sharp-toothed beak was snapping at his face before he had time to react.

"Geddoff!" he yelled.

Toothbirds were enantiornithiforms the size of crows. Having an angry one on his chest was terrifying.

He swatted at the little horror, and it dug in its claws and jabbed at him with its beak.

"Get it off of me! Get it off!"

He was running, blindly, not caring where.

Chuck was running too, and stumbling, using his hat to try to ward off the creature. It flew in tight angry loops between him and Tamara, aiming always at their heads, their eyes. She plunged ignominiously through the bushes at the edge of the clearing, and disappeared.

Then Leyster too found himself immersed in the gloom of the deep woods. The archaeopterygian launched itself into the air. It flew angrily back to its young, screeching threats over its shoulder.

Leyster straightened warily. He looked around, and saw his friends shamefacedly approaching. Chuck shrugged, and grinned sheepishly.

"Well," Tamara said. "We didn't exactly cover ourselves with glory this time."

"This one definitely doesn't go in the autobiography," Chuck agreed. "You okay?"

"Yeah, fine." He'd been bitten on both of his hands and on one cheek. The bites ached like blazes. "Only, I think maybe we should go around this particular clearing."

Toothbirds rarely nested alone. There might be dozens of nesting pairs further in.

"Let's get those wounds bandaged up," Tamara said, digging out her water bottle and eying a nasty-looking gash on Chuck's forehead. "Before the smell of blood draws something *really* mean."

Leyster nodded. From where they stood, they could still see the meadow, bright in the sun and framed by shadows, like a Victorian oil painting of the Garden of Eden, and like the Garden of Eden a place to which they could not return. How much did a toothbird weigh? Maybe nine ounces? It was a sobering thing to contemplate in a world containing predators weighing eight tons and more.

Though he said nothing, he was beginning to wonder if maybe this trek wasn't going to be quite as easy as they had all confidently predicted.

15

Adaptive Radiation

Terminal City: Telezoic era. Eognotic period. Afrasia epoch. Orogenian age. 50 My C.E.

From a distance, Terminal City was mesmerizing. Molly Gerhard had once been to Petra, the "rose-red city half as old as time," on a Bible Lands tour. She'd thought then that nothing could be more magical than those columned facades carved from the mountainside, those graceful roofs hewn from solid stone.

She'd been wrong.

Watching the cold Aegean tumble through the narrow cleft between the golden halves of Terminal City while the afternoon light played across the fractured strata of its surface filled her with the same bewildered sense of wonder that an infant feels on first seeing a Mylar balloon. It took the breath away. When she closed her eyes, the river and mountains disappeared but the City remained, burned into her memory forever.

That was the outside. The *inside*, however . . .

The inside had all the charm of a badly-lit warehouse. The Unchanging scurried like Medieval monks through twisting corridors so murky that Molly Gerhard was continually being startled when one suddenly loomed up, silent and grim, out of the darkness. There were no signs or directions anywhere in this drab labyrinth. The Unchanging knew where to go without them.

It was her job to make sense of it, though. So she had. She had mentally mapped out the main corridors well enough, anyway, to lead Dr. Salley where she wanted to go. The paleontologist, she noted, was in an even worse mood than she had been an hour ago.

"Why are we doing this?" she asked.

"Because I asked you to," Salley said.

"Why did you ask me to?"

"Because I have something to show you."

"What?"

"You'll see when we get there." Salley flashed her a bright, malicious glance. Something had filled her with energy and purpose. Molly Gerhard assumed it was somehow related to her problems with Griffin.

Whatever the source, she was a bitch on wheels today.

Waving a hand at the gray, unornamented walls, Salley resumed an earlier monolog: "All this I understand. It's as plain as the interior of a wasp's nest, and as functional too. Nothing but what's needed. The inside is everything it ought to be. What baffles me is why the exterior is covered with *gold.*" She spoke the final word with distaste, as if the conventional beauty of the substance offended her esthetic sense.

"I think—"

"Please don't." Salley strode straight ahead, trailing a hand lightly against the passing wall.

To Molly Gerhard's uneducated eye the walls looked to be concrete. But, no, Salley had said, they were made of fine-grained coral, most likely grown in slabs for that exact purpose. They passed open doorways through which might be glimpsed a Victorian fernery, or a barrel-vaulted hall crammed with subway cars and garden gnomes, or perhaps one holding endless rows of filing cabinets whose opened drawers would reveal thousands of neatly-organized salad forks. She knew because Sally darted in and opened several.

It was easily the strangest structure Molly Gerhard had ever been in, less a city than some mad collector's wet dream of a private museum.

"I *think,*" she repeated, "that there could well be a functional purpose for the gold." Her father was an electrical engineer, and she had inherited much of her logical sense from him. "Gold is an excellent conductor. The river flowing through the city must set up an enormous static charge. Maybe the entire structure acts as a passive electric generator. If so, they could get all the energy they needed, just by tapping the shell."

"Huh," Salley said flatly. "Fancy that. You're not as brain-dead as you look."

Molly Gerhard bit her tongue. Salley knew something. She was determined to find out what.

Five Unchanging passed them without word or a glance. One held a large red fungus in a bell jar. Another cradled a piece of Etruscan sculpture in its arms. Two more effortlessly carried a red-and-white Indian motorcycle between them—a 1946 Chief, by the looks of it. The last held a mahogany-and-brass gramophone. Nothing she ever saw came from her future. There were systems in place, they'd been assured, to prevent that from happening.

Salley sniffed loudly as the Unchanging passed. "Smell that?"

"I don't smell anything."

"Exactly."

"All right, dear," Molly Gerhard said, "I give up. You win. I'm not as smart as you are, I admit it." She felt an urge to slap the woman. "This I-know-a-secret act is getting old. Why don't you just tell me what you're trying to say?"

"The data are laid out before you," Salley said complacently. "The rest is left as an exercise for the student."

The corridor twisted and then split in two. Thinking murderous thoughts, Molly Gerhard chose the wider corridor, leading downward.

The deeper they went, the more Unchanging they saw. They were as indistinguishable as worker bees. All were clad in identical robes, like those worn by Buddhist monks, but white rather than orange. In the dim light, they seemed to glow.

"They do look extraordinarily like people, don't they?" Salley said abruptly.

"Um . . . yes. Of course." She had been thinking that they looked as beautiful and impersonal as angels. Griffin, who was raised a Catholic, had made that comparison. Molly was a Baptist, however. She thought the Unchanging were creepy. Their lack of suspicion annoyed her. They were all patience and predetermination. So far as she could tell, they had no curiosity whatsoever. "I mean, they must be mammals, right? They're obviously related to people. Somehow." She hesitated. "Aren't they?"

"How many of them do you think there are?"

"Here in the City? Maybe a hundred thousand? Two?"

"That's just a frazz on the high side." Salley was openly smirking now. "In my humble opinion."

They came to a five-way splitting of the corridor that didn't look familiar. Molly Gerhard paused to work it out. Two of the corridors were too narrow for the kind of traffic that the time funnel generated. A third led upward. She listened to the fourth: Silence. Down the fifth, she could hear the scuff of footsteps.

That was the one.

"You're not going to explain yourself, are you?" she said when they were underway again. "You're just going to keep making cryptic little comments and laughing at me when I can't decipher them."

"Yep."

"I begin to see why so many people find you irritating."

Salley stopped. "Irritating?" she said. "Just what do you *mean* by that?"

Another Unchanging emerged from the darkness, leading something that was Percheron-tall, fifteen feet long, and obviously a predator. It was black-lipped, hyena-ugly, and possessed of the longest jaw, sharpest teeth, and pig-stupidest eyes Molly had ever seen in her life. That great head rolled around to look down at her as it went by, and she shrank back against the wall.

In a flash of fear, she saw herself as that thing saw her: as meat. To it, she was nothing but a small monkey, two bites and gone, something it would gladly have snatched up and eaten if it hadn't been controlled by its torc.

The acrid stench of it lingered in its wake.

"My God!" she gasped. "What was *that?*"

"*Andrewsarchus,*" Salley said impatiently. "Late Eocene, from Mongolia. The largest known terrestrial carnivorous mammal. It could eat lions for breakfast." She gazed solemnly after it. "Wasn't it lovely?"

"That's . . . one term for it." Repulsive son-of-a-sea-cook being another. Then, figuring Salley was now in as good a mood as she was ever going to be, she said, "What you want me to see—is it something about the Unchanging?"

"Oh, yes." Again, that superior look. "It took me a while, but I've finally got them figured out. I know what they are now. And if you're a patient little girl for just a few minutes more, I'll prove it, okay?" The corridor ended in a cavernous darkness. "Hey, is this the place?"

They'd reached the heart of Terminal City.

Here, deep below the river, were the endless arrays of openings that served as the confluence of every branch of the time funnel in existence. Here, she could feel the power that the city contained, the living pulse so low and deep that the world hummed to its vibration. Gates crashed open and shut in the darkness as the Unchanging came and went. The din was astonishing.

Salley inhaled deeply. "Now this is more like it!"

Everything that had come through this dull granite-and-brushed-steel space had left its trace: Fusel oil and forsythia. Creosote and brine. Uintatherium dung and primate musk. Salley was waving another clue under her nose. Of all things that had passed this way, only the Unchanging had no smell.

It was obviously significant. But of what, she had no idea.

They stood at the end of the hallway, just outside the open space. The nearest funnel was only a few steps distant. The way to it was blocked by a single Unchanging. It studied them alertly, incuriously.

There were many entrances, but only theirs was guarded. To Molly, who had put in decades working the predestination game, this was a far more effective deterrent than any show of force would be. Its mere presence said that they had no chance of getting past it.

"Okay," she said. "This is as far as we can go. What was it you wanted to show me?"

"This." Salley reached up to her neck and then dumped something in Molly Gerhard's hands. Her mutilated torc. Molly looked up just in time to see

Salley flash a piece of paper at the Unchanging guard and stride past it.

"Hey!" Molly Gerhard started after her.

But her way was barred by the Unchanging. "You cannot pass without authorization," it said.

"That woman has no right to use the time funnel," she said quickly. "You've got to stop her."

"You cannot pass without proper authorization."

"But she doesn't *have* proper authorization! Whatever she showed you was either forged or stolen." Briefly, she considered trying to shove her way past. Then she remembered how easily the two Unchanging had carried that cruiser motorcycle between them, and decided it was wiser not to try.

"You cannot pass without authorization."

"You're not listening!"

"You cannot pass without authorization."

Salley seized the iron gate of the nearest funnel entrance. It crashed open. She stepped within, turned to face forward.

"Wait!" Molly cried after her. "Where are you going?"

"Someplace more interesting than this." Salley waggled her fingers. "Toodles."

The gate slammed shut.

"Damn," Molly Gerhard said.

Whatever it was that had just happened, she *knew* that Griffin was going to be pissed.

Griffin stood out front of his cottage, staring at a smoldering trash fire. There were charred box springs at its center. Molly Gerhard recognized the stench of burning mattress stuffing. Beside her, Jimmy wrinkled up his nose.

Griffin did not look up at their approach. "She's gone," he said.

"I know," Molly Gerhard said. "I was just at the time funnel. I saw her leave."

Griffin grunted.

"Maybe she'll come back," Jimmy suggested. "Women have been known to change their minds."

"She's not coming back. I've been through two divorces. I know the signs."

Griffin was holding his wrist in one hand. Slowly, he forced the hand open and moved it away, so he could stare down at his watch. By the look on his face, it told him nothing.

"Well?" he said at last.

Molly, unsure what he wanted, didn't respond.

"Where did she go? Why did she go there? What does she know that we don't?"

"I really don't—"

Jimmy squinted up at the sun. "It's too hot out here for this kind of conversation," he said. "Let's go inside."

They talked in the village pub. It was, Jimmy had firmly pointed out to them, not a reproduction of a real pub, but rather a reproduction of an American imitation of one. Molly Gerhard didn't care. She'd been in phonier. At least this one didn't have cardboard leprechauns taped to the mirrors.

Griffin sat hunched over the bar. He looked like he could use a drink. She'd heard he had a problem there. In all her years working for him, she'd never actually seen Griffin with an alcoholic beverage in his hand. That could just be discretion, though.

She sat at a table, and Jimmy lounged by the window.

It seemed to Molly Gerhard that Salley would be pleased by how she dominated their thoughts in her absence, as she never had while she was here. She was one of those people who discredited their own ideas by the force with which they argued them. With her gone, they were able to give her speculations the serious consideration they deserved. They were able to admit that she might well be right.

"Salley's the key to everything," Molly said.

"How so?" Jimmy asked coolly.

"She's figured it all out. Exactly what's going on. Why we haven't gotten anywhere in our negotiations. Everything."

"You're sure of that?"

"Yes. She as good as said so any number of times."

Griffin sighed, straightened, turned. *Tick-tock,* Molly thought. Like a machine resuming its function. This was one of the reasons she was leaving for the private sector. She didn't like what manipulating destiny did to people, how it coarsened them. He took up the reins of the discussion. "We're getting ahead of ourselves. Let's begin by establishing the precise order of events."

Griffin got the ball rolling by telling how he had come back to the village from yet another futile and unproductive meeting with the Unchanging to find both Salley and his All Access pass gone. Then Molly Gerhard related how she'd been conned into leading Salley to the time funnel. "I didn't see what harm she could do," she said shamefacedly. "I honestly didn't think she was that devious."

"Where did she go?" Griffin said.

"I don't know. Forward, presumably." With the AA pass, she could have gone anywhere. But if she had returned to the Cenozoic or Mesozoic, her return would have been logged into the system. "If she'd gone back, the Old Man would be here now. Since he's not . . ." She shrugged.

"How far forward?"

"I don't know."

"Could you identify the exact entrance to the funnel she used?" Jimmy asked.

She closed her eyes, thought. "Yes."

"Then we can follow her."

"What? How?"

"Let's just say we have our ways. Technically speaking, I'm not even supposed to know about them."

"No, you're not." Griffin glowered at his subordinate. Then, to Molly: "Why would she go forward? What's she trying to accomplish?"

"Hard to say. But she's headed all the way to the end of the line. To the *real* source of time travel. Sometime many, many millions of years beyond Terminal City."

"She told you this?"

"Not directly. She tried not to say anything. But that's not easy for her. She was dropping hints constantly."

"That's true," Jimmy said. "She was bubbling over with things unsaid."

"After a while, I gave up on trying to get a straight answer out of her, and just began assembling her pronouncements. I've been sorting through them in my mind, and I think I've put them into some sort of order."

"Go on," Griffin said.

"She kept referring to how quiet it was. How clean and unspoiled. She talked about how much she wanted to get out into the local ecosystem, but she never said a word about the fact that there don't appear to be any large animals in it. It suggests she didn't want us to realize that we're in the aftermath of a major extinction event."

"She said something to me about how quiet it was," Jimmy said. "I didn't think it meant anything."

Molly Gerhard reminded herself that she couldn't expect Jimmy to be of much use here. This wasn't his arena of action. "It means everything," she said. "To begin with, there hasn't been the time for the adaptive radiation of species."

Jimmy cleared his throat. "You're losing me,"

"Evolution," Griffin said, taking control again, "is not like an arrow, with a fish crawling out of the water at one end and a white male in a business suit on the other. It is a radiation in all directions, provided only that there is room to evolve in the indicated direction.

"Usually, there isn't. In a healthy ecosystem, all niches are filled. A desert mouse wanders into the grasslands and finds there are field mice there already. It can't harvest the grass seed as efficiently as they can, or dodge the local owls and foxes as well. So it's either driven back into the desert, or it dies.

"After a major extinction event, however, there are empty niches everywhere, devoid of predators or competition. So elements of a single species can radiate out in several directions to fill them. They get larger, they get smaller, they climb trees. Before you know it, there are mice the size of gophers, mice the size of hippopotami, otter mice, bison mice, with sabre-tooth mice and grizzly mice to prey on them.

"It's a fast process. It only takes ten million years or so for the niches to fill up again. So the fact that they haven't, means we're in the aftermath of a major extinction event. Which means that this can't be the Unchanging's home time." He scowled. "I should have seen it myself. I would have, if I hadn't been so tied up in negotiations."

"Okay," Molly said. "So we're all agreed that this isn't the Unchanging's original time period?"

"What is it, then?" Jimmy asked.

"It's a quarantine station for animals being transshipped forward, and a holding space for items they've acquired and only occasionally need to refer to."

"Hold on. If they're our descendants, why couldn't they have simply survived the extinction event?"

"Salley said that they weren't people."

"They look like people."

"Salley said that too. She also made a big deal about how they didn't smell. She said it often enough that I finally asked myself what kind of animal doesn't have a smell." She paused, half expecting Jimmy to make a wisecrack. He did not.

"Well?" Griffin said.

"An artificial one. The Unchanging approached us with time travel in one hand, and a list of restrictions in the other. Naturally, we assumed it came from them."

"Christ on a crutch!" Jimmy said suddenly. "Will you look at this fucker?"

She turned. Jimmy was staring out the window at a grotesque, long-jawed giant of a predator that was padding slowly down the river road.

"I saw that same creature inside Terminal City! It scared the daylights out of me."

"It's only an *Andrewsarchus*," Griffin said irritably. "So it's big! Something has to be. There's really no reason to make such a fuss over it. Sit down, Jimmy. In a chair, with your back to the window."

Meekly, Jimmy obeyed.

"Continue," Griffin said to Molly.

"That's pretty much it. But it explains why they're all of a height and a size and an appearance. Why they have no genetic variety at all. Why they look so pleasing to the eye. They were simply created for a job—dealing with us. And it explains why the negotiations have gotten nowhere. We've been talking to the wrong folks. The Unchanging aren't our sponsors. They're just our sponsors' tools."

For an instant, no one spoke. Then Griffin said, "We need to talk with the Unchanging."

The door opened.

An Unchanging walked in. "You require me," it said. "I am here."

"Yes," Griffin said. "But what use are you?"

It regarded him with polite, bland patience. Molly Gerhard recalled that Griffin had once told her that one of his chief tools was boredom. *Sitzflesh,* he said, was even more important to a bureaucrat than it was to a chess player. Many a concession had been made by a negotiator who simply couldn't face running through the same excruciating drivel for the seventeenth time. Yet he had never been able to out-sit an Unchanging. He could not match their perfect lack of expectation. He could not rattle them, nor insult them. They never displayed emotion.

"We've been discussing you," Griffin said. "It has been suggested that this is not your proper time."

"I am here. Time is always proper."

Griffin grinned. He was a warrior, Molly Gerhard realized, and this was his field of combat. However discouraged he might have been mere minutes ago, the possibility of victory exalted him. "It has been suggested that you are an artificial construct. Is this true?"

"Yes."

"How were you made?" Molly Gerhard asked.

"I was grown from human genetic material, suitably altered for the purposes to which I am put."

"Who made you?"

"I am not authorized to tell you that."

"Then we must talk to those who made you."

"I cannot authorize that."

"Who can?"

"I am not authorized to tell you that."

Tick-tock, she thought again, her suspicions confirmed. The Unchanging was just another machine. Nothing more. Nothing less. They could stay here forever arguing with the thing, and not make a single inch's headway.

Griffin, unfortunately, was a battler. It took three hours' repetitive argument for him to give in.

"Can anything at all be resolved through you?" he finally asked. "Have you the authority to make decisions without precedent? Can you, under *any* conditions, send us forward on your own cognizance?"

"No."

Griffin looked disgusted. "Then leave."

It turned to go. Suddenly, Molly remembered another of Salley's hints. "Tell me something," she said. "Exactly how many of you are there?"

It paused. "One."

"No, not you personally. I mean of the Unchanging. How many Unchanging are there in Terminal City? How many are there in the world at any given time? How many exist if you add up every one of the Unchanging no matter what era in time it inhabits?"

"One," it said. "I am all there is. I perform all tasks, fulfill all functions, suffice for all that must be done. Only me. One."

When the Unchanging was gone, Molly Gerhard said, "Yikes."

"What annoys me," Griffin said, "is the very real possibility that the Pentagon has had this information all along, but didn't deem it important that we share in it."

Jimmy scratched his head. "Let me get this straight. There's only one of them."

"Yes. One single individual, looped through time a thousand, a million, however many times it takes to do all the tasks that need doing."

"Like that old notion that there was only one single subatomic particle running from one end of time to the other and back, over and over, until it's woven an entire universe out of itself?"

"Yes."

Jimmy stood, scraping his chair back on the floor. "Then I know what to do. Gather up everything you want to take with you. We're leaving."

When they came to the center of Terminal City and saw the guard waiting for them, Griffin said mildly, "I hope that whatever you plan doesn't require our getting past the Unchanging. Without my pass, we won't be allowed anywhere near the funnel."

Molly Gerhard felt a sudden chill. Without access to the funnel, they had no way go get home. "Ever?" she asked.

"Now don't you worry one least bit," Jimmy said. "Let me show you how we handle problems like this back in Belfast."

Unhurriedly, but not slowly either, he walked up to the Unchanging on duty before the cavern's entrance. "Excuse me just a sec," he said. "I have something here that—"

He was alongside the Unchanging now. His hand came out of his pocket and moved with uncanny speed toward the being's back. Then he stepped away.

There was surprisingly little blood. Just a spreading crimson stain on the robe where the knife hilt stuck out of the Unchanging's back.

Quietly, without protest, it fell.

It was quite dead.

"If there's only one of him, then he has to end somewhere," Jimmy commented. "And if he ends here, then he couldn't see it coming."

He started toward the funnel. "Come on."

16

Buddy System

Lost Expedition Foothills: Mesozoic era. Cretaceous period. Senonian epoch. Maastrichtian age. 65 My B.C.E.

When sunset came, they set up the poptent in a sheltered spot in a grove of sycamores and fell asleep almost immediately.

In the morning, Chuck was the first out, whistling cheerily. The instant he left the tent, however, the whistling cut off.

He stuck his head back in and, with quiet urgency, said, "Don't make any fast movements or loud noises. Grab your things and get out of the tent. Now."

"I hope this isn't another one of your—" Tamara began, crawling out, spear in hand and blouse only half buttoned. "Oh, shit."

A herd of geistosaurs had moved into the grove. It was hard to count their numbers in the dawn light, but there were at least forty of them. They were unhurriedly stripping the leaves from the lower branches of the sycamores.

The geistosaurs were almost dead white, with blotchy black markings scattered across their bodies and thick black rings around their eyes. Those rings should have made them look comic, but did not. Their markings, combined with their absolute silence (*Geistosaurus* was the only mute hadrosaurine Leyster knew of) gave them a spooky solemnity, as if they were spirit animals that had wandered into reality from the totemic lands of the dead.

They dared not try to slip away. Any large animal was potentially dangerous. And though a geistosaur was no more aggressive than a Brahma bull or a water buffalo, it was considerably larger. If they startled one, it could easily trample them all.

Nor would climbing a tree be of any use. It might save them from a ceratopsian, but not a hadrosaur. When they reared up onto their hind legs, the geistosaurs could reach all but the highest branches. Those, they could shake savagely enough to dislodge anything clinging there.

So they sat scrunched up against the trunks of the sycamores for several hours, hoping to escape notice, while the ghostly white-and-black giants browsed their way through the grove, pale animals among the pale trees. "Under other circumstances," Chuck muttered underneath his breath, "I'd be enjoying this. We've got front row seats here."

"I can't get a handle on their social interplay," Leyster whispered back. "As a rule, the smaller adults seem to be subordinate to the larger. But—"

"Would you two kindly shut the fuck up?"

Tamara whispered. "We don't want to stampede them."

At that instant, the phone rang.

As one, every geistosaur in the grove lifted its head in alarm. For a long, frozen instant, nothing moved. The phone continued ringing, an alien noise completely unlike anything these animals could ever have heard before.

Then they fled.

They scattered like pigeons. Briefly, they were everywhere, enormous, terrified. The juveniles dropped to all fours first, and trotted briskly off to the east and north. Then the adults, herding their young before them.

In its haste, a geistosaur brushed against the poptent, sending it leaping up a good six feet into the air. By the time it bounced back to earth, the grove was empty.

The phone was still ringing.

Shakily, Leyster stood. He stretched his aching muscles, then retrieved his pack, so he could answer the phone. It took a minute to unwrap the thing. "Yes?"

"This is Daljit. Lai-tsz called and told us she's built a device for detecting infrasound and . . . Hey, how far have you guys gotten?"

"Not as far as we were hoping. But we'll make up for lost time this afternoon. How's Jamal?"

"It's just a broken leg," Jamal said in the background.

"I think it's infected," Daljit said. "Did you remember to bring antibiotics?"

"Of course we did." Their last, though Leyster

didn't mention that. "Oh, and you'd better watch out for Chuck. He's got hold of a theory."

"Uh-oh. What is it?"

"I'll let him bend your ear when we get there. Right now, tell us about the infrasound."

While he listened, Chuck and Tamara repacked their gear. When he finally hung up, Tamara said, "We were lucky. The only thing that was broken was one of the tent's support struts. We can make a replacement from a sapling."

"Thank God," Leyster said.

They were midway through the slow process of losing everything they had brought with them. The solar shower device went first, followed quickly by (of course) their consumer electronics—game players and music systems—and the batteries they required to function. Then a knife went missing, and a comb, and the next thing they knew, they were suffering serious inconvenience, and facing the possibility of genuine hardship. When one of his cameras died, Patrick went into mourning for a week.

Bit by bit, they were losing their grip on the machine age and sliding back into the stone age. It was a terrifying prospect not only because it was irreversible, but because they lacked the complex mastery of paleolithic technology that a stone age hunter had. Nils had spent most of the rainy season trying to make a bow before giving it up as a bad job. He hadn't even been able to manufacture shafts straight enough for the arrows.

"Let's go," Leyster said, shouldering his pack. "I can tell you about the infrasound on the way."

* * *

Lai-tsz had jury-rigged two recorders to detect infrasound. On their very first day using them, the crew back home had been able to establish that the valley was full of sub-audible communications. More, according to Daljit, the messages were profoundly moving.

"They *sing!*" she'd told Leyster. "No, not like whales. Much lower, much more vibrant. Oh, it's exquisite stuff. They played some for us over the phone. Jamal says we should be sure to hang onto the copyright. He says he's sure a music company would be interested."

"I was joking," Jamal said weakly in the background.

"Oh, hush. You were not. Fortunately, our original equipment included directional microphones. Since Lai-tsz rigged up two recorders, it's possible to point one at a tyrannosaur and another at a herbivore, record both simultaneously, and then play them back to see if you've got anything that looks like interspecific communication."

"So, do they?"

"Well, it's a little early to say . . ."

"Don't be a tease, Daljit," Jamal said.

"But yes, yes it really does look like there is."

When Leyster finished relating the conversation, Tamara said, "That is so *neat!*"

"Aw, c'mon," Chuck said in a mock-hurt voice. "How can you be so impressed by something we already suspected, and not by my theory? I mean, let's face it, it's got the K-T extinction, continental drift, the Chicxulub impactor, and mass dinosaur madness all in one sexy package."

"Yes, but those are just ideas. Forgive me, Chuck, but anybody can come up with *ideas*. What the guys back home have done goes way beyond ideas. They've established a new fact! It's like the universe had this secret it's been keeping since forever, and now it's been found out. It's like reading the mind of God."

"*Now* who's being grandiose?"

"Louis Agassiz once wrote that a physical fact is as sacred as a moral principle," Leyster said. "I'm siding with Tamara on this one."

Chuck shrugged. "Anyway, they've established that different species talk to one another infrasonically. I consider that step one toward proving my theory."

"Whoah, whoah, whoah! That's not the way science works. First you gather the data, then you analyze it, and *then* you come up with a hypothesis and a plan for testing it. In that order."

"And yet scientists come up with idiot notions and set out to prove them all the time," Tamara said. "I could name names, if you want. Your system works fine in theory. But things are different in the real world."

"I'm going to move to Theory someday," Chuck said. "Everything works there."

"Sometimes you guys make me question my ability to teach. You can't *prove* a hypothesis in paleontology—you can only test it to see if it can be destroyed. If, over time, a hypothesis resists every attempt made to falsify it, then you can say that it's extremely robust and would require an extraordinary mass of data to unseat it. The germ theory of disease is a good example of that. The evidence for it is compelling. People bet their lives every day that it's true. But it's not proven. It's simply the best available interpretation of what we know."

"Well, given what we know, I think my hypothesis is the best available interpretation of the facts."

"It's not parsimonious, though. It's not the simplest possible explanation."

Arguing and keeping a wary eye out for predators, they made another few miles' progress through the forest.

They were following an old hadrosaur trail when the woods opened out into a bright clearing. It had recently been browsed almost to the ground, and was covered with new growth, fresh green shoots shot through with white silkpod blossoms and red-tipped Darwin's broomsticks. A stream ran through it. On the far side of the stream, the woods resumed with a stand of protomagnolia trees in full bloom. Their scent filled the clearing.

Birds scattered as they stepped out of the darkness. They waited cautiously for a moment, then took a step forward. Then another.

Nothing attacked them.

Gratefully, Leyster let his knapsack slip to the ground. "Let's take a break," he said.

"Second the motion," Tamara said.

"Moved and carried." Chuck plopped to the ground.

They put their packs together, and sat leaning against them with their legs stretched out. Leyster rolled up his pants legs and checked for ticks. Chuck took off a shoe and rubbed his foot.

"Let's take a look at that," Tamara said. Then, "The sole is practically falling off! Why didn't you say something?"

"I knew you'd want to tape it up, and we've got so little left."

Leyster already had the duct tape out of his pack. "What do you think it's for?" The shoe had been repaired before, but the tape had abraded where the sole met the upper. He rewrapped it with generous swaths of new tape overtop the old. "There. That should hold for a while."

Chuck shook his head ruefully. "We have got to start making new shoes."

"Easier said than done," Leyster said. "We can't do oak tanning because we haven't found anything that looks to be ancestral to the oak. And the problem with brain tanning is that dinosaurs have such tiny little brains. We'll have to harvest a lot of them."

"Sounds like the pioneer method for making a toothpick," Chuck observed: "First, you chop down a redwood . . ."

Everybody chuckled. They were silent for a while. Then Tamara lazily said, "Hey, Chuck."

"Yeah?"

"You don't really believe that stuff about the Chicxulub impactor making the Earth ring, do you?"

"What's so difficult about that? The Earth rings for two to three weeks after a major earthquake, and the force of the collision was six times ten to the eighth power stronger than any earthquake. Now, most of that force went into heat and other forms of energy. If less than one tenth of one percent of that went into elastic energy, as seems entirely plausible, then the elastic wave propagation would be enough to make the Earth ring for a hundred years."

"Oh."

"The only question is how much the heat energy changed the properties of the crust. If it became more viscous and less solid, then the more viscous crust would damp out the elastic waves. However, I do not think that happened. *Extremely* unlikely, in my humble opinion. Though I am open to new interpretations, if the data are there to support them."

Leyster smiled to himself. Chuck had a good mind. He'd make a fine scientist as soon as he learned to stop jumping to conclusions. He sighed, stretched, and stood.

"Time to go, kids." Leyster took a reading, pointed toward the protomagnolias. Tamara came after him, and then Chuck.

They splashed through the stream and back into gentle shadow.

"Keep alert," Chuck said. "Don't be distracted by how peaceful it all looks."

He had barely finished speaking when the dromies attacked.

Dromaeosaurs were not particularly large as dinosaurs went. They were the size of dogs, somewhere between knee- and hip-high to a human, but, like dogs, they were nothing you wanted to have attack you. This particular pack was covered in tawny green feathers, all short save for the wrist-fans on the females, which were used to shade their eggs when brooding. The feathers, the savage little teeth in their whippet-narrow heads, and the oversized claws on their hind feet combined to make them look like Hell's own budgerigars.

They were ambush hunters.

As one, they burst out of the bushes and leapt down from the trees. The air was filled with flying bodies and protomagnolia petals.

Chuck screamed once.

Leyster spun and saw Chuck go down, covered with dromaeosaurs.

Instinctively, he dropped his compass and snatched out the axe. Hollering and swinging, he ran toward the swarming knot of dromies.

Tamara ran past him, yelling at the top of her lungs. She'd thought to drop her knapsack, where Leyster hadn't. Her spear arm was cocked back, and there was murder in her face.

The dromies scattered.

There were enough of the creatures to kill Tamara and Leyster both. But they weren't used to being challenged. Faced with a situation totally outside their experience, they retreated across the clearing and toward the shelter of the woods beyond.

Tamara hadn't dared throw her spear while the dromies were on top of Chuck. She threw it now, shifted her second spear to her throwing hand, and threw that as well.

One spear flew wide. The other caught its target square in the chest.

At the verge of the clearing, a dromie turned to chatter defiance and was almost hit by a stone Tamara flung. Angry and alarmed, it darted back into the forest. Briefly, the brush was filled with dark shadows milling about in confusion. But when Tamara dashed in under the trees after them, they were nowhere to be found.

She turned back toward the meadow. "Chuck?"

Chuck had twisted as he fell. His body lay face down under the protomagnolias. Leyster knelt beside it and felt for the pulse, though he knew what he would find. There had been somewhere between six and nine of the little gargoyles, and they'd all gotten in several bites before being chased away. Chuck had been bitten in the legs, arms, and face. His throat had been torn open.

"He's dead," Leyster said softly.

"Oh . . . *crap!*" Tamara turned away and started to cry. "Damn, damn, damn."

Leyster started to turn Chuck's body over. But it didn't move quite right when he shifted it, and something started to slide loosely from the abdomen. He remembered then how dromies would latch onto their prey with their forelimbs and use those enormous claws on their hindlimbs to eviscerate their victims. Chuck's abdomen would be ripped open from crotch to rib cage.

He eased the body back into his original position, and stood.

Tamara looked stricken. He put his arms around her, and she buried her face in his shoulder. Her back heaved with her sobs. But Leyster found he had no tears in him. Only a dry, miserable pain. Living in the Maastrichtian, with violent death an everyday possibility, had made him harder. Once he would have felt guilty for surviving. He would have blamed himself for his friend's death, and sought after a reason why he should have been spared when Chuck was not. Now he knew such emotions to be mere self-indulgence. The dromaeosaurs had chosen Chuck because he was last in line. If Leyster had been limping, or Tamara had been having her period, things would have gone differently.

It was just the way it was.

In survival training, they'd called it "the buddy system." To survive an attack, you didn't have to be faster than the predators—just faster than your buddy. It was a system that served zebras and elands well. But it was hell on human beings.

Leyster unhooked Chuck's knapsack, so they could redistribute his things in their two packs. Mastering his revulsion, he went through Chuck's pockets for things they might yet need. Then he removed Chuck's shoes and belt. Until they mastered tanning, they couldn't afford to abandon the least scrap of leather.

"I found the compass," Tamara said. Then, when he shook his head in puzzlement, "You dropped it. I picked it up."

She held the compass up for him to see, and began crying again.

"There are plenty of rocks in the stream. We should build Chuck a cairn. Nothing fancy. Just something big enough to keep the dromies off his corpse."

Tamara wiped her eyes. "Maybe we should let them have him. That's not an entirely bad way to dispose of a paleontologist—by feeding him to the dinosaurs."

"That might be good for you and me. But Chuck wasn't a bone man. He was a geologist. He'll get rocks."

Leyster wasn't sure how many miles he and Tamara got under their belts before the night overcame them. Less than they'd planned. More than could be expected. They walked in a kind of daze, tirelessly. Later, he couldn't remember whether they'd kept an eye out for predators or not.

Just before turning in, Leyster called Daljit and Jamal. He didn't want to speak with them at all. He really wasn't in the mood. But it had to be done. "Listen," he said. "We had a little setback, so we'll be later than we were expecting to be. But don't worry, we'll be there."

"What happened?" Daljit asked. "You didn't lose the antibiotics, did you?"

"The antibiotics are fine. We'll tell you the details when we get there. For now, I just didn't want you to worry."

"Yeah, well, you guys better get here soon. Jamal's not doing that well. His fever is up, and he's delirious."

"All I want is a bicycle," Jamal muttered in the background. "Is that too much to ask?"

"Him and his damned bicycle! I'm going to ring off now. Give my love to Tamara and Chuck, okay?"

Leyster winced. "Will do."

He stowed away the phone and returned to the fire. He hadn't gone far from it. Just enough that there wouldn't be any chance of his dropping the phone where it might get scorched.

"You didn't tell her?" Tamara said.

"I couldn't." He sat down beside her. "Time enough when we get there. She's got enough to worry about, as it is."

They said nothing for a long while, silently watching the fire burn slowly down to coals. Finally, Tamara said, "I'm going in."

"I'll join you in a bit," Leyster said. "I want to sit and think for a bit."

He sat, listening to the night. The syncopated music of frogs, and the steady pulse of crickets. The lonely cry of the moon-crane. There were other noises mixed in there as well, chuckles and distant warbling cries that might be dinos and might be mammals and might be something else entirely. Ordinarily, he found these sounds comforting.

Not tonight.

There were more than three hundred bones in the skeleton of a triceratops, and if they were all dumped in a heap in front of Leyster, he'd be able to assemble them in an afternoon. The sixty-three vertebrae would all be in the proper order, from the syncervical to the final caudal. The elaborate fretwork of the skull would be knit into one complex whole. The feet would be tricky, but he'd sort out the bones of the pes, or hindfeet, into two piles of twenty-four, starting with metatarsals I to V, arranging the phalanges in a formula of 2-3-4-5-0 beneath them, and capping all with an ankle made up of the astragalus, calcaneum, and three distal tarsals. The manus, or front foot, almost simple by contrast, contained five metacarpals, fourteen phalanges arranged in a formula of 2-3-4-3-2, and three carpals—still, it was a rare ability to sort them by sight. Leyster knew his way around a skeleton as well as any man.

He knew, as well, the biochemical pathways of the creature's metabolism and catabolism; many of the subtleties of its behavior and temperament; its feeding, fighting, mating, and nurturing strategies; its evolutionary history; and a rough outline of its range and genetic structure. And this was but one of the many dinosaurs (to say nothing of non-dinosaurs) he had studied in depth. He knew everything it was possible to know, with the resources at hand, about the life and death of animals.

Except, perhaps, the central mystery. All he had were facts, and none of his knowledge was necessary. The bones found their proper order with every triceratops born. The biochemical pathways policed themselves. The animals lived, mated, and died quite successfully without his intervention.

Chuck was here and he was gone.

It seemed impossible.

He didn't understand it at all.

The forest was black upon black. It made his sight swim. It made him feel small, just one more transient mote of life moving inexorably toward death.

For all his knowledge, he knew nothing. For all he had learned, his understanding was nil. He stood at the lightless center of a universe totally devoid of meaning. There were no answers here, no answers within, no answers anywhere.

He stared off into the darkness. He wanted to walk straight into it and never come back.

So great was his unhappiness at that moment that it seemed to him that the night itself was sobbing. All the bleak forest and starless sky shook with a low, muffled noise that was the perfect embodiment of misery. Then, with a start, he realized that the sound was Tamara weeping softly in the tent.

She hadn't gone to sleep after all.

Well, of course she hadn't. After what had happened to Chuck, how could she? Even if she hadn't seen it happen, even if they hadn't been close, his loss reduced the human population of the world to ten. It was an unparalleled catastrophe. It was cause for terrible grief. Which made it his duty to go into the tent and comfort her.

His spirit quailed at the thought. I can't, he thought angrily. I don't have any comfort in me. There's nothing here but misery and self-pity. He had no strength at all, no power to endure. He felt that if he took on a single grain more of the world's pain, it would crush him flat.

Tamara went on crying.

Well, let her! Maybe it was selfish of him, but he wasn't going to subject himself to anything more.

He couldn't! What did she *expect* of him? Tears were running down his cheeks, and he despised himself for them. What a fucking hypocrite he was! Of all the people there ever were, he was the last one that anybody would turn to for solace.

Still, Tamara did not stop crying.

You have to go in, he told himself. He couldn't go in.

He went in.

17

Type Specimen

Ultima Pangaea: Telezoic era. Mesognotic period. Chronic epoch. Epimethean age. 250 My C.E.

Jimmy was the first one out of the time funnel. He glanced around quickly, then moved aside so Griffin and Molly Gerhard could follow. They stepped out onto the sward after him.

It was night.

To one side was a copse of trees with low, tangled limbs—"climbing trees" Jimmy would have called them in his youth. Downslope was a lake. In the sky above its black waters hung a glory of stars. Colored lights rose and sank among them like lanterns.

The clearing was ringed with a dozen palely luminous gates. The funnel stood at its center.

A light breeze ruffled the waters of the lake. Molly Gerhard shivered, and finally spoke. "Which way now?"

Jimmy pointed toward one of the gates, where

two dim figures, identical in size and height, waited. He said nothing. A touch of action always made him feel particularly calm and alert afterwards. He didn't want to spoil that by talking.

The two figures resolved into women at their approach.

"Hello, Griffin," Salley said.

"Hello, Griffin," Gertrude said. The moon-shaped scar at the corner of her mouth sailed sardonically upward.

There was a quick exchange of glances in which Jimmy read anger, defiance, hauteur, hurt pride, and astonishment.

Molly Gerhard, who knew the history of that scar on the older woman's face, gave voice to the last of these. "*Tell* me this is you from your own future . . ." (But Salley was already shaking her head dolefully.) ". . . and not the woman who got us into this mess."

"She's—" Salley began.

"I am the original me, and yes, I take full credit for all that's happened."

"That's impossible."

"Only to small minds," Gertrude said.

"We can explain," Salley said.

"I was *told* that divergent time lines could never meet," Molly Gerhard said with an edge in her voice. "How can the two of you possibly exist in the same reality?"

Jimmy, watching, had to admire how efficiently she worked. Gerhard invited correction. She wasn't afraid to sound foolish. And she directed her question at the older woman—Gertrude—while ignoring the younger—Salley. Thus driving the thinnest of wedges between the two and creating a division she might later wish to widen.

"Within your frame of reference, that was true," Gertrude said. "Things are different on this side of Terminal City. You've been there. Surely you understand. Anyone with a modicum of perception would realize that its chief function is to reconcile the products of divergent time lines into a common reality."

Salley's eyes flicked toward her, then away.

"To what purpose?" Griffin asked.

"If nothing else, it enables us to meet." Gertrude turned away. "Let's go to my place. I'll explain everything to you there."

She stepped into the nearest gate and vanished. After the briefest of hesitations, Salley did likewise.

They had no choice but to follow.

Gertrude lived in a floating tower at the center of a ring forest in the Interior Sea. A soft, sultry breeze passed through the open windows, carrying with it the salt smell of the unseen sea. A sliver of new moon hung low in the sky. It had not been visible from the mouth of the time funnel. So Jimmy Boyle knew that the gate had transported them a goodly distance. Not so far, however, that it was not still night.

"Exactly where are we?" Molly Gerhard asked.

Gertrude snapped her fingers, and a map appeared in her hands. She opened it. "This is Ultima Pangaea. Continental drift has joined the scattered continents once more into a single landmass. It is surrounded by a world-spanning ocean and embraces at its heart a solitary inland sea." She tapped a fingertip where the equator bisected the inland sea. "We're right here. In a sense, I live at the exact center of the world."

Of course, Jimmy thought. Where else?

The others were prowling about the room, examining things, opening drawers, displaying a curiosity that Gertrude ignored complacently, though Jimmy would never have allowed it in his digs. "You've got quite a few books here," Griffin observed.

"All mine."

"She means she wrote them," Salley said.

"Yes, of course. What else would I mean?"

"What are *these* creatures?" Molly Gerhard asked.

One wall was nothing but windows. The wall opposite it was taken up by an earth-filled terrarium. A labyrinthine structure of tunnels and dens could be seen through the glass, with pale, hairless animals the size of mice within. "Naked mole birds," Gertrude said. "They lost their feathers *and* their endothermy, and acquired a communal social structure. A fascinating case of convergent evolution. Behaviorally, they're almost identical to naked mole rats. Yet their most recent common ancestor was a pre-Mesozoic creature that looked like a lizard."

Molly Gerhard stared with undisguised loathing at the pallid creatures, climbing clumsily over one another, some few scrabbling at the dirt with needlelike talons and tiny beaks. "Why would you have such things?"

"For their inherent interest."

"They have inherent interest?"

Gertrude snorted. "Bloodedness has always been the paleontologist's Afghanistan," she said. "Any number of scientists have marched off boldly to determine whether dinosaurs were warm-blooded or cold-blooded, and lost themselves in a wilderness of definitions. It turns out that bloodedness is not so simple as it looks from the outside. It's not a single thing, but several families of strategies.

"Body temperature can be either constant or variant, regulated internally or externally, and in service to a high resting metabolism or a low one. Maintaining a constant body temperature is called homeothermy. Variant temperature, usually close to the variation in ambient temperature, is poikilothermy. Internally regulated temperature is called endothermy. Externally regulated temperature is called ectothermy. An animal whose resting metabolism remains at a high level is tachymetabolic. One whose resting metabolism slows to a low level of activity is brady metabolic.

"Got that? Good.

"Now, a 'warm-blooded' animal is generally homeothermic, endothermic, and tachymetabolic, where a 'cold-blooded' one is poikilothermic, ectothermic, and barymetabolic. The naked mole bird, however, is homeothermic, ectothermic, and tachymetabolic. Is it cold-blooded? There are insects whose body temperatures, at rest, reflect the ambient temperature, but whose wing muscles raise their temperatures much higher than that during flight. They're poikilothermic, endothermic, and brady metabolic. Warm-blooded or cold-blooded? How about hibernating mammals? Homeothermic, ectothermic, brady metabolic. Do they shift between bloodednesses?

"Moreover, when you begin to look into the *mechanisms* of all these things, you'll realize that I've been oversimplifying furiously. It's all a lot more complicated than I've made it sound.

"So I've decided to take a whack at straightening the whole mess out."

All the while she talked, Jimmy noted, Salley stood to the far side of the room, sad-eyed and silent. She had only spoken the once, and then without addressing anybody directly. Nor had she looked at Griffin, save casually and fleetingly.

Well, that was easy enough to decipher. It was a terrible blessing she'd been given, to see herself the way everybody else did. He imagined it was humbling. What Jimmy couldn't figure out was why Gertrude was being so talkative.

Griffin listened silently, head down, flipping through book after book. "Leather bound," he said, when Gertrude wound down at last. "Steel engravings. You're certainly being treated well. And this place of yours. Do all the inhabitants of this era live in towers like this?"

"Some do. Most don't."

"Then you're being indulged," Molly Gerhard said. "Why? By whom?"

"Our sponsors. I cut them a deal."

"What for what?" Molly asked crisply.

"You already know what I got: permission to change my personal past. Otherwise you wouldn't be talking with me now. My life here is not what I bought, but rather the price I paid. I serve easy masters. They allow me to engage in activities I find rewarding—research, mostly—and in return I remain available for examination, should any questions about human beings arise."

"Yes, but what do you do?" Molly Gerhard insisted.

"I'm the type specimen for *Homo sapiens.*"

Jimmy made a face, and Griffin explained: "When Linnaeus first set up his system of binomial nomenclature, he defined species with an abstract type—a written description of their features. So he felt free to replace his specimens with superior examples. But, as always, mistakes were made. Which occasionally led to the absurdity of a species being represented by a sample from another species entirely.

"So nowadays, when a species is described, it's done from an individual organism, called the type specimen, which is carefully collected and preserved, and then referred to whenever there's any question as to the taxon's attributes."

"I'm not sure I . . ."

"You can think of Dr. Salley as being the physical definition of humanity. She is the yardstick by which all human beings are measured."

"Wait." Jimmy spoke at last, and as he did so felt that fine top-of-the-world mood collapse to nothing within him. Back to the workaday world again. "You mean to say that my humanity is judged by how closely I resemble *her?*"

"And what's wrong with that?" Gertrude asked.

It was a question that required a day's response or none at all. "Maybe it's time you told us why we're here," Griffin suggested.

"First a drink," Gertrude said. "Then I'll tell you everything."

She poured them glasses of a clear and refreshing fluid. A moment before, Jimmy had been thinking that Griffin and Molly Gerhard looked tired and ready for sleep. But after that drink, they brightened right up. He himself felt ready to climb mountains. He couldn't help thinking that a case of the stuff would make a fine souvenir to bring home.

"I was on the original Baseline expedition," Gertrude said. "Terrible though it is to say, even with the deaths, I was happy. I had dinosaurs. I had Leyster. I had everything. If I hadn't alienated Leyster, I could have stayed in the Maastrichtian forever."

"How did you alienate him?" Molly Gerhard asked.

"I was a fool."

When the bomb went off, Gertrude was engaged in folding up the rocket launcher. Birds were chirping in the trees, and she was marveling at how familiar-yet-strange their song sounded. Like birds everywhere, and yet oddly scored. None of the cries of this age were known to her yet. But they were obviously as sophisticated as those of modern birds, sixty-five million years hence. Music, it seemed, was basic. It arose first among the small, feathered but flightless dinosaurs. The oviraptor had a pretty song.

Then came the explosion.

She ran through the smoke and confusion, and found three bodies lying on the ground: Chuck, Daljit, and Tamara. Two of them were already dead. The third, Daljit, had lost most of an arm.

Leyster was already kneeling at her side, making a tourniquet.

Gertrude ran to get the med kit. She flipped an ampule of morphine into a syringe, found a vein, and shot the painkiller into Daljit's good arm.

The others were milling about uncertainly, hovering over the bodies, asking each other what they should do. Gertrude looked up, and snapped, "Don't just stand there! Pitch a tent. Make up a bed for Daljit. Clear away these bodies. Somebody check and see how much of our supplies have been destroyed. Jesus fucking Christ! Do I have to do everything myself?"

The students scattered in purposeful action. Helping Leyster try to staunch the flow of blood, Gertrude felt a small twinge of satisfaction. Work was the best thing for them, she knew.

Work would keep them all alive.

Daljit's injuries were too extensive to be successfully treated in the field. She died that night.

They buried her body next to the others with a minimum of ceremony. The graves were positioned away from the camp, to avoid drawing in predators, as well as for reasons of morale.

Then, to keep the crew from dwelling on their

loss, Gertrude set them to building log cabins for everyone. There was some grumbling because hers and Leyster's was bigger than the others. But they were a couple by then—they slept together for the first time the night of the disaster—and naturally they needed the room.

It was not difficult keeping everybody busy. There was more than enough work that needed doing, if they were to survive. The trick was to provide everybody with a sense of purpose. With so much equipment destroyed by the bomb, they couldn't hope to perform a fraction of the research they'd originally intended. Still, they could do some. At her instigation, Leyster built a blind on Barren Ridge where they could observe the tyrannosaur nest.

She and Leyster, being the best qualified, traded off on the tranny watch. Sometimes, as a reward for good work, she let one of the others assist.

Jamal came to Gertrude one day when she was in the blind. She was watching Boris and Bela, the runts of the clutch, mock-battling one another, snapping at each other's snouts until one of them got a purchase and they rolled over and over, kicking with their feet like kittens. "Fishing good?" she asked, without putting down the binoculars.

Young tyrannosaurs were a hoot to watch. They were curious about everything. A shiny pebble, a lizard they had never seen before, a mangled wristwatch hung from a limb in a place where Gertrude knew they would confront it—any novelty was a toy and a diversion to them. They would cock their heads and stare at it with their glittery little eyes.

Then they would kick at it with one taloned foot, if it were on the ground, and bump it with their heads if it were higher. Sooner or later, they'd try to eat it. Immature trannies would put anything in their mouths. They lost a lot of teeth that way.

Adults were different: surly, aloof. They reacted to anything new in their environment with disdain and suspicion. Their behavior was rigidly set. They avoided novelty in all its forms.

"Look," Jamal said. "Everybody's a little concerned about the way things are going."

She lowered the glasses. "We're alive. We have food. What's to complain about?"

"To put it bluntly, we do all the work, while you two get to sit around all day and make observations."

"You're grad students, for pity's sake. What else do you expect?"

"We're working our butts off. You should too."

What really irked her was the unfairness of his accusation. She and Leyster each worked twice as hard as any of the rest of them. But she bit down on her anger. "Leyster and I are the only fully trained researchers here."

"Just who are we doing all this research *for?* The beacon's smashed. We're never going home. Who's ever going to read our findings?"

"We're scientists. If we don't do any research, then why are we even here?"

"Sometimes I wonder," Jamal said grimly.

He turned and strode away.

That night, she told Leyster about the encounter.

Leyster looked drawn and pale. His responsibilities were wearing him down. "I don't know," he said. "Maybe he has a point."

"No, he does *not!* He's just an ambitious young beta male with delusions of alphahood. He wants power and double rations, is all. This whole thing stinks of primate politics."

"Yes, but maybe we should—"

She silenced his mouth with kisses. Then they made love. Leyster was not at his best that night, and immediately afterwards he fell into an exhausted slumber. But he really did love her. That sort of thing was impossible to fake.

A week later, Jamal walked away from the camp, taking half the expedition with him.

Only Lai-tsz, Gillian, and Patrick stayed. Katie, Nils, and Matthew went with Jamal. With them went all the supplies they could carry.

Their departure doubled the work load for everyone. Two camps needed two people to cook, two people to wash the dishes, twice the labor to make two of anything that was needed. They had to put off building the smokehouse indefinitely, though that would have saved them enormous labor in the long run by making it possible to store meat for more than a day at a time. It was insanely inefficient.

They gave up the tyrannosaur blind, of course. They had to. Science had become a luxury.

The dissidents didn't go far. They came back periodically, angry and sheepish, looking for tools or supplies they hadn't thought to bring along.

"The axes stay," Gertrude said the first time it happened. She figured the worse their privation, the sooner they'd come limping home. "They're not private property. They were bought for the expedition with public funds."

But Leyster, blind to the larger picture, said, "Of course you can have an axe, and anything else you need. We're not enemies, you know. We're all in this together." He still had notions of winning them over with kindness.

He was unworldly, was the problem. He was too good for his own good.

Things went from bad to worse. Gillian left them for the dissidents. Then, two months after the rift, Nils died in some kind of accident. The rebel camp didn't want to talk about it, so Gertrude never did find out the details. But they all got together for his funeral.

It was a tense encounter. The groups didn't mingle, but stood a way apart from each other. When Gertrude managed to get Katie aside and tried to talk her into coming back, she'd burst into tears. "Jamal wouldn't like it," she said, shaking her head. "You don't know what he's like when he's angry."

It was classic cult behavior: the charismatic leader whose word was law, the unreasoning obedience, the pervasive fear. Leyster wouldn't listen, but Gertrude grew convinced that Jamal was holding the others against their will, keeping them bound to him by psychological means.

Five months after the accident, they were barely managing to hang on. They'd all lost a lot of weight. Leyster in particular had deteriorated badly. He never smiled or joked anymore, and he sometimes went for days without speaking. It hurt Gertrude's heart to see him so diminished.

Then, six months less one day after the bomb, Patrick was killed, mobbed by a pack of small theropods while he was digging for turtle eggs.

He wouldn't have died if they'd been able to spare somebody with a spear and a sack of rocks to watch his back.

So, over the course of a long and sleepless night, Gertrude decided to take action.

The dissidents had built a trench latrine just far away enough from the new camp that they wouldn't be bothered by the flies and odors. Bright and early the next morning, Gertrude found a hiding place by the path leading to the latrine and settled down to wait.

First Katie walked up the path and back. Then Matthew. Jamal was third.

His face darkened when she stepped out in front of him. "What do you want?"

"I brought you a shovel."

She swung it at him as hard as she could.

A look of profound surprise overcame Jamal. He didn't even think to duck away from the blow. The blade of the shovel slammed against his shoulder and then, glancingly, the side of his head.

He staggered. She swept the shovel around again, at the back of his knees.

He fell.

"No, wait," he said weakly from the ground. He held one hand up in supplication. "For pity's sake, don't."

"Damn you!" Gertrude said. "You took everything that was good and fine and fucked it up. You filthy, ignorant son of a bitch." She was crying so hard she could barely see, and the corner of her mouth was bleeding. In all her wild swinging, she'd managed to cut herself with her ring. "Die, you bastard."

She raised the shovel in both hands, blade pointed at his throat. She had thought it would be difficult, but now that she came to it, she was so filled with rage that it was not difficult at all. It was the easiest thing in the world.

"Jamal!" somebody shouted joyfully. The voice came from behind her, from the new camp.

It was Leyster. He was running up the path, waving his arms.

"We've been rescued!" he shouted. "They're here! We . . ."

He saw her standing over Jamal, shovel raised, and came to a dead stop.

The story ended.

"So how did you wind up here?" Molly Gerhard asked.

"I put together a few rumors, and figured it out that whoever was in charge was headquartered in the very far future. So I stole Griffin's access card—"

"How?"

"It wasn't difficult." She glanced knowingly at Griffin. "I stole his card and took the funnel as far into the future as I could go. Then I cut a deal with the folks here."

"Just who are 'the folks here'? What are they like?"

"All in good time. It's easier to show than to explain. Wait a couple of hours and I'll arrange an introduction."

"There's one thing that makes no sense to me," Griffin said, leaning forward. "What's in it for you? When you changed your past, you also cut yourself free from it. Why did you do it?"

Gertrude lifted her head and stared down her nose at Griffin. Like a bird, Jimmy thought. Very much like a bird. "I wanted Leyster," she said. "I decided that if I couldn't have him in one time line, I'd have him in another."

She turned toward Salley, who seemed to shrink from her gaze. "I did it for you," Gertrude said triumphantly. "I did it all for you."

Salley stared down into her lap. She said nothing.

The sun was coming up over the ring forest. At Gertrude's invitation, they all went out onto the balcony.

The ring forest was a circle of green a mile across with open water at its center. It smelled as different from the forests Jimmy knew as an oak forest smelled different from a pine forest. Birds nested in the branches and fish swam among the roots. There were ponds and lakes within the forest, natural openings above which ternlike birds hovered and struck, sending up sharp white spikes of water as they penetrated the surface.

"This is lovely," Molly Gerhard said.

Gertrude nodded and, without a grain of irony, said, "You're welcome."

Jimmy Boyle remembered how, in an earlier age, Salley had gone on and on about the waterbushes and what a significant ecological development they were. He wondered if these things were their descendants. He supposed they were.

"The forests cover all the continental shallows," Gertrude said. "These trees are adapted for deeper water. Their holdfasts can't reach the ocean floor, so they serve as sea-anchors. They entangle, and form a rich variety of habitats sheltering many distinct species."

As she spoke, Griffin and Salley slipped away. They stood apart from the others, quietly talking. Jimmy positioned himself so he could unobtrusively eavesdrop, while still seeming to be listening to Gertrude.

"How long have you been here," Griffin asked, "with her?"

"One month."

"It must have been difficult."

Salley moved a little closer to him. "You have no idea," she said angrily. "That has to be the single most arrogant and self-centered and . . . and *manipulative* creature in existence."

Griffin smiled sadly. "You haven't met the Old Man yet."

"Oh God," Salley said. "I am so ashamed."

"You shouldn't be ashamed of something you did not do," Griffin said.

"But I am! I am! How could I not be, knowing that she's *me?*"

Suddenly Salley was crying. Griffin placed his arms around her, comfortingly, and she let him.

"It's funny," she said. "I swore to myself that I'd never let you touch me again, and yet here I am, clinging to you."

"Yeah," Griffin said. "Funny."

"I can't keep a single god-damned resolution I make," she said bitterly. "Not to save my life."

Jimmy moved away. There was nothing more to be learned here.

Gertrude was still talking, of course.

"Did you ever notice," she said, "how all the stations are set at the end of an age? Just before a major extinction event? Did you ever wonder why the station in Washington should be different?"

"Biologically speaking," Jimmy said, "our home age is in the middle of one of the greatest extinction events in the history of the planet. Even if not a single species more died off after our time, it would still be one of the Big Six." He'd been around scientists long enough to have picked up that much, anyway.

"Perhaps," Gertrude said. "Yet look around you. "We're extinct, humanity, I mean, and have been so for a long, long time."

"How?" Molly Gerhard whispered. "How did we die off?"

"That," Gertrude said firmly, "I'll leave as an exercise for the student."

There was an odd look on her face, triumphant and yet yearning. She was lonely, Jimmy realized. The old thing had been living here in splendid isolation so long she'd almost forgotten how to get along with other human beings. But she still felt the lack of their company.

He felt terribly sorry for her. But at the same time, he didn't feel called upon to do anything about it. That wasn't part of his job.

A chime sounded.

"What was that?" Molly Gerhard asked.

"It's time," Gertrude said, "to meet our sponsors."

The gate was located in a small room at the center of Gertrude's tower. Now a door opened, and one of the Unchanging emerged. "We have come," it said, "to take you to the meeting." To Gertrude: "Not you." To the others: "Now."

18

Peer Review

Lost Expedition Foothills: Mesozoic era. Cretaceous period. Senonian epoch. Maastrichtian age. 65 My B.C.E.

The raft trip down the Eden was slow and languid. They were not disturbed once by crocodilians, though they saw many. And because the migrations were not entirely over yet and the river meandered through more varied terrain than existed back in Happy Valley, Leyster was able to add several rare dinosaurs to his life list. He got clear sightings of betrachovenators, cryptoceratops, fubarodons, and jabberwockias. Once he even saw a *Cthuluraptor imperator* in all its terrifying splendor. They were species he had never seriously hoped to see, and it put him in a good mood.

Jamal was still a little weak from the aftereffects of his fever. But his broken leg had begun to knit over the weeks that it had taken to build the raft. He was looking forward to the day when the splint came off. There were times, in fact, when he insisted that his leg was already healed, and the thing could be removed immediately. But Daljit refused to allow it. "After everything I put up with, watching over you," she said, "I am *not* taking any chances a repeat performance. I am not going to be Florence fucking Nightingale ever again. Got that?"

They had considered other means of returning home, but settled on the raft as being the safest method of transporting Jamal. It broke Leyster's heart to cut up an entire coil of rope to lash the logs together, but there was no helping it. Tamara christened it the *John Ostrom,* after the man who had established dinosaurs as active creatures and the ancestors of birds, and she stuck an upright stick with a handful of bright dinosaur feathers tied to its tip between the logs at the bow for luck.

Their trip began early in the morning, when they loaded all their possessions onto the raft, loosed the moorings, and used long poles to push it out into the river. Water birds were diving for fish in the smooth brown water. They exploded into the air at the raft's approach.

Tamara stood at the stern manning the sweep, and Leyster squatted a few paces fore of her with a weighted line. Periodically he took a reading. The Eden was muddy, wide, and slow, which meant that it was also shallow in spots, and they were constantly in danger of running aground. Daljit and Jamal were both sunbathing at the front of the raft.

Leyster was thinking about the infrasound paper and idly admiring the sculptural beauty of their bodies, when a pterosaur's shadow touched the raft, then soared toward shore.

He turned quickly, and caught the briefest flash of the animal disappearing behind a massive bank of willows, into a rookery that he could hear but not see. In that lucid instant, everything came together for him.

Interspecific infrasound communication in a late Maastrichtian community of predator and prey species

"Okay, I'm ready to start composing the paper," Leyster announced.

Composition was, of necessity, a mental exercise. Of all their dwindling resources, the rarest and most valued was paper. They had communalized all notebooks and passed an iron law that nothing could be written in any of them without the consent of all.

As a result, Leyster had had to train his memory so he could compose their scientific papers in his head, recite them to the tribe to get their feedback, and then, only when all objections had been dealt with, transcribe the words in his tiniest, neatest hand.

"What's the title?" Tamara asked. Daljit and Jamal sat up to hear.

He told them.

"Not very catchy, is it?" Jamal said.

"It's not supposed to be catchy. It's supposed to convey information in as clear and specific a fashion as possible."

"Yeah, but . . ."

"Oh, Jamal just wants it to be commercial," Daljit said. "So he can license the gaming rights and market a set of plastic action figures to Burger King."

Jamal flushed. "I withdraw my objection."

She gave him a squeeze. "I'm just teasing you, sweetie-pie. I know you're not like that anymore." Then, as an afterthought, she said to Leyster, "You're not going to include Chuck's goofball notion, are you?"

"I might."

"Refresh my memory," Jamal said. "Exactly what was his theory again?"

"To begin with, he posited that since the major dinosaurs are capable of hearing infrasound, they would also be able to hear the mountains shifting and the continents moving underfoot. That movement is so slight and regular that they could then orient themselves by it. It would provide a sonic compass for their migrations—they'd simply head toward where the world sounded right to them.

"Now, when the Chicxulub impactor struck the Earth, it would have set up reverberations that lasted for years. That's elementary. Major earthquakes do that all the time.

"But Chuck speculated that, since the impact was so much greater than any earthquake, dinosaurs would then be deafened to the steady noises that tell them where they are. They wouldn't know where to go for the migrations. He further speculated that the noise might be great enough that they would no longer be able to communicate. Thus rendering their feeding strategies useless.

"Their very strengths would then be turned against themselves. Overadapted as they are, they could not survive the difficult times after the disaster. Less specialized taxons like crocodiles and birds manage to survive into the new era simply because they *are* less specialized. They could adapt, where non-avian dinosaurs could not."

Jamal shook his head. "Chuck was a sweet guy, but his theory is full of it."

"It is *not!*" Tamara said. "What's wrong with it?"

"It's not falsifiable, to begin with. There's no way you can test it."

"That's not—"

Leyster turned away from the others and returned his attention to the mountainous forests gliding by. The voices faded to a background murmur in his mind. Ahead, a grandfatherly old tanglewood tree stretched arthritic limbs out over the water. As they passed it, tree-divers—crocs no larger than his hand, with iridescent membranes stretched between their front and hind feet—rained down into the river. They launched themselves from the limbs, glided downbank in twisty aerial paths, and plunged into the water with a soft noise.

Plop. Plop. Ploplop. Plop. Ploploploploplop. Plop.

It was a rich world, filled with fascinating creatures he would never have time enough even to begin to study. Leyster sighed, and let his mind wander freely over the data they had gathered so far.

The central fact of their discovery came first. They had observed and then confirmed by instrumentation that several different species of dinosaur "spoke" to each other by means of infrasound. Rather than enumerate all the species they had documented as communicating in this manner, he synopsised them as "several major dinosaur groups." The species involved could be mentioned when he came to specific interactions, and this way was more concise.

The dirty little secret of scientific journals was that not only did they not pay for the papers they printed, the authors had to pay *them* a fixed rate of so much per page. Not that money alone could get you into a serious journal; you still had to write a paper that would get past peer review and impress the editors enough to want it. But, particularly if you were just starting out, you might delay publication of some papers for years, while waiting for your financial situation to clear up.

The system, for all its faults, did have one positive effect, though: It kept the papers terse. The irony was that now, when the economics of scientific journals was irrelevant, the limits of his ability to memorize text imposed an equally strict need for economy.

When he was satisfied with the wording, he announced that he'd come up with the first section of the paper, and recited it aloud. The others abandoned their argument to consider it.

"That should be 'field observations' rather than 'observations in the field,' " Daljit said. "It's shorter."

"Good thought. I'll change it."

"Why 'major dinosaur groups?' " Jamal asked. "Why not simply 'dinosaurs?' "

"Because we don't know that *all* dinosaurs engage in the behavior. In fact, we're pretty certain that some—birds—don't."

"Point taken."

The phone rang.

"Yes?" Tamara said. "It's Gillian," she told them. Then, to Gillian, "Leyster's working on the paper. Yes, already. Well, obviously he thought we had enough data. What? No! Well, it's about time. Hey, everybody! Lai-tsz's gone into labor!"

"She has?"

"You're kidding me."

"Outstanding!"

"They're all happy and everybody sends their love. When did it start? Uh-huh. How's she doing? Well, of course." She was silent for a bit, then said, "Okay, I'll ask him."

She turned to Leyster. "Gillian wants to know if you're going to use Chuck's theory."

The raft lurched. "Oh, cripes!" Daljit said. "Who's navigating?"

It took them over an hour to get the raft off the sand bar, and it was dirty and difficult work doing so. They all had to climb into the water (except Jamal, who stayed aboard and fretted) so the raft would ride higher in the water, and then wrangle it over toward deeper water.

Dirty and tired, and yet exhilarated by their eventual success, they shucked off their clothes and spread them out to dry. Daljit bullied them into raising poles at the rear and lashing a canvas to them to make a canopy to keep from getting sunburned.

They were amiably finishing up their comments on the opening of the paper—it was the simplest part, and there was the least room for disagreements of interpretation—when Tamara suddenly held a hand up and said, "Shhh!"

"What is it?" Leyster whispered.

She pointed to the left bank. A *Stygivenator molari* was walking briskly downriver along its margin, moving at a speed that kept it parallel to them. Every now and then it would glance over at them, its eyes bright and avaricious.

Leyster shivered involuntarily. A stygivenator was one of the larger predators, as large as a juvenile tyrannosaur but with the reflexes of an adult predator.

"What's it doing?" Jamal asked quietly.

"Pacing us," Leyster whispered back. Fortunately, most theropods were lousy swimmers.

"So what should we do about that?"

"Keep quiet, and be very careful not to let the raft drift too close to it."

Then the river bent, and they all had to frantically man the poles to keep the raft from running aground. The forest thickened at the bend, and the trees hung far out over the water, forcing the stygivenator inland. By the time they'd regained the center of the river, it was gone.

There were termite mounds on the right-hand side of the Eden—a metropolis of them. On the left, Leyster saw a marsh hopper prying open a freshwater clam with its tiny claws and furred paws. Suddenly a troodon that neither Leyster nor the marsh hopper had suspected was lurking there, snapped up the small mammal. It shook its head twice to snap the marsh hopper's spine, then lifted its neck and swallowed down the unfortunate animal whole.

While it was thus occupied, the stygivenator emerged from the wood, moving at top speed. Its jaws closed upon the troodon before the smaller predator knew what was happening. One crunch, and the bugger was dead.

It was an incredibly violent era, sustained only by the enormous number of offspring almost everything here produced. Which was what made it so astonishing that so many *did* reach adulthood. The network of interspecific cooperation—the tyrannosaur as farmer—resulted in a staggering efficiency, which allowed a greater population of the largest life forms than would otherwise be possible.

He couldn't help thinking again of Salley's talk, so long ago and so far in the future, when she had said that ceratopsians were farmed by their predators. He smiled. It was so typical of her to impress him with his own work. In some ways she was not a very good scientist: impatient with data, too ready to leap to conclusions, apt to judge an idea not by its merits but by its sheer niftiness.

But paleontology needed her, as leavening if nothing else. Science needed leapers as well as plodders, visionaries as well as detectives.

She was a kite. She needed only the most tenuous connection with the ground in order to fly, a sure string of logic with a reliable hand at the end of it to make sure she didn't take a nosedive straight into the ground. More than anything he wished he could be the hand at the end of her kite string.

Watching the banks flow by, he slid off into a reverie. He didn't notice when Jamal took the lead away from him, and moved to the bow to take readings. He didn't notice how careful the others were to avoid disturbing him.

The cycle began with the spring migrations, when flights of tyrannosaurs, living off their winter fat, spread across the land looking for territory to establish. These were the breeding males. The females followed at a more leisurely pace, sparing themselves the initial hardship, and arriving well-fed and ready to breed.

The Lord of the Valley (they could identify him by his scars) returned to claim the previous year's territory and, because he was experienced and in his prime, faced only a few challenges from younger males. He paced off the perimeter of his valley, singing, both to warn away competitors and to call in the titanosaurs.

The titanosaurs, those vast eating machines, drifted slowly through the valley, guided by its resident tyrannosaur toward the most productive areas. They stripped vast swaths of the upper-story vegetation, splintered trees, and enabled a bloom of understory vegetation. Now and then, the females deposited hundreds of eggs in a subsoil clutch before wandering away and forgetting about them entirely.

When the titanosaurs finally left, the understory was flourishing and the tyrannosaur was free at last to call in the herds of hadrosaurs and triceratopses.

Leyster held the whole in his mind now; he set about to boil it all down to the least number of words.

"Biocybernetic . . ." said Daljit. "*Is* there such a word?"

"There is now."

"Does it mean anything?"

"Actually," Jamal said, "The word *cybernetic* refers to feedback loops occurring not only in machines but also in and between living organisms. So there's really no need for the neologism."

Leyster blushed. It had been a long time since he'd been caught out in a mistake of terminology. "I'll change it."

"What I want to know," Tamara said, "is why you don't mention the incident Katie and Nils saw. With the troodons."

Katie and Nils had reported seeing a small flock of troodons actively drive some hadrosaurs away from a titanosaur nesting site. The savage little beasts, they reported, had rousted hadrosaurs ten times their size. They concluded that it had been done to protect the eggs.

"Its meaning is ambiguous," Leyster said.

"Not to Katie and Nils."

"Also, it only happened the once."

"That anybody saw."

Judiciously, Jamal said, "When you report the behavior, you say, 'It is possible that . . .' Where's the problem?"

"I *hate* to include speculation in a scientific paper."

There was a brief silence. "So," Tamara said. "I guess that means you're not going to include Chuck's speculation?"

"I didn't say that. I haven't made up my mind yet."

While Leyster thought about the paper and Daljit manned the sweep, Tamara trailed a fishing line, and caught a tiger-striped catfish. Jamal cleaned and gutted it, and they had sushi for dinner.

As they ate, they discussed the section of the paper which Leyster was working on. Here he got into more problematic behaviors.

The herds of hadrosaurs and triceratopses moved continually up and down the valley, feeding. Lai-tsz, whose ear for the sped-up recordings was better than the others', was able to establish that when the local vegetation was in danger of being overgrazed, the Lord or his Lady would seek out greener areas, and call the herds to them. Leyster had been skeptical of this at first, but then Lai-tsz had repeatedly demonstrated her ability to predict when the herds would disappear from established territory, and where they would go, based on the recordings. So he'd had to admit it was so.

He planned to cite this as an example of "ranching" behavior.

"Exactly what is the difference," Daljit asked, "between domestication and ranching?"

"Domestication is the process whereby the predator species have rendered the prey species docile to their will."

"Are you even sure they *are* domesticated?"

"Several times we've seen the Lord of the Valley approach a herd, of various species, singing. They huddle, with the young in the center. He walks around and around them. They turn to face him, cluster tighter, jostle each other. Tighter, closer, more assertive, until one individual gets expelled from the pack. Always the oldest, or weakest, or sickest. His Lordship surges forward, and—*snap!*—it's dead. Thirty minutes, start to finish." Leyster grinned. "Beats hunting, doesn't it?"

"Okay, and ranching?"

"Ranching is the set of behaviors by which it cares for the herds—moving them between pastures, keeping away rival predators, and so on."

"Well, you'll have to make sure that's spelled out clearly in the paper."

"Teach your grandmother to suck eggs."

They tied up for the night to a sandbar island overgrown by a snarl of young tanglewoods. Tamara waded ashore and chopped clear a section of the island to make a fire. She began to brew them some sassafras tea.

The phone rang.

"I'm not here," Leyster said. "If anybody asks, I'm at a meeting and you don't know when I'll be back in the office."

Daljit picked it up. She listened briefly, then put her hand over the receiver. "It's a *boy!*" she shouted.

Whoops and cheers.

Leyster took the phone. "So, does he look like anyone in particular?" he asked. Feeling a strange mixture of hope and apprehension.

"What does it matter?" Katie said. "We all love the little brat. You will too, as soon as you see him."

"I know it doesn't matter, I'm just curious. Come on, you'd ask the same question yourself, if you weren't there."

"Well . . . judging by the color of his skin, I'd have to say the father was either Jamal or Chuck."

"The father is either Chuck or Jamal," Leyster said, hand over the receiver.

"I'm a father?" Jamal said.

"*Maybe* a father," Leyster said.

"You're half a father," Daljit elaborated.

"I'm a fath!" Jamal said. "I'm a ther!"

He danced a clumsy little jig that made Daljit snap, "Watch the damn splint!" Tamra seized him, and kissed him deeply.

Leyster found that, for all he was happy for his friend, he felt a pang of jealousy as well. That could have been *his* son. The thought of what might have been stirred complex emotions within him.

The next morning, they cast off and headed downriver again. It was another beautiful day. Leyster felt alert and invigorated, and he had the paper pretty much whipped into shape by lunchtime.

Last of all, he composed the abstract:

Field observations reveal that major dinosaur groups in the late Maastrichtian communicated both intra- and interspecifically via infrasound. Communications between species are of particular note since they suggest cybernetic feedback loops operating within and helping to shape the ecosystem. Domestication and "ranching" behavior were observed. The advantages of this cooperative behavior to the predators are self-evident. Benefits to the prey species, though less obvious, are postulated to be equally compelling. It was a complex system working to the maximum benefit of all.

"I'm done," he said.

Jamal applauded. "Well, let's hear it!"

"No, I should give the first full reading to everyone. That's only fair."

Groans.

"You told us what you had yesterday," Daljit pointed out.

"Yes, but yesterday we were nowhere near our destination. Today we're—how far is it we have yet to go?"

The mapping satellite was low in the sky, but they were just able to get a location from it. Daljit and Jamal huddled briefly over the maps, argued, then concluded that they'd reach the confluence of the Eden and Styx rivers sometime in early afternoon.

"Well, that settles it. With any kind of luck, we should be home by nightfall. We can have the inquisition then, with everybody present." Leyster stood. "My turn at the sweep, I think.

Within the hour, the bioregion along the river was looking familiar. The land opened up. The towering forests retreated to the far distance, and the rich soil was overgrown with shrubs, ferns, and cycads, dotted with the occasional copse of hardwoods.

They were back in the farmlands.

It was this very familiarity, perhaps, which made them overly confident. Leyster was holding the raft steady in the gentle currents of the Eden, staring alertly ahead for shallow water, when Daljit said, "Uh-oh."

They had seen the triceratopses from a distance, studding the landscape like huge, placid cattle. It was only when they got close that the number of them registered, and they were able to see how restless the creatures were.

They were getting ready to ford the river.

Crossing water was not something that triceratopses did happily or often. They were afraid of the stuff, so they milled about, advancing and veering away, feinting at the river and then retreating from it, until they'd worked themselves up into such a frenzy of hysteria that they plunged into the river in a torrent of flesh, smashing anything unfortunate enough to be in their way.

Such as the raft.

"Maybe we'll slip past them," Jamal suggested quietly. Daljit put her hand over his mouth. When the brutes were in this state, they were easy to spook.

Silently the raft floated down past the herds. The river was straight here, and the current steady. It took the lightest of touches on the sweep to keep the raft on course.

It would have been bucolic, if it hadn't been for the terror they all shared.

Ten minutes passed. Twenty. At last they could see the end of the herds. They were almost out of danger now.

There was a noise behind them.

Daljit sucked in her breath.

Turning, Leyster saw a white spume of water, as the first stream of triceratopses plunged into the river. Galvanized, the body of the herd streamed up the bank to follow. Below them, a second stream of bodies entered the river. A third.

At the very end of the herds, just parallel with the raft, a fourth stream of triceratopses hit the water.

"Oh, fuck," Tamara said.

Briefly, there were horned dinosaurs all about them. Their massive bodies churned the water, rocking the raft. One of the brutes bumped against one side, making them all stagger. A second barely missed them on the left, brushing gently against the logs as it swam by. Then, because it was just the tag end of the herd and thus the smallest of the streams—two dozen, possibly three, of the beasts—it was over.

Except for one final triceratops.

The very last of the herd was too confused to veer away from them. It plunged straight ahead of itself, smashing into the raft and lifting one side up into the air.

The raft leaned, hesitated, and flipped over.

Everything was in flight. With what seemed to be excruciating slowness, Leyster saw their baskets and knapsacks, axes and smoked meat, tents, blankets, and cooking gear, all raining down into the water. Daljit had scrambled across the moving deck and launched herself into the river with a fast, flat dive. Tamara followed less surely, with her spear in one hand and a backpack in the other. Jamal went over in a tangle of limbs. Leyster saw him look astonished as his head struck the edge of the raft. He disappeared into the water.

"Jamal!" Leyster heard himself scream, and then he was in the water too.

Choking, he fought his way to the surface. There were logs everywhere, moving as if alive. Triceratopses splashed and surged, churning up the mud, and he discovered when his feet touched the bottom that the water was only chest-deep.

Jamal was nowhere to be seen.

He took a deep breath and plunged beneath the water again. He swam with his arms outstretched in the direction he thought he had last seen Jamal.

He kept his eyes open, but he saw nothing.

The water moved by slowly, and more slowly, and stopped. He burst through the surface again, gasping for air. His lungs burned and his chest ached. The river stretched to infinity to either side of him.

It was hopeless. There was not a chance in hell of finding Jamal in all this water.

One more time, he thought bleakly. One more dive, and I'll know for sure he's not going to be found.

He dove.

The brown water swam past him, as before. Then, abruptly, there was a darkness at its heart. His arms touched something soft, and at that same instant his face collided with Jamal's body.

Jamal wasn't moving.

He put his arms around the man's chest and strove for the surface. Almost instantly, his feet touched bottom and his head was in the air.

Suddenly, miraculously, the body in his arms shuddered.

Water exploded from Jamal's mouth, and he gasped for air. He began to struggle. Leyster found himself in danger of being fought down beneath the surface.

"You're okay!" he shouted. "You're fine! Just let me walk you to shore!"

Jamal twisted in his arms. "I'm what?"

"You're okay!"

Jamal stopped moving. Then, with enormous effort, he said, "You've got one hell of a strange idea of okay."

Laughing and gasping, they stumbled to the shore. Daljit appeared under Jamal's other arm, and together they carried him in.

"I'm fine!" Jamal protested weakly. "I'm fine, really."

Tamara appeared, carrying a wet pack. "I managed to save one." She held up the pack, looking embarrassed and wild. "But the others are lost. I'm sorry."

Leyster thought of all that had gone down to the bottom of the river: the two cell phones, both axes, all their shoes. So much of it was irreplaceable. But he couldn't manage to feel the loss.

He still had one arm around Jamal's shoulders. Now he lifted the other and Tamara, dropping the pack, slipped under it. They all four of them gathered together in one hug, then, teary and unashamedly sentimental. "We got off easy," Leyster said. "We got off easy."

So they had. He knew in that instant that he would have given every axe they had to keep Jamal alive.

And in that same instant, he mentally added to the abstract:

It is possible that by its very success, this cooperative behavior contributed to the extinction of the non-avian dinosaurs at the K-T boundary.

19

Lazarus Taxon

Carnival Station: Mesozoic era. Jurassic period. Dogger epoch. Aalenian age. 177 My B.C.E.

The Old Man sat in a dark room, alone.

The world outside was arguably the most interesting time in all the Mesozoic, an age when dinosaurs were challenged from a surprising direction, almost lost their place in the ecosystem, and then successfully fought their way back to dominance again. He did not give it a thought. All his attention was focused on the visions he called up, one after another, in the air before him. He had been given tools that were inexplicable in their effects. The one he was using now enabled him to eavesdrop on select events that were, to him, of particular interest. It was like owning God's own television set. So far as he knew, he was the only human being who had one.

Half a billion years in his future, Griffin and company were finally about to meet their sponsors. They stepped through a gate and onto the same grassy sward where they had first set foot in the Epimethean.

He leaned forward, and all his surroundings vanished as his identity dissolved into theirs.

Jimmy's "climbing trees" were further from the gates than any of the party had thought. The tangle was as tall as a cathedral, and as complexly buttressed. The closer they got, the more elaborately structured it appeared, and the less like anything they had ever seen before.

The Unchanging led the company into the shelter of the trees. They walked down twisty pathways into ever-deepening shadows. There were rustling noises and furtive movements all about them. A great many living things dwelled here.

"I can't decide if this is natural or artificial," Molly Gerhard said, gesturing toward a splay of branches that spiraled up one trunk like a staircase. Water dripped down from above to fill a basin that grew out from another trunk, level with her chin. A drinking fountain for very tall children? "Or whether that's even a valid distinction here."

"What's that smell?" Jimmy asked.

The tree was permeated with a sweet and sickish stench, reminiscent of theropod hatchlings before they've lost their down, of maple syrup on sweaty flesh, of zoo cages never perfectly cleaned. It was an uneasy-making smell.

Something dropped from an opening above, and stood before them for the briefest of moments.

It was humanoid only by the most generous reading of the term: bipedal, upright, with two arms, a trunk, and a head, all in the right places. But the arms folded oddly, the trunk canted forward, the legs were too short, and the head was beaked.

It favored them with an outraged stare, stamped its spurred feet, and *screeched*. Then it was gone.

"Dear God!" Molly Gerhard gasped.

"What the fuck was *that?*"

"Avihomo sapiens," Salley said. "The second intelligent species ever to arise on this planet. Gertrude calls them Bird Men."

"Birds," Griffin said flatly. "They're descended from birds?"

"Yes. I'm afraid we mammals have been relegated to the evolutionary fringes once again."

The Unchanging gestured toward an arched cleft. "This way," it said.

They stepped through and the tree opened up. Branches intertwined overhead to create a high ceiling. Soft globes of light floated among them, gently illuminating the space below. At the center of the room was a table. Behind it, their hosts stood waiting.

There were three Bird Men, ungainly and proud. The least of them was half again as tall as the humans. They were covered with fine black feathers that rose to a spiky crest at the backs of their commodious skulls. Their beaks were white as sun-bleached bone. Their eyes were stark red.

Their arms, scrawny and oddly jointed, were

much like those of mantises but with the long hands bent downward. They were nothing like wings; their kind had clearly lost the ability to fly long ages ago. It seemed to more than one of the party a sacrifice much greater than that made by their own ancestral hominids when they descended from the trees.

One of the Bird Men shook its head rapidly, then made a low, chuckling noise.

"I will translate," the Unchanging said.

The Bird Men's faces were unreadable; they displayed no visible sign of emotion save for the fast sudden movements of their heads. The one which had spoken before made a brief warbling sound.

"He says: We know why you are here. We know what you want."

Griffin cleared his throat. "Well?"

"He says: No."

"No?" Griffin said. "What do you mean, no?"

There was a prolonged exchange between the Unchanging and its masters. Then it said, "He says: No means no. No. You cannot have what you came here for."

Griffin sucked in his cheeks, thinking. Then he said, "Perhaps we're getting a little ahead of ourselves. Let's start at the beginning, shall we?"

The Old Man leaned back in his chair with a wry smile of appreciation. This was an elementary tactic of bureaucratic infighting: When somebody won't give you what you want, pretend you think he simply doesn't understand what you're asking for, go back to the beginning of your argument, and go over every aspect of your case again in excruciating detail. Then repeat. It was trial by boredom: Sooner or later, somebody would give in.

He had spent many hundreds of hours of his life locked in exactly such combat with a counterpart from DOD or GAO, slamming heads together like two bull pachycephalosaurs.

It wouldn't work this time, though. The Bird Men were simply too far divergent from the human genome. They were immune to primate psychology. They didn't even understand how it worked.

He delicately slid the time forward an hour, and leaned back into the narrative.

"He says: That is what we did. It can be traced in time as a four-dimensional spiral. Was there an alternative? No. We could have done otherwise, but we decided not to."

"What," Salley said, "the fuck does *that* mean?"

Griffin made a hushing gesture. "Can you clarify?"

One of the Bird Men, the tallest, slammed a hand down on the table with emphatic violence.

"She says: Why are we discussing this when otherwise, we are not discussing this?"

The humans exchanged glances. "Perhaps," Griffin said, "you are suggesting that there is no such thing as free will?"

The Bird Men clustered, heads darting so emphatically that it seemed miraculous that none of them was stabbed by their slashing beaks.

"They say: It is free, yes. But is it will?"

That small part of the Old Man that remained himself while he was immersed in the experience, felt an old and familiar exasperation. If a lion could talk, Wittgenstein said, we couldn't understand it. It was true. He had dealt with the Bird Men countless times, and their thoughts were not like human thoughts. They did not translate well. Perhaps they could not be translated at all.

The Unchanging were merely obstinate and maddeningly unimaginative. The Bird Men processed information in a manner completely alien to human thought. Only rarely was there true understanding between the two species.

There was a knock on the door. Jimmy stuck his head in. "Sir?"

He withdrew from the experience. "What is it?"

"You asked me to tell you when we had Robo Boy's confession."

"Well, it hardly matters now. Did he name his superiors?"

"Oh, yes. He sang like a canary, sir. He sang like Enrico fucking Caruso. We've been in contact with the FBI. They say it won't be any trouble getting the warrants."

"That's something, I suppose." He waved Jimmy out of the room and slid the time forward another hour.

The humans were sitting on chairs now. They had finally thought to ask for them. All of them but Griffin looked annoyed and resentful. Only he had enough experience hiding both anger and humiliation to hold himself with aplomb.

"Explain your project to us."

Here at last was the core question. The Old Man leaned out of the conversation. What followed was necessary for their understanding. But it was old news to him, and he didn't care to hear it again.

The Bird Men had given time travel to humanity for one reason: in order to study human beings. The gift enabled them to place the Unchanging, a tool designed to be minimally disruptive, in close proximity to humans, so that it could observe and record their behavior.

But there was a second reason for the gift as well.

The Bird Men wanted to study humans engaged in typical human activity. Their curiosity was broad-ranging, but by logging the comings and goings of the Unchanging, the Old Man had been able to determine that the two activities they considered quintessentially human were bureaucracy and scientific investigation.

Of the two, they were significantly more interested in science. So they had created a controlled situation in which humans might engage in it. They had given them the Mesozoic.

This pleased him almost as much as it had pleased him, as a child, to learn that dolphins genuinely *liked* people. Human beings could be real jerks. It was encouraging that another species deemed them worth liking. It was reassuring that somebody with nothing at stake believed that finding things out was central to the human enterprise.

It made him feel vindicated.

He slid the vision up to the end of the explanation, and then froze time motionless while he wrote and posted a memo. When he unfroze the vision, a second Unchanging came in and said a few words.

Salley and Molly Gerhard followed it out of the room.

It was a small act of mercy on his part. The conference would go on for hours, and they were both bored to tears. So he'd arranged for them to be given a small tour.

"Look!" Molly Gerhard said. "Little models of floating towers, like the one we were on."

"No." Salley pulled one from the water, and held it up so the other woman could see the underwater bulb that gave the tower it buoyancy, and the tangle of holdfasts that rendered it stable. "They're not models. They're saplings."

They were deep in the tangled roots of the Bird Men's cathedral habitat, and so of course there were many, many pools of water. They were black and still. The air above them smelled of cedar.

"So you're saying they *grew*—"

A Bird Man burst from the water, neck extended. Molly Gerhard gasped and drew back in alarm. The creature strode from the water, shook itself like a duck, and then disappeared down a corridor.

The Old Man skipped ahead. Now the two women were high in the crown of the tree. Gold coins of sunlight danced all about them as a light breeze stirred the branches overhead.

Molly Gerhard wrinkled her nose. "With all

their technology, you'd think they'd do better." There were white-streaked nests all about them, carelessly made things filled with the din of screeching hatchling Bird Men.

"You have to look at it from their perspective," Salley said without conviction. Then she shrugged. "I—"

He skipped ahead again.

Now they were standing on a parapet not far from the top of the trees. The Unchanging gestured to direct their attention outward, toward the horizon. Molly Gerhard turned, laughing, and froze with astonishment and awe. Salley stood silent behind her.

Impatiently, the Old Man switched his attention back to Griffin and Jimmy. He was not interested in mere wonder. What he cared about was results.

"He says: Yes, we could give you the equipment you request. Yes, you could rescue your friends. Not at the first resilience point. Not at six months. That is on record as not having happened. But at the second resilience point. At two years.

"But you would not want it."

Griffin straightened. Hours had passed. He was visibly weary. "What do you mean? Of course we want the equipment. Thank you. We'll take it."

There was a very long silence.

"Why *wouldn't* we want it?" Jimmy asked.

Now there came a low growl so uncertain that Griffin could not tell which of the three had made it.

"He says: You would not want it because the project is over."

"What?"

"He says: The line in which we gave you time travel is being negated."

"When?"

"He says: Immediately after this conversation."

There was a certain amount of squabbling and logic-chopping following the Bird Men's revelation, simply because to argue was human. It would do no good. The Old Man skipped over most of it.

"But what about Gertrude? *She's* from another time line, and yet I met her," Salley was saying when he dropped back into her consciousness. The Old Man had made sure she and Molly both would be back for the end of the discussion. "Surely that proves you can reconcile time lines. So why close down ours? Why can't you do the same thing—whatever it was—for us?"

The Bird Man spoke for a long time.

The Unchanging said, "She says: It was only temporary. Even if it were possible, it would not be possible."

"I'm not following this."

"She says: The time line that contains our field of study contains us as well. We knew this from the start. We knew that to study you meant that we must ourselves dissolve into timelike loops when the work is done. That is the price. Time travel is not available under any other terms."

"Then why?" Jimmy asked. "Why bother at all?"

The Bird Man jabbed a beak first at Salley and then at Griffin. "She says: *They* understand."

One of the Bird Men turned, and walked to the

back of the room. A second followed him. There was a still pool of water there. One after the other, they plunged into it and were gone.

Before the third could start after them, Griffin said, "Listen to me!"

It peered at him intently.

"If it doesn't matter . . . If nothing matters . . . Then give us the machines so we can rescue our friends."

The Bird Man and the Unchanging exchanged what sounded like clucks and squawks.

"She says: Why?"

"It's a human thing. You wouldn't understand."

The Bird Man screamed, a noise so loud it made their ears hurt.

There was a long silence, while the four humans resigned themselves to failure, and then at last the Unchanging spoke. "She says: It shall be done." It paused. "Also, it has been—" It paused again. "A rare honor. To stand in the presence of a human being. How beautiful you are. How delightful in your curiosity and your courage both."

The Bird Man made a rattling sound.

"She says: You are scientists. She also is a scientist. All her life she has spent trying to understand mammals."

A shriek.

"She says: You are noble creatures. The world is a poorer place without you."

The Bird Man unfolded one grotesque forelimb and stretched it across the table. The three fingers on its terrifying hand separated, extended.

"She says: Can we shake hands?"

* * *

The Old Man toyed with the idea of following Griffin's company on their journey home, and decided against it. He shut down the one vision, and called up another. A window opened on the latter days of the Maastrichtian, a mere hundred and twenty-two million years in his future.

It was the day they had chosen for their harvest festival, and the camp was filled with the smell of a whole young ankylosaur roasting slowly on a spit over a bed of coals.

Leyster was sitting in the long house scraping swamp tubers and idly watching Nathaniel play with a rattle Patrick had made him. Daljit was plucking a small feathered dino. He glanced at the carcass in her hands and froze. "That's not a . . . what *is* that thing?"

"It's just a nothing-special little brush dino. It'll make a nice side dish."

"No, seriously. I don't recognize it. Is that a new species? Let me see its teeth."

"No dissecting dinner!" Katie laughed. She was taking palm leaves from the kettle where they'd been soaking, and wrapping them around the scraped tubers, so they could be baked in the coals. "Keep scraping."

"Oh, come on. It has to be gutted anyway. It could be significant."

Daljit put the carcass down. "Listen," she said tensely.

"I don't . . ." Katie said.

"Shush!"

From outside, there came the sound of voices. They were not familiar.

"Oh God, where's my blouse?" Daljit cried.

Katie scooped up the baby and ran outside without saying a word.

Leyster was the second out the door. Daljit came close on his heels, buttoning furiously.

Their rescuers were U.S. military, for the most part, young men with short hair and socially awkward demeanor. But they'd brought along a documentary camerawoman, and she was already moving among the paleontologists, interviewing them.

"What is the one thing you most regret?" she asked, camera on her shoulder. Several of the tribe hung back shyly, intimidated by the novelty of an unfamiliar face. She pointed her microphone at Jamal. "You?"

"I guess the thing I most regret is that we didn't bring along a botanist. There's a prejudice in our field in favor of animals, vertebrates in particular, and we certainly paid the price for that. We really could have used somebody who was familiar with the properties of the local plants."

"Amen to that!" Katie said fervently. "There must be something around here with tannin in it. Do you have any idea how difficult brain tanning can be? And dyes! Don't get me started on dyes."

"And you?"

"I'm sorry I never managed to make a decent clay pot," Daljit said. "The kiln was good. I just couldn't manage to get the right clay or the right temperature."

"You?"

"I'm sorry I didn't bring along a spare time beacon," Nils said. Everybody laughed. Then, more seriously, "If I'd known how long I was going to be stuck here, I would've brought along a lot more pharmaceuticals. And I would have learned some crafts."

"Like what?"

"Like how to make knap flint. Have you ever tried to make a flint knife? It's not easy!"

"What," the woman asked, focusing her camera first on Nathaniel and then panning up to Katie's face, "is the first thing you plan to get or do when you get back to the present?"

"I want a steak."

"A milkshake!"

"A cup of tea—with lemon and extra sugar."

"A shower! With hot water!"

"Oh, yes."

"I'm going to turn off my brain and sit down in front of the television for a week."

"I'm going to read a book I've never read before."

"I'm going to talk to a stranger!"

Standing apart from the others, Leyster muttered fervently, "I'm going to kill Griffin for putting us through all this. Then, if there's time, I'll get Robo Boy as well."

But he spoke quietly, to himself. Only the Old Man heard him. And when, a half hour later, the coals soaked with water and the half-roasted ankylosaur laid out for the scavengers, they lined up to step through the gate and out into the Crystal

Gateway Marriott, Crystal City, Virginia, only he saw Leyster very carefully pick up a rock and slip it in his pocket.

The Old Man sighed, and opened the file folder on the desk before him. There were eight memos within. He read through them all carefully, then lifted one between thumb and forefinger and tore it in half.

Things had worked out much better the second time around. There had only been two deaths. He had to admire Leyster for that. The man had done much better with his charges than he had the first time through.

He regretted Lydia Pell's death, of course, and that of the young man as well. But what was done was done. Second chances were so rare in this world to be almost miracles.

He decided to take one last look at Gertrude, solitary and splendid. She was a *rara avis*, perhaps the rarest in his private aviary of colleagues, and he liked to look in on the old bird from time to time.

A Lazarus taxon was one that disappeared from the fossil record, as if extinct, only to reappear later, as if rising from the dead. It pleased him to think of Dr. Gertrude Salley as humanity's own Lazarus taxon. So long as she existed, the human race wasn't really dead. Occasionally he paid her a visit, just to maintain her tenuous connection with humanity.

Sometimes they played chess. He always won.

Thus reminiscing, he opened a window into Gertrude's tower, where she sat at her writing desk, working. Once, when he had done so, she had sensed his presence (she also had been given extraordinary tools) and, looking him directly in the eye, winked sardonically. Not today, though.

It was just as well. This was too solemn a day for laughter. This was the day when everything ended.

He signed off on the last of the memos, and dumped them into the tray for outgoing mail. The enterprise was over. As of this instant, he was as good as retired.

Slowly, he stood. The leather chair creaked as he did so, as if in sympathy for him. His body ached, but such pains came naturally with age. He was used to them.

There was only one thing left to be done.

20

Extinction Event

Crystal City, Virginia: Cenozoic era. Quaternary period. Holocene epoch. Modern age. 2012 C.E.

If the story could be said to have any end at all, then it ended on a bright spring day in Crystal City at the Crystal Gateway Marriott when some two hundred paleontologists gathered by invitation in the ballroom to watch army personnel assemble machinery unlike anything any of them had ever seen before and open a temporary gate through time.

"Stand back, please," an officer said. There was some shuffling about, but nobody moved away. "Please! Gentlemen. Ladies." He was clearly unused to dealing with civilians, and his urgings had little effect. Finally, exasperated, he turned to his second-in-command and muttered, "Oh, the fuck with it. Throw the goddamned switch."

The switch was thrown.

Something hummed.

There was a flat metal plate on the floor, connected by thick cables to the alien equipment. The air above it puckered, crinkled, gleamed. A flat, circular area filled with sunshine as it opened into a brighter reality. The scientists squinted and shaded their eyes with their hands, straining to get a good look at what was happening.

"I think I see—" somebody began, and was silenced by a chorus of shushings.

Through that glowing disk stepped, one by one, the survivors of the stranded expedition. Leyster came first, scowling and clutching their field notes, and Tamara after him, with her spear. Jamal burst into a smile as he saw everybody waiting for them. Then came Lai-tsz, looking anxious, with Nathaniel on her shoulder, and after her Patrick, Daljit, and all the rest.

Somebody began to applaud softly.

Everyone joined in. A roar like surf filled the ballroom.

A bald old man with a flamboyant white mustache hobbled forward and, with the utmost respect, took the notebooks from Leyster's hands. Then, with sudden flair, he raised them high over his head, grinning.

The applause redoubled.

Tamara was clutching her spear tightly in one hand, blinking at the flashing cameras and feeling disoriented, when she was suddenly overcome with the awareness of how bad she must smell. She looked around the ballroom, and then at the spear, and in a fit of revulsion, said, "Somebody take this thing away from me."

A dozen hands reached for it. "We'd like to include this in one of our displays, if you'd allow us," a woman said. A lifetime ago, Tamara had known her. Linda Deck, was that her name? Something like that. From the Smithsonian. "And . . . maybe your necklace?"

Tamara touched the tooth that Patrick had pierced for a length of cord and scrimshawed with a rather good likeness of the photo of her standing triumphant above the juvenile tranny. She flashed her teeth, and in a low, intense voice, said, "Over my dead body."

The woman took a step back in alarm, and in a moment of sudden empathy Tamara realized just how *fierce* they had all become. "Hey, never mind me," she said, as kindly as she could. "Just point me toward a shower and three bars of soap, and I'll be fine."

"We've booked a room for you." The woman handed her a key card. "We booked rooms for everybody. There's fresh clothes in there, too. Things you picked out for yourself next week."

"Thanks," Tamara said. "Keep the spear."

Patrick carried his photo disks, wrapped with obsessive care in scraps of their softest troodon leather, in both hands. All the storage space on them had been used, and much of it had been overwritten three to seventeen times. A man in a suit started to take them away from him and then, when he yanked his arms away, laughed and said, "Now, is that any way to treat your editor?"

"What?"

The man took the disks and gave him a presentation copy of the book that would be made from them. Disbelieving, Patrick leafed through it. Ankylosaurs wallowed in the river mud. A tyrannosaur looked up suspiciously from its kill, blood streaming from open jaws. Pterosaurs skimmed low over the silvery surface of a lake. An unlucky dromaeosaur was caught in the act of being trampled under the feet of a charging triceratops.

He looked up from a photograph of titanosaurs at dusk. "This was printed too dark. You can't make out the details."

"Now, Patrick, we've already been through all—" The editor stopped. "At any rate, *I've* been through all that already, and I'm not really anxious to go over it again, particularly on a Sunday. Tomorrow morning you can drop by my office and start raising hell over color values. You'll come over to my side by the end." Then, ignoring Patrick's obstinate look, "Let me buy you a drink. I'll bet it's been a long time since you've had a beer."

Lai-tsz had been worried that her son would be frightened by the flash cameras, the noise, and the pervasive unfamiliarity of an age dominated by humans and their technology. She held Nathaniel in her arms, watching him crane about, those big brown eyes drinking everything in with calm intelligence. Then somebody stepped forward with a bouquet of Mylar balloons, and presented them to her.

Nathaniel laughed and crowed at the sight of them.

The modern world didn't faze him a bit.

She was completely involved in her son's wonderment when a tall and lanky young man walked up to her and said, "Hi, Mom."

He enfolded the astonished Lai-tsz in his arms and kissed her on the forehead. "My little mother," he said fondly. Then, "Hey, is this me?" He scooped up Nathaniel and hoisted him into the air, the both of them laughing. "I sure was a cute little fellow, wasn't I?"

Jamal was luxuriating in the simple privilege of being home again, when a woman presented him with her business card. "I was told you'd be the one to speak to," she said. "You fellows have lived through an extraordinary adventure, and I think it only fair to warn you that the buzzards will be circling soon. You need representation."

"Representation?" he said blankly.

"An agent. You've got an incredibly valuable story here. Don't throw it away on the first media offer you get."

A minute ago, he had been thinking how strange it would be to inhabit a commercial universe once more, and how lacking in the requisite skills he would be. Now, in an instant, they all came flooding back.

The first thing to do was to establish Nathaniel as a member of the expedition, and set up a trust fund to handle his share of the income. That way, if everybody got weird later on, the expense of his upbringing wouldn't all fall on Lai-tsz. Come what may, his education would be taken care of.

That presupposed, of course, that they maximized income now, while public interest was at its greatest.

He took the woman's arm. "Let's talk numbers, shall we?"

Katie and Nils seized a quiet moment and slipped away from the others, out into the hallway, to talk.

"It's kind of the end of an era, isn't it?" Nils said.

"Yeah. Were you listening to that woman who was with Jamal? She was saying something about making a movie out of what happened to us."

"Well, if there's a movie, I guess there's parts that'll have to be left out."

"You mean, uh . . . ?" She blushed ever so slightly.

"Yeah." He dug a toe awkwardly into the carpet. "I guess that's another thing that's come to an end. I mean, I can't imagine us all renting a big suite of rooms and . . ."

"No."

"It would be tacky. Like those swingers' clubs they had back in the last century."

"Yes."

"But you know . . ." He took a deep breath, and finally met her eyes. "Just because everybody else is breaking up doesn't mean that we . . . That you and I . . ."

It took them some time, and a great many words more. But they finally arrived at the understanding they had each known all along they would.

Raymond Bois, standing in the crowd, realized suddenly that there were security people standing to either side of him. He took a step backwards, and bumped into somebody. The Irishman put a hand on his shoulder and said, "Steady there, son."

The man's grip was firm to the point of being painful. Raymond Bois looked wildly beyond him, and there was somebody who could only be Molly Gerhard, though she looked decades older than she had the last time he'd seen her.

"Good to see you, Robo Boy," she said. "It's been a long time."

Her eyes were like flint.

Gillian and Matthew were hustled away from the others by a quiet-voiced security officer, who identified himself as Tom Navarro. "This will only take a moment," he said. "We need you to make an identification. We have reason to believe that the terrorist who planted the bomb that killed Lydia Pell is present in this room. If you would be so kind as to take a quick glance around—"

He stopped, placing them directly in front of Raymond Bois.

"My God," Gillian said. "That's him!"

"It's Robo Boy!" Matthew said. He was dimly aware that a woman with a digicam was filming them, but paid her no mind. "He's the one! He left a message, we all saw it, we'll all of us testify to that. I—"

But already, as if all that were needed was their nod, Robo Boy was being taken away, kicking and struggling, by the security people. "It wasn't me!" he cried in a panicked voice. "I didn't do anything!" He tried to bite one of them, and was punched in the stomach. He doubled over in pain, weeping, as they half-carried him rapidly toward the door. The camerawoman scuttled along, focused tight on his face.

"Thank you," Tom Navarro said. "That will be all."

Amy Cho leaned heavily on her cane. Her hip ached. She had put off her operation in order to be here, and now she regretted it. A martyr, however mistaken in his cause, should go sweetly to his fate. He should put his faith and trust in God, and consign everything else to the Devil. He should be an inspiration to the world.

Raymond Bois was a terrible disappointment to her.

She wasn't as fast as she used to be. The best she could do was a kind of difficult and painful shuffle, no faster than a healthy person's normal stride. Nonetheless, she hurried to intercept the security people. "Wait!" she demanded. "I have something to say."

Jimmy Boyle recognized her voice, and stopped for her. Turning, his people held up their sobbing prisoner so she could see him. The camerawoman stepped back to get them both in frame.

Amy Cho had raised her cane wrathfully, as if she were about to bring its knob down upon the young man's head. "Stop blubbering! Paul was arrested in Antioch and in Ephesus and in Rome and God only knows where else, and yet it only strengthened his faith. He endured persecution. He reveled in his suffering. Can you do less?"

Robo Boy gaped stupidly at her.

She shook her cane furiously. "You have murdered and you have deceived and you have been weak in your faith. You must pray, young man. Pray for forgiveness! Pray for redemption! Pray for the restoration of your faith!"

Amy Cho was a firm believer in the redemptive power of faith. God didn't require that you read His will correctly in every particular in order to be accepted as His own. She could easily imagine a Crusader and one of Saladin's knights being welcomed into Heaven together, Christian and Mohammedan both, though they had died at each other's hands. "Tell me you'll pray to the Lord, damn you. *Tell* me you will!"

Raymond Bois straightened in the arms of his captors. He squeezed tight his eyes, and then gave his head a shake to free them of tears.

Then, curtly, he nodded.

Amy Cho stepped aside, and the security people took him away.

Maybe, she reflected, there was hope for him after all. God never gave up on anybody, not even the least of His creations. Nor must she. She would visit Robo Boy in prison. She would explain a few things to him. She would show him where he had gone wrong.

Incarceration could well turn out to be the best thing that ever happened to the boy.

Daljit felt as if she were both here and someplace else entirely. Everything was strange to her. She was slowly coming to the realization that she didn't belong in the modern world anymore. Not that she wanted to go back. Not really. Not yet.

Still . . . the greatest adventure of her life was over and done for. She had returned from Never-Never Land, from Middle-earth, from El Dorado. The dragons were slain, the treasures dug up and hauled away in wagons, the swords and bright banners packed in trunks and stowed in the attic. Nothing she ever did would ever be as vivid and meaningful again.

She couldn't help but feel saddened by that.

She had been happy in the Maastrichtian. It had been a lot of work and suffering, sure. But there were satisfactions. Time and again, she had proved her own competence both to herself and to the others.

She might not be the jock Tamara was, but she had good survival skills. She knew how to make seven different kinds of snares and deadfalls. She could catch fish by hook, spear, or by hand. She could skin and butcher a fresh-killed hadrosaur and get away with as much meat as she could carry in less time than it took for the predators to arrive. She might not be the paleontologist Leyster was, but she could identify almost any dinosaur by sight or sound or, in some cases, smell. Most of the herbivores she could identify by flavor. She could pick up a shed tooth and identify not only its former owner, but where it had been in the jaw, and make a few shrewd guesses as to the creature's age and health.

She could build a house and know it would stand up. She could sing a song in an entertaining manner. She had re-invented the loom, working from half-forgotten memories of a model she had made as a girl, and then she had taught herself and the others how to use it.

More than that, she had gone rafting down the Eden. She had faced down the largest animals ever to walk the Earth. She had tended to a dying woman in her final days and nursed an ailing man back to health. She had known tears and laughter, toil, love, sweat, and danger.

These were the primal satisfactions, the things that made life matter. What did Washington, D.C., in the twenty-first century have to offer that could compare with them?

Patrick came up from behind and linked arms with her.

"Come on," he said. "This poor, deluded fool is my editor"—the man smiled and nodded—"and, being pig-ignorant of the drinking habits of paleontologists, he has rashly promised to buy us all the beer we want. There's an Orioles game going on right now, and he tells me the bar has a wide-screen TV with state-of-the-art speakers. It just doesn't get any better than that."

She let herself be led away. "Do they have baskets of those little pretzels?" she asked anxiously. "It's not really a proper game without them."

"Not to worry," the editor said soothingly, "If they don't, we can always send out for some."

Leyster had spotted Griffin standing against the far wall of the auditorium, and automatically taken the stone out of his pocket. Now, unobtrusively, he put it back. Whatever inchoate plan he might have had for vengeance had disappeared in an instant. He was in a different world now. That wasn't how things were done here.

There were people everywhere about him, hands grabbing at him, voices making demands on his attention. It was hard sorting them all out. Somebody thrust a pen and an open copy of *Science* at him, and it was only after several had been signed and snatched away that it registered on him that he was autographing copies of the infrasound paper.

He needed air.

"Excuse me," he said, moving toward the hall. "Excuse me, please. Excuse me." He'd always hated crowds; how had he gotten away from them in the past? "I need to use the men's room."

"End of the hall to the left," somebody said.

"Thanks."

He fled.

There were people in the hall too, though not nearly so many as in the ballroom. Most were strangers. One, however, he recognized.

Salley.

He walked straight toward her, heart pounding, not knowing what he was going to do when he arrived. She stared at him, her eyes stricken, fearful, like a sacrifice waiting for the knife, or a woman who knows that someone is about to hit her.

Wordlessly, he took her hand and led her away.

They went into a blind fuck on the floor of the hotel room, just inside the door. It was fast and hard, and when they were done, their clothes were in tatters and Leyster realized that the door was not entirely closed. He kicked it shut, and in so doing found that he still had his shoes on.

So they untangled themselves and began removing those items of clothing that had been pushed out of the way rather than removed or (in some cases) ripped to shreds. "My poor blouse," Salley said. She wriggled out of the panties that Leyster, too impatient to wait, had ripped down the crotch. "I'll have to send out for new clothes."

"Don't do it for my sake," Leyster said. "I like you just fine the way you are."

"Beast," she said lovingly. "Brute." She picked up the complimentary newspaper they'd kicked aside on their way in, and aimed a swat at his head.

Leyster wrestled the paper from her hand, kissed her, kissed her again, kissed her a third time. Then he glanced at the paper and burst out laughing.

"What's so funny?"

"The date. It's only been five days since the first time I was here. That first conference after I was recruited, when Griffin explained about time travel." He stood. "You gave the keynote address. Of course, you were older then."

"Hey. Where are you going?"

"To do the *other* thing I've been thinking about every day of my life for the past two-and-a-half years."

Leyster ran a bath, while Salley pretended to sulk. Then, as he lay soaking, she climbed in after him. By the time they were done screwing, there was more water on the floor than in the tub. After which, they dried each other off with the thick hotel towels, and finally made it all the way to the bed.

There, at last, they made love.

Afterwards, Leyster said, "Now I feel complete. All my life, I've had a kind of tension. A feeling that there was something I really ought to be doing but wasn't. Now . . . well. I guess I'm finally happy."

Salley smiled lazily. "You were waiting for me, dear heart. You and I were fated to be together from the beginning of time, and now here we are."

"That's a pretty thought. But I don't believe in fate."

"I do. I'm a Presbyterian. Predestination is dogmatic."

He looked at her curiously. "I didn't know you were religious."

"Well, I don't knock on people's doors and give them pamphlets, if that's what you mean. But, yeah, I take my faith pretty seriously. Is that a problem?"

"No, no, of course not." He took her hand, kissed the knuckles one by one. "Nothing about you is a problem for me."

She drew her hand away. "There's something you have to know. I've been putting off telling you. But now it's time."

Leyster listened patiently, while Salley told him about the Bird Men's decision, and all that had led up to it. When she was done at last, she said, "You don't look surprised."

"Of course not. I've known from the beginning that none of this was possible. The numbers never did add up on the whole time travel thing. Maybe the others could kid themselves about it. Not me."

"Then why did you go along with it? Why didn't you just refuse to play?"

"And miss out on seeing dinosaurs?" He laughed. "I've lived my life as I wanted, I've gotten answers to questions I thought I'd never know, and now I've had your love and known your body. Why should I want more? Why should I . . . say. Whose room is this, anyway? Yours or mine?"

"It's yours."

"Then my things should be in here somewhere, right?" He began opening drawers, rummaging through piles of clothes. "And if my things are here, then there ought to be . . . Aha! Here it is!"

An opened drawer yielded up his volume of the collected Shakespeare. He picked it up, leafed rapidly through its pages. "This is from *The Tempest.*"

He read:

"Our revels now are ended. These our actors,
As I foretold you, were all spirits, and

Are melted into air, into thin air;
And, like the baseless fabric of this vision,
The cloud-capp'd towers, the gorgeous palaces,
The solemn temples, the great globe itself,
Yea, all which it inherit, shall dissolve;
And, like this insubstantial pageant faded,
Leave not a rack behind. We are such stuff
As dreams are made on, and our little life
Is rounded with a sleep."

He put down the book. "That pretty much says it for me."

Salley smiled again, not at all lazily. "Come here, you. We've got things to do before we fall asleep."

"How much time do we have?"

"Not long. A few hours, subjective time."

"Time enough."

Griffin stayed after everybody else to see the rescue team off through the gate. Immediately after which, because the team had already returned safely with the lost expedition, the soldiers in the support crew began dismantling the equipment.

It was all over.

He had decided at the last minute not to say anything about the Bird Men's decision to the returning paleontologists. What could they do with their remaining time better than what they were doing now? They were all happy. Let them be happy.

Their generous patrons from Ultima Pangaea had granted him the boon of one last passage through time. He went to the front entrance, and found a limo waiting there for him.

It was time for his final trip to the Pentagon.

Griffin stepped out of the time funnel into a station that had been officially decommissioned the day before. He walked through the silent building and out the door. It was a bright, foggy morning. He could hear dinosaurs singing to one another. In the distance he saw the gray outlines of apatosaurs gently steaming in the mist.

His responsibilities were over now. He had fought the good fight. He had lost. Any second now, he fully expected to be weighed down with the crushing awareness of defeat. Yet, oddly enough, it did not come.

Instead, a great surge of glad emotion rose up within him. God, but he loved the Mesozoic! Particularly here and now. He couldn't think of a time and place he'd rather be.

Griffin was staring out into the dazzling fog when he heard footsteps. He did not turn. He knew who it had to be.

The Old Man came up behind him, and placed a hand on his shoulder.

"You've done a good job," he said. "Nobody could have done better."

"Thank you," Griffin said. "Now tell me that there was some point to all of this. Tell me I haven't spent all my adult life knocking myself out for nothing."

For a long moment he thought he would get no response. Then the Old Man said, "Imagine that you've been imprisoned, either justly or injustly, it makes no difference, for the rest of your life. You've been locked in a small room with one tiny barred window. You can't see much—maybe a bit of sky, that's all.

"But one day a bird comes to the window with a bit of straw in its beak. The next thing you know, it and its mate have built a nest right there in your window. Now, there are any number of ways you could respond to this. You could capture the birds and attempt to train them. You could steal their eggs to vary your diet. You could even kill them and smash their nest to punish them for being free when you're not. It's all a matter of temperament.

"What would *you* do?"

"I'd . . . study them. I'd try to learn everything I could about them. How they mate, what they eat, their resting metabolism, the developmental patterns of their young."

"If you're never going to get out of that cell, then what the hell good does your study do?"

"I don't have an answer for that. Except that I'd still like to know. Just for its own sake."

"Knowing is better than ignorance," the Old Man said.

Griffin weighed the statement judiciously, nodded. "That's true. But is it enough?"

"To justify your life?" The Old Man was silent for a while. Then he said, "I can't speak for anybody else. But for me personally, life doesn't need justification. It just is. And as long as I'm here, I want to know . . . simply *to know*. Yes, I honestly believe that's enough."

"How much time do we have left?" Griffin asked.

The Old Man cleared his throat. "I don't think that question has any meaning."

"I suppose that's so." He looked down at his watch without seeing it. Carefully, he removed it from his wrist and slipped it into a pocket.

"It's a lovely day, isn't it?" he said.

"Yes," he answered himself. "Yes, it is. If we've ever had a nicer, I can't remember when."